New book donated
87 year-old to a
terminal cancer
welcome -
brilliant thing... ~

CW00381297

NEXT TIME

A novel by

Adam Grace

By the Same Author

The Square Triangle

All in the Same Boat

The Tina Project

Keep Breathing

The Maturity Contract
(film screenplay)

Overalls to Ermine
(co-author with Lord Garfield Davies CBE)

Ye must be born again -- **John 3.7**

For Jean

CONTENTS

ONE

'Where've you been, Breen?'

The luminous green eyes regarded him with a slightly amused expression. He had danced with her briefly a fortnight earlier at the Odeon Ballroom and his mind had been in meltdown ever since. But his job had kept him away from the weekly dance the following Saturday and he'd wondered if he'd ever see her again. Now as they waltzed on the crowded dance floor sprinkled with splashes of light from the overhead glitter ball, he could barely control his excitement. She knew his surname. Could it be true that she'd actually missed him?

'Oh, they made me work at the office.' He tried to sound casual but his voice let him down.

'You're a reporter, aren't you?'

He felt his pulse quicken. How did she know? He hadn't told her. 'That's right, for the local rag.' His voice still sounded cracked

'I know, a friend told me. Do you have to work weekends?'

'Yes, I'm just a trainee. We get pushed

around something rotten!'

She smiled and squeezed his arm sympathetically. 'One day you might work for a national newspaper like the Times or the Telegraph.'

The prospect had dominated his dreams for years before the image of her flawless teenage beauty brushed it aside. He grinned. 'I'd settle for the Guardian or the Daily Mirror!'

'Oh no, not *them*!'

They laughed and all too soon the waltz was over. He escorted her back to the table where her friends were sitting. Protocol required that he returned to his own group nearby but he could not let her go. Other youths were hovering in the background, waiting for their chance. As a cub reporter not yet 18 he'd already learnt the value of persistence. It was part of his training. You had to be determined -- seize the moment.

He felt an overwhelming compulsion to stay by her side as she rejoined her chattering young friends. It was as if a physical force held him in a vice-like grip. There was no alternative. This was what he had to do. He took a deep breath. 'Can I get you a drink?' he heard himself say.

He'd seized the moment. It stood still, submissively. The lights, the band, the twinkling glitter ball, the glamorous blondes, brunettes and redheads, the awkward youths, his louche rivals... all froze in a blank, expectant hiatus...

She turned and looked at him, uncertain of her response. Her head told her she wasn't thirsty but her heart told her she was -- that she *had* to be. It was preordained. Her heart won and she smiled brightly. 'That would be nice, Breen... I'll have a pineapple juice with ice please.'

The spell was broken. He pushed his way through perfumed and sweaty bodies to the buffet bar. Although unlicensed it offered enticing multi-coloured beverages of special appeal to teenagers. A single slow-moving barman was in no hurry to serve him. By the time he'd returned to her table with their drinks the next dance, a quickstep, was well under way and she was nowhere to be seen.

Then he spotted her dancing with one of the rivals, an overweight kid trundling her slender figure round with the grace of a navvy. He was not in her league, that was obvious. There was nothing for it but to sit and watch the unedifying spectacle. At last she returned, laughing and fanning her face with both hands in mock relief as her clumsy partner, seeing Irving at her table, faded away.

She flopped onto a banquette and crossed her elegant legs in a tight-fitting beige silk skirt, decorously slit above the knee. They sipped their alcohol-free pina coladas self-consciously and she dabbed her face with a dainty handkerchief. 'Thanks for the drink,' she said. 'It's so hot in here.'

He took another deep breath. 'You know my name but I don't know yours.'

'Emily Shannon.' The cool green eyes beneath delicately arched eyebrows still looked slightly amused.

'Irving Breen.'

They shook hands gently with mock politeness.

The amused expression dissolved into girlish delight. 'Now we've been properly introduced!'

The lights dimmed for a slow foxtrot and once again she was in his arms, this time a little more closely, the scent of her fair shoulder-length hair driving the intense drumbeat of his heart. She could certainly dance. But then, so could he.

The band's female vocalist was singing:

Dancing in the dark
Till the tune ends
We're dancing in the dark
And it soon ends
We're waltzing in the wonder
Of why we're here
Time hurries by, we're here...
And gone

TWO

The tar was bubbling in the road on the day he was born. He knew because his mother never tired of telling him. It was one of those pre-war summers that produced regular heatwaves long before the days of global warming. Susan Breen had been in labour with her firstborn for over 20 hours, during which she vowed several times never to have any more children. Nurses at the private maternity hospital were in constant attendance. The doctors had insisted on that. There'd been problems during the pregnancy, serious problems affecting her long-term health.

Half way through a sweltering afternoon the seemingly endless ordeal was over. As a grandfather clock in the nursing home's hallway chimed the hour the anxieties, pain and tears gave way to blissful relief. Relief all round -- for Susan, for the doctors and the perspiring nurses. But most of all for the baby.

Months of fear over his mother's difficult pregnancy were resolved. A moment of alarm when a doctor tentatively used the word *abortion* had quickly passed. The all-encompassing darkness of the womb bore an uncanny resemblance to his passage across infinite space-time but felt more comfortable. Then a tiny white light appeared. It grew gradually larger until it flooded his entire being as he dived headfirst through the opening into the world. He felt intense pain and euphoria in equal measure. He had survived the multi-dimensional quantum leap. He was back in the land of the living.

Somewhere a clock was chiming. Three-o-clock.

Perfectly healthy baby, the nurses declared. Weight seven pounds four ounces. Mother and child both doing well. Gently they bathed and powdered him, wrapped him in a soft blue blanket and tiny bobble hat and, as his loud cries subsided, handed him to his proud mother. She held him tenderly to her heart, an overwhelming surge of love obliterating all memory of months of suffering.

Throughout the labour, as the contractions intensified, she had longed for her husband's comforting presence but that was not possible. David Breen, a ship's officer, was somewhere in the Baltic and was not expected home for another week. She would call him later by radio telephone and she knew he would be thrilled by the news. They had both wanted a son. Ultrasound pregnancy scans had yet to be invented.

Susan missed her husband acutely but now helplessness and dependence gave way to joy and empowerment. She had become a mother. Never in her whole life had she experienced such emotional intensity.

The nurses who had seen it all before but for whom the event never failed to resonate with their own ineffable life-giving instincts, formed an admiring gallery. 'Isn't he gorgeous!' 'Such a handsome little chap'... 'All that hair -- the lad's a free spirit to be sure!'

They never said a truer word.

Susan kissed him softly and gazed at the perfect little face with its tiny, heart shaped birthmark -- the classic beauty spot -- on one cheek, and breathed the sigh of fulfilled mothers down the ages. Yes, he was handsome all right, just like his father. He had David's chin and David's nose. But when she looked into the eyes, the likeness faded.

They were the eyes of a very old man.

They named him Irving, after his grandfather. Private Irving Hubert Breen had answered Lord Horatio Kitchener's emotive call to patriotic duty and cheerfully marched off to war with his boyhood pals as a carefree Lancashire Fusilier. He survived the Battle of the Somme without an enemy-induced scratch -- a feat achieved through a unique combination of circumstances. But when he came home he was a changed man.

His wife, Bridget, hardly knew him. Gone was her extrovert, hard-drinking spouse without a care in the world. In his place was a serious, skilled mill weaver content with cultivating his allotment and who rarely drank more than a single Scotch at weekend. Like others who had survived the horrendous conflict, it had left no physical scars but the cerebral ones ran deep.

He became a steward at his local Methodist chapel, giving out hymn books, taking the collection plate and singing in the choir. He also helped out at the manse where the ageing pastor, the Rev Gerald Williams, lived alone. On the arrival of Irving Junior his grandfather lost no time in organising the baptismal service. Susan and David regarded him as a natural choice for the role of godfather.

The christening ceremony was a simple affair in the austere chapel with the Rev Williams struggling to remember the baby's name as he sprinkled him with holy water. After a few short prayers and exhorting the parents and godfather to raise their son in the somewhat spartan and abstemious Methodist tradition it was all over. Irving Junior had slept throughout.

The family posed for the obligatory photographs, David, the proud father, resplendent in full dress naval officer's uniform, mother Susan, her restored slender figure stretching the sort of floral frock all the rage in the 1930s; David's mother, Bridget, and father, Irving Senior, in their Sunday best. Susan's parents had died when she was a teenager and she had no brothers or sisters. Her only family representative was her crossbred collie, Bobby, who she insisted should be included in the group.

David had missed wetting the baby's head on the day of his birth but made sure the baptism was properly celebrated at the couple's modest semi in the once affluent but now decaying middle class area of Brawton, north Manchester. He'd smuggled in some genuine Russian caviar to go with the canapes of smoked salmon and cucumber, plus a couple of bottles of vodka to supplement the sherry and port. Two young fellow officers, also in dress uniform, and several neighbours crowded into the parlour with its upright piano, old-fashioned gramophone in a polished walnut cabinet and art deco-patterned standard lamp.

They played the latest dance music on the gramophone -- Benny Goodman, Ambrose and Glenn Miller classics -- and by the time they'd reached the vodka everyone had mellowed, even Bridget who normally frowned on alcoholic indulgence. A lifelong member of the Temperance movement, she was a strict opponent of the demon drink. She stuck to apple juice and simply raised an eyebrow but said nothing when her husband relaxed his one-drink rule and asked for a sherry top-up. This was a special occasion after all.

Irving Senior, the greying ex-Lancashire Fusilier with a full moustache waxed to a point at each end, smiled at her and patted her hand. The demon drink had nothing on his own personal demons. If Bridget had seen what he had seen on the battlefield and felt a fraction of the paralysing fear... if she was sometimes wakened at night by the cries of dying men calling for their mothers... she would never begrudge him another drink. Mercifully, her soul remained unscarred by such horrors.

Now it seemed the horrors were about to be repeated. Every day there was talk on the wireless about political turmoil in Europe and the growing threat of war. God forbid that the old soldier's innocent little godson would be caught up in another conflict. He had promised to ensure the boy was brought up in the Christian faith and live a life based on sound moral and ethical foundations. It was his solemn duty to steer him away from misguided notions of patriotism preached by a ruling class of cynical capitalists. Cannon fodder, that's what his generation had been taken for. He vowed with steely determination that his godson would never be subjected to similar manipulation. He'd make damned sure the boy grew up with a mind of his own.

The mind of Irving Breen Junior was already developing along independent lines. Although his surroundings were vaguely familiar, memories of a previous existence had been blocked by the trauma of birth. The little white light that guided him unerringly through the lonely, empty darkness of space-time had left him.

Now oblivious to all that had gone before the three-o-clock chimes on a summer's afternoon, he was trying to work out where the sound of a gentle pitter-patter was coming from. He was lying snug and warm in cocooned comfort and could feel a sensation of regular movement that was not unpleasant. Every so often the movement stopped and his mother's face would come into view, gazing into his old man's eyes and smiling. Occasionally, other smiling faces would appear and smile. The pitter-patter sound would cease and then resume. He found the sound strangely soothing and without any effort went back to sleep.

Susan Breen found pushing her son's pram through the rainswept suburban streets exhausting. The shops were less than a quarter of a mile from home but the heavy showers, puddles, uneven pavements and an increasing collection of shopping bags slowed progress. At intervals she encountered neighbours as well as total strangers who insisted on admiring little Irving, sleeping safe and warm and protected from the weather under the raised hood of his pram. How adorable the swarthy babe looked, a cosy little bundle oblivious in his infant's bliss to yet another round of menacing challenges lying in wait for him.

Although Irving quite enjoyed being a baby, the centre of attraction whose every need was catered for with alacrity by doting parents, it seemed no time at all before he became a toddler. His needs were still adequately catered for although there were moments of anxiety when it came to learning to walk and distinct unpleasantness involving potty training.

He also had serious concerns over his father's indulgence in robust horseplay involving swinging him round his shoulders, pretending to drop him and catching him at the last moment. But the practice he found really hair-raising, in every sense of the word, was riding on his Dad's shoulders, clutching for dear life the thinning hair surrounding a circular bald patch with both hands. His proximity to the ceiling with its central light fitting induced an alarming sense of vertigo and he tried to express his fears by kicking his father's shoulders but that seemed to suggest he was enjoying the ride, so Dad did it some more.

The trauma of birth may have blocked memories of what had gone before but it had not completely erased them. Fragments of a higher consciousness remained floating around Irving's psyche like spiritual after-birth. Together they formed a subliminal message: that he was no ordinary person. His life had a special purpose. There was important unfinished business to attend to.

But first he needed to grow up, which sowed the seeds of impatience in his subconscious mind and a desire to leave childhood as quickly as possible. Whenever his parents and their friends gathered for a party or celebration, their laughter and infectious enjoyment of life sparked a sense of resentment that he was unable to join in.

They would make a fuss of him, of course. They passed him round from one to another like a parcel, bounced him up and down on their knees, tickling and teasing him. It seemed to make them happy -- but not him. He wanted to be treated as one of their equals, not talked down to and patronised. All he could do was seek refuge in withdrawal. He failed to respond to their ridiculous baby noises and would turn away when they tried to make him laugh.

'Oh, isn't he shy,' they'd say. 'Such a handsome little chap but so shy!' They'd give him a lollipop. At least that was acceptable. He wasn't really shy, just impatient. Buried deep in his DNA there was a dim awareness that destiny was calling and here he was happily sucking a lollipop.

In his haste to grow up he amazed his parents by almost eliminating the crawling stage of his development. He was up on his feet and staggering around after only 10 months, repeatedly falling over and sometimes hurting himself but rarely crying. His mother and father captured his more successful moments on their Brownie box camera and kept the snaps for decades in the family album.

Another important part of growing up was learning to talk. By the age of 15 months he had acquired a vocabulary of about a dozen words, although the art of assembling them in the right order proved elusive. He would string whole sentences together but nobody could understand them except Bobby. The family's faithful pooch had shown signs of jealousy at Irving's arrival but soon took a protective interest in the baby. He would sit at his little master's side and listen attentively to his garbled soliloquies as if he understood every word. Maybe he did -- and it was just the adults who lacked comprehension.

You needed to be on the right wavelength to relate to young Irving on a meaningful level, something which his mother soon realised. Her effective wavelength was music. She had a delightful contralto voice and sang with her local amateur operatic society. Whenever she broke into song while cooking or doing the house-work, Irving instantly responded. He would try to join in and their duets would dissolve into helpless laughter. Sometimes Bobby would also throw back his head and howl causing even greater hilarity.

One of the popular songs at the time was *If You Knew Susie*, a lively swing number that Susan and David used to dance to before they were married.

If you knew Susie
Like I know Susie
Oh! Oh! Oh! What a girl
There's none so classy
As this fair lassie
Oh! Oh! Holy Moses
What a chassis...

Whenever the record was broadcast on the old cabinet wireless set in the living room, mother and son would burst into a loud ren-dition, with Bobby offering rousing support. For Susan it brought back happy memories of their courting days, when the handsome young naval officer swept her off her feet. They still went dancing when he came home on leave. They were like a couple of newlyweds. Absence clearly made their hearts grow fonder.

David would hire a car, a big Austin drophead tourer, quite a luxury in those days, and they'd drive to the seaside -- Blackpool, Southport or New Brighton. Irving would sit next to his mother and Bobby on the back seat, well wrapped up as heaters were unheard of. In no time he would be lulled to sleep by the drone of the engine.

On the beach they'd build sand castles and go paddling. Bobby would chase tirelessly after a ball and had to be kept away from the donkeys. They sat Irving on one of the docile animals and a lad led it gently towards the sunlit sea. Another taller youth walked alongside to ensure Irving didn't fall off. Their charge nervously clutched a metal handle on the front of the saddle, peering between two large pointed ears at the approaching panorama of sea and sky. Something about the desolate encircling emptiness triggered emotions buried deep in his subconscious. The tinkling of the donkey's bells swelled into a loud ringing in his ears. Panic took over and he burst into tears. The lads swiftly turned the donkey round and headed back to his anxious parents.

As summer mellowed into autumn the little family would spend hours in their neat patch of rear garden with its tiny lawn, two flower beds filled with marigolds, petunias and pansies, and a single cherry blossom tree that produced a brief glorious display each spring. David was not much of a gardener and his efforts while on leave were short-lived. He relied on his father to mow the grass and keep things tidy. Irving Senior and Bridget lived close by in an older terraced house and the old man was happy to help out. The task was minimal after tending his much larger allotment and it allowed him to visit his grandson regularly.

Irving Junior fascinated his grandfather -- now called Grandpa by the whole family including Nana (Bridget). He was growing so fast and there was something different about him, something special Grandpa couldn't quite put his finger on. 'The boy's a free spirit all right,' he told Susan. 'He'll go far,' never realising the perspicacity of his words.

It was not long before, at Grandpa's insistence, Irving was enrolled in the beginners' department at Brawton Methodist Sunday School. It was held in a large classroom with semi-panelled wooden walls, a battered upright piano and several tiny chairs for the diminutive pilgrims. Along one wall was a curtained internal window and after handing Irving to one of the young women teachers his mother would leave the room but then peep from behind the curtain at her son. Sharply observant even at such a tender age, Irving wished she wouldn't do that. It made him feel uncomfortable among his companions, wriggling and giggling and some toppling off their perches onto the polished wood floor, crying then comforted by the teachers.

His mother had given him one old penny (1d) which he was instructed to place in a glass jar when they came round with the collection. He found the act inexplicable. He'd discovered that the coin could be exchanged for a small chocolate bar or, in the summer, a tiny ice cream cornet. You got nothing in return for placing it in the collection jar.

Led by an elderly teacher playing an old tinny-sounding piano they all sang:

Hear the pennies dropping!
Listen while they fall;
Ev'ry one for Jesus,
He will have them all,

Dropping, dropping, dropping,
From each little hand;
'Tis our gift to Jesus,
From his little band.

The jar was passed round but when it reached Irving he declined to offer up his penny. One of the teachers, a smiling teenage girl, gently prised the coin from his hand. His face crumbled and dissolved into floods of tears. Susan hurried into the room to console him.

After the tears were wiped away and his mother had given him a sweet, the toddlers listened to a story about Jesus and how much he loved all children throughout the whole world -- not just in Brawton. Some of the children in foreign countries were black as well as white. Some were brown and others were yellow. Many were sick and suffering from terrible hunger. There was not enough food to go round and the pennies from the collection went towards buying food for them and saving their lives. Irving and like-minded supporters were convinced. The rebellion was crushed.

The knowledge that his penny was helping to save the life of another little boy in a far-off country helped to cheer up Irving and his classmates, some of whom had shared his reluctance to surrender their precious pennies.

THREE

Shopping in Manchester department stores with mother and Nana was another memorable highlight of Irving's early years. Sometimes they would travel 'into town' by bus but they usually took the electric train to the city's Victoria Station. There was a slot machine on the platform at Brawton Station and, as Irving had discovered, one old penny (1d) would buy a small bar of white chocolate. Susan would demur about giving her son chocolate on the grounds that it was not good for him but Irving knew how to respond. He would cosy up to Nana, take her hand and tearfully plead with her until she finally said: 'Oh for heaven's sake let him have one. It won't do him any harm.' The two women would fall out briefly over the issue of whose son he was but then their train would arrive and he would be happily scoffing his prize.

The chaos and cacophony of Victoria Station always fascinated Irving. As his mother and Nana led him towards the exit, he would marvel at the crowds of people hurrying in different directions, the porters pushing trolleys loaded with luggage, the smoke and hiss of the monstrous steam engines, the guards' shouts and whistles. This was another world outside Brawton and once again he could not wait to be part of it.

They'd take the tramcar along Market Street to Lewis's, one of the city's magnificent emporiums -- five storeys of every kind of consumer perishables and durables imaginable from cabbages and pineapples in the food hall to gramophones and grand pianos on the furniture floor. Rows of lifts offered customers instant rides to the floors of their choice but Irving liked it best when they took the escalator. Holding his mother's hand they'd wait for a suitable moment to jump on the moving stairway and it was even more fun timing the right moment to jump off.

Shoes and clothes were generally on the shopping list and the two women would spend hours on their purchases. Sometimes they would admire expensive jewellery although they never bought any. Irving found it all very boring and had a tendency to wander off to explore other attractions. He got lost once among all the shoppers and a sales assistant took him to a nursery full of toys -- rocking horses, tricycles and pedal cars. They gave him an ice cream and a picture book while an announcement of a lost child was made on the store's loudspeakers.

His mother and Nana soon appeared, both distraught. They had searched frantically for him, blaming themselves for his split-second disappearance and fearing the worst. They hugged and kissed him tearfully, and apologised profusely to the nursery staff. Irving could not understand what all the fuss was about. He was having a great time and would not mind getting lost more often in future. That was not going to happen, of course. Never again would they let him out of their sight.

All too soon, of course, the time came when Susan did have to let her son leave her side, not for an hour or two with Nana but for days at a time with strangers. Pre-school nurseries like car heaters and mobile phones still belonged to the future. There was no way of rendering the process painless. Irving's first day at primary school was an event etched on both their memories for the rest of their lives. It was raining heavily and they should have parted at the school gates but the teacher, a stern faced young woman with a hair bun and holding a large umbrella, relented when she saw the boy's distress. She allowed the pair to enter the school but only as far as its hallway.

His mother took his hand and once again assured him that the teachers would take good care of him. He would meet lots of other boys and girls. They would play games and have fun together. There was nothing to worry about. She would come back and take him home again a few hours later. She promised.

Irving was not convinced. He didn't like the look of the teacher and as he glanced round the hall, echoing with the clamour of boisterous infants, he didn't much care for them either. He clung on to Susan as she kissed him goodbye and she literally had to tear herself away with the teacher's assistance. Sobbing quietly, she hurried out into the rain. Irving watched her go through the glass panelled door as she crossed the playground. On reaching the gateway she turned and waved. He half raised a hand and tried to wave back but the tears were flowing down his face faster than the raindrops on the window.

'Come along, Irving,' the teacher said, taking his hand and drying his eyes with a large handkerchief. 'Come and meet your new friends.' But the last thing Irving felt was friendly. He cried steadily throughout the morning and nothing the teachers could do would console him. His heart was broken. He simply could not believe that his mother had left him. How could she do a thing like that?

Susan couldn't believe it either. She also wept throughout the morning, comforted only by Bobby. The hours dragged by until it was time to collect her son. It had stopped raining and she waited with the other mothers at the school gates. When the children came running out, Irving was among the first. He stopped and searched the faces of the waiting women. Then he spotted her and ran to her. They embraced like long lost lovers. She had kept her promise. His faith in her was restored.

Irving proved a quick learner at primary school, soon mastering the alphabet and times-tables, thanks to his mother's pre-school instruction. But elements of the curriculum were to develop which she could not have anticipated. Workmen began excavating the school's playing fields to install a large communal air raid shelter covered by a huge bank of earth. The teachers then held practice alerts, leading their pupils into the structure's damp, dimly lit interior where they sat on wooden benches and sang hymns and patriotic songs.

The children found it fun. It made a change from ordinary lessons. There was more fun when they were introduced to their junior gas masks. They struggled to put on the grotesque rubber contraptions and laughed at the sound of their muffled voices. When they tried to recognise each other it was like playing a new party game.

It was all just a practice drill, parents were told. Such was the escalating political crisis across Europe and Germany's increasing belligerence that the threat of war could not be ignored. The air raid shelter, like those being in-stalled in people's gardens, and the gas masks were necessary precautions. God forbid that they would ever be needed.

The topic was on everyone's lips. Was there really going to be another war? Memories of the last one had barely faded. The politicians had called it 'the war to end wars'. How con-temptible and utterly foolish they all were. You could not believe a word they said. When Hit-ler invaded Poland the threat became a reality. Suddenly people seemed much more serious. At Christmas everybody exchanged gifts and you could still smell roast turkey, cigars and pine needles. Mother and father still sang and played carols on the piano and Bobby got his extra large bone tied up with a blue ribbon.

But Irving could tell it wasn't quite the same. The grown-ups were scared. They kept asking each other how long the war would last. What was Mr Churchill going to do about it? They would need bedding for the bunk beds in the air raid shelters being hastily erected in their gardens. They would need blankets, candles, food and drink, iron rations. Nana and Grandpa were more philosophical. They had seen it all before. There was no way they were going to get up in the middle of the night and run outside to a shelter. If their time was up, that would be it. It would be God's will.

With the outbreak of war, David Breen

was redeployed to a different ship and promoted to the rank of captain. He was now in command of the SS Angelo, a venerable 20,000 ton freighter commissioned by the Admiralty as a supply ship for the warships protecting Atlantic convoys from German submarines. Night after night there were reports on the wireless of merchant vessels being torpedoed by U-boats as the Germans' strategy of starving the British people into submission began to take shape.

At the same time the Luftwaffe also launched nightly raids on Britain's towns and cities, exacting their deadly toll on innocent civilians. While her husband performed his perilous duty in the Atlantic, Susan Breen faced her own personal challenge at their home on the outskirts of Manchester -- one of the main targets for the German bombers. The eerie wail of the air raid sirens would rouse her and Irving from their warm beds regularly during the winter months of the prolonged Blitz. She would gather him up in her arms and carry him out into the freezing night to the shelter, along with Bobby.

As searchlights swept across the sky and anti-aircraft guns began pounding they could hear the sinister throb of the German bombers overhead and occasionally the steadier engine note of the RAF Spitfires. They would hear the thud of exploding bombs, mostly distant but others alarmingly close. Susan tried to put a brave face on it all, pretending it was a big adventure. Irving was too young to understand but he knew there were men up there trying to kill them and all they could do was pray. He felt his mother's fear as she held him close and whispered a prayer:

Lighten our darkness,
we beseech thee, O Lord,
and in thy great mercy defend us
against the perils of this night.

Mother and son and dog huddled under their blankets in the bitterly cold and dismal shelter, the light of a few candles showing condensation dripping down the corrugated iron walls. During lulls in the raids they'd keep up their spirits by singing *There'll Always be an England* and popular songs like Vera Lynn's *We'll Meet Again.* The war would soon be over and they'd all meet Daddy again, Susan would say brightly. Then they would go away for a long holiday by the seaside and build some more sand castles because the sea had washed away those they'd made last time. She tried her best to sound cheerful and there were times when she almost convinced her son -- but not quite.

It would often take hours before the all-clear siren brought relief. They would stumble shivering back to bed while the dawn sky grew red over Manchester. Brawton had survived another raid but many long-suffering Mancunians had been less fortunate.

As if the climate of fear enveloping the nation were not enough, full-scale war also inflicted a double whammy in the shape of crippling austerity. Almost overnight, rationing was imposed on food and clothing. Even children's sweets were rationed. Every man, woman and child was allocated a ration book by the Ministry of Food. They contained coupons to be exchanged for meagre weekly supplies. These supplies were only marginally more than starvation rations. Each person was allowed only one egg per week, a single one-inch square piece of cheese and similar size portions of margarine, tea, sugar and jam. Bread of very poor quality was rationed later and fruit such as oranges and bananas disappeared almost completely.

Irving was both indignant and mystified when his weekly sweets allowance suddenly shrank to a tiny two-ounce bag and that there were no longer any bars of chocolate in the slot machine at Brawton Station. But he never went hungry. In later years he came to realise that this was mainly due to the ongoing sacrifices of his mother and grandparents. There were times when, in giving him their pitiful rations, they *did* go hungry although Grandpa played a crucial role in their survival by cultivating a highly productive allotment. Responding to the government's slogan 'Dig for Victory', he worked long hours on his hillside plot to minimise the hardship.

To undermine national morale still further, domestic coal was also rationed. Central heating was an almost unheard-of luxury. Nearly every home relied on open fires for warmth and hot water and the winters of the early 1940s were among the harshest of the century. Grandpa could not bear to see his half-starved family suffer intolerably when their meagre fuel ration ran out, as it did every week.

He did some reconnaissance of the marshalling yard at Brawton Station and discovered that railway wagons loaded with coal were left unguarded in a siding running parallel to a public footpath. All that separated them from the path was a tall wooden fence. It was too high to climb but if he were to lift a lightweight accomplice over, a young boy for example...

Irving was about nine years old at the time. As he recalled, he had little input in the planning of the enterprise. Nana and Susan were consulted and both were aghast at the idea. It was stealing. What if they were caught? They'd be arrested. They could go to jail. And what if they were caught in the middle of an air raid? But Grandpa talked them round. There had been no air raids for three months and the authorities were saying more were unlikely in the near future, although the blackout would continue. The RAF's heroic Fighter Command had inflicted heavy losses on the Luftwaffe in the Battle of

Britain. Hitler had now turned his fire power on the Russian front.

As for 'stealing', it was a victimless offence. The police were not going to investigate the disappearance of a few lumps of coal. The railway company would not even notice they'd gone. Nobody used the footpath at night and the sidings were not patrolled so the chance of being arrested was negligible. In that unlikely event he would take full responsibility. No-one would come to any harm, least of all young Irving.

The old soldier rested his case, sat back in his favourite armchair and sagely twirled the waxed ends of his moustache with his gnarled arthritic fingers as he did when he had made a point. His doubters were swayed by his eloquence. It was either that or being pushed beyond the limits of human endurance for the rest of the winter.

Grandpa, redolent of tobacco smoke, sat the boy on his knee and explained the gravity of their situation. It was not a problem of the family's making. It was not their fault that they didn't have enough coal left. They had money to pay for some but the government would not supply them with it. They needed the help of a brave young man to put things right. When the grim scenario was explained in these terms Irving considered the plan to be entirely logical. He was proud of the trust the grown-ups were placing in him. It also meant he could stay up late. But most of all it sounded like fun.

There was a hard frost and a thin sliver of Moon on the night the conspirators set out by torchlight along the darkened streets of Brawton. All street lighting was extinguished as part of the continuing blackout and no light escaped from windows draped in heavy opaque curtains. An old man with a walking stick led his elderly wife and their daughter-in-law pushing an empty pram and holding the hand of her young son along the pathway circling the railway sidings. The area was deserted. Not a mouse moved in the frost-bound scene. Not a sound broke the eerie stillness. At a point where the wooden fence separating the pathway from the wagons dipped slightly, the motley group stopped.

The women turned and kept an anxious lookout as the old man hoisted the boy effortlessly on his shoulders. From there, with the agility of a natural cat burglar, the lad bounded over the fence and on to a wagon piled high with coal. Within seconds he was lifting heavy lumps of the precious fuel in his gloved hands and lowering them to outstretched hands below. The pram was quickly filled and the women hissed for Irving to return. There was a heart-stopping moment when the young hero slipped on the frosty fence. But he quickly regained his balance and dropped into his grandfather's strong arms. The heist had taken no more than five minutes.

It took another 20 for the gang to make their getaway along the blacked out streets. The pram, weighed down on its slender springs, was difficult to push and there would have been some awkward moments if they'd encountered a patrolling policeman. But they reached Grandpa's house undetected and unloaded their booty in the coal shed where it achieved instant legitimacy.

There was relief all round as the criminals collapsed into armchairs in the front parlour with its upright piano, aspidistra and picture of Private Irving Hubert Breen, his three campaign medals glinting in the flickering gaslight. 'Never again,' Nana said with feeling. But the two Irvings were happy. They had forged a special bond of comrades in arms who'd faced danger together and come through unscathed.

'Mission accomplished,' the older Irving declared, blue eyes twinkling and moustache bristling. He lit up his briar pipe amid clouds of smoke. 'Told you there was nothing to worry about.'

Nana made the obligatory pot of tea to steady their nerves and passed round slices of her home-made apple pie. Everyone relaxed. It was well past all their bedtimes, especially young Irving's, but just as thoughts were turning to sleeping arrangements there was a loud knock on the front door. Fear returned to all their eyes. Who could be knocking at this hour?

Had someone seen them after all and reported them?

Frowning, Grandpa opened the door. Standing outside was a police constable. He looked sternly at the old man and beyond him into the hallway. Its startled occupants stared back, fearing the worst. 'Morning, all,' the officer said. 'Sorry to disturb you but there's still a blackout you know. There's a gap in your curtains and you've got a light showing.'

FOUR

On a hill not far from Nana and Grandpa's house stood the Brawton War Memorial. The hill was known as Spion Kop, in commemoration of the Boer War battle in 1900. It was a battle the British had lost but that did not seem to concern the locals. Every Remembrance Sunday the Brawton branch of the British Legion held their annual parade to the memorial and civic dignitaries would lay their poppy wreaths at the white stone cross in its small neat garden.

Crowds of people, diminishing over the years, would attend the ceremony, hold a two-minute silence at 11am in keeping with services at similar cenotaphs throughout the country, then solemnly return home and get on with the lives denied to their 'fallen' fellow citizens. Their names were inscribed on the bronze plaque at the foot of the cross. All local men, many of them little more than boys, who had marched off to their deaths in the service of an elite ruling class who regarded them as cannon fodder.

The memorial, enclosed by a white picket fence, would remain deserted and neglected for the remainder of the year. But Grandpa did not ignore it. Every day he pushed his wheelbarrow along a path skirting the site on his way to his allotment on the far side of Spion Kop. As he passed he would stop, stand to attention for a moment and salute before resuming his progress. They had been his comrades. Some he had known personally, classmates, teenagers still bantering and joking in his mind's eye. Age would not wither them.

But it was starting to wither him. Trundling his barrow between home and allotment was becoming steadily more arduous and the digging, planting and weeding were taking a heavy toll on his arthritic joints. He needed a strong enthusiastic helper and his grandson filled the role admirably.

At weekends and during school holidays young Irving proved he was as green-fingered as his grandfather. The new hobby suited his independent nature perfectly. He was a loner with few friends among his age group. Most of them were deadly boring. He knew they found him an oddball but so what? A special destiny awaited him beyond their little world of football, comics and model aeroplanes.

Harvest time particularly appealed to the boy. The digging up of potatoes, carrots, parsnips and beetroots, lovingly watered and tended throughout the summer, proved a rewarding experience that none of his contemporaries would understand. The peas and beans and soft fruits also fascinated him. His lifelong love of strawberries began on Grandpa's allotment.

At dusk when work was done the pair would sit outside the little hut used to store tools, and drink glasses of dandelion and burdock. Grandpa would light up his pipe and puff contentedly while regaling his willing listener with advice on horticulture and life in general. Irving would press him for stories of his war service but the old veteran would not be drawn. Such horrors were not for the ears of a young lad, even one as precocious as his grandson.

But he did tell him one story of his remarkable escape from annihilation during the Battle of the Somme. After weeks under continual fire in the trenches his unit was withdrawn, traumatised, covered in mud and lice, for a recovery period behind the lines. A surprise visit to the war zone by Manchester City football team helped to restore morale and a match was organised with the troops. Grandpa played as a winger but broke his ankle in a tackle. He was stretchered off to a field hospital full of casualties from the front. Two days later his unit was deployed to the trenches but he was left behind in the hospital with his leg in plaster.

The evening sun slanted through the smoke from Grandpa's pipe as the old man paused for an emotional moment. 'What happened next, boy, is very painful to tell you. When my comrades went over the top they were all killed by the German machine-guns. Every single one of them. So you see, if I hadn't broken my ankle I'd most likely not be here now!'

The profound implications of his grandfather's story were not lost on young Irving. They also explained the large blue and white rosette along with a horseshoe on the door of the hut. 'Is that why you support Manchester City, Grandpa?'

The old man laughed and wiped his moustache with the back of his hand. 'That's right, boy. Used to support United but City saved my life!'

'Everyone supports United,' Irving said. 'All the boys at school. United keep winning and City keep losing. But I'll always support City!'

Sometimes when it rained the gardener and his apprentice would huddle in the hut amid the tools, sacks and seedlings smelling of damp earth and tobacco smoke, and Irving would listen attentively to views at some variance to the received wisdom of the age. The Great War had changed everything. Previously society had been based on mutual respect, chivalry and moral fibre, Grandpa told him. 'Morals are things of the past these days along with honesty and respect. Immorality and mendacity are everywhere.'

Irving had an idea what immorality was. His mother and father were always saying there was too much of it in the newspapers and on the wireless. A couple who lived nearby in their road were getting divorced and their children would be bound to suffer as a result. But mendacity was a new one. 'What does mendacity mean, Grandpa?'

'It means lying and dishonesty,' his grandfather said. 'We live in a capitalist society. That means everything is based on money -- and the love of money is the root of all evil. Some people will do anything to get their hands on it. The mill owners pay their workers starvation wages and the Tories put up our taxes, so we're left with next to nothing. And there are still people who try to cheat us out of *that*.'

Irving had noticed that when they went shopping, his mother always counted her change. She had warned him that shopkeepers often made mistakes and every time the mistake was in their favour. 'Do you mean like shopkeepers short-changing you?'

'Yes, always check your change, boy. But others will try to deceive you as well, bankers, landlords, politicians... the toffs. They'll all try to take your money because deep down they don't like working class people. It's our honesty they can't abide. They think we should all be bent, like them. Don't trust them, least of all the politicians. They're very plausible... try to fool you by using big words that make them seem clever and important. They're just cheap liars and shysters really.

'You must always tell the truth -- like your mum and dad have taught you, like they teach you at Sunday school. Be polite and respectful but don't let the toffs push you around. They're no better than you are. Learn plenty of big words yourself. You're going to need them later in life. Don't let anyone browbeat you. You've got a mind of your own -- use it!'

Still impatient to grow up, Irving listened carefully to his grandfather's prophetic advice. He got the message.

During the summer holidays Grandpa took him on day trips to the seaside. The odd pair -- the old man with his cloth cap, knapsack and walking stick, and the young boy in school cap and blazer -- would take the steam train from Central Station in Manchester to Liverpool Lime Street. There they'd catch a tram to the Pier Head and from there board a ferry to New Brighton on the opposite bank of the Mersey estuary. The service was operated by two ancient steamers, The Royal Daffodil and The Royal Iris, both of which fascinated Irving.

If the weather was fine he and Grandpa would sit on the outer upper deck savouring the sea air and salt spray while watching shipping traffic along the busy river. If inclement they would choose the cosy saloon with its comfortable upholstered seats. Visibility there was restricted but you could feel the throb of the engines and hear the clanging telegraphed commands from bridge to engine room. This was the life, the schoolboy thought. He resolved to be a Mersey ferryboat skipper when he grew up.

On other outings grandfather and grandson would take the train to quaint Cheshire towns then strike out into the surrounding countryside and walk for miles. Irving would often tire before the old man did and they'd stop for a break near a stream for a picnic. The old soldier would produce sandwiches and a billycan, fill it from the stream, light a fire and brew tea which they drank from tin mugs. When they'd rested they'd damp down the embers and leave the campsite as they found it.

'You've got your second wind now so stand up straight, boy, take a deep breath and pick your feet up!' Grandpa would exhort. He may never have been a sergeant major in the Army but he certainly acted like one on the duo's route marches.

At other times they would board a tram and rattle uncomfortably to Belle Vue zoo and amusement park on the other side of Manchester. Grandpa was fascinated by the caged animals and birds. He would stand for what seemed like hours, watching the multi-coloured parrots on their perches and the wide-eyed monkeys swinging to and fro. Irving soon grew bored with the zoo. He wanted to go on the helter-skelter and the dodgems, and later the rowing boats on the lake when the old man would let him do the rowing while he steered.

When Irving's father returned to his ship at Liverpool docks following home leave, Grandpa and Nana escorted the family to see him off. On one occasion, they were given a tour of the ship. As the dockside cranes lowered essential supplies into the ship's four cavernous holds, they were shown round the engine room with its vast tangle of gleaming machinery and pervasive diesel fumes, the navigation bridge featuring the vessel's original ship's wheel, polished brass compasses, sextants and engine telegraph equipment with ahead/astern dials plus the chart room and two flimsy looking lifeboats.

Years earlier when the Admiralty requisitioned the ship, an anti-aircraft gun had been installed at the stern but Captain David informed them it no longer worked, not that it was much use when it did. He was still waiting for the Admiralty to fix it or replace it but understood their priority had to be warships rather than merchant vessels.

A row of bullet holes across the deck, the handiwork of a Messerschmitt dive bomber, reminded the visitors of the perils facing David and his crew. 'We were in convoy off Madeira when it happened,' he explained. 'He might have finished us off but we had air cover. One of our

Hurricanes intercepted, thank God.'

They were all served afternoon tea in the officers' mess and Irving, then aged 11, was mightily impressed when he was addressed as 'Sir' by the stewards. From that moment a career as a Merchant Navy navigating officer seemed marginally preferable to that of Mersey ferry boat skipper. He had forgotten, for a time, that destiny had other designs on his services.

It was with profound sadness when the SS Angelo set sail again, laden down with victuals and ammunition for the Royal Navy in the latest war zone. The Breen family stood on the quayside waving tearfully as the vulnerable old freighter with its useless rear gun slowly disappeared over the horizon

FIVE

Another year would pass before the vessel returned -- a year in which a nation on its knees found the courage to get up and start fighting back. The transformation was largely due to the inspirational leadership of the Prime Minister, Winston Churchill, whose regular broadcasts on the wireless effectively banished any lingering notions of capitulation to the encircling Nazi war machine.

When the air raids diminished they were replaced as an ever-present threat to life and limb by crippling austerity. People were living on their nerves and on the verge of starvation but nightly news bulletins gave them hope. The tide seemed to be turning in our favour. The Eighth Army, led by Field Marshal Montgomery, was pushing the enemy back in North Africa. The Germans were retreating...

And the SS Angelo was steaming back to port, battle weary like its crew. There had been narrow escapes when, watched by its helpless sailors, a U-boat's torpedoes twice surged a few yards past its rusting hull. Captain David had sought refuge in his faltering Christian faith at such times and he recalled moments when he observed hardened atheist crew members on their knees in prayer -- though they refused to admit it later.   The Admiralty had notified the Breen family by telegram of the ship's imminent return and Susan, Nana, Grandpa and Irving all braved a blizzard at the dockside, along with other crew's families, as the embattled old steamship lumbered into view and inched painfully into its berth like an exhausted creaking and groaning giant.

The gangways were lowered and the families streamed on board for their emotional reunions. David had grown a beard and Irving barely recognised him. Tea in the officers' mess was embellished with champagne to celebrate a successful homecoming. Sea-going exploits vied with home news in that spirit of relaxed bonhomie found among people who've shared a traumatic ordeal and lived to tell the tale.

Everyone had a story to tell. Susan, who had learned shorthand in her youth, had taken a part-time job as a shorthand-typist at the Co-operative Wholesale Society in Manchester. Nana had joined the Women's Institute and knitted khaki jumpers for the troops. Most excitingly, Irving had passed his 11-plus and was lined up for grammar school.

Only Grandpa's news was less than cheerful. He'd been diagnosed with diabetes and angina so had to cut down on his allotment work. David noticed that his father had lost weight, his eyes had sunken and the bristling moustache had turned white. He did not like the look of him at all.

Irving was 12 years old when the war ended. He and his mother had been glued to the wireless for a week since the news of Hitler's suicide on 30th April 1945 -- wait-ing for the official announcement of Germany's unconditional surrender. It came on 7th May, followed next day by Victory in Europe Day (VE Day) and after six years of hell it seemed all heaven was let loose.

A nation not given to showing its feelings threw off its inhibitions in a tidal wave of emotion. Out came the flags, bunting, banners, streamers and balloons, the secretly hoarded supplies of Spam, tinned fruit and jellies for the street parties and children's fancy dress parades. Thousands of people went to church for the first time in their lives. Thousands more flocked to the pubs with their extended opening hours, sang and danced in the streets until dawn.

The war was over. People simply couldn't believe it. Susan kept telling Irving and Bobby: *'We won the war! We won the war!'* and hugging them both. Grandpa scotched his one-Scotch rule and even Nana was persuaded to take a few sips.

Unbridled joy and relief flowed in equal measure throughout the whole of society. Huge crowds gathered in London on the afternoon of VE Day. In a speech in Trafalgar Square Winston Churchill told the multitude: 'This is your victory.' The crowd roared back: 'No, it's yours.'

However, for many people mourning a loved one killed in service or in an air raid, it was a bittersweet moment. Victory had come at a price. After the parties were over there was a feeling of anti-climax. Some felt they had lost a sense of purpose in their lives. Rationing would remain for another nine years. The war had ended but the misery lingered on.

SIX

Some people manage to avoid confronting death until well into their adult lives, when they are better able to cope with it. For others the realisation that they are not going to live for ever hits them during their formative years and childhood comes to an abrupt end. Irving was 14 when Grandpa died. He realised his grandfather's health was failing when their outings became less frequent and then stopped altogether. And when Grandpa was suddenly confined to bed he knew it was serious. The whole family did but when the cerebral haemorrhage finally struck it still came as a shock.

'Into every life a little rain must fall,' the Rev Gerald Williams told the family when preparations were made for the funeral. But for Irving Junior it felt more like a prolonged deluge. Grandpa lay in an open coffin in his home's front parlour and neither Nana, Susan, David nor the elderly pastor could decide whether it was desirable for his grandson to view the body. In their grief and distress they all feared death, Irving could tell. Even the Rev Williams. They wanted to protect him from a frightening experience.

In the end the decision was left to the boy. He still couldn't believe Grandpa was dead. He wanted to remember him in life, smoking his pipe on the allotment and telling him to be brave and stand up straight. At the same time he couldn't just walk away from his dear old friend and mentor without saying goodbye.

The front window curtains were drawn and they switched on the light as he entered the parlour, gripping his mother's hand tightly. At first he couldn't bear to look at the coffin but glanced instead at the old soldier's picture on the wall with his row of campaign medals. Then his gaze fell on the seemingly sleeping figure, the features grey and drawn but the white moustache as splendid as ever. It was too much for the young boy. He didn't feel fear
-- just suddenly very lonely. Tears welled up in his eyes and he ran from the room.

He'd learned at Sunday school that good people who believed in Jesus went to heaven when they died and there could be no doubt that Grandpa was a good person. But nobody, not even the Rev Williams, could tell him where heaven was, although everyone agreed it was 'a better place'. 'He's just gone on ahead,' the pastor said comfortingly. 'You'll meet him again one day.' Irving thought he didn't sound too confident.

A British Legion bugler sounded *The Last Post* as Private Breen's Union Jack-draped coffin was lowered into its last resting place. The small group of mourners threw handfuls of earth into the grave followed by a single red rose from Nana and Captain David, of the Merchant Navy, saluted smartly.

When the Rev Williams led the solemn prayers closing with the words:

'Eternal rest grant unto him, Oh Lord,'

Irving's fragile composure cracked and he sobbed loudly. It set everyone else off. Hugs and condolences were shared all round and Irving was sure he heard a voice sounding remarkably like Grandpa's telling him to

'Stand up straight, boy.'

Irving had been doing well at Whitefield Grammar School. Although baffled by mathematics he excelled at English and French, and was fascinated by history and geography. But when Grandpa died that all changed. For a time he suffered headaches and ringing noises in his ears. The family GP prescribed painkillers which eased the headaches but not the head noises. He diagnosed tinnitus, an unusual complaint in one so young. It played havoc with Irving's school progress. He could no longer concentrate on his lessons and lost interest in all the subjects, even

PE and games.

From an early stage his maths teacher had realised he had little aptitude for the subject. But when his pupil started gazing out of the classroom windows for long periods during lessons, it was the last straw. A strict disciplinarian with a sadistic streak, he would drag the boy out to the front of the class by his hair and make him chalk some incomprehensible formula on the blackboard.

When the task proved too much, he would make fun of his efforts and encourage the class to laugh at him. They needed no encouragement. Almost all Manchester United supporters, they taunted him mercilessly for his support of City which proved what a loser he was. In later more enlightened times such bullying by teaching staff and pupils would never have been tolerated. Remembering Grandpa's advice -- 'don't let anyone browbeat you' -- Irving developed his own form of intolerance. He started to skip school.

After breakfast, his mother would leave the house before him. She would hurry off to catch the bus into Manchester and her part-time job at the CWS. Irving would stay home instead of catching the bus to Whitefield, in the other direction. He would read his *Beano* or *Hotspur* comics, perks from his early morning delivery round for the local newsagent, and listen to dance music on the wireless. The elderly Bobby would watch him reproachfully as if sensing all was not as it should be.

Then before his mother was due to return home he'd slope off to Brawton Plaza, the local cinema, to watch the matinee, using his bus fare and dinner money to pay for his ticket. Westerns were his favourite films. He had a soft spot for Roy Rogers and his horse, Trigger. There were times when he was the only customer in the entire cinema. It seemed the whole performance was being screened specially for him. That suited Irving perfectly.

He made sure he returned home at the usual time. If his mother asked him about his day, he pretended he'd enjoyed the maths lesson and was beginning to understand algebra. He hated lying to her but became quite plausible at it. She never suspected a thing. At other times he would use the money he earned from his paper round to venture further afield. He'd take the tram to Belle Vue, retracing the route he and Grandpa used to take but avoiding the parrot and monkey houses. Instead he'd make for the rowing boats and row round the deserted lake, imagining it was the limitless ocean and he was alone in a world free from all overbearing authority, school bullies and people generally.

The illusion would fade when an attendant using a megaphone told him his time was up, so he paid sixpence more for another hour. Then he'd go on the dodgems and the ghost train before ordering waffles and coffee in the cafe, making sure he saved a shilling for the tram fare home.

A trip to the coast was more expensive. There were train, tram and ferryboat fares to pay plus the cost of meals and amusements. But the call of the sea in the shape of the Mersey ferryboats was too strong to resist and he could no longer wait until he'd saved enough money. On one of his truant days, after his mother had left the house for work, he sat at the dressing table in her bedroom admiring the reflection of a handsome dark haired 15-year-old with a pale complexion and tiny birthmark from different angles in the triple mirrors.

Then he reached for the top drawer in which he had seen his mother keep her cash. He knew what he had in mind was wrong and even as he thought about it he felt the start of a headache and the ringing head noises. But he slowly opened the drawer and within seconds had located the small bundle of banknotes under some handkerchiefs. There were two large white five pound notes, several pound notes and ten shilling notes.

For a long time he looked at the money. The pain and tinnitus grew worse but the temptation became irresistible. A pound would supplement his funds for the day's excursion. Hopefully, his mother would not notice the absence of a single pound note. Then again, a ten shilling note would hardly be missed either. He eased the two banknotes from their pile, rearranged the handkerchiefs and closed the drawer carefully. It was like a sort of loan really, he told himself as he hurried from the room. He'd pay his mother back one day when he had a grown-up job. But there was no way he could look at himself in the mirrors again.

For Irving, New Brighton was at its best out of season. It was like a ghost town. He wandered round the deserted amusement park, riding on the dodgem cars when there were no other cars to dodge and spending his pennies on the slot machines in the near-empty arcades. He found the cafe where he and Grandpa had lunched and ordered meat and two-veg for three shillings and sixpence.

Throughout the meal members of staff kept an anxious eye on the solitary fresh-faced kid in his school uniform. They seemed relieved and touchingly grateful when he paid up afterwards, complete with a generous tip of sixpence. He realised they half expected him to do a runner but such dramas would never occur to him. He may be a loner but he wasn't bent. Then he remembered the pound and ten shilling notes. Well, not really bent. He'd pay his mother back one day after all.

If there was time before catching the train

back to Manchester, Irving would take in a short film at the local news theatre and it was here that his solitary lifestyle showed its vulnerable side. As he was about to buy his ticket at the box office a short middle aged man with spectacles and a comb-over sidled up and insisted on paying for both of them. Irving found it strange but didn't object. Maybe it was just the guy's good deed for the day.

He did find it odd when his benefactor sat next to him in the darkened and almost deserted auditorium but he seemed harmless enough. He had a strong Scouse accent and made intelligent comments on the newsreels and laughed with him at the cartoons. But then he found an arm round his shoulder and the conversation took on a more personal note.

'Shouldn't you be at school?'

Irving drew away from the man but was prepared for that sort of question. 'Got the afternoon off... teacher was taken ill.'

'Are you Everton or Liverpool?'

'Manchester City.'

'Not from round here then?'

'Nope.'

'Do you have a girlfriend?'

'Nope.'

'How come a handsome young man like you doesn't have a girlfriend?'

Irving began to feel uncomfortable. 'I'm not old enough.'

'Course you're old enough. Maybe you're too shy, eh?'

Irving said nothing. The guy was right about that but he wasn't going to say so. His companion produced a magazine and moved a little closer. His expression was cheerful but there was a steely glint behind the spectacles. 'I bet some of the girls in here would soon turn you on. Want to have a look?'

'No thanks.' The conversation was becoming embarrassing. He'd taken the odd sly glance at similar magazines on his newsagents' top shelf. His curiosity had left him with a deeply disturbing sensation. He was in no hurry to repeat it, certainly not with this
weird stranger old enough to be his father.

The man laughed quietly. 'Bet you do really. We can look at them in the gents if you like.' He got up. 'I'll go in first, you follow in a couple of minutes.'

As soon as the creep had left, Irving fled the cinema. He took the next ferry back to Liverpool. The wind was getting up and the Mersey was choppier than usual. The ringing in the ears he experienced at times of stress returned, along with the dull headache. He sat with the pensioners in the saloon, pulling his blazer tightly round him. Growing up had suddenly become a lot less fun.

What Irving needed, of course, was a permanent father figure in his life and when David finally secured a shore-based Admiralty job in Manchester after much lobbying, his son's truancy came to a swift end. One of his father's first tasks was to arrange a meeting between Susan and himself and the headmaster of Whitefield Grammar School. The couple were shocked to learn of Irving's erratic attendance and poor academic performance. Susan blamed herself for failing in her duty to her son while preoccupied with her CWS job and taking care of Nana after Grandpa's death.

David was quick to console her. He maintained the teaching staff were to blame for not bringing the absenteeism to her attention. Their feeble excuse had been that they had to deal with far worse cases. Some pupils bunked off school for weeks at a time. Irving had slipped through the net as he had only taken odd days off. It was the sort of disciplinary shambles which David would never have tolerated aboard his ship but, back on land, he realised standards were alarmingly slipshod.

He set about mending fences by helping Irving with his homework, in particular his maths, an area where Susan had been helpless as she also found the subject baffling.
With his father's expert assistance their son

finally got his head round algebra, an achievement that coincided with the appointment of a new maths teacher for the fifth form. Dad took him to Maine Road to watch Manchester City and the team actually won a couple of matches but remained rooted near the bottom of the second division while United were top of the first.

There was a brief hiccup in the rehabilitation process when Bobby died. At the grand old age of 15 the Breen family's faithful cross-bred collie finally succumbed to acute distemper. Several desperate visits were made to the vet's surgery, each time an injection delaying the inevitable for a little longer. But the day soon came when they had to look into the sad brown eyes and cuddle their long-suffering pet for the final time. He seemed to understand and his tail wagged weakly. Tearfully, all three of them left Bobby with the vet who assured them he would take good care of him. Everyone knew what that meant.

Having a live-in father turned Irving's life around with a spin-off of contentment for both Susan and Nana. Susan was able to give up the CWS job and concentrate on being a full-time housewife. Nana. whose osteoarthritis was now limiting her movement, came to live with the family at Susan's insistence, sleeping in the spare bedroom. She could still bake a mean apple pie and strum out old songs and hymns on the family's piano, while singing along in a quavering voice. One of her favourite hymns was *Fight the Good Fight* which they often sang at church on Sundays.

The good fight was a frequently recurring theme in conversation with Irving. Taking over from where Grandpa had left off, the grey-haired matriarch instilled into her grandson the vital need to stay clean in an increasingly murky world. Life was an ongoing battle between good and evil. You had to stand up for what was good.

Irving's problem was that as he stood on the threshold of adult life he had yet to learn how to tell the difference.

The first major purchase David made on becoming a senior executive with the Admiralty, was a top-of-the -range Austin limousine with a six-cylinder engine, walnut dashboard, luxurious leather seats and most impressive of all, a heater and radio. Family outings resumed on a more restrained note with Grandpa and Bobby conspicuous by their absence.

David had seen enough of Liverpool but still enjoyed Blackpool, the Pleasure Beach and the Winter Gardens. Further north, the Lake District and Yorkshire Dales worked their charm on the family. As they toured the Aire Valley with its rolling meadows and quaint stone cottages, David and Susan agreed it would be the ideal location for retirement in a few years' time.

Irving, of course, had his whole life ahead of him. Past lapses forgotten, his school work improved out of all recognition. With David's help he retrieved all lost ground and sailed through matriculation at the age of 16. Armed with a School Certificate that had earlier seemed out of reach he could not wait to leave academia behind. There was no way he wanted to stay on at school in the sixth form and progress to university. He was ready to make his mark on the real world, the university of life. The only question was: doing what?

He still fancied a career in the navy but his father talked him out of it. His own experience had taught him that a sailor's life was far from the romantic image it enjoyed. Apart from the unpredictable behaviour of the sea itself, with 10 foot waves one day and flat calm the next, life at sea was hard work. Discipline on board was strict, with little room for individualism and self-expression. It did not agree with sensitive souls. To be a sailor you needed a tough, obedient disposition as well as a cast iron stomach. David knew his son possessed neither. He was not cut out for life at sea.

What was the boy really good at, his father wanted to know. The answer was English. He had gained distinctions in both English Language and English Literature in his School Certificate. His essays had been highly commended by the teachers. David had read them and realised his son had a natural flair for writing -- a 'way with words' which he himself, being more maths-inclined, respected. "Why not be a journalist?" he suggested and his son's destiny was decided.

The idea instantly appealed to Irving. His visits to the cinema had featured several films about American newspaper reporters tracking down dangerous criminals and achieving exciting scoops for their hard-bitten editors. The reporters tended to be dynamic young men, hard drinking and smoking, with trilby hats on the back of their heads and admired by beautiful young women. It seemed like a glamorous lifestyle.

The only drawbacks, as far as he could see, were the need to learn shorthand and typing. There was also the little matter of finding a newspaper prepared to employ him as a junior reporter. You couldn't just walk into the Daily Mirror, the Times or the Telegraph and ask for a job, you had to start with a local paper. It was long before the days of university courses in journalism.

His father suggested writing letters of application to editors of weekly newspapers in the area and some further afield and he set about the task with enthusiasm. It steadily diminished as the editors either replied that they had no vacancies for editorial trainees or failed to respond at all. It turned out to be useful experience for the young hopeful as constant rejections, rudeness and hostility are part and parcel of a journalist's life.

As is often the case, however, just when he was about to give up hope and apply for a job as a shoe salesman, his luck changed. A vacancy had arisen for a junior reporter at the Brawton Chronicle and he received a letter from its editor-in-chief, Mr Wilfred Andrews, offering him an interview. It was the break he'd been looking for and in his home town for good measure. Excitedly the Breen household set about preparing him for his big adventure.

There was no shortage of advice on how to behave and what to say at the interview. He would need to wash round the back of his neck, comb his hair neatly, clean and file his fingernails, wear a clean shirt and tie, and freshly pressed trousers. His shoes would have to be polished to a shine all the way round including the back. Attention to all these details was essential, his father assured him. It was what employers wanted to see in their junior staff.
If they took care of their appearance it was likely they'd be equally conscientious in their work. Timekeeping was even more important. No employers would tolerate persistent lateness however smartly dressed you were.

To make sure Irving arrived for the interview punctually his father drove him to the Chronicle's offices in the family car and parked round the corner from the main entrance. He could sense his son's nervousness. 'Just take a few deep breaths and you'll be fine,' he told him. 'Speak clearly and be polite. Be confident even if you don't feel it. Tell them you want to be a reporter because you're good at English and you're keen to know what's going on in the world. I'd like to come in with you but that would defeat the object. They want someone who can stand up for himself. You're on your own now, Irving. Good luck!'

So, at the tender age of 16 and armed only with his School Certificate and a character reference from the Rev Williams, Irving took his first faltering steps into the mysterious world of journalism. On the stroke of 3pm, punctual to the second, he was ushered into the old-fashioned wood panelled office of Mr Wilfred Andrews JP, the paper's proprietor.

The white-haired septuagenarian, an archetypal newspaper editor in waistcoat and shirtsleeves, was studying a page proof on a large ornate desk and barely looked up as Irving entered. 'Sit down, son,' he muttered. The fresh faced, smartly dressed teenager sat on a plain uncomfortable chair and waited.

'So you want to be a journalist?' the old man said, looking up over rimless spectacles.

'Yes, sir,'

'Why?'

'Well, I want to know what's going on in

the world, and I'm good at writing. I got a distinction in English in my exams. This is my School Certificate.'

The venerable editor took the document, untied the blue ribbon and studied its contents. 'Interesting,' he said after a pause. 'Do you understand what the work entails?'

'I think so, sir.'

'It's a tough job, long hours, some night work. Council meetings, court reporting... can you do shorthand?'

'Not yet, but I can learn -- at night school.'

'Any references?'

'Yes, sir.' Irving extracted the Rev Williams' glowing testimonial from his jacket pocket, unfolded it and handed it over. 'This is from the minister at our church in Brawton.'

'Trustworthy, honest and reliable,' Mr Andrews read aloud. 'You need to be all those things as a journalist. You also need initiative and an enquiring mind -- and to write accurate copy quickly under pressure. Do you think you can handle that?'

'Yes, sir. I'm confident I can.'

'That's what I like -- confidence. Go over there by the window where I can see you.'

Irving got up and walked to the window.

The old man swivelled in his chair and regarded the boy standing in the afternoon sunshine. 'Turn round,' he ordered.

Irving thought the command strange but

turned round smartly. Perhaps the backs of his shoes were under inspection.

'Fine,' Mr Andrews said. 'You can start next month as a junior reporter. Your wage will be two pounds ten shillings a week for a six-month probationary period. Then three pounds weekly, providing your shorthand is up to scratch. It's a five-year apprenticeship scheme with annual pay increases subject to satisfactory performance. Any questions?'

'No sir. Thank you very much.'

'My secretary will send you a letter to confirm the starting date. Many leading journalists began their careers with the Chronicle, Irving. I hope you'll be one of them.'

'So do I, sir!'

SEVEN

The year was 1950. The Second World War had been over for five years but to maintain capitalism's insatiable appetite for international conflict, a new war had broken out in Korea. The Labour Party, led by Clement Attlee, won the General Election by a drastically reduced majority compared with its landslide victory five years earlier. Manchester City were languishing in the Second Division while Manchester United were riding high in the First. The average UK wage was £7 a week, slightly higher than the National Union of Journalists' minimum rate for qualified staff on the Brawton Chronicle.

That autumn, two sixteen-year-old trainee reporters joined their ranks at the union's probationary rate of £2.10 shillings. One was Jamie Lee, from Whitefield. The other was Irving Breen, from Brawton. Both were starting their careers straight from grammar school and were studying shorthand and typing at evening classes. Both were beginning a learning curve that would take them to top jobs in Fleet Street but for the present they were innocents at large, on the brink of a big, very bad world and about to be thrown in at the deep end.

One of the paper's senior reporters, Alistair McKenzie, was delegated as their mentor. A quietly spoken Scot with thinning sandy hair turning grey, he had worked for almost every publication in Fleet Street. If anyone could keep the novices afloat during their sink-or-swim initiation it was this seasoned wordsmith. 'Well now, my brave wee laddies, so you want to be jairnalists,' he greeted the two tyros as they presented themselves nervously at his desk in the cramped editorial office. Jamie and Irving were far from 'wee'. Jamie was a gangling six-footer while Irving was slightly shorter and slimmer. But both were trying their best to look brave.

For the time being, they would be sharing Alistair's desk with its ageing Remington typewriter, telephone and well-worn contacts book as space was limited. The newsroom was partitioned off from a larger composing room containing linotype printing machines and smelled of ink and newsprint. It housed six staff including Alistair and Jack Hurst, the news editor who doubled as a sub-editor, plus four reporters. They were middle-aged Gordon Lomas, Roy Clarke, a plump Brian Simpson, doubling as a sports reporter/editor, and a young woman -- unusual in those days -- Rita Kennedy, whose tousled auburn hair framed an oval, acne-plagued face. Most were heavy smokers, Rita in particular relying on her Players Medium cork-tipped cigarettes for support as deadlines approached.

Their desks were close together and when everyone was present, such as on press days, moving between them could be awkward. Plans were afoot to extend the newsroom into the printing area to accommodate more staff. Alistair managed to squeeze two chairs, one each side of his desk, for the trainees and presented them with two pristine reporters' notebooks and ballpoint pens. Armed with the tools of their trade, they took down practice dictation in rudimentary shorthand, with Alistair reading slowly from that week's edition of the Chronicle. They could barely keep up with him.

'What's you shorthand speed, Irving?' Alistair asked.

'Forty words a minute.'

'And yours, Jamie?'

The same. Forty words a minute.'

'That's no bad for starters. I expect you to be up to 100 words a minute after six months.'

It sounded a daunting challenge but after a few sessions on the Press bench in Brawton Magistrates' Court alongside Alistair, Irving was surprised how his verbatim note-taking improved. This was mainly due to the pedestrian pace at which justice was dispensed, with solicitors frequently told to slow down their questioning while the JPs made their own laborious notes in longhand.

The case lists varied little from day to day -- drunk and disorderly larrikins now sobered up and shamefaced, bus and train fare dodgers, speeding motorists and pathetic shoplifters pleading poverty and saddled with fines making them even poorer.

Occasionally there'd be people accused of serious sex and violent crimes. Irving's 'deep end' moment arrived with the case of a drug addict accused of attempted murder by swinging his baby son round by his legs and battering his head against a wall, causing irreversible brain damage. He denied the charge but pleaded guilty to GBH. The magistrates remanded him in custody for trial at Manchester Crown Court.

Irving, still a boy fresh from school, was visibly shaken by the case. Half way through the hearing he asked to be relieved from covering it but Alistair was unsympathetic. He described the accused as 'the dregs of society'. There were plenty more where he came from so Irving had better get used to it.

Then there were meetings of Brawton Urban District Council held in the ornate Victorian debating chamber at Brawton Town Hall, when self-important local councillors held forth on such matters as planning applications, street lighting, dustbin collection and road widening schemes as if they were vitally important affairs of state. Debates were usually conducted at a slightly faster speed than in the law courts, with speakers keeping one eye on the green baize-covered Press table to see if the young reporters were keeping up with their eloquence.

When Alistair was unable to supervise them due to his own workload, Irving and Jamie were never idle for long. Jack Hurst, the overbearing news editor, saw to that. When they were not answering the telephone or making tea for the hard pressed editorial staff they were drafted into the proof readers' tiny cubby hole adjoining the composing room. They would sit and read from edited copy while the two ancient proof readers, Mr Coppuck and Mr Hall, corrected the numerous printing errors in galley proof form. Both were retired school teachers and keenly interested in the trainees' academic performances. During their time as proof readers they'd seen numerous journalistic hopefuls come and go but both agreed these two were among the brightest.

There was also the dreaded chore of compiling wedding and funeral reports from report forms filled in by members of the public. These reports followed a rigid template along the lines of:

The wedding took place on (date) between (bride's name) of (bride's address) and (groom's name) of (groom's address) at (name of church etc). The bride wore a dress   of (describe material and style) and the bridesmaids (state names) wore dresses of   (describe). The bride's mother (name) wore a dress of (describe)... and so on,   including names of the best man, officiating clergy and all the guests, plus details of   the reception and honeymoon destination.

Funeral reports followed a similar pattern, including rambling biographies and long lists of mourners. Often the handwriting would be barely legible and the forms stained with tea, beer, ketchup and in the case of funerals, tears. Details would be confused, with numerous spelling mistakes, alterations and crossings-out. It was up to the cub reporters to convert it all into accurate copy, bearing in mind the first golden rule of journalism drummed into them by Alistair:

SPELL PEOPLE'S NAMES CORRECTLY

Mistakes would be pounced on not only by irate telephone callers the following Monday but by Mr Hurst himself using equally obnoxious language.

When it came to coverage of everyday news stories, Alistair taught them the basic formula of 'who, what, where and when' plus the importance of the word 'alleged' in police inquiries and court reporting.

'Who did what, where did they do it and when did they do it?' the veteran wordsmith told them. 'You need to answer all these questions high up in your story. Then there's the equally important question of *why* did they do it. So many reporters fail to deal with this. Take the case of a protest march by jobless people. It's not enough to say when and where the demo took place, roughly how many people took part, what the weather was like, how many arrests were made and so on -- the real story is *why* they did it!

'Mingle with the marchers, talk to them and they'll tell you their grievances... hair-raising stuff about lay-offs, victimisation, cuts to their dole money, unable to feed their kids, strong-arm police tactics. Get to know the organisers, the trade union leaders and you'll hear the inside story.'

'You need lots of contacts, don't you?' Irving offered.

'I was coming to that. The more names and phone numbers you have in your contacts book the better. They don't all have to be bigwigs. Sometimes people lower down the pecking order know more about what's going on than their bosses. Always check your facts and then double check. Take nothing at face value. Question everything, especially stuff you're told 'off the record'. Beware of people who say "to be honest" or "I'll be totally honest with you" -- it could mean they're *not* always totally honest.'

'Surely that's just a figure of speech,' Jamie said.

'Aye it's a figure of speech and it's also a Freudian slip, laddie. It gives them away for what they are -- dodgy. Another dead giveaway is the word "refute." I'm working on a story right now about a cowboy market trader accused of selling counterfeit goods. He keeps saying he refutes the allegations. He means he denies them but he's looked up '"refute" in the dictionary and found it means "disprove." He's counting on people not knowing the real meaning of the word. If we fall into his trap and report that he has refuted the allegations he can then say we've confirmed that he's disproved them!'

'Smart operator,' Irving said.

'Street-smart. It's a favourite trick of cheap jack lawyers everywhere. So we've got to be street-smart too and avoid these pitfalls or we'll be in trouble.'

Three months with more tricks of the trade thrown in elapsed before Alistair felt confident Irving and Jamie were likely to make the grade as journalists. That was when he introduced them to the second golden rule of their craft: the vital importance of joining the union.

'To survive in this job you need to be in the NUJ,' he told his charges on one of their newsgathering rounds -- pub crawls as they were called. You chatted to landlords, your contacts, and bought them drinks on expenses but drank little yourself.

The trio were seated in the Swan Inn, a

popular local venue with its own billiards room and bowling green, Alistair with a half of bitter, his pupils with their Cokes and ice. Their instructor dug into his jacket pocket and produced two Press cards. 'Now you represent the Brawton Chronicle and going solo quite soon you'll need identification,' he told them. He handed them the National Union of Journalists' cards, each with a blank space for their photographs.

'The NUJ issue these cards for probationary members. They're recognised by the police, fire and health authorities just like full members' cards. Whenever you cover a story it's important to tell people who you are, the paper you represent and show them your Press card. That way they can't say they didn't know they were talking to a reporter.'

Irving was immensely proud of his Press card. He regarded it as his own form of status symbol. Other teenagers in his neighbourhood bragged about their expensive racing bikes and Manchester United season tickets but he possessed something more impressive. His Press card boosted his self-esteem. It opened doors which remained closed to others. He was a professional journalist -- albeit still a trainee -- and he was earning money for writing in newspapers instead of delivering them.

Alistair recognised the symptoms of delusions of grandeur in both his apprentices. It was a normal response from juveniles who had still to experience the hard knocks of their chosen profession. All too soon there would be times when possession of an NUJ Press card would lead not to respect but abuse and hostility, frequently heavy-handed.

In another tutorial in the Swan, he told them: 'In this job you have to take the rough with the intolerable. Doors will be slammed in your face. People will hang up on you on the phone. They'll accuse you of telling lies and misquoting them. That's why your shorthand notes are essential. They'll demand to know your sources -- and that's where the third golden rule of jairnalism comes in.'

He took out a well thumbed copy of the NUJ Code of Conduct and handed it to Irving. 'The union's code of conduct spells it out. Read it out loud for us, laddie.'

Irving took the booklet and read: "The foundation on which all confidential information is exchanged between a journalist and a source is mutual trust. The ability of journalists to act in the public interest is contingent on their ability to honour commitments made in good faith to a source of confidential information.

"The highest level of protection, under international law, must be afforded to journalists in respect of privacy in their communications and in respect to the right to protect confidential sources of information received and published in the public interest."

Alistair stopped him there. 'In other words, we have a solemn duty to protect the identity of our sources at all times -- regardless of who may be pressuring us to tell them. And that includes the police. Jairrnalists must be prepared to go to prison if necessary to protect their sources. Some have done so. The union always looks after them and their families.

'If you think that's tough remember that the job's a lot more challenging in other countries. Do you know how many jairnalists have been killed in the line of duty during the last 20 years?'

They had no idea.

'Over a thousand -- reporters and media staff just doing their jobs. Places like South America, Russia and Israel where they shoot first and ask questions afterwards. Just thank your lucky stars it's no like that here.'

'We won't be needing bulletproof vests just yet then,' Jamie grinned. He was a happy-go-lucky lad and a bit of a practical joker. He rarely took anything seriously.

'No but when you get on the nationals you soon realise there are plenty of unsavoury characters in this country who hate us -- because we bring into the open what they would rather stay hidden. When you progress to Fleet Street you're likely to face harassment and threats, even bribes to cover up the truth.'

'They'll say they're protecting their right to privacy, won't they?' Irving said. He had done some homework on the subject.

'That's what they call it but really they're just trying to hide their dark secrets. Don't let them kid you about their right to privacy. The public have a greater right to know what's going on in the world. They pay their taxes and need to know how their leaders are spending their money, how they're dealing with crime and corruption. It's our job to tell them.'

'I've been thinking about that,' Irving said. 'Who do we really serve as journalists? Do we serve our proprietor or our readers?'

'Or the advertisers?' Jamie put in.

'We sairve all of them and none of them,' Alistair answered. 'We work for Mr Andrews, our dear proprietor, of course. He pays our wages. We also work for the advertisers, they *help* to pay our wages.'

'So do the readers,' Irving reminded him. 'They buy the paper, they pay us to tell them the news.'

'So they do. But they also pay us to tell them the truth. Above all, y'see, jairnalists are sairvants of the truth. Don't ever forget that, laddies.'

The shortage of space in the Chronicle's editorial department was the sort of minor irritation that could escalate at edition times on Thursdays -- press days. Linotype operators and compositors in their ink-stained overalls added to the traffic with their demand for copy from reporters under pressure to meet their deadlines. Collisions were unavoidable and could lead to bad-tempered exchanges. It was significant that these involved one printer more than others.

His name was Mike, a short balding linotype operator aged about 50 with protruding eyes. He had already upset Gordon Lomas and Brian Simpson by pressing himself against them as they passed each other, with Brian threatening robust consequences if it happened again. But then Mike appeared to single out Irving for similar treatment, brushing against the youth several times. When it happened again, with Mike pressing hard on the boy's buttocks, Irving complained to Alistair, who told Jack Hurst, who was far too busy sub-editing stacks of late copy to do anything about it.

On a less busy day during their lunch break Irving mentioned Mike's behaviour to Jamie. The pair had polished off fish and chips at a nearby cafe and with half an hour of their break left were playing snooker at a billiards hall. Jamie, a few months older than Irving, gave his junior colleague the benefit of his worldly wisdom.

'Mike's a queer,' he said. 'Best to keep out

of his way.'

Irving felt foolish. He didn't know what a 'queer' was. In his 16 years he had never heard of homosexuals. Jamie had to spell out in graphic detail what sodomy meant.

It was the rookie journalist's first encounter with gut-wrenching revulsion. Still a naive schoolboy at heart, he simply could not believe it. But then the memory of a middle-aged man who'd accosted him years earlier in a New Brighton cinema flashed across his mind. He felt his fish and chips lunch churning in his stomach and fled to the toilets where he was violently sick. Years later, in a more upside-down society, such a reaction would be deemed 'homophobic' but he couldn't help it. The queasiness never failed to assail him when obliged to report on 'gay' issues.

A few days after his eighteenth birthday, with Irving now 'going solo' as a junior reporter writing fluent shorthand at over 100 wpm, his National Service call-up papers arrived. Having completed his probationary period without blemish and now earning the princely wage of three pounds a week, a promising journalistic career lay ahead but for now the RAF's need of him was greater than the Brawton Chronicle's.

The editorial staff gave him a rousing send-off at the Swan, when he was allowed to down a full pint of bitter followed by a whisky chaser for the first time. The spotty Rita Kennedy, who had developed a protective instinct for him, gave him a lingering kiss on the cheek -- which he discreetly wiped off at the first opportunity -- and Alistair a rousing lecture on the need to watch his back as a greenhorn conscript.

'We'll keep your job open for you, laddie,' the Scotsman told him. 'Don't get any ideas about running off to Fleet Street when your two years are up. You need to finish your time here.' Irving's fellow trainee Jamie had received the same lecture several months earlier when his own call-up papers arrived from the Army.

Slightly inebriated, Irving travelled home in the luxury of a taxi. National Service lasted for two years but something -- call it intuition or an alcohol-fuelled premonition -- told him he'd be back in the Chronicle's smoke-filled newsroom much sooner than expected.

Irving's middle ear defect was not picked up during the initial medical examination at RAF Padgate, near Warrington. He was passed fit for service as an Aircraftsman Second Class along with the rest of his intake after a rudimentary check-up. There followed three months of gruelling square-bashing led by an obnoxious drill sergeant and fatigue duties such as peeling potatoes and cleaning toilet blocks. Evenings in the barracks were spent polishing his boots to a mirror finish and looking at girlie magazines passed round by recruits given to boasting about their sexual experiences. Irving knew it was all bravado and that, like him, they were mostly virgins.

When the NCOs were satisfied he could march in a straight line and come to an abrupt halt at the same time as everyone else, they marched him off to RAF Hornchurch in East London as an aircrew candidate. Here he was subjected to stringent aptitude tests. Using dummy aircraft controls he was required to keep a dot of light in a central position on a screen despite the light suddenly darting away. The object was to test the speed of a recruit's reactions. Other tests involved rapidly inserting square and round pegs into suitable holes on a board in a given time, to assess speed and co-ordination.

Irving found he was quite adept at these exercises and looked forward to the next stage of the training programme -- basic flight simulation. However, a further more rigorous medical check-up was necessary. Before learning to fly an aircraft costing millions of pounds the RAF had to be sure their pilots' sight and hearing were not just adequate but 100 per cent perfect. Sophisticated tests on eyes and ears were performed using flashing lights and symbols plus different sound frequencies. They showed Irving had flawless vision but less-than-perfect hearing, due to a middle ear abnormality.

He could hear most sounds however faint but failed to detect others on certain wavelengths. The condition was likely to deteriorate, leading to acute deafness, the doctors told him. So he was discharged as 'unlikely to become efficient on medical grounds' -- despite passing everything else and being told that otherwise he was considered ideal officer material.

It was disappointing for all concerned, not least for Nana who had visualised her grandson fighting the good fight in the best family tradition. She had reserved a special place on her mantelpiece for a photograph of him in RAF officer's uniform and pilot's wings. Irving senior would have been so proud. But fate clearly had other plans. There was no shortage of good fights facing the young man as an officer in the service of truth.

They welcomed him back with open arms at the Brawton Chronicle -- those of Rita Kennedy being particularly accommodating He noticed that her acne had almost cleared up and she'd had her hair permed. He also noticed -- for the first time -- that she had rather shapely legs, thanks to a short, tight-fitting split skirt.

'We've all missed you, lover boy, Rita said, her intense blue eyes telling him she really meant it. She reached for her 20-pack of Players Medium and offered him one although she knew he didn't smoke.

'You're not going to tempt me, Rita,' he said.

'One day,' she replied. 'Give it time.'

She was a few years older than him and he'd never regarded her as anything other than a disorganised and feisty colleague. But now she'd worked on her appearance, she no longer seemed unattractive. In fact...

Immediately the image of Emily flashed into his mind and the pain of their enforced separation during his brief career as an aircraftsman second class returned. No way, he decided. Absolutely no contest.

EIGHT

The band at the Odeon Ballroom was playing a slow foxtrot. The velvet smooth saxophones, the muted brass and the gently pulsing rhythm section offered perfect backing for the mellifluous female vocalist, singing a popular ballad of the day, *Where or When?*

It seems we stood and talked like this before

We looked at each other in the same way then

But I can't remember where or when...

'Where've you been, Irving?' Emily asked.

He smiled and held her closely as they swayed on the crowded dance floor. At last she'd stopped calling him by his surname. 'Oh, exciting places... Hornchurch... Padgate... I failed my RAF medical.'

She drew back and the green eyes widened. 'Why, what's wrong with you?'

'They say I'm going deaf but I can hear perfectly!'

'So you're back for good?'

'Sorry, what did you say?'

They laughed together in shared delight, as young lovers do.

The clothes you're wearing are the clothes you wore
The smile you are smiling you were smiling then
But I can't remember where or when

It was love all right. The real thing. How could they be sure? It was the first time for both of them, after all.

Or was it?

Some things that happen for the first time
Seem to be happening again
And so it seems that we have met before
And laughed before and loved before
But who knows where or when?

The music ended and the lights went up but they clung to each other for a long moment. The song's lyrics had left Irving strangely light-headed and breathless. Could he and Emily have loved and laughed before in another world? Were they simply recognising each other from last time?

Maybe that's what true love was -- recognition. Caring for someone in a previous existence must be the only memory strong enough to survive the trauma of rebirth and the process of relearning life. It was what made you soulmates.

Suddenly he knew what Emily was going to say: 'So I've got you and the Air Force haven't.' He just knew. The certainty sent a shiver up his spine.

She took his hand and led him back to their table. 'So I've got you and the Air Force haven't.' The guileless eyes danced mischievously. 'Which would you rather have?'

He knew what he would answer as if it had been scripted for him. 'What a question... absolutely no contest!'

She had stopped calling him by his surname, as if he were a classmate, on leaving school. All too soon her carefree sixth form days of chemistry, her favourite subject, cookery, hockey and netball were over. She took a job as a laboratory assistant at a Salford pharmaceutical company and started using make-up. With a workmate, Gwen, she began ballroom dancing lessons and met boys, also fresh from school, who took her to the cinema and awkwardly tried to kiss her. None of them applied the slightest tug to her heartstrings. Until she met Breen.

Or rather, Irving.

Irving was different. Very different. Darkly handsome with soulful brown eyes and a shy smile. Flawless complexion -- he'd only just started shaving -- except for a tiny birthmark next to an eye. His beauty spot, as she called it. Whenever she thought of him, which was often, she went weak at the knees. Other boyfriends were dull, tongue-tied, rough and clumsy dancers. Gwen could have them. Irving was a prince by comparison. He was an intelligent talker with a glamorous job and an infectious sense of humour. He was also a sensational dancer -- and an even more sensational kisser. She was just 18, still naive and unworldly, but intuition drove all doubt from her mind. A compelling voice told her that he was THE ONE.

It was time to introduce him to her parents.

Fred and Lilian Shannon owned an off-licence and grocery store in Brawton, a mile from the Breen's and close to the border with down-market Salford. They lived above the shop with Emily and an elder son, Daniel. Their apartment was spacious and comfortable though not luxurious. Prominent among the lounge furniture was an upright piano -- a standard feature in almost every home however humble. The instrument was a Bluthner, an aristocrat of its species, and the couple's pride and joy. Emily had learned to play it from childhood and often accompanied Daniel, who was learning to play the guitar, as well as her father. Fred, the middle-aged head of the musical family, who had a fine tenor voice.

They made a fuss of Irving when Emily shyly brought her 'young man' home to afternoon tea. With Daniel looking after the shop, Lilian plied their visitor with strong tea, sausage rolls and buttered crumpets. The best china crockery was called into service and Fred produced a special vintage port wine from stock and cut glass schooners. It wasn't every day they welcomed a journalist -- albeit a junior reporter -- into their home.

'We've heard a lot about you,' Lilian said. 'What's it like being a reporter... is it like you see in the films?'

Irving was reluctant to disabuse her but it wasn't a bit like that. 'Not really, I'm just a trainee. There are two of us. We do all the boring stuff like wedding reports and funerals... not very exciting! Sometimes we cover the magistrates' court but not the juicy cases, just the drunks and petty thieves.'

Fred wanted to know about Irving's career prospects. 'You'll be on a good wage when you've done your training won't you?'

'I'll get the union rate plus expenses. But the real money is with the Manchester papers, like the Evening News and the nationals. The nationals pay their northern staff Fleet Street rates plus expenses and car allowance. That's where I'm aiming for -- a staff job on one of the nationals.'

'You're ambitious. That's good.'

'Irving's hoping for a job on the Guardian,' Emily said.

Fred frowned and ran his hand through receding grey hair. 'Not our kind of newspaper, I'm afraid. We're Catholics. They don't like Catholics. We take the Daily Mail here.'

'I'd settle for the Mail,' Irving said, tongue in cheek. 'But they're not ready for me yet. And I'm not ready for them. I need more experience, get a byline and some scoops.

'Scoops?' Lilian asked. "Like we use for ice cream?" Everyone laughed.

'Exclusives -- stories other papers have missed. I also need a car. I'm saving up for one and learning to drive. The lessons are expensive and I need a car to practise on. Dad won't let me use his. He says it's too powerful for a learner-driver.'

Fred had two vehicles, an old Ford van he used for business and a small Wolseley saloon. A lifelong Manchester City fan, he took an instant liking to his daughter's young man when he discovered he was also a 'true blue'. The lad supported City so he must be all right. 'You could practise in my car,' he told Irving. Which was exactly what Emily was hoping he would say.

On their nights out together, dancing or

going to the pictures, she and Irving went everywhere by bus. Neither of them smoked but even the smoke-filled top deck of a bus could be bathed in a magical glow for the starry-eyed couple. True to its reputation, it rained regularly in Manchester but Emily and Irving hardly noticed. The weather under their umbrella was permanently golden. Grim, grey, rainswept Manchester was their El Dorado.

But when it came to serious smooching, the back row at the cinema and shop doorways had their limitations. Sometimes, oblivious to the passage of time, Irving missed his last bus home and had to walk back, a distance of nearly two miles. She dreamed of the day he would pass his driving test and own a car.

The idea of driving a car herself never occurred to her or her parents. This was the 1950s, long before the era of the two-car family. Few women went out to work and even fewer drove cars. Those who did were frowned on and the subject of frequent jokes. A woman's place was in the home, caring for her husband and family. It would be up to Irving to provide the car and do the driving. That's when their love life, such as it was, could be expected to blossom.

But again, this was some 10 years before the permissive society known as the Swinging Sixties. There was an unwritten moral code for 'courting couples'. Sex before marriage was still taboo. Passion took you so far but no further.

You learnt self-control and restraint. True love waits you were told, but the waiting could be agonising and deeply frustrating. Still, Emily figured, canoodling, as her mother liked to call it, would be more fun in a car and a lot more comfortable.

The driving lessons in Fred's sedate Wolseley took place once or twice a week depending on Irving's fluctuating newsgathering duties and the equally fluctuating trade at the Shannon's busy off-licence. Thursdays, press days at the Brawton Chronicle, and Fridays, pay days for most of the store's customers, had to be avoided. Sundays were out as Emily and her family went at different times to Mass at St Peter's, their parish church.

Due to lack of practice in three-point turns, Irving failed his first driving test but passed second time. Off came the L-plates to be ceremoniously consigned to the dustbin and they cracked open the champagne. The following Sunday after Mass, with Daniel in charge of the shop, Irving and Emily set off for their maiden outing, with Emily in the front seat and Fred and Lilian in the back so there could be no 'hanky-panky'.

The Wolseley was not built for speed. It was designed for comfort, with leather seats, walnut dashboard and sunroof. There was even a rather primitive heater but, unlike his father's luxurious limo, power and acceleration were not its strong points. All the same, Irving's driving style might best be described as positive and several times Fred had to tell him to slow down.

'Just because you've passed your test doesn't mean you can drive like Sterling Moss,' he said. 'You're young and you've got quick reflexes but you must observe the speed limits like everyone else -- *almost* everyone else' he added, as a red sports car driven by a woman swept past. 'Women drivers!' he sighed, with a shake of the head.

Irving became a frequent visitor to the Shannon's off-licence and general store. In addition to beer, wines and spirits, it sold a wide range of groceries, greengrocery, hand-sliced bacon and cooked meats, milk, bread, eggs, cakes and confectionery. Sometimes, when they were short-staffed, he helped out behind the counter, with Daniel showing him the ropes.

Emily's brother, in his early twenties, had worked full-time in the store since leaving school at 16. He knew the price of everything, how to operate the beer pumps without spilling a drop, how to carve meat to perfection on the bacon slicer, how to make sure the old-fashioned weighing scales always showed generously more than the amount requested at no extra cost. He seemed to know the names of almost every customer and those of their children, who invariably received extra sweets for their pocket money.

Daniel was over 6ft tall so could easily reach all the mineral water bottles and cordials on the top shelves without difficulty. He grew his light brown hair to shoulder length and sported a wispy beard to match his gentle personality. In his spare time, not that he seemed to have much of it, he played the guitar. You could have called him an archetypal hippie -- some ten years before the species appeared on the cultural landscape.

Like the rest of his family, Daniel was a devout Catholic and a regular Mass attender at St Peter's, where he did voluntary work in the church's centre for poor and homeless people. Mass was celebrated four times on Sundays, morning and evening, and the Shannons were able to fit in services around the shop's opening hours. At some Masses when there was no organist. Daniel led the hymns on his guitar, though the delight of younger members of the congregation was not always shared by their elders. Guitars in church -- whatever next!

Daniel was a self-taught guitarist heavily into the skiffle and rock 'n roll, musical styles rapidly transforming the pop scene. Irving would sometimes sing along in impromptu concerts in the lounge with Emily on piano. Emily's favourite song was *Come - For it's June*. and she sang the lyrics as she played:

Wake from your dreaming my sweet, my sweet,

Open your wonderful eyes...
Come to your window and watch the sun
Watch it arise -- arise!
Fountains are playing so fair, so fair
Fragrant and cool in the balmy air
Roses are blossoming everywhere
Oh come -- for it's June -- it's June!

After a hard day covering the seamy side of life in Brawton Magistrates Court, her performance had a magical effect on Irving. It was like the sun coming out from behind dark clouds. Here was a world far removed from the baseness of human nature and the murky pressures of modern society. There were still people in it like Emily, the darling girl fate intended him to marry. Just how lucky could a young man get!

David and Susan Breen were not exactly thrilled about their son's romantic attachment at an age when his journalistic career had barely got off the ground. He and his girlfriend were not yet 20 after all. What could they possibly know about love at such an age? In the words of the latest pop song, *Too Young*, played on the wireless every hour or so, love was a word they'd only heard and couldn't begin to know the meaning of. They had their whole lives ahead of them yet it seemed Irving had his heart set on the girl and there could be no room for reason and common sense in romantic affairs.

But there was another deep-seated concern about the relationship. It seemed that Emily was a Catholic, and a devout Catholic at that. She and her family went to Mass every Sunday. Neither David nor Susan was a staunch Methodist. They attended their church in Brawton only at Christmas and Easter and on special occasions such as weddings, funerals and baptisms. But their families had always been Protestant in one form or another and tradition died hard.

There was no bigotry or animosity involved although it was a different story in Northern Ireland. In England it was a case of live and let live. Everyone on both sides was polite about it. But the unwritten law remained inviolable: Catholics and Protestants kept themselves to themselves.

On meeting Emily for the first time, however, Susan and David's doubts quickly evaporated. They were completely won over by her beauty, intelligence and natural charm. It was a Sunday and after polite conversation over afternoon tea, Emily sat at the upright piano in their lounge and played a selection of hymns from the Methodist hymn book which had Catholic and Protestants literally singing from the same hymn sheet.

As the religious divide dissolved, Emily accompanied them to Brawton Methodist

Church at Easter, with Irving driving the limo and David only slightly apprehensive as a back seat passenger. Later on, Irving drove Emily and members of her family to Mass at St Peter's and sat with them during the service, although he wasn't allowed to receive Communion.

He found the two versions of the Christian faith fascinating, the one in an austere setting with a plain altar and lusty hymn singing, the other in a quieter, more restrained atmosphere induced by flickering candles and luxuriant floral arrangements. The difference between the two officiating clergy was also striking. The Methodist pastor, the Rev Colin Gowland, who had replaced the ageing Rev Williams, was dressed in a suit with open-neck shirt and had a casual throwaway manner, standing with hands in his pockets while leading prayers. In complete contrast, Mass was more formal, the priest, Father Michael Keenan, wearing his robes with reverence-inspiring dignity.

Irving was saddened by the change in his old chapel since his Sunday school days. What were they doing to the faith he grew up with? The answer appeared to be 'modernisation'. Since the Rev Williams had retired services had become 'happy clappy' with hand-waving and shouting from the congregation. Grandpa Irving would have hated it. Grandma Bridget had stopped going, along with others of her generation.

He felt himself gravitating to Emily's church, a feeling reinforced by a meeting with Father Michael at a dance in St Peter's social club. He and Emily were taking time out over their iced Cokes listening to the jukebox when the priest joined them at their table. He was in his 40s with thick prematurely greying hair, gold-rimmed spectacles and a scholarly presence. Irving half expected some serious talk but was pleasantly surprised. Father Michael had heard all about him from Emily and was full of admiration for the journalistic profession.

'Great job you do,' he said with a slight Lancashire accent. 'Thought about it myself when I was young. Decided against as I couldn't keep up with their hard drinking!'

They all laughed and relaxed. Irving took a sip of his Coke. 'We're not all heavy drinkers. Some are, I know, but most of us can't afford it.'

Father Michael eyed their soft drinks. 'Just kidding. You won't go far wrong if you stick to those.' He asked after Emily's parents and brother. 'Daniel's a wonderful help at our homeless shelter but we've not seen him for a while. Is he okay?'

'He's not been well, Father,' Emily told him. 'He suffers from migraines as you know. The last one was nastier than usual. It lasted for days but he's getting better now.'

'That's good, I'll say a prayer for him.' The priest turned to her boyfriend. 'Written any interesting stories recently, Irving?'

As it happened Irving had that day interviewed a young mother of three children whose husband had just been sent to prison for theft and was facing eviction from her home. She was penniless and had applied for a national assistance grant at her local employment exchange but was told she would have to wait a week.

It would be four days before the story was published in the Brawton Chronicle. By then she and her starving children could be homeless. Irving had given her ten shillings from his own pocket and pointed her in the direction of the Salvation Army but she was ashamed to go there because of what she called her 'past sins'. She was not prepared to tell a young newspaper reporter what the sins were.

The priest listened attentively. When Irving had finished he said: 'It's always the wives and families who suffer when their men go to jail. Send her to St Peter's. We'll help her. No questions asked.'

NINE

The film was *How to Marry a Millionaire* at their local cinema. Apart from starring Marilyn Munroe as a gold-digger chasing a rich husband, the comedy had appealed to Emily and Irving as it was the first to be screened by the much publicised CinemaScope widescreen process. It had the desired effect on both of them -- it made them laugh and at the same time painted a rose-tinted image of matrimony.

Now that Irving had the regular use of Fred's Wolseley the days or rather nights of travelling by bus on such occasions were over. They drove back to her home in the car and parked outside the darkened off-licence under a street-lamp. Irving had bought and installed a radio to complete the car's refinements. They relaxed in each other's arms in the comfort of the back seat and listened to Mario Lanza singing *Be My Love* competing with the rain drumming on the roof. It was followed by Elvis Presley's *Jailhouse Rock* and yet another performance of the current hit, *Too Young,* in the honeyed tones of Nat King Cole.

They try to tell us we're too young
Too young to really be in love
They say that love's a word
A word we've only heard
But can't begin to know the meaning of

'Are we really too young, Irving?' Emily asked dreamily, curled up in his warm embrace.

Irving withdrew his face from hers and looked into the green eyes, deeply seductive in the half-light. 'Silly question,' he whispered. 'Our spirits are ageless. I will always love you.'

She kissed him tenderly. 'I will always love you too, darling.'

'It's our destiny... we're meant for each other. You believe in fate, don't you?'

'I believe in God.'

'Same thing... God is fate personified.'

The moment he said it, he wondered where such profound words had come from. He felt déjà vu kicking in... the electric frisson and the shortening of breath. But then the certainty of knowing what he had to say next... and exactly what Emily's reply would be. 'Now I've got another question for you, darling.'

She straightened up and turned her flushed face towards him. 'Go on.'

'Will you marry me?'

She threw her arms round him and burst into tears. 'Oh Irving, I thought you were never going to ask!'

He took that as a Yes.

'Love bears all things, believes all things, hopes all things, endures all things.' Father Michael was quoting from the Bible as part of Irving and Emily's marriage preparation class. It was the third and final session held in the priest's cosy living room at St Peter's presbytery. 'The key word here is "endures". Holy matrimony is the sacred union between husband and wife *and shall remain unbroken.*

'It is the joining of two hearts, bodies and souls... husband and wife who need to support one another in times of happiness and times of adversity. *And there will be adversity.* It is there to be overcome not to run away from as some people do through divorce. Marriage between two people who love each other in the way you both do is all about a journey -- through good times and bad -- towards completion.'

'For better or for worse,' Emily said.

'Exactly! That's the deal. It's what you solemnly vow to do before God.'

'For as long as we both shall live,' Irving added, stroking Emily's hand with its tiny solitaire diamond ring -- all he could afford on his junior reporter's salary. One day, when he'd made his name in Fleet Street, he'd buy her a ring fit for a princess.

Father Michael nodded. 'It's a lifetime commitment. And as you go through life, you will be blessed with the gift of children, God willing. It's a condition of marriage in a Roman Catholic church that all offspring of the union are raised in the Catholic faith. You do understand that, don't you, Irving?'

'Yes, that's been explained to me.'

'You're not a member of our church but you're thinking about converting. May I ask why?'

'Well, it's just that our church -- Methodist -- is not like it used to be. It's gone all happy clappy.'

The priest smiled. 'They just like a bit of excitement with their religion.'

'It doesn't seem right to me somehow. I've stopped going.'

'You'd be very welcome to join us when you feel ready. But if you remain a Methodist you must agree to any children of your marriage being baptised as Catholics.'

Irving had problems visualising himself as a father at such a tender age but was unconcerned about the prospect of Catholic baptism. 'I've absolutely no problem with that, Father.'

Catholic baptism may not have been a problem for Irving but for the rest of the Breen family it represented a controversial grey area. Nana, in particular, was not short of impassioned rhetoric on the delicate subject. She had just finished helping Susan and David prepare Saturday afternoon tea and the family were seated in the lounge, listening to the football results on the wireless. (Manchester City had lost again).

'I'm surprised at you, Irving,' she declared when the conversation turned to the forthcoming nuptials. 'I can't believe you'd even think about converting to the Catholics. Why can't Emily convert to the Methodists? There'd be no problem then.'

The idea of the Shannons joining in happy-clappy liturgy amused Irving. He smiled patiently. 'There's no chance of that, Nana.'

'The Bible says keep the Sabbath day holy but they don't. They go out to the pictures, drinking and dancing straight after Mass. Drinking's bad enough but drinking on a Sunday... how sinful is that?'

Her grandson didn't believe there was anything unholy about the cinema, dancing or drinking in moderation but knew better than to interrupt her in full flow.

'What would Grandpa have said about marrying a Catholic? And the Reverend Williams, God rest their souls.' Their retired former minister had 'passed away' a month earlier, signalling the end of an era for the Breen family.

Susan and David were torn between

Nana's biblical eloquence and their charming future daughter-in-law. In the end they agreed to a more broad minded, ecumenical approach. David said the different Christian denominations should forget their divisions and unite against the common foe -- evil. It was high time they got their act together because the enemy was showing disturbing signs of winning.

Nana said nothing. Neither did Susan nor Irving. Deep down they all knew he was right.

It wasn't as if Irving had no experience of weddings. He had written enough wedding reports for the Chronicle to last a lifetime. But he had never actually been to one. Now he was about to do so -- his own. This was totally different. This was the day his life took a fateful step along its predestined path. It was a grey day in early September which he would always remember as the day he grew up.

Harbouring a sense of foreboding, the morning became darker and light rain began to fall. The rain grew steadily heavier and a knot began to form in Irving's stomach to match the one in his silk tie that he could not get straight. His mother came to his assistance, fussing over her fledgling about to leave the nest. At last, uncomfortable in his best dark blue suit and black shoes polished to a shine all the way round, he was ready.

His father had cooked him breakfast,

something he had never done before in his life, but he could not eat. The nerves really kicked in when Susan pinned the wedding carnation to his lapel before kissing him gently and hugging him tightly.

When the car came for him, a bright yellow vintage Rolls with rain splashing off the windscreen wipers, he took a deep breath and tried to smile. His father clapped him on the back and gripped his shoulder in a gesture of paternal solidarity before handing him an umbrella. He may not have been the most demonstrative of men but there were tears in his eyes just the same.

The rain had stopped when the Rolls arrived at St Peter's but the sky remained overcast. A splendidly robed Father Michael welcomed the pale and apprehensive groom with a broad reassuring smile and a firm handshake. Jamie Lee, his best man, smartly suited and debonair, took his friend's elbow and steered him into the brightly lit, red carpeted church. Softly playing organ music added an air of expectancy to the ethos of holiness.

'Too bad about the weather, Irving,' Jamie said. 'But it'll brighten up later, according to the forecast.' They took their seats in front of the flower-decked, candle-lit altar and tried to relax. 'This is the tough bit, the waiting,' Jamie said helpfully. Beneath the confident exterior he was almost as nervous as Irving. He made a clumsy attempt to ease the tension. 'Scored twice in a five-a-side match the other night.'

Irving was not impressed. 'Have you got the ring?'

Jamie felt in his jacket pocket. 'Oh Lord, it's gone.'

Irving felt sweat break out on his forehead. 'For God's sake, Jamie!' He mopped his face with a handkerchief.

Jamie tried the other pocket and pulled out a small box. 'Oops, wrong pocket! Sorry.'

'Open it, Jamie. Let's make sure there's a ring inside.'

Jamie did. And there was.

They sat in silence. Brides were always late. It was part of tradition. The organ music stopped and then started again. Irving looked round. The pews had filled up. Sitting in the row behind were his mother and father, along with Nana. David wore his Sunday best striped grey suit and Susan a beige dress with a frothy cream coloured straw hat. Nana was soberly dressed in a dark coat, her grey head hatless. She clutched a handkerchief and smiled weakly, not relishing her first visit to a Catholic church.

Across the aisle sat Lilian and Daniel, Lilian in a light blue outfit and matching hat, also with a handkerchief at the ready. She waved happily and blew a kiss to her future son-in law. Daniel managed to look untidy in a new blue suit but had tied his hair back fastened in a ponytail.

The organ played on and there was still no sign of the bride, her father and her bridesmaids. Then someone tapped Irving on the shoulder. It was Alistair McKenzie.

'You're the story now, laddie,' the newshound grinned. 'Front page, first edition: Chronicle Star Reporter Weds.'

Irving had to laugh. 'Fame at last!'

'And you get to write the wedding report yourself.'

'No way, Alistair, I'll be on my honeymoon.'

'Then Jamie can write it.'

Before Jamie could say thanks for the honour, there was activity at the doorway and the organ swelled with the strains of Wagner's *Bridal March*. All heads turned as one of life's time-honoured spectacles slowly unfolded. The bride, all in white, a half-glimpsed vision of ethereal beauty behind her veil, carried a bouquet of red roses. She seemed to float down the aisle in slow motion escorted by her proud and smartly suited father. There followed an enchanting trio of bridesmaids also in dazzling white with multi-coloured floral head-dresses.

The procession took less than two minutes but for Irving time stood still. As Emily arrived at his side and smiled at him he felt a tightening in his chest and he struggled for breath. This was Emily as he had never seen her before, the purity of her girlhood shining through the delicate veil. Taking Grandpa's advice, he was learning plenty of big words but he struggled to find the right one. Breathtaking was literally true. Elegant. Stunning, Surreal all flashed through his chaotic thoughts. But when Emily handed her bouquet to Gwen, her friend and chief bridesmaid, and lifted her veil, the trainee wordsmith found the right word.

It was Spiritual. God, in his amazing generosity, had just presented him with one of his angels.

The choir was singing *This is the day... this is the day that the Lord has made, that the Lord has made...* He took her hand and they stepped forward before a beaming Fr Michael to make their vows, their immutable vows. Her hand was cold and trembling slightly. He realised she was as nervous as he was. Hardly surprising really, this was a first for both of them after all.

Or was it?

Was this day, this special day that the Lord had made, a one-off? Or was it one of a string of special days stretching across eternity? The thought of all that cosmic energy made him feel dizzy and his tinnitus returned louder than ever. But then cutting through the cacophony he heard the voice of an old man. It was Grandpa.

'Take a deep breath and stand up straight, boy.'

He took a deep breath and stood up straight.

The next voice was the priest's, intoning the opening words of the ceremony: 'Dearly beloved, we are gathered here today in the sight of God to join this man and this woman in holy matrimony...' The words echoed through Irving's confused consciousness.

'... holy matrimony...'

'Marriage is a sacred union between husband and wife and shall remain unbroken.'

'... remain unbroken...'

'Who gives this woman in holy matrimony to this man?

Fred said in a loud voice: 'I do.'

The effect was startling. Everyone seemed to wake up. Had they all been suffering from déjà vu as well? The priest was asking Irving a question. Would he take Emily to be his lawfully wedded wife, to live together *forever...*

That was a very long time, he thought.

... in the estate of holy matrimony... to love, comfort, honour and keep her, in sickness and in health, for richer or for poorer, for better or for worse, *for as long as they both shall live?*

. He heard himself say determinedly: 'I will.'

Of course he would. How many times did he have to say so?

As the choir sang the prayer of St Francis, *Make me a Channel of Your Peace*, the timeless soulmates signed the register, then slowly but unsurely progressed to face a dystopian, disorganised world in which the only certainty was an all-pervasive uncertainty principle.

It kicked in right on cue. The moment the radiant couple emerged from the church, the grey clouds parted like curtains and dazzling sunshine illuminated the scene. It was a moment of pure theatre. No film director could have timed it better. The cameras clicked, the confetti swirled as the clamour of wedding bells announced Act One of a very special world premiere -- and an omnipresent cosmic audience held its breath.

The reception was in St Peter's Church social club with Daniel and his semi-pro group supplying the music. Fred had dug deep and the wine was soon flowing freely. Nana was persuaded against her better judgment to sample a drop of red as it was a once-in-a-lifetime occasion. By the time they had finished the carrot soup she was beginning to revise her opinion of Catholics. She considered herself a connoisseur of carrot soup and this was the finest she had ever tasted. Following the roast pheasant and a dessert of peaches in brandy she had lost all resistance to toasting the happy couple in champagne. Catholics were not so bad after all.

Tradition dictated that the speeches were mostly of a personal and bawdy nature and Jamie, ever the comedian, was in his element. There were cracks about Irving's capacity for ale and his talent at snooker compared with his own lack of it. 'My highest break is minus seven,' he said proudly. Irving corrected him. 'Not true, Jamie. You once made a break of plus five but then went in-off.'

The jokes continued with Jamie quoting an old newsroom favourite about celibacy being a very hard thing to handle, which not everybody understood. He saved his best for last. 'There were these two old codgers sitting on a promenade bench overlooking a nudist beach. After watching all the naked cavorting, one turns to the other and says: "Remember those tablets they gave us in the Army during the war -- to take our minds off women?"

'His mate says yes he remembers.

"Well, I think they're starting to work!"

Glasses were raised for the bridesmaids and then it was Fred's turn. Giving his daughter away in marriage on this wonderful occasion had filled him with mixed emotions. Much as he admired Irving and much as he liked the idea of a journalist as a son-in-law, he still felt indignant about giving her away -- for nothing!

'Well, look at her... isn't she worth a million dollars? When we were on holiday in Morocco a few years ago, an Arab gentleman offered me a dozen camels for her hand in marriage.'

Emily burst out laughing. She remembered it well.

Fred turned to Lilian in mock enquiry. 'We were tempted, weren't we?'

His wife joined in the fun. 'But we had nowhere to keep them!'

Fred went on: 'All Irving can offer me is free copies of the Brawton Chronicle for life!'

'One day, Fred... one day,' Irving called out, 'it might be the Daily Telegraph...'

'That would be more like it. But you never know... it might be the Daily Mirror or worse still, the Guardian. Anyway, that's in the future. You'll go far whatever you do. And speaking of going far, Lilian and I have decided to help you do just that.'

He reached into his jacket pocket and produced a small bunch of keys. 'The keys not to Paradise but to the next-best thing -- our Wolseley saloon.' He tossed the keys to Irving, who deftly caught them. 'As you already spend more time in it than we do, we've decided to give you the car as a wedding present.'

Irving was overwhelmed. There was no limit to his new in-laws' generosity. He got up and impulsively hugged both of them. The emotion was contagious. Everyone clapped and cheered. When the applause subsided Lilian produced a surprise of her own. She reached into her handbag and took out a small jewellery box from which she extracted a gold crucifix and chain.

'It's not over yet,' she announced brightly. 'This is an entirely unscripted moment. I also have a gift for my handsome young son-in-law. He may not be a Catholic but I'd like him to accept this crucifix as a token of my admiration and to protect him from all the wickedness of the world.'

She reached up and placed the fine chain over Irving's head and around his neck before kissing and hugging him. He was almost lost for words but not quite. 'Thank you for this truly beautiful gift. There's certainly a lot of wickedness in the world and I need all the help I can get. I may not be a Catholic -- at least not yet -- but I'll treasure it all my life.'

TEN

The West Country in early September can be recommended as the ideal location for a honeymoon. The sea around north Devon is as blue as the Cote d'Azur. It reminded Emily of a family holiday in Monte Carlo as a child. The warm climate was gentler than the scorching heat of southern France and Ilfracombe was every bit as nice as Nice. The same applied to other quaint resorts of Westward Ho, Woolacombe, Bideford, Bude, Lyme Regis and Minehead that they visited in Fred's diligently purring wedding present.

The touring newlyweds stopped for the night where the mood took them. With the holiday season almost over there was no shortage of accommodation. They preferred small hotels overlooking the sea and if there was a honeymoon suite on offer so much the better. Not that they cared much for their creature comforts or noticed the nods and winks of their indulgent hosts. This was their time, the magical time they had dreamt of during the frustrating moments of courtship when restraint had seemed agonising and unreasonable. How brilliant and inspired those moments seemed now! True love waited and this was its rewarding moment of truth.

The first time Irving saw Emily in just her diaphanous negligee he was blown away. The excitement of physical arousal sent his pulse racing and his mind spinning, rekindling the nervousness of his wedding day. Something would go wrong. It was bound to. As they lay together locked in love the urge for physical consummation became steadily less urgent. It was enough to just lie there, two virgins naked in body and soul, lost in the purest form of sensuality.

Love not lust. Was there a difference? All the difference in the world. Lust seemed like a crude invasion of innocence. He couldn't bear the thought that he might hurt his angelic wife. Yet it was all too evident that she *wanted* him to hurt her in that special way that would seal their love for ever.

Their breathing became more measured. She seemed to read his mind. 'Just relax, darling,' she whispered. He rolled out of bed and went to the bathroom. Looking into the mirror, he saw the flushed face of a handsome young man deeply concerned about his wilting manhood. As he'd feared, something had gone wrong virility-wise. Then, out of the recesses of his memory he heard a voice. For the second time in a week it was Grandpa's.

'Stand up straight boy!'

He splashed himself with cold water and smiled at the innuendo. Not exactly what Grandpa had meant but it did the trick. He was standing up straight now. Straight as a poker. The overpowering urgency of his desire for her came flooding back. Returning to bed, they started over again. Lust would not be denied. This time there were no doubts or inhibitions. He was on the threshold of manhood. Gently at first but then powerfully he pushed open the door.

They moved in with Emily's family above the shop. There were two spare rooms on the second floor and a bathroom and kitchenette they shared with Daniel. Fred and Lilian asked only a nominal rent. They were more than happy with the temporary arrangement, until the couple could save enough for a deposit on a home of their own. A new housing estate was being built less than a mile away and Emily had her eye on a three-bedroom semi-detached with twin luxuries of a garage and a small garden. There was a park nearby with squirrels. Above all, she thought dreamily, it had a children's play area.

Her job as a laboratory assistant had been upgraded and she earned almost as much as Irving. Between them, after living and travel expenses had been budgeted for, Mr and Mrs Breen managed to salt away a chunk of their joint income towards the all-important deposit. Homes on the estate were for sale at around £2,500 in the days before the housing market rocketed into inflationary orbit from which it never recovered. Mortgages were available from several building societies repayable over 10 and 15 years and a 10 per cent deposit was all that was required to secure one.

After a year of penny pinching self-denial they'd saved over £200 towards their target. They needed another £50 and the estate agent had become impatient. The houses had been built and there was a queue of potential buyers. He imposed a deadline for the full £250 deposit. If the couple could not deliver it within one month, their place in the queue would be lost and their mortgage application rescinded. Time was running out. They needed one final push.

Irving had just covered a story about a jobless bricklayer who'd won over £1,000 on the horses with a shilling accumulator and he decided to have a go himself. He didn't need to win thousands, just £50. One of the regular customers at the off-licence was a 'bookie's runner' (betting shops had not yet been legalised) and helped Irving select shilling accumulators from the day's race cards.

Their combined efforts failed to pay dividends, based as they usually were on rank outsiders. Irving decided to raise the stakes and place single bets on more fancied horses -- the sort tipped by the Daily Telegraph's racing expert, Goldspur. The November Handicap meeting at Manchester racecourse, Castle Irwell, provided an ideal opportunity so he persuaded Emily, Lilian and Daniel to join him for an afternoon's racing.

With Fred minding the shop, they drove to the course in the Wolseley and paid for entry to the silver ring enclosure, nearer the winning post than the cheaper enclosures. It was a fine day with a blustery wind and the going was officially described as 'good'. That was essential for backing winners, Irving assured the others with his newly acquired knowledge of the Turf. None of them had been racing before. They found the experience fascinating; the magnificent highly strung horses, the diminutive jockeys in their colourful silks and the bookmakers shouting the odds adding to the air of excitement.

They studied their racecards and tried to decipher some of the jargon. A letter D next to a horse's name indicated that it had won over the same distance as the race it was entered in. C meant it had won at the same racecourse and C/D that it had won over the same distance at the same course. 'Horses for courses, that's what you have to look for,' Irving declared knowledgeably.

'What does BF mean?' Daniel asked with a

grin.

'Beaten favourite.' Irving translated. 'Last time out it was favourite and it was beaten.'

Then there were the mysterious odds offered for the various runners. Favourites were the most heavily backed horses and usually at short odds such as 2-1 or lower, 6-4 for example. That meant you put £4 on it to win £6. If it won you profited by £6, plus the return of your £4 stake.

Emily and Lilian preferred to bet in shillings rather than pounds and were more interested in each-way investments -- bets offering returns on horses finishing in the first three places. They also preferred to make their selections based on the horses' names rather than on their form. They placed their modest bets at the Tote windows while the men, making their investments more logically, boldly wagered as much as a £1 note on their selections with the trackside bookies.

Afrer the first three races, the only member of their party showing a profit was Lilian, who was 15 shillings to the good on her each-way transactions. Then it was time for the Big Race, the November Handicap. It had a large field and the prices on offer were higher than usual. Goldspur of the Daily Telegraph had tipped Sir Marcus, an improving four-year-old colt, to beat the high class favourite, Arctic Storm. He made the horse his star selection for the meeting.

It had won over the distance at Castle Irwell earlier in the season and was currently second favourite at 11-2. The four novice racegoers watched the runners circle the parade ring and it had to be admitted that Sir Marcus looked the most impressive of them all. Its beautifully groomed chestnut coat shone with health and it was clearly on its toes, full of confidence.

Not only did the animal look an all-over winner but its form showed it had won its last race by five lengths. At 11-2 it looked outstanding value compared with Arctic Storm, the favourite priced at 11-4. Irving felt an increasingly strong premonition on the outcome of the race. It was another of those electric moments. So compelling was the feeling that he decided to take the plunge and back Sir Marcus with his last £4. He was already calculating his winnings. That would be £26 he'd be taking away -- half what was needed to clinch the deposit on their new home.

Lilian had other ideas. Using her own system, she surveyed her racecard looking for a name that took her fancy. And there it was: Number 18, one of the outsiders at 25-1. Its name was Too Slow. 'That's the winner,' she told Irving confidently and he burst out laughing. The others joined in. Her choice, a grey six-year-old gelding, lived up to its name. It plodded round the ring seemingly lacking all interest in proceedings. But the name appealed to Lilian and she liked the way the grey's tail had been plaited. I'm in front so I'm thinking of betting 10 shillings each way on it,' she said.

Irving felt it his duty to protect his mother-in-law from such an ill-considered action. 'It's got no chance... unplaced in its last two outings, never won at this racecourse and its jockey is 1 lb overweight. 'That's why it's a 25-1 shot. Don't waste your money, put it on Sir Marcus instead. You can still back it each way if you like.'

Lilian was in two minds. The grey had no form, it was true. And it didn't look too keen on the job in hand. Its jockey was overweight. Backing it was clearly illogical. Yet her feminine intuition had no place for logic. It was more into metaphysics. With such a name, fate owed it a favour. If it were to win it would be poetic justice. On the other hand, the Daily Telegraph had made Sir Marcus its star selection. Also, her son-in-law was a journalist and seemed to know what he was talking about. Swayed by his eloquence but against her better judgment, she took his advice.

The die was cast. From their position high in the stands the Shannons and the Breens watched the runners line up and the tapes rise. In the words of the race commentator over the loudspeaker, they were 'orff.' From the start, Too Slow shot into the lead as if galvanised. Experienced racegoers nodded sagely. The grey was just setting the pace. It would soon tire and the better horses would then take over. But by the halfway stage, where the track bordered the River Irwell, the outsider was still setting the pace. In fact, it now led by some eight lengths from the favourite, Arctic Storm.

Sir Marcus was in fourth place, its tail swishing vigorously -- not a good sign according to a punter nearby watching through binoculars. Irving began to feel uneasy. His grip tightened on the bookmaker's ticket in his pocket. But it was early days yet. Sir Marcus' jockey was just biding his time. Once they were into the home straight he would come with a late run and finish an easy winner.

Sadly, fate was writing a different script. On rounding the home turn, with two furlongs to go to the winning post, Too Slow had increased its lead to 10 lengths from Arctic Storm, struggling in second place. Sir Marcus was nowhere to be seen. Even the race commentator sounded surprised when the grey crossed the winning line, slowing down to a canter: 'Number 18, Too Slow, is the easy winner, leading from start to finish. He's proved too fast for all of them!'

Irving felt physically sick. So much for the Telegraph's racing 'expert'. And so much for his own psychic powers. They no longer seemed to work when it came to gambling -- just when he needed them most. He tore up the sweaty bookmaker's ticket and tossed the pieces in a bin along with the hopes of countless other disillusioned losers. What was the old saying about a fool and his money? They were soon parted. How foolish he'd been to talk Lilian out of her inspired hunch.

But Lilian took it very well. She waved away her son-in-law's abject apologies. 'Never mind, young man. You meant well, I know.' She gave him a motherly hug. The others were similarly forgiving. They'd all taken his advice and backed Sir \Marcus. 'Look at it this way,' Daniel said cheerfully. 'It didn't finish last.'

'Where did it finish?' Irving asked, not really caring.

Goldspur's star selection for the November Handicap had finished next to last.

They drove home in silence. There was no point in staying for the remaining races as all were suddenly without resources to put it politely, or to put it less delicately in Emily's words, skint. Irving knew she would remind him later of the damage to their precious budget. She was right, of course, it was a setback but only a minor one. He would make it up to her one day. He'd buy her a proper engagement ring as soon as his financial problems were over.

He also needed to make it up to Lilian whose faith in him had cost her heavily. If she had bet 10 shilling's each way on Too Slow at 25-1 as she'd intended, she would now be over

£16 better off. What could she have bought with that, he wondered? A new dress from Lewis's? She was always saying that's what she needed but could never afford. He'd take her to the store and buy her one. Soon. Definitely. And what about Daniel, who was also skint? He'd go along to St Peter's and help out at the night shelter where his brother-in-law spent most of his free time helping the homeless.

Meanwhile, there was the little matter of raising £50 -- a substantial sum at a time when the national average wage was £8 a week -- with less than a month to do it in. Some evening over-time was available in the form of amateur dramatic productions and concerts but after three exhausting weeks of covering every excruciating performance on offer he was still only half way towards his target. With a week left before the estate agent's inflexible deadline they still needed another £25. The agent was becoming overbearing and Emily was going spare. Desperate times called for desperate measures.

He'd not had much luck so far as a gambler but he reckoned he deserved a second chance -- if only to prove he hadn't lost his rare gift of extra sensory perception. You couldn't abandon such a talent on the strength of one failure at the race-course. All the excitement there was too much of a distraction. Research showed ESP needed a calm, more relaxed atmosphere to realise its full potential -- a casino for example seemed the ideal setting. He drew out £10 from the joint piggy bank in their bedroom without telling Emily. She was babysitting for a friend and would assume he was working overtime. He'd tell her when he returned with his winnings. Then he headed for the tables of Salford Casino.

The Wolseley's fuel gauge was showing empty as usual so to save money on petrol he took the bus. It was early evening and the casino with its plush red and gold decor was almost empty. With the casual air of a seasoned gamer but feeling acutely nervous Irving cashed in his precious £10 for 10 round yellow £1 chips at the cashier's window before strolling between the lines of fruit machines towards the roulette and blackjack tables. He was waiting for inspiration. Which game should it be? The action around the roulette wheel looked slightly more lively.

He took a seat and read a helpful card explaining the different odds available on various combinations of numbers. They seemed complex and not really conducive to an exercise in ESP. A more realistic test lay in the straight choice between red and black or between odd and even numbers. They were offered as even-money bets.

He studied the play for several minutes and noticed that red came up five times in succession. Perhaps black was due now bearing in mind the law of averages. Tentatively, he placed a yellow chip on black. The little white ball seemed to take an age circling the wheel before kicking and bouncing into the number seven slot -- red.

That was six times in a row. Surely the law of averages would work now. *Rien ne va plus,* the blonde girl croupier in a low-cut red dress intoned and they were off again. Red again. A bald, middle aged gambler seated alongside seemed to read his mind. 'I once saw that happen 16 times in a row. The law of averages doesn't work in roulette.'

Irving took the advice as the sign of an ESP premonition. He placed his next yellow chip on red. Twenty, black. His neighbour grinned and threw up his hand in a gesture of resignation. 'Maybe you should try the numbers.'

Judging by his pile of chips, numbers seemed to be working well for the guy but his system of placing multiple bets on different combinations conflicted with Irving's method. It needed to be an even bet -- odd numbers or even numbers. Was there a clue here somewhere? As the betting odds were evens then why not back the even numbers? Yes, that was it. That was the hunch he'd been waiting for.

It worked immediately. The even numbers came up four times in succession. Each time he doubled his stake. When odd numbers came up he halved his stake. Then it was back to doubling up on the evens. Before long his stack of chips had outgrown his neighbour's. The yellow chips now included two pink ones, each worth £20. He was on a roll. He'd turned his original £10 stake into over £60. The house deposit was assured and he could even fill the car's petrol tank

He looked at his watch. Two hours had passed in a blur. The room had filled up and smoke from dozens of cigarettes, pipes and cigars hung around the gilded chandeliers. He suddenly felt very tired, as if he'd done a day's work. It was time to quit while he was ahead. But a small voice he hadn't noticed before had started to nag him. Why leave now when you're on a lucky streak? Seize the moment. Just one more bet -- double or quits -- and all your worries would be over. You'd not only fill the petrol tank but buy Emily a proper engagement ring, a new dress for Lilian. Maybe a new guitar for Daniel....

He paused on his way to cash in his chips. It was his lucky night after all. And fortune favoured the bold. No need for another two hours' graft. Just one more throw. It was a proper engagement ring for Emily that swayed it.

He returned to the table. Odds or evens? Red or black? His mind went blank. The hubbub of the casino subsided and once again at a pivotal moment in his life time seemed to stand still. One more throw. Did he have the guts? Yes, he did, but what he also required was a sign of some kind... even a hunch would do. Where was déjà vu when you needed it? All he could see was a croupier in a red dress. She caught his eye and smiled.

That was it! That was all he needed. Red. It had to be red.

Rien ne va plus. As soon as the little white ball hurtled off on its fateful orbit he felt sick. A frisson of real déjà vu arrived seconds too late. The ball was not going to land on a red number. It would not even land on a black number.

'Zero,' the blonde croupier announced, raking in all the chips on the table.

She was still smiling.

Irving trudged out of the warm brightly lit casino into the cold dark night. The wind was getting up and it had started to rain. It would be a long walk back to the off-licence because the last shilling he'd kept for his bus fare had gone the same way as his roulette chips. He lost it in a fruit machine -- the last throw of a desperate loser.

Still cursing his luck, he turned up the collar of his jacket and set off on the long march home. The girl had smiled at him for heaven's sake. Fortune had smiled on him, then kicked him in the teeth. The premonition had arrived too late. If it had shown him the ball landing on zero a minute earlier he could have been taking a taxi home, his pockets bulging with winnings. So near and yet so far!

The rain grew heavier, soaking his hair and stinging his face. It was no use blaming Lady Luck. He had just been greedy. He'd had a winning streak and, as a novice, failed to grasp the basic principle of gambling: quit while you're in front. It served him right. He'd know better next time -- not that he was contemplating a repeat experience.

He needed to find a less risky way of raising the necessary cash -- which had now increased by £10 to £35. All he could think of was a loan. He could ask the bank but they'd be unlikely to help. There was no way he would approach his parents. David had taken early retirement and they'd moved to a cottage in the Yorkshire Dales. They'd had to pay cash for the cottage and were living on his father's modest Admiralty pension. The last person he wanted to ask was Fred after all his selfless generosity. That left Daniel. Maybe his brother-in-law could come to the rescue.

First off, however, he had to make his peace with Emily. It was well past midnight when he finally reached the off-licence, looking like the survivor of a shipwreck. She'd waited up for him and her intuition told her something was wrong. She was relieved he hadn't had an accident but shocked by his appearance.

'Darling, you're saturated,' she said. 'Where've you been? You'll really have to give up all this overtime.' She took a towel from the kitchen and dried his hair vigorously.

He peeled off his soaking clothes -- even his underwear was wet -- and put on a dressing gown. 'It's a long story,' he said wearily. 'I've not been working. I've been to the casino. I had to walk home...'

She feared the worst. 'Skint again?'

He nodded. Best not to tell her all the details. The bottom line was enough. 'I lost £10. I'm so sorry, darling. It seems we're not intended to win any money.'

He'd half expected an emotional rollicking but she took it bravely. 'Well, it could be worse, I suppose. You could have lost all our savings. So what do we do now? We have to find that deposit somehow.'

'We'll have to ask for a loan.'

'Who can we ask?'

'Maybe your brother could help.'

'I don't want to ask Daniel. He's as hard up as we are. I asked him the other day why he never has a girlfriend and he said he couldn't afford one. That's because he gives all his money to the down-and-outs at St Peter's. Also, he's not well. He's been getting more of his severe headaches.'

'I can't ask anyone at work. They're all skint too.'

'Do you suppose I could pawn my engagement ring?' She stretched out her hand and the tiny diamond glinted faintly.

Irving visualised the sort of ring he'd

planned to buy with his winnings and forced back tears. It had come to this -- his poor, innocent wife obliged to pawn her engagement ring and the harsh reality that she would never raise £35 for it. His face was the picture of misery. 'That just breaks me up.'

'Me too, but it's better than selling it outright. I'll get it back one day, when we pay off the pledge. And I still have my wedding ring. There's no way I'd part with that!'

He took her hand and squeezed it tightly. 'No way.'

She smiled brightly and kissed his still damp forehead. 'I'll find a pawnshop tomorrow.'

Her husband sneezed twice. He'd started to shiver. 'What if we don't raise enough?'

'Then I'll have to ask Daniel. There's no other way. Now you get to bed, my love, you've caught a cold.'

Finding a pawnbroker in Brawton was a problem so Emily took the bus to Salford where there were three brass balls hanging from almost every street corner. But getting a realistic valuation on her engagement ring was another matter. At the third attempt she settled for an advance of £15, the highest offer. That left £20 still needed to secure the deposit.

Irving was in bed with a hot water bottle and classic flu symptoms when she returned to their bedroom. 'How did it go?' he asked anxiously.

She sat on the side of the bed. 'All done and dusted.' She handed him the pawn ticket and banknotes.... £15 for the ring and £20 from Daniel. We've reached the target at last!'

'Thank God for Daniel. An interest-free loan?'

'Oh no, nothing like that. I told him we were determined to pay him back but he wouldn't listen. He insisted on giving us the money -- as a gift.'

ELEVEN

Throughout the long waiting period while the couple were saving their deposit they had watched their dream home being built, brick by brick from foundations to the roof in all weathers, rain or shine. Once they had paid the estate agent the hard-earned deposit and the deal was finally done their dream home was ready to move into. What was needed now was more money for carpets and curtains plus, of course, beds for the two main bedrooms -- and a cot for the third.

Emily was three months pregnant when they finally moved in. Hire purchase was in its infancy and still frowned on by many retailers but as they were both working they found dealers happy to set them up with the essentials plus a second hand three-piece suite, dining set and the obligatory upright piano. The luxury of a refrigerator for the kitchen came later following Irving's second pay rise at the Chronicle.

Maternity leave was still unheard of and Emily struggled with increasingly frequent bouts of nausea and vomiting for as long as possible. But after being reduced to living on ice lollies and anti-sickness medication she had to give up work six weeks before the baby was due. Pressure was also building on Irving. He was helpless to ease Emily's distress in any meaningful way. Their moments of blissful intimacy had gone out of the window. A peck on the cheek was all she could bear. The last thing she wanted was sex.

Now the sole breadwinner, the need to increase his income became ever more pressing. He'd had two wage rises since their wedding and been promoted to the ranks of fully fledged general reporter. His shorthand was fluent and he was regularly assigned the top stories. But pay days couldn't come round fast enough. Setting money aside for Emily's layette and a pram and cot for the baby had left him permanently strapped for cash. More overtime offered a partial solution but it wasn't always available.

What he desperately needed was a job in the 'big time' in Manchester, the hub of Britain's newspaper industry, where the nationals were paying twice his present salary. He put out regular feelers among contacts and started attending monthly meetings of his local NUJ branch but found fraternal solidarity only stretched so far. Other hopefuls had the same idea and everyone was keeping tight lipped. The meetings took place in a room above the Grapes Inn, opposite

the offices of the Daily Mirror and Daily Telegraph -- so near yet so far. They inevitably adjourned to the bar where he was expected to buy
his round. There was no way he could claim for
the bill on expenses. Worse still, he developed a
taste for the local brew so the exercise quickly
became alarmingly counter-productive.

Most seasoned hacks will tell you, after a
few pints, that the moment their careers took
off was due to a large slice of luck -- that and the
priceless value of contacts. It was this time-honoured formula that eventually came to Irving's
assistance. Seated in the Swan after putting the
Chronicle to bed, Alistair plonked two pints of
the amber nectar in front of his protégé and
flopped into his seat. It had been another action-
packed press day.

'Cheers! Quite a balls-acher, eh laddie?'

Irving sipped his beer. 'Cheers! It gets no
easier. Just like home, in fact!'

'Having a bad time?'

'You could say that. Emily's morning sickness has started to last all day.'

Alistair's son and daughter were both
grown up but he could remember the trials of
childbirth. 'It'll pass, you'll see. But then there's
the joys of babyhood, the crying and the sleepless nights. You think you've got problems now!'

'Thanks for that, Alistair.'

'But I do have some good news for you.' He
drew closer to the young reporter and lowered

his voice. 'A mate of mine on the Telegraph news desk in Manchester is going to take early retirement. George Taylor. Fine jairnalist. Going back home to Falkirk. Told me yesterday. No-one else knows. Hasn't handed in his notice yet. But any day now...'

Irving was all ears. The Daily Telegraph! What a break that would be. Although a Tory paper it was widely regarded among journalists as a top newsgathering organisation. Then the doubts set in. 'Wouldn't they want someone more experienced than me?'

'Not necessarily, laddie. What they look for on the Telegraph is talent and integrity.'

'Not public schoolboys?'

'Maybe in London but Manchester's different. Godfrey Myers, the northern editor, is a grammar school lad himself. He's a hard nut. Doesn't stand for any nonsense. Insists on staff with initiative, writing ability and capable of meeting deadlines. You've got all three.'

Irving took a long drink. It seemed like the gilt-edged tip-off every journalist dreamt of. 'You really think they'd have me?'

'Sure thing but you'll need to get your skates on. Write to Godfrey applying for the vacancy he doesn't know exists. That should impress him. It would certainly impress me. Once George hands in his notice they'll advertise the job and it'll be up for grabs. Beat everyone to it!'

It was one of those pivotal moments in

Irving's life that matched the excitement of a scoop -- and this one might outshine them all. The Daily Telegraph of all papers! A real newspaper of record. You couldn't get any higher than that except for the Times and they didn't have an office in Manchester. What did he tell his father-in-law at his wedding reception? 'One day it might be the Daily Telegraph.' How prophetic could that turn out to be?

The moment he reached home he took out his Olivetti portable typewriter and set about composing the letter of his life:

Dear Mr Myers

I believe a vacancy is about to arise on your news desk and should like to offer

my services as a general news reporter.

I am 23 years of age and was educated at Whitefield Grammar School where

I obtained my School Certificate with distinctions in English Language and English Literature. My shorthand and typing speeds are 130 and 60 words per minute   respectively.

For the past five years I have been employed as a general news reporter by the Brawton Chronicle. I can provide numerous specimens of my work -- including   bylined exclusives -- if you will kindly grant me an interview.

In the event of your appointing me I am confident you would find me a keen,   competent and versatile addition to your reporting staff.

Yours sincerely
Irving Breen

Then he hurried off to catch the late collection at the local post office.

In the following days Irving waited anxiously for a reply but none came. Instead, anxiety of a deeper kind kicked in. After an exhausting press day he was ready for an early night. It was not going to happen Emily had cooked shepherd's pie for dinner and even managed to eat some. But then, as they listened to the nine o'clock news on the wireless, the pain started. This time it was stronger than usual but after a few minutes it subsided. Then a short time later it returned even stronger.

'I think the contractions have started,' she gasped, clutching her swollen stomach. 'Can you call an ambulance?'

Her fear was contagious. He rushed to the telephone in the hall. A calm voice assured him an ambulance would arrive in ten minutes and advised him to relax. The advice worked for a few seconds but then he found Emily doubled up in a heap on the floor. 'They'll be here in ten minutes,' he told her, gently easing her into a sitting position. He found himself perspiring as freely as his wife. What if they took longer?

What if the baby arrived before they did? He had no idea what to do. Nobody had given him any instruction. Childbirth was the exclusive preserve of women and husbands were expected to keep their distance.

In the event, the ambulance arrived promptly and Emily was helped inside, draped in a blanket, by its attentive two-man crew. 'She'll be fine, sir, don't worry,' one said. 'You can follow us in your car, if you like. Or stay here and keep in touch by phone. It could be hours before the baby's born.'

He followed in the Wolseley, locked on to the ambulance's tail lights as if by radar. This was the big moment they had awaited with rising excitement and now it had arrived it had turned into panic. Boy or girl? They hoped for a boy but had no means of knowing. Pregnancy scans still lay in the future. Would the child be healthy? Again, they could not tell although their GP and hospital doctors were reassuring.

He had just worked on a story about a mother giving birth to a severely handicapped baby. The impact it would have on the family did not bear thinking about but the mother remained impressively resilient. Emily had suffered so much during her pregnancy. What if their own child was born handicapped in some way? How would Emily cope with that? How would *he* cope with it?

What else could possibly go wrong -- apart from crashing into the back of the ambulance if it were to brake sharply?

The ambulance turned into the hospital's maternity wing and Emily was wheeled on a trolley through the darkness to a brightly lit reception area. She tried to smile at him but her angelic face was creased with pain. He parked the car in a near deserted car park and hurried back to her. She had been taken to a ward and he followed in a lift. A plump middle-aged nurse met him as he stepped out and took him aside. His wife would be fine, she said, guiding him to a small sparsely furnished waiting room. There was no cause for anxiety. Childbirth was a perfectly natural event and Emily was in the best place for her delivery.

She made it sound as if they were expecting a parcel, Irving thought, as he took a seat on a well worn armchair next to a table piled with out-of-date magazines. This was where he would have to wait until the 'delivery'. The idea of husbands being present at the birth of their children was still unheard of. Tradition dictated that they paced up and down, smoking furiously and telling each other jokes to keep their spirits up.

Irving had never smoked but if someone had offered him a cigarette right now he would have lit up straight away. Not that there were any other expectant fathers to share a joke with.

It seemed everyone's deliveries had arrived except Emily's. He was alone with his thoughts, all deeply depressing.

He tried worrying about something else apart from the daunting prospect of fatherhood. The Wolseley's petrol gauge was hovering just above empty as usual. Would there be enough in the tank to see him, Emily and child safely home. What a start to family life that would be, to run out of petrol on your way home! The thought made his head ache and he started to sweat. He loosened his collar and tie and tried to read a magazine.

A nurse came in with a cup of tea and toast. At least he'd have some supper! He noticed it was a younger nurse this time, with fair hair and freckles. It was past midnight and the late-night shift had taken over. How was Emily? Were there any developments? His wife was still 'fine', the nurse said. She was now asleep. The doctor thought it would be some hours before the birth. He was advised to return home and get some sleep himself. They'd phone him if there was any news.

There was no way he'd go home. Fatigue started to kick in and he tried to doze in his chair but it was too uncomfortable. His confused thoughts turned to his mother and father, and Emily's parents. He'd forgotten all about them in the unfolding drama. He should tell them they were about to become grandparents but it was too late to call them now. It would have to wait until morning.

He still couldn't get his head round the idea of fatherhood. It was something that happened to other men, older more mature men who grew beards and smoked pipes. He looked at his watch. It was 2.50am. He staggered to the toilets and splashed his face with cold water. In the mirror looking back at him was a pale, clean-shaven lad with weary, anxious eyes. It was the image of a work in progress -- of a boy about to grow up. But stick a pipe in that young mouth? Ludicrous!

It was still dark outside though the gaunt hospital skyline was streaked with a faint cheerless light. Dawn was not far off. The wind had got up and rattled the sash window of the waiting room. Suddenly he was back at the Chronicle office and Rita was offering him a cigarette. Gratefully, he took it and she gave him a light from her lighter. When he inhaled the smoke he felt calm and relaxed. Everything was going to be 'fine', she said. The 'delivery' would go ahead smoothly although he would be required to sign a receipt. But then Rita disappeared and his mother was at his side. 'Why didn't you tell us we had a grand-daughter?' she demanded crossly and shook him by the shoulder.

He woke up swiftly and stiffly in the uncomfortable chair. The freckle-faced nurse stopped shaking his shoulder. She didn't seem cross. She sounded happy.' Wake up, Mr Breen, it's a girl,' she announced. 'Your wife has given birth to a daughter. Mother and baby both well.'

He was still half asleep, A girl. Not a son, after all. Throughout Emily's pregnancy, the fears of fatherhood had eased at the prospect of taking a son to Maine Road, both wearing City scarves, as he and his father had done years ago. The slightly blurred image faded. He could still do that with a daughter, of course, but it didn't seem the same somehow. Then he remembered the dream. He must phone his mother immediately. There was a public telephone in the corridor and he rang his parents' number. After a lengthy delay a sleepy voice answered.

'Hello, grand-mama,' Irving said. 'I'm at the hospital. It's a girl.'

Susan was wide awake now. 'That's wonderful, Irving. Is everything OK?'

He thought she sounded disappointed. 'So I'm told. Mother and baby both well.'

'Wonderful.' she said again. 'But I don't feel old enough to be a grandmother!'

'I don't feel old enough to be a father!'

She laughed. 'I'll phone Fred and Lilian. What are you going to call her?'

'Search me, Mum. We were hoping for a boy.'

'I know, dear, so were we. But you'll love her just the same, you'll see. They bring their love with them.'

He could open his eyes properly now but it all felt like a dream as the nurse led him to Emily's bedside. Bright dawn sunshine streamed through the ward's windows and almost dazzled him. At first he didn't notice the tiny cot with its even tinier occupant. He only had eyes for his poor, long-suffering wife. She was sitting up in bed, smiling radiantly, her arms open wide for his embrace. Her classic face, without a trace of make-up, had never looked lovelier than at that moment. Motherhood clearly became her. The green eyes, darker and more lustrous than usual, were filled with tears but they were tears of relief and joy. Gone was the pain and anguish that had marked the long pre-natal months.

He tried to think of something original to say but not for the first time, words failed the wordsmith. But then, the occasion was too great for words. They clung together in that spiritual silence that renders words superfluous. 'Darling,' he whispered at length and dried her eyes with his handkerchief before dabbing his own with it.

She gestured toward the bedside cot. 'She looks just like you -- without the birthmark!'

Irving looked at his hour-old daughter for the first time. Unaccountably, the word 'papoose' sprang to mind. The tiny olive skinned baby sleeping peacefully was tightly wrapped in a lacy blanket with a light blue bobble hat partly covering thick black hair. The only likeness her father could see was a resemblance to Carmen

Miranda, a swarthy Latin American singer of the time. Hirsute was the word but better not convey such ideas to Emily.

'I like the hat. She's a City supporter from birth!' He realised the inadequacy of the words as soon as he said them.

Emily sensed his nervousness. She smiled indulgently. 'Would you like to hold her?' The thought simply hadn't occurred to him. Fatherhood was taking its time to sink in.

'If that's OK,' he said, doubtfully.

Emily lifted the baby from her cot. 'Of course, it's OK darling. She's your daughter.' She handed the slumbering form to her husband. He took the papoose in his arms and held her gingerly. She was lighter than he expected but he was terrified of dropping her.

Your daughter... he still couldn't get his head round the enormity of the words. 'Hello, daughter,' he said, kissing the cherubic face tenderly. The baby opened her eyes, moved her head and the tiny lips twitched.

'Wow, you got a smile,' Emily exclaimed as she carefully took back her daughter. She suspected the twitch was just wind although Irving would be none the wiser. 'She's going to be Daddy's girl all right. But what are we going to call her?'

Irving turned his tired eyes across the ward and out through the window into a world full of challenges but also bright with hope. He

felt a surge of protective love for the child relying on him for survival. His mother was right.
Their little papoose had brought her love with
her. A new day was dawning and a new life lay
ahead for the three of them. It was another of
those surreal moments when he knew what he
was going to say next.

'Let's call her Dawn.'

They got home without running out of petrol.
Fred's van and David's limousine were parked
outside. Both sets of grandparents were waiting,
along with Nana, Daniel, a freshly brewed pot
of tea plus a plentiful supply of bacon butties
in the making. Nana, now living in sheltered accommodation since suffering a stroke, was determined to see her great grand-daughter 'before
I die'. Daniel had closed the off-licence, leaving
a notice in the window: CLOSED FOR FAMILY
REASONS -- BACK SOON. Business was business
but there were some things in life money could
not buy. The birth of a niece was one of them.

Dawn, the star of the show, was awake
and full of curiosity as she was introduced to
her admiring family. She looked long and hard
at each new face as if trying to recognise them.
All seemed to win her approval except Nana and
Daniel. When Nana's old, pain-lined face came
into view Dawn immediately burst into tears.
Emily took her and cuddled her, kissing her

and drying her eyes. The tears subsided and she handed the baby to Daniel. He took her gingerly, pushing his face close to hers and smiling his gentle smile. Dawn looked uncertainly into the kind eyes and softly bearded features framed by shoulder-length hair. She seemed about to smile back but then changed her mind and the tears returned.

'I think she needs another feed,' Emily said although she had breast-fed her just before leaving the hospital. She carried the baby to her bedroom for more nourishment. Nana could not hide her sadness. Some babies were born with the gift of second sight. The tears might mean she would not be around much longer. The same applied to Daniel, although his only health problem was his recurring migraine attacks. Carefree as ever, he just laughed it off.

Fred declared it a time for special celebration as it was the Dawn of a new era and everyone laughed. He produced a bottle of his most expensive champagne, along with cigars for the men, as was the custom. The two grandfathers lit up, filling the room with an exotic evocation of Christmas. The younger men did not smoke. They kept the cigars as souvenirs.

The conversation soon turned to baptism and Irving made a mental note to phone Father Michael at the first opportunity. Everyone agreed that Dawn was an inspired name for the new arrival but shouldn't she also have a middle name? After much animated discussion, it was unanimously agreed that the middle name should be Bridget, after her great grandmother. Nana at last smiled with delight.

TWELVE

Godfrey Myers, known to everyone at the Telegraph as God, was not your archetypal national newspaper editor. Embellishments such as Eton, Harrow or Winchester were absent from his educational credentials as were references to Oxford, Cambridge or any other university. He had come up the hard way, from copy boy at the age of 16 through the ranks of reporter and sub-editor, backbench executive and night editor before stumbling exhausted across the editorial summit, gin and tonic in hand, and firmly pulling up the ladder behind him.

As northern editor of the London-based broadsheet, he was a far cry from his Fleet Street counterpart but the noble lord who owned the paper regarded him as a safe pair of hands who could be trusted to supervise northern editions with as little disruption as possible from the powerful print unions.

His office on the third floor of the Telegraph building in central Manchester was an oasis of calm in contrast to the frenetic atmosphere of the adjoining newsroom, filled with the clatter of typewriters, the clamour of telephones and a perpetual haze of cigarette smoke. Its deep blue carpet and book-lined walls spoke of authority and probity while a large clock, accurate to the second, provided an ever-present reminder of merciless deadlines.

Middle aged, short and wiry, with receding grey hair and dark, world-weary eyes behind rimless spectacles, Godfrey sat almost dwarfed by his imposing mahogany desk and studied Irving's job application. He'd been away on holiday when it arrived over two weeks earlier and a mountain of work had built up in his absence. But when he finally got round to reading it he had to admit he was intrigued. After a lifetime writing about human nature nothing surprised him any more but the lad's letter came close.

Seated opposite was the lad himself. Irving looked immaculate in his dark wedding suit, freshly laundered white shirt, silk tie and black shoes polished to a shine that would have impressed his RAF drill sergeant. But just as nervous as that first interview at the Brawton Chronicle years earlier.

Godfrey fixed his youthful visitor with the stern stare that instantly disarmed interviewees. He came straight to the point. 'It seems you know something I don't, young man.'

Irving was not disarmed. It appeared George Taylor had yet to hand in his notice. He took a deep breath, as Grandpa had instructed, and tried to smile. 'About your news desk, sir?'

'Exactly. I was not aware we had a vacancy.'

'I think you will have shortly, sir.'

'Do continue...'

'I believe one of your reporters is about to resign.'

'Which one?

'George Taylor.'

'How do you know?'

'A tip-off, sir.'

'From whom?'

It was the key question and Godfrey waited with half-closed eyes for the answer.

'I'm sorry, Mr Myers, but I'm not at liberty to say.'

The editor smiled thinly. The lad was shaping up well. He tried one more time. 'You can tell me in strict confidence, you know.'

Irving felt his freshly starched collar tightening. Surely he could reveal his source to the northern editor of the Daily Telegraph. Then he remembered the third golden rule of journalism: you protected your sources regardless of who wanted to know. Even when a possible job with a leading national newspaper was in the balance.

'With respect, sir, I'd rather not.'

Godfrey was impressed. Irving had passed the test. Here was a bright young man with a nose for news who could be relied on to protect his sources under intense pressure. In other words, ideal Telegraph material. Only one more question remained. Grinning broadly, he got up from his desk and shook Irving's hand. 'When can you start?'

Dawn Bridget Breen took a dim view of proceedings at her baptism in St Peter's Church. She hollered throughout the ceremony until the moment of her christening, when holy water was poured on her hirsute head in the name of the Father, the Son and the Holy Spirit. Then she instantly fell asleep. Father Michael said that was a good sign and everyone was impressed, Catholics, Methodists and atheists alike. Irving, handsome in his dark wedding suit, was touched by the reverence of the service. The baby in her long white christening robe, cradled by his beautiful wife, wearing an elegant green two-piece to highlight her flowing fair hair, filled him with a sense of paternal pride he had not felt a few weeks earlier. As his mother had said, Dawn had brought her love with her.

Her grandparents, Susan and David, Lilian and Fred, plus Nana, all in their Sunday best for the occasion, completed a perfect tableau in front of the flower-decked altar for photographs at the end of the Mass. Daniel, hirsute and otherworldly, was the archetypal godfather. He took his duties very seriously, vowing to help raise his niece according to the Catholic faith. That didn't just mean regular Mass attendance but also practical aid for the poor and underprivileged.

Fred and Lilian took care of the catering at the reception in St Peter's social club in their inimitable style. There was a large cake covered in pink icing with the names Dawn and Bridget in fancy white piping and the champagne flowed freely. Cards and generous gifts were gratefully accepted by the proud parents. All contributions would help towards the formidable expenses of parenthood and a new post-maternity wardrobe for Emily. But now the need for them was no longer pressing. With the offer of a job on the Daily Telegraph in his pocket, Irving's permanently worried expression had been replaced by a relaxed smile. And for the first time in several years the needle on the Wolseley's fuel gauge pointed to Full.

'So this time you're definitely leaving us?' Rita drained her pint glass of best bitter and regarded Irving with a mixture of scepticism and regret.

Irving had served his month's notice at the Chronicle and was bidding farewell to colleagues at the Swan for a second time. 'Yep, this time it's for good. You're finally getting rid of me.'

Rita lit up one of her Players Medium without offering him one. Her auburn hair had been restyled in a shoulder-length and he noticed she'd started using lipstick. 'I always said you'd go far, you know.'

'Yes, the further the better!'

They laughed at their shared joke. 'Seriously though, how did you manage to land a job like that? I mean, I've been working my balls off all these years and I'll never get near a national.'

Irving smiled sympathetically. Everyone worked their balls off at the Chronicle, even those who didn't have any. 'I dazzled them with the cuttings of my exclusives.'

They both knew that wasn't the real reason. This was the 1950s and national paper newsrooms were no place for women. Their place was in the bedroom -- and the kitchen.

'Old boys' network, more like. One day we women will take over, then you'd better all watch out,' she said prophetically.

'Sounds scary, Rita. Actually, I told old Godfrey Myers something he didn't know.'

'I'm all ears.'

'That one of his reporters was about to leave.'

'Really? Who told you that?'

He tapped the side of his nose. 'Naughty, naughty.'

Jamie, his fellow rookie, joined them at their table. 'Cheers, Irving,' he said, raising his glass. 'Couldn't have happened to a nicer chap -- albeit a City supporter!'

They talked about their personal lives with the engaging frankness of their profession. Both were 'knackered' but for different reasons. Fatherhood was taking a heavy toll on Irving. Repeated sleepless nights and Emily's postnatal depression meant their sex life was non-existent. Jamie on the other hand was 'getting plenty;' with his long-term girlfriend, Olive. By the sound of it, Olive was an insatiable lass and her demands were leaving him exhausted.

Jamie was leaning towards sports reporting. His coverage so far was limited to amateur football matches where the Press sat on a touchline bench next to the trainer's bucket and sponge, and tried to keep their notebooks dry when it rained. His chief ambition was a seat in the Press box at Old Trafford. 'It will come,' he reminded Irving, not for the first time. 'Today Brawton Rovers, tomorrow Manchester United.' They clinked glasses at the dazzling prospect, distant if not improbable.

'You never know, it might be the Press box at Maine Road,' Irving said.

'Never, not even if they paid me!' City had lost again and were once more flirting with relegation.

Then Alistair popped up alongside. 'What have I always said about you, laddie?'

Irving laughed. 'Better not answer that, Alistair.'

'No stopping you now, you'll see.'

'Thanks to you Alistair -- for the tip-off and for everything you've taught me.'

His ever-patient tutor knocked back his Scotch and reeled off a well-worn office joke for everyone's benefit. 'I've taught him all he knows and he still knows nothing!' When the laughter died down, he grew serious. 'One last piece of advice laddie: be nice to people on your way up -- you'll meet them again on your way down!'

His other colleagues -- now former colleagues -- Gordon, Roy and Brian, weighed in with their own banter and back-slapping farewells. Then after a couple more drinks and slightly the worse for wear they ordered taxis.

A tearful Rita was the last to shake his hand. 'We'll meet again, lover boy,' she said, hugging him briefly. She kissed him tenderly on the cheek.

This time he didn't wipe it off.

It was a word Irving disliked intensely. But he had to admit he was gobsmacked by the scale of the Daily Telegraph's Manchester publishing operation. The vast open-plan newsroom consisted mainly of sub-editors' desks dominated by the senior executives' 'back-bench', and divided into sections for news, sport, features, pictures, parliament and city desks. Beyond a glass partition a large wireroom housed teleprinters extruding cables from all over the world, and telephonists with headphones typing home news stories.

The newsroom had a complement of 120 staff journalists -- almost as many as the paper's London office. Publishing in Manchester meant front page treatment for important northern stories which London would usually tuck away on inside pages. The 'London bubble' mentality considered anywhere north of Barnet a foreign country and anywhere beyond Carlisle as inside the Arctic Circle. The Telegraph's Manchester operation covered the whole of Scotland, northern England and North Wales. It offered a national newspaper with a unique 'northern flavour' commanding almost half of the paper's total circulation of 1,500.000 copies. Ultimately this 'northern flavour' was irretrievably lost when The Daily Telegraph closed its Manchester newsroom in 1987, and circulation has nosedived ever since.

On his first day with his prestigious employer, Irving reported to Godfrey Myers' inner sanctum in mid-afternoon to meet the news editor, Trevor Unwin. Tall, spare, prematurely balding and with a permanently harassed expression, Trevor offered him a limp handshake and ushered him to his seat on the news desk. The other reporters had yet to arrive so he was handed a batch of Press Association stories to rewrite under the byline of 'Daily Telegraph Reporter' for submission to the sub-editors.

As afternoon turned to evening, the room gradually filled up, activity increased and the tempo began to rise perceptibly. By 7pm the full, all-male reporting team were in place on the news desk. All were in shirtsleeves. Most were middle aged, some smoking cigarettes and one or two slightly redolent of alcohol. They included well-known names, such as Maurice Williamson, just returned from America as the paper's New York correspondent, Brian Hall, industrial correspondent, and George Taylor, finally working his notice before retiring.

A few jocularly remarked on the boyish appearance of their new colleague. George led the wisecracks. 'So this is the bright spark who's replacing me,' he said, affecting surprise. 'I thought he was a messenger. I was just going to ask him for a brew.'

Charles Clarke, the paper's bald, tubby and amiable chief reporter, who was doing the introductions, winked at his baby-faced recruit.' Take no notice, Irving,' he said. 'It's just banter. Everything's in fun here... keeps things in proportion. If we didn't have a laugh we'd all be nervous wrecks.'

Irving wasn't fazed in the slightest. It had been the same at the Chronicle. You took none of the banter seriously. The job was serious enough -- reporting on death, destruction and disaster. A 3D job they called it. The main difference between the Chronicle and the Telegraph was that at the Telegraph the pressure got to you every night, not just once a week.

As the first edition's 10pm deadline approached the buzz of mounting urgency started to kick in. Typewriters chattered so furiously they seemed in danger of overheating, Telephones rang dementedly, mingled with shouted instructions from the backbench to the sub-editors about pictures, story length and headline type sizes. The youthful messengers hurried between desks with cables and phone copy from the wire room, galley proofs from the composing room, endless mugs of tea from their outsize kettle and bacon sandwiches from the canteen.

At 9.30pm the pressure took a vice-like grip as toiling sub-editors wrestled with desperate last-minute changes to the front page -- a time of barely organised chaos when most mistakes were made. In the basement purring, freshly oiled presses revolved slowly, ready to pounce on their prey. And after the final semi-circular stereo plate was fitted a foreman in the control room pressed a red button. The Manchester first edition of The Daily Telegraph was up and running. For better or for worse.

'What do you think of it so far?' Charles Clarke asked his new staff reporter when a brief calm descended on the newsroom.

Irving had spent the last hour helping out on the pictures desk, writing captions and checking proofs. He mopped his brow with a theatrical gesture and shook off imaginary sweat. Some of it was real. The pressure made weekly press days on the Brawton Chronicle seem almost sedate. And it happened every night. 'Phew. I could use a drink,' was all he could say.

'It's supper time,' Charles said. 'We all go to the pub.'

They made for the lift as the editorial floor swiftly emptied except for a skeleton staff in case of emergencies. They were joined in the lift by the sports editor, Howard Miller, and chief sub-editor, Alan Trent. 'Another balls-acher,' Trent declared feelingly. 'Those of us unfortunate enough to survive the night will go through it all again tomorrow.'

'You've been warned, young man,' Miller added with a broad grin.

Irving's youthful confidence would not be shaken. The adrenaline had started to flow. He neither knew nor cared about the size of the mountain he was about to climb. He was hooked.

'Bring it on!' he laughed.

Although now enjoying the NUJ rate of pay for a national daily newspaper reporter -- almost twice his income at the Brawton Chronicle -- Irving spent his first weeks at the Telegraph as a news desk dogsbody. All the messy, unwanted tasks came his way, such as weather round-ups with heat waves and/or flooding a frequent cause of travel chaos. Football pools winners 'living the dream' and others going bankrupt were also a useful source of copy on slow news days.

The chore nobody wanted was answering readers' telephone calls. During daytime office hours, these were fielded by Trevor Unwin's secretary, Irene. They tended to fall off during the evenings but could pick up again in the early hours, especially at times of a full Moon. In Irene's absence all reporters manning the news desk were required to deal politely and efficiently with callers. However muddled, eccentric or weird they might sound, there was always the possibility of a story lurking in the details.

Irving's nose for news remained firmly in place when taking all calls, especially from readers with story tip-offs. These were the calls to be taken seriously. They were passed to Trevor for evaluation. But he found it difficult to keep a straight face when dealing with readers' complaints. Most concerned spelling and other errors which, he pointed out, would have been corrected in later editions. In cases where the errors occurred in the final edition, printed at 4am, the complaint would be relayed to the chief sub-editor.

Failure of the paper's business experts

to predict share price fluctuations and sports writers to forecast score-draws for the football pools were sympathetically referred to the city and spots desks respectively. A surprising number of people complained about baffling clues in the paper's celebrated cryptic crossword. They would read out the clue and expect Irving to come up with an instant answer as if he had the solution in front of him.

Trying to sound sympathetic, he advised them to contact the London office's crossword editor. When he mentioned the puzzled puzzlers to Charles Clarke, the chief reporter told him: 'Half our readers buy the paper for the crossword. Be nice to them. If we were to stop publishing the puzzle, we'd go bankrupt.'

According to the latest socio/economic ratings, the bulk of the paper's readers were to be found in classes A, B and C1. 'In other words,' Charles said, 'the upper and middle classes. Some seem to have nothing better to do than telephone the Telegraph with their pet hates and expect us to do something about them.

'I've had people complaining about men with beards, men wearing brown shoes with blue suits, boys wearing caps the wrong way round, swearing on the radio and TV, and failing standards of courtesy among shop assistants. Then there's the nature lovers, going on about the nesting habits of swifts and why you should talk to plants to help them grow. You mustn't laugh but it's hard not to.'

Irving laughed. 'What do you tell them?'

'That's easy, dear boy. Just suggest they write a letter to the editor in London. You can't guarantee it will be published but you're sure he'll find their views fascinating.'

The real oddballs were people who called in the early hours of the morning, usually when there was a full Moon. Many and lurid were their conspiracy theories concerning the corrupt government, international financiers, religion and the influence of astrology on world events. They were mostly loopy. It was best to tell them they'd made some interesting points, worthy of consideration at a higher level. Suggest they write to their MP. Others were just lonely and needed someone to talk to in the middle of a sleepless night. You did your best to comfort them. As a last resort, if the conversation turned to suicide, you gave them the number of the recently-formed Samaritans.

'It's all about passing the buck as politely as possible,' Charles said. 'We're journalists, after all, not psychiatrists.'

Roughly half the Daily Telegraph's news output originated from the Press Association. Breaking news stories were tagged 'snap' and 'rush' by the agency's staff to indicate degrees of newsworthiness. So when a Home Office blunder resulted in over 100 inmates being released prematurely from different prisons it carried only a 'snap' label. It seemed like another example of routine incompetence in government departments. However, the tale took a bizarre twist when many of the freed convicts turned up at police stations pleading to be taken back into custody. Suddenly the snaps became 'rushes'. Irving was sent to interview one of the men in Oldham, outside Manchester.

When he knocked on the door of the terraced house in the shadow of a monstrous cotton mill, he was met by a bald, heavily tattooed gentleman who was only too pleased to be interviewed. Irving could hear a baby crying and a woman screaming in the background. The man half closed the door behind him. He told the reporter he'd handed himself in at the local police station along with several others but had been freed on police bail because all the cells were full.

'I know my rights,' he snapped. 'I was due for another year inside but they gave me my release papers.'

'But that meant you were a free man,' Irving said.

'Yes, but I'd settled in, you see. Three hots and a cot, a roof over my head and no bills to pay. Can't beat it. Better than being outside!' Three hots and a cot meant three hot means a day and your own bed.

'How did you get back home?' Irving asked.

'Police van... at taxpayers' expense.'

'How long do you expect to be here?'

'Can't say, mate. There's no room at the local nick. They say they'll send a taxi to take me back to Strangeways.' That was the name of the prison in Manchester.

On his return to the news desk, Irving phoned the Manchester police Press office. He was told the prisoner was still waiting for his taxi. Meanwhile, the phone calls were pouring in from irate members of the public who had heard the news on the radio. There were impassioned complaints about Home Office incompetence and calls for much tougher prison conditions. What did it say about the penal system when criminals preferred the comforts of prison to earning an honest living in the community, etc.

Irving included their comments -- made anonymously in most cases -- in a composite, pull-together story, using accounts from freelancers in other regions. It had been a balls-acher to catch the first edition and he hoped the chief-sub would allow him his first named byline. But his heavily subbed copy appeared on an inside page attributed, as usual, to Daily Telegraph Reporter.

Another story Irving regarded as a potential scoop suffered a similar fate. He sometimes helped out at St Peter's all-night shelter for the destitute. He would finish a late shift on the news desk and head for the church to relieve Daniel and his fellow volunteers of working through the early hours. That was when most of the down-and-outs turned up for soup and a bed for the night. It was Irving's way of repaying his brother-in-law for his generosity over the house deposit.

On one such rainswept winter night, there was an unusual surge of homeless people seeking refuge in the shelter -- whole families, adults and children, deeply distressed and in need of urgent help. There was insufficient room in the church annex and the main building had to be opened to accommodate them. It turned out they had all been evicted by a local landlord at a moment's notice because he wanted to demolish their humble terraced homes to make way for a block of luxury flats.

It was a gift-wrapped scoop if ever there was one and Irving scribbled numerous quotes in his notebook as he helped settle the refugees down for the night on the church pews, cushioned with padded kneelers and cocooned in blankets. The tenants had held out for weeks against pressure to quit their homes from the landlord -- a titled property tycoon -- but he had finally lost patience and taken out court orders for immediate eviction.

After only a few hours' sleep Irving was

back at his typewriter the next day and had the whole exclusive story wrapped up in good time for the first edition. Surely it deserved a byline. When the messengers brought the first edition copies up to the newsroom he eagerly scanned the front page headlines: Rail strike continues; More bullets flying in the Middle East; Prince breaks elbow in fall from horse. ('At least he now knows his arse from his elbow,' Charles declared amid loud guffaws). But there was no sign of Irving's exclusive. He checked the inside pages. No sign of it there either. Then he spotted it -- a three-paragraph filler at the foot of page six. EVICTED FAMILIES HOUSED IN CHURCH. No byline. Not even a DTR. That's a ruling about disclosure and transparency.

It was all in a day's work -- or in this case a night's work -- for a Telegraph reporter, Charles explained sympathetically. 'Class element, dear boy. No place for rapacious landlords here, they're a protected species, especially titled ones. You're lucky the story got in at all.' Fortunately for the homeless families, their ordeal received more realistic treatment from the Daily Mirror. The paper picked up on the story for its final edition, making it the front page splash. A few days later, shamed into urgent action, the local council had found emergency accommodation for them all.

Irving began to wonder if executives on the editorial 'backbench' had it in for him as the new boy -- their way of telling him bylines did not come easily on the Telegraph as they did on some newspapers. But Godfrey Myers had been monitoring his protege's progress closely and was encouraged by what he saw. After conferring with Trevor Unwin, it was decided the young man was ready for his first major story with front page potential.

THIRTEEN

The 1950s were a time of newsworthy change at home and abroad, and in Manchester, always at the forefront of innovation, the face of higher education was changing rapidly. The city's Municipal College of Technology had been elevated as an independent university-level institution and a major centre of scientific research. It was renamed the University of Manchester Institute of Science and Technology (UMIST) and Irving was chosen to cover its prestigious inauguration ceremony.

The Press corps consisted of reporters from all the national newspapers, TV and radio stations. They were shown round the lecture halls, laboratories and students' quarters by Prof Frank Jordon, an expert in cosmology, who taught in the physics and astronomy department.

The young lightly bearded professor proved an insightful guide to the assembled media. There had been a spate of UFO sightings in recent weeks and the reporters wanted to know if he believed there was intelligent life elsewhere in the universe.

'Of course. There has to be,' he said. 'There are billions of galaxies in the universe. Our university's radio telescopes at Jodrell Bank are trying to count them all. Let's say at a conservative estimate there are 10 billion galaxies in the observable universe. The number of stars in a galaxy varies. Assuming an average of 100 billion stars per galaxy that would give a total of around 1 billion trillion stars in the observable universe.'

Irving struggled to write the figure in his notebook. 'How many noughts is that?'

'Let me show you.' The professor led them into an adjoining lecture room and chalked on the blackboard:

1,000,000,000,000,000,000.000

'That's just stars, of course. There are countless planets going round them. So you see there has to be life elsewhere in the universe. I cannot possibly believe that we are alone.'

The journalists were uncharacteristically subdued. 'What about UFOs?' one asked.

'They have no place in astrophysics. They belong more to the realm of science fiction. It's possible alien life forms are taking a peek at us. They'd be well advised to give us a wide berth -- we're toxic!'

Irving wanted to know about parallel

universes. 'Does quantum physics also belong to the realm of science fiction?'

'Far from it. It's the latest thing in astrophysics. We're still trying to get our heads round it. Basically, it overturns classic laws of physics by suggesting there are countless universes as well as ours. with worlds almost identical to Earth in them.'

'Does that mean all of us people exist in these different dimensions?'

'That's the popular interpretation. I believe it to be very probably true.'

'So there are replicas of us all -- like clones -- in other versions of UMIST out there at this moment trying to make sense of what you're saying?'

'Lots of you, almost identical, maybe wearing different coloured socks.'

Irving asked about quantum moments and the uncertainty principle.

'The theory is that quantum moments are happening all the time. For example when a footballer draws his leg back to shoot for goal -- that's a quantum moment. Just for a second it's uncertain whether the ball will enter the net, whether it will miss the target or if the goalkeeper will save it...'

'If he's a City player it'll go over the bar,' a wag called out amid laughter.

'Or it could hit a post,' another said.

'Exactly. In different universes there'll be

different results. It's like tossing a coin... uncertain which side it comes down. It'll be heads in one world, tails in another.'

A sceptical voice asked: 'Isn't it all speculation really? It doesn't prove the existence of parallel universes does it?'

Prof Jordon raised a hand in acknowledgement. 'No, not yet. But I'm confident it will.'

Irving remembered his own quantum moment of feeling sick as a white ball whizzed round a roulette wheel but at the same time was quietly thrilled to meet a distinguished scientist who shared his own instincts on things not being what they seemed. He would be a valuable addition to his contacts book.

The story appeared on the paper's front page along with pictures of academics, VIPs and students. Speculation about parallel universes and quantum moments were not mentioned as the backbench decided they would go over readers' heads. Speeches by other luminaries, recorded verbatim by Irving's polished shorthand, were also ruthlessly cut by the sub-editors to fit available space. But none of the mutilation concerned Irving unduly since his report carried the byline:

by IRVING BREEN.

He'd arrived. He'd taken his first step on the ladder. Many more remained to be climbed but for the present, as he carefully cut out the story for his scrapbook, he was happy to have become a member of the Daily Telegraph's prestigious family.

There remained the small but important matter of his expenses. The Wolseley was due for its annual service so he travelled to the venue by public transport. As he'd been out of the office for most of the day he qualified for a subsistence allowance in addition to travel expenses. He claimed for one meal (lunch) plus bus and third class rail fares. The total came to one pound, four shillings and sixpence. He left the claim form in the chief reporter's in-tray. A short time later Charles called him over and Irving feared the worst. Was he about to get a rollicking for claiming too much?

'This won't do, dear boy,' Charles said, indicating the expenses slip. 'It's much too low. Daily Telegraph staff journalists never go anywhere by bus. We use taxis. And when travelling by train it's always first class, not third. For all-day assignments we're allowed to claim for breakfast, elevenses, lunch, afternoon tea, dinner and supper.' He added a nought to the total. Irving took a look. It now read £10.4s.6d

For a time the Suez crisis dominated the front page as Anthony Eden, along with the French and Israeli governments, vacillated over military intervention when Colonel Nasser nationalised the waterway. With the canal blocked to international shipping, oil imports quickly dried up and it was not long before petrol was rationed. Motorists were allowed only 200 miles worth of fuel per month. A black market sprang up instantly and contraband petrol began to figure on the case lists of magistrates' courts along with illegal drugs.

Major news stories of the period competing for front page space included the formation of the EEC in the Treaty of Rome, Asian flu, Sputnik the first space satellite, the launch of Premium Bonds and in America the birth of rock 'n roll. Bill Haley and the Comets -- a group of middle aged gents in dinner jackets -- ushered in a riotous era of pop music that changed the world for ever.

There were few opportunities for home news exclusives for Irving and his news desk colleagues but that all changed when the turbulent fifties careered into the decadent sixties. According to most historians this was where the rot set in. Sexual morality, religion and respect for authority were the first casualties of lovable, guitar-strumming hippies obsessed by a drug culture that would ultimately overwhelm the nation. The Tories were in office, Harold Macmillan was Prime Minister and Elvis Presley was King.

Handkerchief-size black and white £5 notes along with farthing coins, used since the 13th century, ceased to be legal tender. The Sunday Telegraph was launched. The Pill became available on the NHS and an unknown group from Liverpool called the Beatles played their first concert in Hamburg. Thousands of people joined CND rallies in London and major cities. On the foreign front, France vetoed Britain's entry into the European Common Market. General de Gaulle declared that Britain lacked commitment to European integration -- a remarkable feat of prophecy.

Daily news lists in the Telegraph's Manchester office led with the Jodrell Bank observatory in Cheshire making contact with the US spacecraft Pioneer 5 over 407,000 miles away; the first episode of Coronation Street beamed from the city's Granada TV studios, drug-fuelled rock concerts and their teenage casualties and Manchester City signing Denis Law from Huddersfield Town for a record fee of £55,000.

'No stopping City now.'

Irving and Jamie Lee were enjoying a late-night drink and a frame of snooker at the Manchester Press Club and conversation had taken its usual turn to football. Irving's confident assertion met with predictable guffaws from Jamie, his fellow cub reporter from their Brawton days. They'd stayed in touch ever since as their youthful enthusiasm matured into the routine daily pursuit of truth. The novelty may have worn off but their sense of vocation had never wavered.

Jamie had taken a little longer to reach the Mancunian equivalent of Fleet Street but was now a seasoned sports journalist with the Daily Mail. Brawton Rovers were a fond memory. He had realised his ambition of full Press accreditation at Old Trafford where his beloved Manchester United were riding high in the First Division. City, forever in United's shadow, were still struggling far below.

'You'll need more than one good player to get you out of the doldrums,' Jamie scoffed, as he lined up an easy red ball only to miss the pot. 'You could do with another ten!'

Irving smiled at the familiar banter and lined up a red ball himself. In it went, followed by the black, another red and the blue. That was a break of 14 for the scoreboard. He ended the frame with pink and black, and a lead of 65 points.

'Just scraped the win again,' Jamie said and Irving grinned. He could still give his old friend a hiding at snooker, which caused him no end of satisfaction.

The drinks were on Jamie and they returned to their seats to watch replays of the Test match against Australia on the club's black and white TV set. Once again, England had suffered a humiliating batting collapse. They were in danger of losing the match together with the Ashes series. Jamie summed up their plight succinctly:

'One gets out and they all fall over, like dominoes. They're just a bunch of losers -- almost as bad as City!'

Irving raised his glass. 'Cheers. One day the tide will turn at Maine Road, you'll see.'

'You've been saying that for years. It never does.'

'One day soon they'll not only win the FA Cup but the First Division championship.'

Jamie spluttered into his pint. 'Pull the other one, Irving!'

'I've been reading up on quantum physics and the uncertainty principle. It's fascinating stuff. The theory is that there are other worlds out there in a different dimension, an infinite number, and we're all in them but different, if you see what I mean.'

Jamie was still chuckling. 'I think you should stick to snooker, mate!'

'Seriously, I've talked to Prof Frank Jordon about it, he's a physics lecturer at UMIST. He's really clued up on quantum theory. It's all about parallel universes, called multiverses. Anything's possible in them. In another multiverse Germany won the war and Hitler is president of Britain.'

'Sounds nasty. Thank God we don't live in that one!'

'But that's just it -- we do. Our characters co-exist in them all, in different manifestations and varying relationships. We're the same people but other things are different.'

'You've lost me mate.'

'For example, if Germany had won the war we'd probably both be resistance fighters.'

'You bet.'

'So you see, our characters would be playing different roles but we'd be the same people in essence.'

'Would there still be football and cricket?'

'Probably -- and snooker.'

'And England whitewash Australia in the Ashes, I suppose!'

'Absolutely. About time! And Manchester City start winning everything in sight!'

'Can't get my head round that one, Irving. You'd need more than another dimension, you'd need a ruddy miracle!'

FOURTEEN

'Chapel meeting in 15 minutes.'

Adam Richardson, a news sub-editor and NUJ office organiser (shop steward) at the Telegraph, strode briskly from desk to desk with the instruction that everyone -- from Trevor Unwin, the news editor, downwards -- was duty bound to obey. Known as Father of the Chapel (FoC), Adam was regarded by the newspaper's management as a political animal, the polite way of saying left-wing activist and a significant threat to their prestigious and highly profitable business operation.

A youthful looking 30-something son of an Army officer, he had a commanding presence despite hippy-length dark hair. He was widely respected by all chapel members with the possible exception of Trevor and a handful of financial journalists in the City department. The news editor, a lifelong Tory, came from Bolton and from childhood had spoken with a broad Lancashire accent. But over the years he'd struggled as a management crony to emulate the southern drawl of fellow executives in the London office. The technique had served him well in his steady rise to his present position of responsibility. But there was still an annoying tendency to lapse into the Bolton dialect under pressure.

In complete contrast, over three-quarters of his reporting staff were down-to-earth, unpretentious socialists, many left-wingers like Adam. This had come as something of a shock to Irving on joining their ranks. He imagined readers being horrified to discover over their breakfast kidneys and kedgeree that their beloved newspaper -- a model of elitism and moral rectitude -- had been produced by socialists to the left of Aneurin Bevan. They would probably have cancelled its delivery immediately. It was the sort of truth you needed to keep quiet about, he reflected as he trooped upstairs with his colleagues for the chapel meeting.

The meeting was held in a sectioned-off area of the canteen. Tables and chairs were drawn up, with Adam as chairman and Aubrey Vickers, an elderly sports sub and chapel clerk, seated at the head of the crowded gathering. Debating society rules applied. Motions to the meeting had to be proposed and seconded before being discussed and finally put to a vote. Questions and points of order were addressed to the chair and the FoC was always referred to as Mister Father.

Adam and Aubrey had returned from a meeting in London with representatives of the newspaper's management. The meeting had not gone well. In fact, it had hardly gone on at all. The paper's editor-in-chief, Cedric Westwood, and senior members of the management negotiating team were conspicuous by their absence. They had more important matters to attend to. It happened to be Royal Ascot week and there was no way they would forsake their private box at the racecourse for a meeting with oiks from the Manchester office.

It was a familiar delaying tactic, tried and trusted over the years. If it wasn't Ascot, it would be Goodwood, Henley, Wimbledon or Lord's. August would herald the unmissable grouse season and in winter months the excuse would be Cheltenham, Twickenham or Klosters.

It was only the NUJ after all. If it had been the NGA (National Graphical Association) the hard-line printers' union, it would have been a different story. The NGA's approach to collective bargaining was to walk out on strike at the drop of a hat and negotiate afterwards. The NUJ's strategy had always been moderate and principled, with industrial action only as a last resort. But moderation was beginning to wear thin as far as Adam Richardson was concerned.

'It's more of the same I'm afraid, gentlemen,' he said, opening the meeting. 'They're treating us with contempt as usual. In the absence of the real decision makers, we met their deputies and were fed the same old story: they cannot afford to give us a pay rise. There is no money. Circulation is falling. Advertising revenue is down. Our request for a review of working conditions and longer holidays in view of the high pressure of our job was also turned down.

'So it's back to square one, where we were two months ago, without the slightest progress having been made. Aubrey and I feel that the chapel's patience is being mistaken for weakness. We think its time to disabuse management of that impression. We are, after all, 100 per cent NUJ membership and as much of a closed shop as the NGA. I'm not suggesting we adopt the NGA's crude tactics -- strike first, talk later. But I do feel the time has come to demonstrate our solidarity in support of our reasonable claims.

'In the absence of meaningful negotiation, we have been forced to consider the prospect of industrial action. There are several options open to us: a work-to-rule that would slow down production and threaten edition times; a partial withdrawal of labour in certain departments; a 24-hour walk out of all departments; a series of such walkouts, or full-blown strike action for an indefinite period. I await the chapel's instructions. It's up to you now, gentlemen. The question is: where do we go from here?'

Trevor stood up and said: 'In arnswer to your question, Mister Father, I suggest we all go back to work.' His statement, predictable though it was, sparked a rowdy response from chapel members and Adam struggled to restore order. When they had all quietened down he addressed the news editor: 'Your comment has been noted, Trevor. Do you wish to propose that as a motion?'

Trevor, who had remained standing throughout the hubbub, replied: 'I certainly do.'

'Is there a seconder?'

The City editor, Denis Delany, one of Trevor's cronies, raised a hand. 'I'll second that.'

'Then the motion is open for discussion.'

'As I was saying before I was rudely interrupted... we have been told the outcome of the FoC's meeting in London. We all know management have severe financial problems and I'm arsking the chapel to show restraint at this difficult time. There is no point in prolonging our meeting. We have already fallen well behind schedule. We should return to work while there is still a charnce of meeting the first edition deadline.'

Trevor sat down and Aubrey Vickers, the clerk, spoke for the first time above a chorus of raised voices. 'Thanks for that, Trevor. This chapel has long regarded you as the voice of its conscience and we take on board all that you have said. However, I believe that the time for restraint has passed. It's over 20 months since we had a salary increase and since then the cost of living has escalated. We have our own financial problems as well as management. We have mortgage payments to make and families to support. Restraint won't pay the bills.

'Despite what we are told, the paper is still profitable. All we are asking for is a reasonable share of those profits since we are the people who work our balls off every night to make them possible. We have shown great restraint and have been offered nothing in return. The time has come for action.'

There were cries of 'Hear, hear' and the tubby figure of Charles Clarke, the chief reporter, bounced to his feet. 'I agree with Aubrey. We've been patient long enough. The time has come for action. I move that the motion be put to the vote.'

'Does anyone else want to speak to the motion?' the FoC asked. Nobody did. There were shouts of 'Vote, vote...'

'Then I will put it to the vote. All those in favour of the motion that we return to work immediately please show.'

No more than half a dozen hands were raised.

'All those against.'

There was no need for a count. It was overwhelming.

'Any abstentions?'

There were none.

'The motion is defeated.'

Nobody had expected it to succeed, least of all Trevor. It had served its purpose. His call for restraint would be placed on record and would impress London management when details of the chapel meeting were eventually leaked to them. The identity of the chapel's mole was supposed to be a mystery but there was little doubt in the minds of members that it was Trevor himself.

'Let's move on now, gentlemen,' Adam said. 'But before we do so, open some windows ... let out the cigarette smoke and some of the hot air!' Everyone took the subtle point. Two of the canteen's sash windows were opened. It was a warm summer evening with the sun low over the Manchester skyline and the sound of traffic from the street far below. Normal people were hurrying home at the end of their day's work while night workers tasked with producing their next day's news declined to start theirs. The journalists' lives were abnormal by comparison, with unsocial hours and rates of pay far below those of the printers. It was a grotesque anomaly that had existed for decades. There comes a time when forbearance ceases to be a virtue. That time had clearly arrived.

Led by their dynamic and cultured officials, chapel members discussed the various methods of concentrating management's mind on their predicament while causing as little collateral damage as possible. It was not easy.

Whatever form of industrial action was adopted there would be a negative impact on the paper's circulation. A work-to-rule seemed the more favoured option. It would affect edition times and slow down production. Thousands of copies would be lost. But the paper would still be published.

The main problem was that it would be difficult to implement. Working to rule was in direct conflict with journalists' innate sense of urgency. It meant observing petty rules and regulations. Their brains were wired to speed things up, not slow them down. As such it would be a blow to their professionalism. But as a short-term measure it seemed the most effective. After much agonised debate the chapel decided on an immediate work-to-rule lasting 24 hours with similar measures to be taken at the discretion of the FoC as considered necessary . Members were about to take a vote on the motion when a curly haired messenger appeared holding an envelope.

'There's a message from God.'

It was time for Godfrey Myers to take a hand in proceedings. Adam thanked the lad, opened the envelope and read out the message:

Dear Adam

Your meeting has now lasted over two hours. If it continues it will be deemed disruptive and deductions will be made from salaries as appropriate.

> Yours ever
> Godfrey
> Northern Editor

There were smiles all round at the affectionate terminology. Godfrey signed all his letters and memos that way. The note was for management's benefit, in the same way as Trevor's defeated motion. Mindful of his humble roots the editor secretly sympathised with chapel members but could never give any outward appearance of doing so.

Adam handed the note to Aubrey. 'The editor's note is placed on record. Any deductions from salaries will result in very serious consequences -- in the form of escalating industrial action. I'm sure Godfrey is aware of that. Our members will now vote on the motion before them, namely:

'In the absence of any meaningful response from management to its claims on pay and conditions, this chapel now instructs members to work to rule for the next 24 hours. It reserves the right to implement further work-to-rule measures at the discretion of the FoC as he may consider necessary.'

'All those in favour please show.'

Apart from Trevor and 'the usual suspects' in City department, the majority was again overwhelming.

Returning to work in a newsroom empty except for messengers was like being brought back down to earth with a bump for Irving after his heady introduction to trade union power. The only chapel meetings he could recall at the Brawton Chronicle had been to appoint officials and collect NUJ subscriptions. They had taken about 10 minutes. The impressive display of collective strength had seemed almost surreal at times -- an institution as illustrious as The Daily Telegraph being challenged by a group of relatively impoverished journalists whose only weapon was solidarity. It was a weapon that would be sorely tested in the weeks ahead now battle lines had been drawn up with the paper's management.

In the journalists' absence cables from the wire room and copy from the telephone copytakers had piled up in everyone's in-trays. These were wire baskets capable of holding voluminous amounts of paper. Trevor's basket had overflowed with paper scattered over his desk and onto the floor. As he stooped to pick it up, Adam gave him a timely reminder:

'We're working to rule now, Trevor. It's the messengers' job to sort out all your incoming copy.'

Faced with a rapidly approaching first edition deadline, a clutch of court reports from

Manchester Assizes, a woman reportedly killed on a level crossing in North Wales and a breaking story of a missing toddler in Carlisle, Trevor was in no mood to start working to rule. 'We're not in a chapel meeting now, Adam,' he snapped. 'This is the news desk and I'm in charge. I'll sort out the basket myself.'

As soon as he'd said it he realised his accent had slipped. He meant 'barsket', of course. The lapse added to his rising stress and he scratched his receding hairline vigorously with both hands. 'I suggest you return to your own department -- there's plenty of copy in need of subbing. Don't rush. The rules say we mustn't hurry.'

The sarcasm was not lost on the FoC. He knew it would be difficult to persuade his colleagues to slow down. A sense of urgency was second nature to them. But it soon became clear that Trevor was fighting a losing battle. Due mainly to the prolonged chapel meeting, the night's first edition was lost. Thousands of readers in Scotland, Northern Ireland and other remote northern areas would go without their morning Daily Telegraph.

The tactic paid off twice more in the following week. It worked particularly well among the news sub-editors. Unclear or ambiguous passages in reporters' copy needed to be taken up with the reporter in question, which was time-consuming and sometimes impossible. Only when the reporter could not be contacted was the sub allowed to rewrite the passage more clearly.

When reference books were required from the paper's library, such as Debrett's Peerage or Who's Who, a messenger would be instructed to bring the book. You could no longer go to the library and check out the volume yourself. Messengers could be dilatory in their duties, especially the younger ones. It was all petty and distasteful to professional journalists but as Adam kept reminding them, 'needs must when the devil drives.'

The speed of management's reaction was unexpected but what really took the chapel by surprise was its draconian nature. 'They're fighting back,' Adam told a hastily convened meeting in the canteen. 'We knew they would, of course. They're not threatening to sack us all -- at least not yet. They're just going to lock us out!'

He read from a memo he'd received from the managing editor:

'Dear Mr Richardson,

Following the repeated action of your members in breach of their contract of employment, resulting in disruption to northern editions of The Daily Telegraph, His Lordship has instructed me to take emergency measures.

Accordingly, I now require an unequivocal assurance that your members will return to normal working forthwith, with no further disruption to circulation of northern   editions.

Unless I receive your undertaking to this effect before 8pm this evening, I will   implement a lockout procedure without further notice. This would require   immediate withdrawal of all NUJ members from the building and suspension of their   salaries.

Yours faithfully
Cedric Westwood
Managing Editor

Adam handed the memo to Aubrey Vickers amid a stunned silence, apart from the distant sound of traffic through the open windows. The journalists' exercise of trade union power had not lasted long. When the shock had worn off, there came the inevitable questions. It was 7.20pm already. If management locked them all out they would not only lose the first edition but all second, third and final editions, the entire night's print run. Where was the logic in that?

Aubrey had an explanation. 'We think they're planning to increase the print run in London -- send extra copies up here to Manchester by train. Sounds like an interesting experiment but it's bound to go wrong.'

'The trains take too long and wholesalers aren't geared up for it,' Adam added. 'They'll lose thousands of copies across the north of England.

It's typical Telegraph mismanagement. They'll take any risks to try and beat us rather than just sit down calmly and discuss their employees' genuine grievances.'

Trevor Unwin had listened to the proceedings with growing impatience but was now on his feet. 'Mister Father... let's be realistic. Time is running out and we're about to find ourselves on the street. Our salaries will be stopped. Most of us have wives and families to support. We're already living hand to mouth. We simply can't afford to lose pay, however temporary. Let's face the facts. Management have called our bluff. Our childish go-slow tactics have failed. We should admit defeat and return to our desks before 8pm.'

He looked at his watch. 'It's now 7.30pm. I move that this chapel's officials provide management with the undertaking requested and return to work -- while there's still time.'

Several hands were raised to second the news editor's motion. Irving's was not one of them although thoughts of Emily and Dawn in their heavily mortgaged home were uppermost in his mind. He had yet to speak at a chapel meeting, preferring to keep his thoughts to himself, but had voted in favour of the original motion to work-to-rule. For all Trevor's impassioned argument, he was not prepared to admit defeat. The issue was clear, the chapel was in the right. They had not broken their contracts of employment by working to rule.

The point was clarified by Adam. 'Let's be perfectly clear about management's claim that we're in breach of contract by working to rule. There is no breach of contract in working strictly to rules of conduct laid down by management themselves. If our salaries are stopped they will be acting illegally. They're fully aware of that. It's just scare tactics. They really should know better... we're journalists not schoolchildren.'

With the motion open for discussion it was clear that chapel members were in no mood to back down. Apart from a few waverers they were prepared for a face-off with a devious and intransigent management, even if it meant losing one or two nights' pay. As Adam said, any salary deductions would be illegal and management would have to restore them. In the meantime the NUJ would ensure they suffered no hardship. The dispute would not last long once it was seen to be hitting circulation. Other papers would gain from the Telegraph's loss. Readers who moved to other titles were difficult to recapture.

Chapel members were still discussing Trevor's notion when, on the stroke of 8pm, a messenger appeared with the customary envelope.

'A message from God.'

Adam read out Godfrey's memo. Management were prepared to grant a 15-minute extension. If the meeting was still in session after that time, chapel members must consider themselves locked out and should vacate the building in an orderly manner. Security staff had been notified accordingly.

Adam handed the note to Aubrey. 'The editor's message is placed on record. Our meeting will continue.'

It continued until 9.45pm when after much robust debate from both sides and the 8pm deadline overtaken by events, the motion to return to work was finally put to the vote. This time a count was needed to determine the margin of defeat. It was still emphatic. Then they all marched out to the Grapes Inn -- a motley collection of reporters, sub-editors, feature writers and photographers, heads held high following a democratically taken decision, while there was still time to buy a few pints. Security staff watched respectfully from a distance. Their involvement would not be necessary.

The lights remained on in the Telegraph offices but there was nobody at home -- apart from the London management team led by Cedric Westwood and his ageing sidekick, Roy Gibson, the finance director. They were frantically trying to organise the transit of an extended print run from Fleet Street. Journey times between Euston Station and London Road Station in Manchester were constantly being shortened but still took over three hours. That meant the first and second editions had already been lost.

If the dispute continued next day the process would start earlier in the evening and they might organise an airlift into Manchester Airport. The paper's Fleet Street presses would need to operate for much longer and that would mean extra payments for their already overpaid NGA operatives. It was not the most uplifting scenario from a management point of view. All that, rather than simply sit down with their long-suffering journalists and negotiate a fair deal on pay and working conditions.

Across the road it was closing time at the Grapes Inn when chapel members regrouped in an upstairs meeting room converted to a campaign headquarters. Adam had called in support from NUJ officials in the Manchester branch office and was organising operations with a military precision inherited from his father. The first step was a press release for other newspapers and broadcasting stations, stressing that Telegraph journalists were not on strike but had been locked out by their employer. All the paper's editorial staff were still available for work at a moment's notice and chapel officials willing to participate in meaningful negotiations. All Messrs Westwood and Gibson needed to do was agree to a meeting.

Then there was the business of organising picket lines outside the Telegraph's building. Branch officials promised to supply leaflets and placards explaining the chapel's position for the following day. They would also consult their London headquarters to organise an emergency fighting fund to alleviate hardship for the journalists' families. Other newspaper chapels throughout the country would be asked to contribute to the fund.

By early afternoon the following day, the FoC had drawn up his battle plans. His troops -- the paper's entire Manchester editorial staff with a few notable absentees -- gathered in their makeshift headquarters to receive their orders. They were drafted into squads of 10 members detailed for picket line duty on a rota basis. Armed with their 'weapons' -- NUJ placards and leaflets -- they would face a largely indifferent and sometimes hostile public for two hours before being replaced by the next squad. At all times there would be a picket line outside the newspaper's main entrance until the early hours. Adam, Aubrey and NUJ branch officials would do their share of picket duty.

When not 'manning the barricades' as Charles Clarke described it, the pickets were obliged to return to the pub so they were immediately available for work in the unlikely event of a management climb-down. Non-alcoholic refreshments were provided by the pub's staff. Only when their editorial shift time had expired could the troops enjoy a pint.

The system worked smoothly that day. And the next. Chapel morale remained high and optimistic. But then, as management's ploy of printing extra copies in London and despatching them by plane to Manchester seemed to be succeeding, murmurs of dissent began to surface. Adam Richardson was ready for them. In a late-night rallying call to his weary followers after last drinks, he recited in ringing tones a poem his father had taught him as a boy:

Say not the struggle nought availeth
The labour and the wounds are vain,
The enemy faints not nor faileth,
And as things were so things remain.

If hopes were dupes fears may be liars,
It may be, in yon smoke concealed,
Your comrades chase e'en now the fliers
And but for you possess the field.

The poem, by Arthur Hugh Clough, brought an impromptu standing ovation. It was a masterly rhetorical flourish at exactly the right psychological moment. Adam had sensed his members' weakening resolve under increasing financial pressure from their families. It was vital to raise their spirits. He'd heard whispers from NUJ sources in London that management were about to cave in. Despite their emergency measures, circulation throughout the north was still patchy and advertisers were withdrawing support. It would not be long before His Lordship's cronies were forced back to the negotiating table.

Clough's rousing words had the desired effect. Irving in particular found the poem inspiring. Along with several colleagues he'd started to doubt the wisdom of their tactics. Dawn had just started at primary school and Emily had almost drained their puny savings to pay for her uniform. There had been no complaints from his wife, although her political views were at some variance with her husband's. She'd supported his actions and understood the vital principle of solidarity when fighting for justice. But Irving, ever in tune with her emotions, could feel her deepening anxiety. Was it time to admit defeat and return to work? Don't even think about it! But for him his comrades were about to possess the field.

It was in this mood of renewed defiance and bolstered by a modest handout from the hardship fund, that Irving took up his position on the picket line the next day, clutching his trusty NUJ LOCKOUT placard and a batch of leaflets. Light rain started to fall, as it has a habit of doing in Manchester, and he pulled on a smart blue corduroy cap that Emily had bought him for his birthday. As he and his colleagues huddled in the Telegraph's arched main entrance, a shiny Daimler limousine drew up at the pavement's edge. The driver, a middle aged gentleman, wound down his window and beckoned towards him.

Some car drivers had sounded their horns in support as they passed so expecting similar encouragement, Irving approached the vehicle. As he leaned forward to offer a leaflet he felt a sharp stinging sensation in his eye. He recoiled, spilling his leaflets on the wet pavement, only then realising he'd been spat at. Without a word the driver wound up his window and the car sped off.

Irving's colleagues had seen the incident and rushed to help him. Hard-bitten journalists, they couldn't believe what had happened. Irving couldn't believe it either. He wiped his eye with a handkerchief and discovered that most of the spittle had landed on his cap. He took it off and wrapped it in a couple of damp leaflets.

He managed a grin. 'Rather get my head wet than wear that again -- at least until it's been disinfected.'

Another picket, Dave Leonard, a fellow reporter, escorted him back to headquarters. 'Elitist scum,' he declared. 'It's class hatred. Can't bear oiks like us standing up to them.' Dave was a member of the chapels' hard Left wing that believed the ruling class formed the scum on the septic tank of capitalism. Irving, more of a moderate, had never considered joining them. Until now.

The pub landlady bathed his bloodshot eye and poured him a brandy despite the rules. Adam called all his troops together and told them what had happened. 'That's Class A readership for you -- what our dear paper is always bragging about. Imagine what they'd do to us if we really upset them! Our colleagues in London should know about this. Its time we had some support from the London chapel.'

The FoC ordered a taxi and sent Irving home.

Emily had just returned with Dawn from primary school when Irving's taxi arrived. She noticed his bloodshot eye instantly. 'Darling, what's happened to you?'

He flopped into an armchair. 'I'm a picket line casualty. Some gent in a Daimler took a dislike to our protest. There was no spittoon handy so he used me instead.'

She was shocked. 'You mean he spat at you?'`

'That's right. Poor aim. Most of it hit my cap.' He took his cap out of his jacket pocket and held it distastefully between thumb and forefinger. 'Mind how you hold it, you might catch something. Better get your rubber gloves.'

She hurried into the kitchen and returned with bright yellow rubber gloves. She took the visibly stained cap with a shudder. 'It's going straight in for washing. You need to bathe your eye, darling. And stop rubbing it, you'll make it worse.'

He bathed his sore eye in the bathroom and washed his face. Then he washed it again as it still felt dirty. He had been injured more emotionally than physically. Insults and hostility were occupational hazards, of course, and by standing on a trade union picket line you were exposing yourself to public scorn. But he had never been spat at before. The experience had had a profound effect on him. Adam was right, the incident had shown the paper's 'Class A readership' in its true light.

Dave Leonard was also right. The 'toffs' didn't just dislike the working classes, they really hated them. Irving struggled to grasp the reason for such hatred. He could understand the poor hating the rich because of their wealth. That could be attributed to envy. But the other way round? What had the rich got to be envious of? He'd always avoided any kind of political extremism, left or right. He was what could be loosely described as moderate Labour, or following more in his grandpa's footsteps, that rare species of journalist, a Christian Democrat.

The vision of homeless families huddled in the pews of St Peter's Church on an icy winter's night was still fresh in his memory. The more he thought about it the more he understood the truth of Dave's words. The landlord had gained nothing by evicting his tenants so callously. It had not brought forward his grandiose expansion plans by a single day. It was simply an act of calculated cruelty in the knowledge it would cause intense human suffering to people who had irritated him. It was what hoarding piles of money did to people. Beneath a thin veneer of refinement there lay a deep capacity for malice.

Grandpa had warned him about it all those years ago. *The toffs hated working people because of their honesty.* 'They think we should all be bent, like them.' So that was the reason for the inverted class hatred, Irving realised. The rich knew that however much money they accumulated, it could never buy them integrity. Deep down they knew they were an inferior species.

'Nothing has changed. It's still us and them,' he told Emily as they lay in bed together later.' I've turned into a raving Leftie!'

She smiled and kissed him gently. 'No, you haven't. What happened to you was disgusting and contemptible but it could have been worse. You've no bones broken, just wounded pride.'

He sighed. 'That's bad enough. It feels like a form of intellectual violence. That's what hatred is, isn't it -- intellectual violence. God knows what that can lead to... racism, fascism, war...' He'd stopped going to church years ago, mainly because of his job's unsocial hours and the need to work at weekends. He had still not joined the

Catholic Church despite his good intentions, although he always wore the crucifix his mother-in-law gave him at his wedding.

Emily still attended Mass every Sunday along with Dawn, who was preparing for her first holy communion. She raised herself on one elbow and kissed his troubled face gently. 'Look at it this way, darling. They hated our Lord. They beat Jesus and spat at him. How do you think *he* felt -- God himself?'

Irving thought for a long moment. 'I don't know, it's beyond our understanding. Deeply humiliated, I should think.'

'Those people... they spat at God! Yet he still forgave them. He even tried to *excuse* them. "Father, forgive them, they know not what they do".'

'But I'm not Jesus. I'm just a journalist,' was all he could say.

'Of course . We're only human. But try to forgive the man and you'll feel a whole lot better.'

The power of her words was compelling. There were times when she was a more skilful wordsmith than he was. The more he thought about it, the more ineffable the incident became. Far from a vile insult the man had done him a special favour. It had provided him with an insight into divine truth. How many people were allowed that? He started to feel better already. He'd forgive the driver of the Daimler.

But he couldn't forget. Grandpa had been right. There was no way he would be browbeaten by the ruling class.

It was a combination of circumstances that finally persuaded management to accept the inevitability of a negotiated settlement. When fog descended on Manchester Airport and hung around for two days, flights had to be diverted to Leeds/Bradford Airport. Among them, of course, were the cargo planes carrying many thousands of copies of The Daily Telegraph published in London. Frantic arrangements were made for fleets of lorries to trek across the Pennines to collect them, then hastily improvising distribution patterns.

Further complications arose when fog also descended on the Pennines. Copies of the paper were nowhere to be seen on the shelves of newsagents throughout the north. But the development that concentrated management's minds most strongly was the prospect of a work-to-rule by the paper's NUJ London chapel in sympathy with their Manchester colleagues. The London journalists were to hold an urgent ballot on the move.

The atmosphere in the continuous chapel meeting at the Grapes Inn lightened perceptibly with news of possible support from their London colleagues. It lightened further a few hours later when Adam announced that management had finally agreed to meet him and Aubrey for 'exploratory talks' at Manchester's Midland Hotel later that day.

'They seem to be cracking at last and not before time,' the FoC declared. 'We now need to draw up an agenda for the meeting at the hotel -- and the first condition must be that there can be no return to work before a new house agreement including all our demands is agreed.'

After a short debate a full statement of the chapel's terms for a return-to-work was proposed, seconded and carried unanimously. It included substantial salary increases, back-dated to the start of the month; reimbursement of all members' pay stopped by management since the dispute began; shorter working hours and longer holidays. Adam and Aubrey were instructed to make no concessions on the pay claim or restitution of deducted salaries but were allowed to compromise, within narrow limits, on the remainder of the package. It was advisable when seeking any negotiated deal to allow your opponents to think they had at least won something.

When their taxi drew up outside the Midland Hotel an ambulance was parked in front of the main entrance but Adam and Aubrey paid little attention to it. They hurried into the opulent lobby and before they could ask at reception for the whereabouts of Mr Cedric Westwood, the managing editor of The Daily Telegraph himself approached them. Tall and dark suited with distinguished silvery hair brushed back, his normally intimidating manner had become agitated.

Apart from limp and perfunctory handshakes there was a marked absence of formalities. 'There's been a distressing occurrence,' he said, ushering the pair into the hotel's crystal chandeliered and gilt encrusted lounge. It was crowded with middle aged, overdressed guests but a small table had been reserved beside a palm tree. A string quartet was playing a rousing Viennese waltz and Westwood was obliged to raise his cultured voice.

'I'm sorry but the fact of the matter is we are no longer able to hold our meeting as arranged. Roy (Gibson) has collapsed and been taken to hospital. You may have seen the ambulance. It happened less than half an hour ago. Just flaked out, poor chap. No warning or anything. They think it's a stroke. Can't say I'm surprised, all the strain he's been under -- thanks to you people.'

He beckoned to a waiter and ordered a single malt for himself. 'What can I get you?' he asked frostily. The two journalists ordered soft drinks and offered their sympathies without rising to the bait of Westwood's last remark. The conversation stalled awkwardly and they listened to the music. When drinks arrived Westwood drained his whisky in one go and asked for another. Then he leaned forward in a more relaxed manner.

'The fact of the matter,' he said again, 'is we now have to wait for updates on Mr Gibson's condition before proceeding. It could be several days before we know so I've phoned his deputy, Oliver Wood, to come up from London. He can't get here before tomorrow. That means another night's disrupted production and heavy losses for the company. These are unforeseen and very difficult circumstances. We ask you to recognise that. Are you and your members prepared to lift your work-to-rule this evening as a gesture of goodwill?'

Adam sipped his iced Coca Cola. 'You do have our sympathy, Mr Westwood, but I have to remind you that we are no longer working to rule because you have locked us out.'

'I know but if we lift the lockout will you lift the work-to-rule?'

'Obviously we'll have to consult chapel members but I feel that would be unlikely without some gesture of goodwill from your side.'

'Please be more specific.'

Aubrey pushed a printout of the chapel's last resolution in front of Adam, who scanned it carefully before replying. There was precious little room for manoeuvre there but he recognised that circumstances had changed since it was passed. If the chapel were prepared to take a more conciliatory view perhaps management would respond in kind.

The two journalists requested a brief time out and adjourned to the bar to confer. When they returned, Westwood was on his third single malt and the string quartet had given way to the gentler strains of a lady harpist. Adam came straight to the point: 'Obviously, we will have to take further instruction from our members but it may be possible to work normally on the strict understanding...'

Aubrey cut in: '... in return for your written undertaking this afternoon...'

'...that our increased pay claim will be met in full -- while other sections of our claim will remain open for negotiation. We regard that as a major concession in the circumstances but I must repeat that it remains subject to the approval of our members.'

Westwood closed his eyes and remained expressionless. After a few seconds he pushed back his chair and rose a little unsteadily. 'I must ask you to excuse me while I make a telephone call.'

'Let's see what His Lordship makes of that,' Aubrey said as he and Adam sat back and relaxed. The harpist finished playing *Greensleeves* and started on *Autumn Leaves*. Before the melody ended Westwood returned, sat down heavily and ordered another single malt from the hovering waiter. It was clear from his defeated expression that the news was not good.

'I am instructed to inform you -- as clearly and as strongly as possible -- that your terms are entirely unacceptable. His Lordship is deeply disappointed by your lack of understanding and instructs me to terminate this apparently futile meeting at once. You will be advised by telephone about tomorrow when Mr Reed arrives. I must now bid you good day gentlemen.'

'Permanently pickled, the lot of them,' Aubrey observed as the two chapel officials, both stone cold sober; returned by taxi to their beleaguered colleagues. 'Still you have to admit they've come up with a new excuse to delay a meeting with us.'

Cynics to a man, their fellow scribes took the same view when the reason for the abortive meeting was reported to them. 'Beats Ascot and Henley,' one quipped. 'And the grouse shooting,' said another. But the one-liner that surpassed them all in terms of black humour came from a reporter who had never said a word during previous chapel meetings. Irving had been drinking with Dave Leonard, his news desk colleague, and was beginning to share his far Left views on the class war. It was another of those tingly moments when he knew exactly what he was going to say about the finance director's affliction before he spoke the immortal words:

'Every trick in the book.'

'Shall I place your comment on record?' Aubrey asked when the laughter died down.

'Why not?' Irving replied. He was long past caring about good taste after his encounter with the Daimler driver.

By the time Ollie Wood arrived in Manchester the next day it was virtually all over. London chapel had voted to work to rule in sympathy with their northern colleagues until an acceptable house agreement could be drawn up. This overdue demonstration of union solidarity left management no alternative but to cut their losses and return to the negotiating table.

With Roy Gibson's condition now stabilised, his youthful deputy found himself making up the numbers at the meeting next day in the Midland Hotel. Damage limitation was now the name of the game from management's point of view. A private room was reserved with plenty of alcohol available in the hope that Adam and Aubrey would over-indulge and lose the plot. No such luck.

After less than two hours the NUJ representatives had clinched a new watertight house agreement that enshrined almost all their demands apart from a few minor concessions on holiday entitlement. The pay increase was met in full with an undertaking to reimburse all salary deductions during the dispute.

The successful generals waited until they returned to their troops before celebrating one of the union's most memorable victories. Then it was drinks all round out of NUJ branch funds. But only one, as it was back to normal working within minutes. The presses were waiting and there was a first edition deadline to be met.

When, sometime later, the union's national executive committee was informed of their members' achievement it issued special commendations to both Manchester and London chapel leaders, as the deal would have taken much longer without the latter's support. And it authorised an award of honorary life membership to one Manchester member. It wasn't Adam Richardson or Aubrey Vickers.

It was Irving Breen.

FIFTEEN

The sleazy sixties slipped into the sober seventies with an alliteration beloved of all journalists. Like a pub landlord calling time on his rowdy customers, the new decade swiftly applied the brakes to the unrestrained hedonism of its predecessor. Prolonged industrial strife brought strikes and power cuts resulting in the introduction of the three-day week. Inflation climbed to 30 per cent triggering a massive financial crisis and a humiliating approach to the International Monetary Fund for a bailout.

But it was also an era of low unemployment and comparative prosperity for most working families -- Good Times, in the words of Chic, an American pop group. The band's hit record was played repeatedly by Emily and Dawn on their new stereophonic gramophone. Its advice to 'leave your cares behind' might have been written specially for them. Poverty, bravely borne, was a thing of the past, a dim memory of pawnshops, wet pavements and inadequate shoes.

As a result of the Telegraph's new house agreement Irving found himself almost solvent for the first time in his married life. The deal increased the number of salary grades from three to five, based on ability and length of service. As he had been with the paper for several years with numerous exclusives to his name, he qualified for inclusion in grade three -- a jump from his former grade one. Along with his substantially increased salary the new deal also improved his car allowance -- plus honorary life membership of the NUJ meant he no longer paid union subscriptions.

After all household expenses including the mortgage and rates there was enough money left to keep his ageing Wolseley properly serviced and comprehensively insured. And when the bills for Dawn's piano lessons, dancing classes and replacement hockey sticks all arrived at the same time there was no need for sleepless nights.

Their daughter was about to move up from primary school to secondary modern and both he and Emily took it as a sign that they needed to move to a larger house in an area containing the right sort of school for her. They had outlived their semi-detached dream home in Brawton. The dream had not disappeared, just faded slightly. It needed upgrading to a more prosperous setting where it could blossom and mature.

Basically they required more space. Emily wanted a larger kitchen to accommodate one of the latest twin-tub washing machines. In more wistful moments there were also broad hints about the superiority of a baby grand piano over her upright model. Dawn was hankering for a dog, a cat and a large garden with a trampoline like one of her friend's.

As for Irving, sad though he was to admit it, the need to upgrade his faithful old Wolseley could no longer be ignored. It was coming to the end of its very long road, using more petrol and oil, and there were problems with the differential. He had his eye on a dark blue, nearly new Rover saloon in a Manchester Deansgate showroom.

They were advised that south Manchester was a 'more prestigious' residential area than the north side. It sounded rather snobbish to Irving but the estate agent informed him it was all about property values and availability of good schools. After viewing properties in Bramhall, Poynton and Altrincham the couple settled for a four-bedroom detached house in Wilmslow, a more up-market area they were assured. It had an integral garage and won Dawn's immediate approval on account of its generous garden. There was a top rated grammar school nearby and a highly recommended secondary modern a short distance away. So when Dawn faced her 11-plus exam, all options would be covered. Of at least equal importance was the proximity of a Catholic church -- St Oswald's just outside the town. The parish priest was a young Father Simon, who happened to be a close friend of their beloved Father Michael.

Both Irving and Emily realised the financial implications of the move. It would stretch their resources to the limit initially but they were making a handsome profit on the sale of their semi. There were ample funds to cover the deposit on the new home and a decent sum left over for the car, washing machine and baby grand piano. They could even fit in a trampoline.

When it came to trading in their faithful Wolseley Emily was too upset to go with him. She said a tearful farewell to their old love wagon and waved until it was out of sight at the end of their tree-lined avenue. Irving was almost as emotional at the car showroom. 'Don't worry sir, your pride and joy won't be scrapped,' the salesman said. 'The bodywork's still sound. It will be fully reconditioned and sold off to someone who'll look after it, I'm sure.'

Driving home through Manchester's traffic in the luxury of the late model Rover, Irving soon brightened up. The car might not have been in the limousine class but it was not far short. It had a powerful two litre engine with overdrive, responsive road handling, soft leather interior and walnut trim, sunroof, adjustable seats, radio and heater as standard and even a cigar lighter. Fred would be impressed.

The Breens' dramatic progress 'up-market' did not end there. Next, it was Emily's turn. The Oldham Street showroom housed what it claimed was the largest collection of grand pianos in the north-west and she insisted on playing all of them before choosing the replacement for their old upright. It was the same make -- a Bluthner -- but a baby grand in polished mahogany that would fit perfectly in a corner of their lounge next to the French windows.

A brand new model was way beyond their financial reach but after playing Beethoven's *Fur Elise* with its resonant bass notes and Fats Waller's *Honeysuckle Rose* with its angelic treble, she knew she had found her instrumental soulmate. It made up for the disappointment she'd felt after Dawn gave up her piano lessons to concentrate on her drama and dancing.

They held the housewarming party a month later. All the family turned up except Nana who was now too frail to travel. Jamie Lee was there with a new partner, Sasha, a vivacious Russian dancer, the insatiable Olive having lost her libido on discovering Jamie was not the marrying kind. Two shy friends of Dawn also came, along with their parents. The sleek Rover saloon parked on the drive, the twin-tub washing machine, the trampoline in the garden and Dawn's newly acquired Labrador puppy (she was promised a kitten when she passed her 11-plus) all received their share of admiration.

But the real show stopper was the baby grand. Of all the status symbols on offer in the materialistic culture of the age, nothing enhanced the quality of a home like a grand piano. Especially when there was somebody who could play it like a concert pianist.

Yet hidden away in this picture of new-found prosperity and domestic bliss there was still one negative niggle in Irving's mind. His father used to say that the road to hell was paved with good intentions and for years he had been intending to buy Emily a 'proper' engagement ring -- one fit for a princess as he had always visualised her. But something always cropped up to prevent it. Emily herself had never mentioned the subject. She seemed happy with the tiny, quarter carat diamond ring he'd scraped his meagre savings together to buy all those years ago.

'It means more to me than anything flashy and ostentatious,' she said when he raised the issue over dinner one night. And she meant it. 'It may not look much but it has great sentimental value.'

'It does for me, darling,' he agreed. 'But it just doesn't look right. It doesn't go with our up-market lifestyle.' He disliked the trendy terminology but it seemed to sum up their dramatic progress up the social ladder. 'We've come up in the world since my Brawton Chronicle days.'

Emily glanced lovingly at the ring, remembering a time when she'd left it with a pawnbroker fearing she would never see it again. The old man had been almost as relieved as she was when she'd called to reclaim it. Yes, they'd come up the hard way and the ring was a powerful reminder of that. She kissed the tiny stone and sighed deeply. 'It's no longer in keeping with the wife of a grand Daily Telegraph journalist -- is that what you mean?'

He reached out and caressed her still slender fingers. 'Nothing like that, Emily. It's just not in keeping with the grand piano!'

They chose their upcoming wedding anniversary to go shopping for the new super ring. A ring fit for a princess, he'd promised her and now there was enough cash left in the kitty he wasn't going to settle for anything less. According to Irene, Trevor Unwin's secretary who had just become engaged herself, the only place to go was the posh jewellers in King Street, Manchester's version of Hatton Garden.

There, after an hour's deliberation, the dazzled couple narrowed the choice down to three enchanting rings -- a one carat solitaire sparkler in an ornate setting; an entwined double diamond creation, and an exquisite diamond flanked by two emeralds totalling one and a half carats. All set in 18 carat gold, of course. The three-stone ring was wildly over budget but it was the one his princess had set her heart on.

So there was precious little left in the kitty after all -- just enough, it transpired, to cover their anniversary dinner at the city's swankiest French restaurant that evening. They ordered lobster thermidor washed down by Bollinger and Irving had to scrape cash together to tip the waiter. Financial life was back to normal after his brief encounter with solvency but somehow it felt more comfortable. What did he need with pockets full of money when, sitting opposite in the romantic candlelight, was a woman whose natural beauty had turned every head on entering that pretentious dining room?

She smiled her loving smile and flashed her dazzling engagement ring. 'At last you've made an honest woman of me, darling!'

Maybe it was a combination of candlelight and champagne but Irving marvelled at the power she still had over him after all these years. She had only to smile at him in that seductive way to make him go weak at the knees.

He took her hand gently and gazed at the lustrous jewels. 'You know what I like about your ring? The emeralds. They remind me of your sensational eyes.'

Rain often stopped play at Manchester's Old Trafford cricket ground, as the England Test team sometimes found to their advantage. But as far as Irving was aware, rain had never stopped play during a snooker match -- which happened when the World Snooker Championship was held at the city's Exhibition Hall in 1973.

Irving, a snooker enthusiast since boyhood, was enjoying the spectacle on his day off when there was a sudden commotion during a quarter final match between Alex Higgins and Fred Davis. The hall had a glass roof and rain was falling so heavily that it started to leak on to the table. The green baize was hastily covered and play suspended. Out came Irving's notebook. Officials of the World Professional Billiards and Snooker Association (WPBSA) told him that over the years play had occasionally been interrupted by lighting failures, spectators fighting, referees being taken ill and once by a streaker but never by rain.

Irving had the little gem of a story all to himself -- a real scoop by 'our man on the spot, Irving Breen'. Once again he was sadly disillusioned. Howard Miller, the sports editor, spiked it with a deft flick of the wrist. 'Nice try old boy but our readers aren't interested in snooker. It's a minor sport.'

When Irving related the experience to Jamie at the Press Club sometime later his old friend was surprised. 'If something happens that's never happened before -- then it's news. We'd have published it in the Mail. We'd have used pictures of Higgins looking pissed off, like he always does.'

When it was their turn to play on the club's table any resemblance to the professional game was sadly lacking, though Irving ran out a comfortable winner as usual. One shot in particular caused Jamie severe discomfort. It was when he had to stretch full length to reach the cue ball. He needed to climb half way on to the table supported by one leg. Of course, he overbalanced and fell off the table. Irving and other club members helped him to his feet and he limped back to his pint.

'Must be getting old, I can't get my leg over any more!'

Irving had never seen Jamie blush before but there was a first time for everything. It was the sort of quote every tabloid hack dreams of. It swept round the room in a gale of hilarity and within moments established itself as a classic in the illustrious annals of Press Club history.

SIXTEEN

Over the years families move house and slowly drift apart. The Breens were no exception. Irving rarely saw his parents, David and Susan, happily settled in Settle on the West Yorkshire border. They kept in touch by telephone. It was the same with Fred and Lilian, still running a thriving north Manchester business. Visits became less frequent, although Daniel acquired a motorbike and on his rare days off drove through the dense city traffic to Wilmslow with 'delicacies from the deli' -- crab pate, stuffed olives and anchovies, with Dawn's favourite dolly mixtures.

Visits to Nana's sheltered flat in Brawton were more frequent on account of her increasing frailty since her stroke. They were usually lively occasions but the one the family made to celebrate her 80th birthday was particularly memorable. She'd said she didn't want a party but people turned up anyway bearing cakes, flowers and bottles. Nana, wearing her best 1920s-style lacy floral dress for the occasion, no longer seemed averse to the idea.

In addition to Irving, Emily, Dawn, Fred and Daniel, the building's warden, a friendly middle aged woman, also turned up with a large bouquet from David and Susan, with apologies for absence. David had recently had a hip replacement operation and Susan could not leave him on his own.

Space in the cramped apartment was limited and further restricted by an overweight grey cat sprawled on an armchair all to itself and in no hurry to move. None of the visitors had seen the cat before. Nana lifted it to the floor and introduced them to her new flatmate.

'She's called Popsie. She belonged to my nextdoor neighbour, Florence, but she's had to go into a nursing home so she very kindly gave Popsie to me. We get on very well, we watch the telly together and stroking her helps to relieve my arthritis.'

Popsie did not take kindly to being moved. She sat on the floor next to the fireplace with its electric logs and scowled at everyone, clearly resenting the indignity. Dawn, who now had a kitten of her own for passing her 11-plus, bent to stroke Popsie but it didn't seem to help.

Dawn had been accepted at the local grammar school and when Nana saw her great granddaughter in her school uniform she forgot all her pain and hugged the girl happily.

'Come here chuck,' she said with tears in her eyes. 'I'm so proud of you, Dawn Bridget Breen. I never thought I'd live to see you get to grammar school. I remember when you were born -- you took one look at me and burst into tears.'

Dawn laughed and kissed the old woman's wrinkled face. 'I'm sorry, Nana!' she said loudly into her hearing aid.

'You couldn't help it, chuck. I just thought you knew something I didn't. But here I still am, as large as life and twice as horrible!'

'You're not horrible, Nana, you're lovely,' Dawn protested.

'Such a sweet child and growing up so fast,' Nana said, turning to Irving and Emily 'She's a real credit to you both. And you Irving, you're doing so well. I tell all my friends and neighbours my grandson is a reporter for the Daily Telegraph, you know. They're all very impressed. They say you can't get much higher than that.'

Irving smiled, leaned closer to her and raised his voice. 'I'm just a general reporter, Nana. If I get promoted, I could go higher up the ladder...'

'You might finish up as the editor,' she exclaimed with an excited wave of her hand.

All things were possible, Irving thought, but somehow he couldn't see himself rising that far. Maybe a sub-editor or backbench executive in the top salary grade, you never knew.

Daniel and Emily were making tea in the tiny kitchen while Fred helped load the living room table with cakes and goodies. When Emily handed her a cup of tea Nana resumed her journey down memory lane. 'D'you know. I remember your wedding day as clearly as if it was yesterday. It was in that Catholic church, wasn't it?'

Emily nodded. 'St Peter's.'

'It was the first time I'd been in a Catholic church and I had my doubts. But it was such a beautiful service and you both looked so young and innocent. You *still* look young and innocent, don't get me wrong!'

Irving and Emily laughed. 'I don't know about that, Nana!' Irving said.

'My memory of the reception is a bit hazy. I'd had some wine, you see, and I wasn't used to it. But one thing I do remember -- and you'll never guess what it was...'

By this time her audience had grown and everyone hung on her answer.

'The carrot soup!'

They all fell about except Popsie, who just blinked.

Nana dabbed her eyes with a handkerchief. 'The things you remember! It was the nicest carrot soup I ever tasted -- before or since.'

Out came the family album and the wedding photos that Nana never tired of showing people -- and which her visitors never tired of viewing, Dawn in particular.

Fred and Daniel expertly mixed champagne cocktails and handed them round. 'A birthday toast to the nicest Nana of them all,' Fred announced, raising his glass. 'Eighty years young!'

Nana, her teetotal background long forgotten, acknowledged the applause with a gracious wave and moments later was enjoying a refill. There was no stopping the flow of muddled reminiscences, anecdotes, political views and religious advice, the gist being the vital need for everyone to fight the good fight in a world growing steadily more sinful.

Irving, Emily and Dawn were the last to tear themselves away. They kissed Nana fondly, repeatedly as she followed them outside to wave goodbye. Popsie allowed herself to be stroked by Emily and Dawn but scowled at Irving when it was his turn. The animal seemed to have taken a particular dislike to him. He scowled back. The feeling was mutual.

SEVENTEEN

Nobody saw it coming, not even Irving in one of his 'psychic' moments. One minute Daniel was handing out mugs of hot soup in St Peter's night shelter, the next he woke up in a bed at Salford Royal Infirmary with his mother stroking his hand. He was dimly aware of Emily sitting on the other side of the bed.

'You had a fit, Danny,' Lilian whispered in his ear. 'You've been working too hard, what with the shop, your band and St Peter's. All those migraine attacks were a warning.'

Daniel tried to sit up but felt a sharp pain in his head and neck. He sank back into his pillows. 'A fit? I'm not an epileptic.' His voice was hoarse and barely audible.

'No of course you're not. The doctors think it could be a symptom of some other illness.'

'Like what?'

'They don't know. They want you to have some tests.'

'How long have I been here?'

'Since last night-- nearly 24 hours.

They've been keeping you sedated.'

'We've been very worried about you,' Emily said, leaning over the bed and kissing her brother.

He kissed her cheek through parched lips. 'I had a gig booked for this Saturday.'

Lilian stroked his long hair, now untidily tousled. 'You'll have to cancel it, Danny. Your dad will tell them you can't go anywhere until you're better.'

A nurse appeared and checked Daniel's pulse and blood pressure. He took sips of water from a cup with a spout and another nurse fitted him with an intravenous drip to keep him hydrated. They gave him painkilling tablets and helped him sit up in bed. Then they brought cups of tea for his visitors. But neither could throw any light on his mysterious illness. The doctors would explain when they'd done more tests the next day.

The following day brought fresh visitors -- Father Michael from St Peter's accompanied by Edgar, a regular customer at the church's night shelter. Edgar, stooped and shaggy bearded, presented Daniel with a huge bunch of flowers, a gift from him and his companions. Daniel was deeply touched. He knew how cruel life was for the homeless, the dispossessed and the rough sleepers he looked after. Yet they had held a whip-round and somehow managed to raise enough for a lavish bouquet. They clearly cared as much about him as he did for them.

A nurse took the flowers and the priest and pauper brought up chairs next to his bed. They asked the usual questions about how long he expected to stay in hospital and if there was anything they could get him. Daniel didn't feel like talking. The pain at the back of his head and in his neck had not gone away despite the painkillers. They had just made him drowsy. And anyway he still had no idea what was wrong with him. He'd had various tests and X-rays. They'd all been inconclusive. He was waiting for some more.

Realising their presence was tiring the patient his visitors rose to leave. 'Give them all my love at St Peter's and thank them for the lovely flowers,' he told Edgar and clasped the old man's hand firmly. Turning to Father Michael, he said: 'Please pray for me, Father, that I may soon get out of here.'

'Of course, Daniel. I'll say Holy Mass for you this evening. Let us pray now.' He crossed himself and Edgar and Daniel did likewise. 'Heavenly Father, please strengthen and heal your servant, Daniel Shannon. Touch him with your healing hands, take away all his pain and restore him to health, we humbly pray for Jesus Christ our Lord's sake.'

All three said: 'Amen.'

Daniel knew enough about prayer to realise it was not always answered immediately. So when the pain remained he was not unduly concerned. He knew that God answered prayer in his own good time and then not always in the way requested. But within days he began to feel constantly sick and a weakness developed on his left side. Doubts crept into his confused, unworldly mind about the power of prayer.

When the doctors finally told him all their tests had failed to provide a firm basis for diagnosis and were transferring him to the Christie Hospital in Manchester the doubts took a firmer grip on his mind, almost reaching his soul. He knew Christie's was primarily a hospital for cancer patients.

So did his family. When they were told the news their first reaction was one of shock. Did it mean a brain tumour? Might it be non-malignant? Could it be cured? When would the doctors come up with answers?

It took the oncologists at Christie's only two days to reach their verdict. Daniel was suffering from something called glioblastoma multiforme, a malignant and aggressive tumour at the back of his brain. They tried but there was no way they could soften the blow. It was the fastest growing and deadliest form of brain cancer with a life expectancy of a few months. Symptoms could be relieved with chemotherapy and surgery in the form of a craniotomy might remove some of the tumour but not all, as it was attached to vital blood vessels.

Fred, Lilian and Emily all agreed that every option should be tried to prolong the life of their beloved Daniel. Soul searching and recrimination were useless but could not be avoided. Why Daniel, of all people? What had this generous and loving free spirit done wrong or failed to do right? If only he had consulted a doctor about his migraines.

Their distress deepened by the day as the weight dropped off him with frightening speed and he was connected to an intravenous pain-killing drip. He became unable to speak and drifted in and out of consciousness. The doctors decided to perform a craniotomy. The delicate operation took several hours and left their patient's face covered with a grotesque surgical mask. Emily could not bear to look and buried her head on Irving's shoulder.

Each successive visit tested the family's devout Catholic faith still further. It was just grossly unfair. Of all people to be afflicted by such horrendous suffering, Daniel was the least deserving. Father Michael administered the last rites and reminded them that Jesus Himself had to suffer. But there were moments when even the priest's faith was challenged although there was no outward sign of it.

They redoubled their prayers. They lit more candles at St Peter's. Mass was offered daily for him. But as hope retreated despair advanced. In their hearts they all accepted that Daniel's devastating illness was terminal and that the end was not far off.

Irving helped Emily to clear Daniel's bedroom in preparation for the inevitable. The room was the way he had left it, full of musical clutter, guitars and amplification equipment. When Irving opened a wardrobe he found a poster pinned inside its door. His brother-in-law was a great admirer of Mother Teresa, the saint who devoted her life to caring for the poor people of Calcutta. The poster displayed one of her famous sayings:

ANYWAY

People can be unreasonable and self-centred

Forgive them anyway

If you are kind, people may accuse you of ulterior motives

Be kind anyway

If you are honest, people may cheat you

Be honest anyway

If you find happiness, people may be jealous

Be happy anyway

The good you do today may be forgotten tomorrow

Do good anyway

Give the best you have and it may never be

enough

Give your best anyway

For you see in the end it is between you and God.
It was never between you and them anyway

-- Mother Teresa

The poster brought tears to the eyes of both Emily and Irving. Daniel's life had ticked every one of the boxes. All hope was lost but even now the family could not come to terms with it. They joined Irving and Father Michael to offer a desperate prayer to God for divine intervention.

Only a miracle could save Daniel now

PART TWO

EIGHTEEN

Deep in the vastness of celestial superspace the white planet collided with the blue one sending it hurtling into a black hole.

'Six,' said the referee.

Irving noticed that the referee was Father Michael, wearing black clerical garb and white gloves

`'I didn't know there was snooker in heaven,' Irving said.

'Oh yes... the best tables, perfect cloths, straight cues, super-crystallite balls.'

'What about the other place?'

'They've got snooker there, too. Exactly the same. Just one thing missing. There's no chalk.'

There was a loud crack as a red planet plummeted into the black hole and Irving woke up in alarm. The bedroom window was open and vivid lightning flashed across the walls and ceiling followed by another loud crash of thunder. Emily stirred in her twin bed but did not waken.

Irving closed the window and drew the curtains. He lay sleepless for a long time as the storm raged throughout the night. It seemed to die away only to return with greater ferocity and repeated torrential downpours. There'd be weather stories to deal with the next day, that was for sure. He smiled at the bizarre dream of celestial snooker refereed by Father Michael but then the memory of the priest saying the last rites for Daniel returned and that was it as far as sleep was concerned.

He went downstairs to the kitchen to find the family pets, Betsy, the Labrador, and Samantha, the cat, upset by the storm. They huddled round his legs as he poured himself a whisky and ginger ale. He did his best to comfort them while he drank and grappled with the impenetrable Telegraph crossword. On the way back to bed he checked Dawn's room. The teenager was sleeping like a baby.

He must have slept for only four hours but when he wakened he felt unusually refreshed. The nocturnal dramas had subsided. He opened the bedroom window and the air was still and cool. In the en-suite bathroom he showered and shaved with his electric razor, taking care to leave no trace of stubble. Men were growing beards now, fearing for their masculinity in response to militant feminism. But no beard for Irving -- however widespread the craze became! Rather than enhancing masculinity it was as if you were trying to hide something. His clean-shaven features were open to the world. He had nothing to hide. Or had he?

As he returned the razor to its cabinet and glanced again in the mirror he could have sworn his reflection winked at him, as if it knew something he didn't. His imagination was working overtime again. But at the same moment he felt hot and a frisson of excitement coursed through him that he hadn't experienced for a long time.

His face *was* hiding something. Something was not visible that should be.

How impossibly weird and completely absurd was that?

He examined his reflection again, this time more closely and from several angles. How *could* something be missing when he looked exactly the same as usual?

The bizarre thought still troubled him as he went downstairs for breakfast. Dawn had left for school and Emily, still nibbling toast and marmalade, was poring over the Telegraph crossword. They exchanged their usual high fives and he kissed her hair briefly. 'Quite a storm last night.'

'Really? I didn't notice. That explains the pools of water all over the garden.'

'You missed a real fireworks display. It was like the end of the world.' He didn't know it but it was the most felicitous simile of his entire career.

His wife just put it down to a wordsmith's fondness for a colourful turn of phrase. She looked up from her crossword. Did you know the word "honestly" is an anagram of "on the sly"? Isn't that weird!'

Irving boiled two eggs, poured some filter coffee and burnt some toast in the toaster. He had a weird problem of his own. Something was wrong with his face and he couldn't work out what it was. Before leaving for work he asked Emily: 'Do I look the same to you as I did yesterday?'

She put down the newspaper. 'Of course, darling, why do you ask?'

'My face just looks different somehow.'

She stood up, went towards him and inspected his face closely. 'Looks the same to me, Irving. Still as handsome as ever.' She kissed him lightly on the cheek.

He thought no more about it as he steered the Rover between large puddles on the way to the office. Some roads were under water where the drains had failed to cope with the tropical storm. Single flow traffic lights were in operation. At one lengthy hold-up he switched on the radio. England were winning in the Test match in Australia. Now that really *was* news.

The day had only just begun. No sooner had he sat down at his typewriter and glanced at the first news list -- full of flooding stories as expected -- than his telephone rang. It was a doctor at Christie's Hospital. He didn't want to raise hopes too high at this stage but Daniel had regained consciousness and his condition appeared to have stabilised. The medic was phoning all relatives to tell them the unbelievable news.

Irving could hardly believe it either. At the first opportunity he drove urgently to the hospital where he met up with Fred, Lilian and Emily, all overwhelmed by emotion. The medical team were almost equally ecstatic. They had never seen anything like it. It couldn't possibly happen to someone in Daniel's advanced terminal condition. Yet it *had* happened. His brain tumour had vanished without trace -- confirmed by X-rays from every possible angle. It defied all the team's combined medical knowledge and experience. There was no possible scientific explanation. Daniel, his head still swathed in bandages, was sitting up in bed sipping a cup of tea.

'It's a miracle!' Fred beamed. 'We prayed for a miracle and we got one.'

Lilian and Emily were both in tears. They clung to each other to reassure themselves they were not dreaming. Then they clung to Irving, their tears turning to joyful laughter. Even the doctors and nurses joined in the elation. They simply could not get their heads round their patient's amazing recovery. Like most of their profession and the public in general, none of them had believed in miracles -- until now.

Daniel, holding the hands of his mother and sister, struggled to speak but the doctors advised him to lie back and relax. Such was the uncharted territory of their patient's recovery they feared a relapse of some kind. Better to take things easy while they kept him under close observation for a day or two.

They sent for Father Michael. He was offering up last rites for another patient in Salford Royal Hospital. When he arrived his face was the picture of spiritual radiance. He had seen prayers answered before but had never seen someone rescued from the brink of death against impossible odds, in circumstances that had challenged even his own sturdy faith.

As Fred, Lilian, Emily and Irving gathered round, joined respectfully by the medical staff, the priest stood at the foot of Daniel's bed and gave thanks to God for what everyone present accepted was a miracle. For some it meant changing the beliefs of a lifetime. There was simply no alternative.

The nurses detached the intravenous drip and carefully removed the bandages around Daniel's shaven head. He grimaced when he looked at himself in a hand mirror but they assured him he was still their star patient even without his hair. One of the nurses, called Megan, was particularly attentive. The agonising ordeal she had witnessed over the past few days had distressed her personally, not just on a clinical level. Seeing him suffer like that had been hard to bear. Previously a religious sceptic, she had been willingly converted to the power of prayer. She also found Daniel rather attractive.

When all his visitors had left and he'd been settled for the night Megan routinely took his blood pressure and checked his pulse. He stirred and held her hand for a long moment. The feeling was mutual.

Suddenly the world seemed an altogether brighter place. At the Telegraph, the agenda of death, destruction and disaster that sustained the daily news lists took a noticeably lighter turn. Charles Clarke, the chief reporter, used to joke amid the encircling gloom that the light at the end of the tunnel had been switched off for economy reasons. Now for a short time at least it appeared to have been switched on again.

England's triumphant cricketers returned home from Australia to a heroes' welcome, splashed all over the front pages of both northern and southern editions. Howard Miller was quick to point out that most of the team came from Lancashire, Yorkshire, Cheshire and Northumberland. The sports editor had played briefly for Lancashire Second XI as a fast bowler in his youth. He would sometimes express the view after a few beers in the Grapes that 'southerners' should limit their sporting proclivities to tennis and croquet.

He was in his element when it came to football, claiming bragging rights over his opposite number on the London sports desk when Manchester City defeated such 'deadleg' teams as Chelsea, Arsenal and Tottenham Hotspur. It was an oft-repeated scenario as Manchester City had suddenly hit a winning streak that had taken them to the top of the First Division where they gave every appearance of remaining indefinitely.

Nobody was more delighted at the transformation than Irving. He took Dawn to a match at Maine Road, both wearing blue and white City scarves. They were invited as Press box guests of Frank Green, the Telegraph's sports reporter covering the game. It was against Manchester United, the local derby match guaranteed to whip up passionate rivalry between supporters of the two teams. Dawn, now studying dramatic arts at Manchester University, had never been to a football match, let alone one attracting a crowd of over 60,000 people. She was caught up in the noise and widespread excitement in the build-up to the kick-off.

In the Press box they met up with Jamie Lee, Irving's fellow cub reporter from way back, covering the game for the Daily Mail. 'Didn't you once tell me you wouldn't be seen dead at Maine Road?' Irving asked him as they took their seats.

Jamie looked shocked. 'You must be joking, mate. True blue all my life.'

Irving could have sworn Jamie was a fanatical United supporter. Had he changed sides all of a sudden? Surely not. Football fans just didn't do that. It was a total mystery but there wasn't time to dwell on it. Frank, their host, elderly and affable, was predicting a close game with a narrow win for City and Jamie forecast a draw. All were City supporters. 'The trick is you mustn't show it,' Frank told them as the teams ran on to the pitch to massive roars from the crowd. 'You have to write a balanced impartial report so no-one would guess you favoured either side -- stay strictly neutral.'

'I imagine that must be difficult,' Dawn said.

'You bet, especially when City score!'

At halftime, with the score at 0-0 they adjourned to the Press room for tea, warm sausage rolls and home-made meat pies. 'No-one does meat pies as good as Manchester City,' Jamie assured them. 'Some clubs hardly look after the Press at all. At Liverpool and Sheffield United you're lucky if you get a cup of tea.'

Dawn wanted to know if either Frank or Jamie had changed their predictions. Neither had. Both expected it to be close. And both were wrong. The second half was as eventful as the first had been boring. Four goals were scored -- three by City who took control of the game with some sustained attacking play. 'Blue Moon, why are you shining so brightly?' sang the massed ranks of home supporters, as the United fans trudged miserably through the exits.

What did Dawn think of her first experience of professional football? Frank asked the question when they toasted the victory in the Press room afterwards. The dramatic arts student remembered a quote from Moiseyev, the famous Russian choreographer, on being asked about the sport. 'It's rather like a cross between ballet and warfare!'

Long after Emily had stopped praying for another child, when she and Irving decided to sleep in separate beds and when Dawn had given up all hope of a brother or sister, the unthinkable happened.

'Guess what, darling,' Emily told her husband after a visit to the family doctor.

Irving didn't need any help from his extra

sensory gifts to guess what she was about to say. He knew she'd consulted the GP after missing a period. He had only to look at her radiantly happy face to guess the outcome. 'I give up,' he said, enjoying the moment.

'I'm pregnant!' She flung herself into his arms like a teenager. 'The pregnancy test's confirmed it.'

If there had been a night to remember they had both forgotten it. Sex was a rare pleasure that happened only when their conflicting lifestyles briefly converged. Irving's working hours, involving regular night shifts, often found him sleeping during the day and Emily's work as a choir mistress and youth club organiser at St Oswald's accounted for most weekday evenings. At weekends she also played the organ at some of the Masses.

Both were now more preoccupied with the future than the past. How would Emily cope with pregnancy in her forties bearing in mind the ordeal she had suffered giving birth to Dawn? The early symptoms were not encouraging. Her breasts began to swell and nausea soon kicked in. There were times when fatigue prevented her attendance at church which particularly upset her. She developed a craving for avocados and stuffed olives. Worst of all were the mood swings and total extinction of her libido. Sex had been rare enough in the past. Now it was non-existent.

'She won't even allow me to touch her,' Irving confided to Jamie at the Press Club. Showing new-found skill on the green baize his previously ham-fisted opponent had just knocked in a break of 38 on the green baize and it was Irving's turn to buy the beers. Jamie was still with Sasha, still unwed and still childless. He sympathised in his usual down-to-earth style. 'Celibacy is a very hard thing to handle!' The oft-quoted newsroom aphorism was delivered with a broad grin 'They do go off it, don't they? Not like us. Can't say I'm all that bothered though...more interested in snooker these days. Scored a 70 the other night. Can't wait to make a century break. That would beat any orgasm!'

Irving, less than impressed by his friend's sexual empathy, had to admire his skill at snooker. But at the same time it felt strange, almost surreal -- as if it couldn't really be happening, yet it was. The deep screw shots with reverse side spin and the stun run-throughs were advanced strokes Irving had never been able to master. Maybe Jamie had been having lessons on the quiet, the sly old fox. But there were other more worrying matters on his mind right now. As a waitress wearing a low cut top bent to collect their empty glasses, all he could think of was sex.

The story had dominated the media for days. A flu epidemic was heading towards Britain from the Far East and Nana had finally been persuaded to have the flu jab. The virus could prove fatal in older people and while the vaccine didn't guarantee immunity at least it provided some protection. Some was better than none, her family advised and for once Nana listened to them.

Irving offered to drive her to the GP's surgery for the afternoon appointment on his way to work. There was the usual long pause when he knocked loudly on her front before she opened it, dressed in her outdoor clothes ready to leave.

'So good of you to come for me, Irving,' she said.

He took her arm and led her haltingly to the lift. 'No problem, Nana.'

'Can we call at the Post Office for my pension while we're out?'

'Sure thing. Where's Popsie, by the way?'

'Oh the warden offered to look after her until I got back.'

When installed in the Rover with the seat belt duly fastened after a prolonged struggle, she asked: 'Why do these epidemics always start in the East -- never in the West?'

It was a good question, he thought, and as a Daily Telegraph journalist he was expected to know the answer. He hated to disillusion her. 'No idea, Nana. Less concerned about hygiene than we are, I daresay.'

She was 20 minutes at the surgery. Irving sat in the waiting room and read a book on quantum physics that Prof Jordon had recommended. Middle age had brought a deterioration in Irving's eyesight and he'd been prescribed reading glasses. They made the book's text clearer although the same could not be said for its content. Described as a beginner's guide to the subject, he found most of it baffling.

Nana smiled cheerfully as she came out. 'Didn't feel a thing.'

Then another 15 minutes at the Post Office. They joined a short queue and he watched as the frail, bent figure pushed her pension book under the glass partition and collected a small pile of banknotes. What an easy target for any mugger, he thought. It was a good job the warden normally escorted her.

They were soon back at the apartment. She insisted on making him a cup of tea as he was still in good time for the start of his shift. As always it was made with full cream milk and came in china cups. It made all the difference. Nobody made tea like Nana. She offered him buttered crumpets and chocolate biscuits. He wasn't hungry but he took a biscuit..

She grumbled about the usual complaints, the arthritis in her fingers made jars and bottles difficult to open. 'Sometimes I think they don't want us to open them,' she laughed.

He knew what she meant. He struggled to open bottles of water at the office and he didn't have arthritis.

'Better be going, Nana,' he said at length and rose to leave.

She extracted herself painfully from her armchair. 'Thanks so much, Irving. You're a good boy... you've always been a good boy.'

There was a knock on the door and he went to open it. A smiling warden stood there holding a lead at the end of which was a small border terrier.

'Hello, Mr Breen,' she said. 'Popsie's been as good as gold.'

Gobsmacked didn't come close. Neither did sandbagged nor discombobulated. Popsie was a cat, for God's sake... or had been last time they'd met. 'What happened to the cat?' he asked. Both women looked blank. 'Cat? What cat?' It was another of those electric moments that defied logical explanation. But there had to be one.

'The cat you had when I last visited.'

Nana was as bewildered as he was. 'You must be mistaken, Irving. I don't like cats.'

'Maybe you're thinking of someone else,' the warden said helpfully.

'No, I remember it clearly. It was a large grey cat. It didn't like me.'

The terrier sniffed at Irving's trousers and wagged its tail. 'Popsie likes you,' the warden said in a further attempt to ease the tension.

Irving had no time for the dog. 'I distinctly remember... ' he began, but then noticed the concern on both their faces. How did they deal with someone as disillusioned as he was? He backed off, raised his hand in a gesture of bafflement and waved them goodbye.

Try getting your head round that, Irving thought as he drove to the office. Could it be a bizarre joke? Surely not, Nana was too old for practical jokes. She would never go to such lengths. Neither would the warden; why should she? Had he dreamt it all about the cat? His dreams could be vivid and extremely realistic. Maybe he was just going out of his mind.

It wasn't the first time he'd wondered about his mental stability. He recalled speculating about delusions while watching his friend Jamie compile a break of nearly 40 on the Press

Club snooker table not long ago. He couldn't believe what he was seeing. Was he dreaming or hallucinating? Jamie had never shown the slightest talent at the game yet there he was playing deep screw shots like a pro. How weird was that?

The feeling that somehow he might be the victim of sophisticated mind games merely served to fuel a new fear -- that of paranoia, heaven forbid. Instinct told him to stay away from his GP who'd be sure to prescribe anti-depressants. Maybe he just couldn't handle the pressures of the job any more. What he desperately needed was a holiday. It seemed like years since his last one.

NINETEEN

'Fancy a week in Blackpool?' Trevor Unwin had called Irving into his office to discuss coverage of the forthcoming Conservative party conference. The paper's political correspondent would be coming up from London and the role of his sidekick -- the journeyman who did all the real work -- had yet to be decided.

'Could be a good career move for you Irving,' the news editor said. The cultured Knightsbridge vowels had inexplicably slipped into a broad Lancashire accent. 'Get you noticed by head office. I've had a word with God and he thinks you're the right man for the job. He's quite a fan of yours.'

Irving found Trevor's change of dialect startling -- more oddness he thought. Maybe his boss was just teasing but it hardly mattered any more. What did matter was he needed a holiday and the sooner the better. He and Emily had discussed Ibiza, Cyprus and the Canary Islands -- among resorts they'd visited over the years. Blackpool had not made the short list -- or even the long list.

It was flattering to be singled out by the editor but he knew the assignment would involve covering all the lesser debates -- transport, agriculture, the arts -- while the London luminary would select the plum issues, defence, foreign affairs, health etc, for himself. He would also be landed with most of the deeply boring fringe meetings. There would be no time for sunning himself on the beach even if the autumn sun were to shine, something you couldn't guarantee in Blackpool.

On the other hand there would be frequent bylines spread over several days which was the name of the game in terms of career advancement. A five-star hotel and generous expense account bar bill helped to concentrate his mind -- until thoughts of Emily and the ongoing ordeal of her pregnancy intruded. There was no way she'd want to go with him to Blackpool. How much longer before she was due to give birth? He consulted his diary. There were still six weeks. With Dawn living at home help would be at hand in an emergency. His daughter had passed her driving test first time. He could leave the Rover at home and travel to Blackpool by train.

'I will get bylines, not a DTR?' he asked, just to make sure.

'Of course, dear boy. God will see to that.'

'OK, then thanks be to God.'

'Amen.'

It was a well worn joke but still good for a laugh.

The helicopter circled slowly under a leaden sky before descending into a gentle touchdown. H B Berry, Political Correspondent of The Daily Telegraph, had arrived at Blackpool Airport on the eve of the Conservative Party conference. Irving, waiting in a taxi to greet the great man, watched as a stout middle aged figure wrapping a sheepskin coat round him and carrying a portable typewriter case, hurried towards the terminal building.

So this was the distinguished scribe, the doyen of Fleet Street who was said to have the ear of cabinet ministers, the great the good and the not-so-good. 'I thought there'd be a car waiting on the tarmac,' he said when Irving introduced himself at the arrivals gate. 'The office did phone in advance.'

'Sorry, Hugo, this is Blackpool, not Heathrow. I've got a taxi waiting,' Irving replied. 'Have you no luggage?'

'No. Travel light old boy. Got a few essentials in here with the old Olivetti.' He tapped his bulging typewriter case.

Their cab sped off to the Metropole, the nearest luxury hotel to the Winter Gardens conference centre. The tide was in and a bitingly cold wind was whipping up the sea, with spray flying over the promenade in places. 'I thought you were above the snowline here not inside the Arctic Circle,' Hugo said, huddled in his sheepskin coat.

Irving smiled at the predictable southern banter. Every Londoner he met had something disparaging to say about the north. They meant no harm. Once outside their protective metropolitan bubble they felt vulnerable in the real world, although Hugo looked the type to survive in any environment. Bald, ruddy cheeked with a neat goatee and impeccable Oxford accent, he had the self-assured bearing of an aristocrat. It stemmed from a family connection to the Telegraph's owners, giving him automatic entree into the highest social circles. Irving wondered if he was a journalist first and aristocrat second. Or was it the other way round?

On checking in at the hotel they headed straight to the bar. The staff had been trained to welcome all journalists with open arms. One look at the Press card and a bar tab was set up instantly. No problem at all. Titled members of the nobility and top-ranking cabinet ministers among the guests could not have received more deferential treatment.

Hugo removed his sheepskin revealing an immaculate light blue Savile Row suit and dark blue tie. 'What are you having, old boy?'

Irving took off his overcoat. Beneath he wore his best brown tweed jacket, freshly pressed grey flannels and NUJ tie. Quite present-able he thought but he could tell HBB was less than impressed. 'I'll have a pint of best Lanca-shire bitter, please.'

Hugo ordered his favourite tipple, a large single-malt, and the bar tabs were up and run-ning like taxi meters. 'Where've they put you, old chap?' he asked his unpretentious sidekick. There was a hint of sympathy in his voice.

Irving took a long pull on his pint. 'Top floor back with the rest of the hoi polloi. Over-looking a building site.'

'Tut, tut... I suppose they're fully booked and that's the best they can do. I'm on the second floor en-suite, sea view, not that one wants to look at the sea of course. Looks the same wher-ever one goes. But I do ask for an en-suite barth.'

He took a cigar case out of his jacket pocket, opened it and extended it to Irving.

'No thanks, I don't smoke.'

'They're Havanas... you don't know what

you're missing.' He selected a cigar and lit up with a gold cigarette lighter, before waving to an elderly gent in a morning suit with a carnation buttonhole. 'Sir Nigel Simms. Top man at the Home Office. Knows everyone worth knowing. Got me in at the Garrick last year. Tell me, old boy, what's your club?'

Irving drained his glass. He suspected he was being patronised. Hugo would have known gentlemen's clubs were off limits to northern newspapermen. 'I'm a proud member of the Manchester Press Club. Turned down an invitation from the Garrick.'

That amused Hugo and they kept the bar tabs ticking over with another round. 'What about the old alma mater... Eton, Harrow or Gordonstoun?'

Now Irving knew he was taking the mickey. 'Whitefield Grammar School, old chap. Yourself?'

'Eton, of course. Like most of this crowd.' With a deprecating sweep of the hand he indicated the bar, rapidly filling up with well-fed capitalists, their elitist hangers-on and heavy with tobacco smoke.

Irving had known the answer. He had the perfect put-down ready. 'They do say Eton is a school for boys not thought bright enough for Winchester.'

Hugo laughed heartily. 'They never spoke a truer word if you arsk me.'

Suitably mellowed and understanding each other better the two scribes got down to the serious business of carving up conference debates between them. As Irving had expected he was allocated education, the arts, housing, agriculture and transport. Hugo would cover defence, health, foreign affairs, the economy and, of course, the closing speech by Margaret Thatcher, the party's leader and Leader of the Opposition.

Evening fringe meetings where extremists of differing persuasions aired their bizarre visions of society would be tackled on an ad hoc basis. Stringers recruited by Hugo would cover meetings of the more delusional delegates including those demanding the restoration of the death penalty and the resurrection of the British Empire. Deadlines were inevitably tight to catch the paper's first editions. Copy to be filed from the conference Press room or when demand for telephones was high, from the hotel.

On arriving at the Winter Gardens conference centre for the opening day's first debate, Irving found the main entrance besieged by a large crowd of people, some bearing placards and chanting slogans. They were a motley collection. Pro-life and Anti-life campaigners, bearded CND activists, Clean-up TV women from the shires, animal rights campaigners in mock hunting gear, middle aged immigration blockers and tattooed militant feminists... all cheerfully rubbed shoulders, united in a common purpose of stopping delegates from entering the hall. A thin line of good natured police officers struggled to contain them. When Irving showed one of the officers his Press card he helped him push his way through the noisy crowd.

'Scary lot aren't they!' Irving said.

'Par for the course, sir,' the policeman replied.

'Who are the scariest do you reckon?'

'Oh, the feminists, by far.'

Inside the vast hall the atmosphere was reassuringly calm. In fact there seemed to be fewer people there than outside. 'Sparsely attended' was the phrase that sprang to mind as Irving took his seat on the Press benches and opened his notebook. There was a long wait before the platform party consisting of lesser members of the Tory hierarchy arrived, to weak applause from the faithful scattered across the auditorium.

The chairman, described as 'the chair' in the Press release, was a stout gentleman wearing a suit at least one size too small. Peering over rimless glasses into the hall for signs of life, he announced the first debate -- on housing. Not enough houses were being built and too many council homes were allocated to immigrants. The 1972 Immigration Act had been only partially effective. Further amendments were needed to give indigenous British citizens priority over foreigners in the housing queue.

A procession of delegates regaled the audience with their own experiences of houses overcrowded with West Indian families while people who had lived here all their lives were pushed down the waiting lists. It was all routine stuff until one elderly gentleman strode purposefully to the rostrum to demand the implementation of the 1793 Aliens Act, strictly prohibiting the entry of all foreigners to this country.

The Act, introduced by Lord Grenville during the Napoleonic Wars, was just as relevant today as it was then. We were still under threat from outsiders bent on destroying our way of life, he declared to rousing applause from a group of supporters waving miniature Union Jacks.

His resolution to invoke the 1793 Act, properly proposed and seconded, was opposed by the platform but when put to the vote was only narrowly defeated. That was enough excitement for one morning and the delegates trooped off for lunch content in the knowledge that they had done their duty in the Tory cause. Irving hurried to the Press room to phone through his report in the full knowledge that it would be hacked to pieces by the sub-editors and consigned to an inside page.

The afternoon debate on the economy attracted a capacity audience with H B Berry representing the Daily Telegraph on the Press benches. His copy had already been flagged for the front page and would receive more respectful treatment from the subs. But as the great man scanned the agenda he realised he would be struggling for a genuinely newsworthy angle.

All the platform could offer was doom and gloom from the Treasury grandee. There was a balance of payments crisis. Prices were escalating, pushing up inflation to over 8 per cent. Unemployment was sky-high, productivity had stalled and the trade unions were to blame for it all. In short, Labour simply wasn't working. HBB gratefully seized on the line for his off-beat intro, headed LABOUR ISN'T WORKING and the Tories' famous slogan was born.

The acrimonious debate culminated in a vote for stringent trade union reforms to outlaw unofficial strikes and to make even official industrial action difficult if not impossible. The resolution -- backed by platform members and enthusiastically endorsed by Mrs Thatcher -- was carried by an overwhelming majority.

The same ideological theme dominated debates over the next two days. Private enterprise was good, organised labour not only bad but downright unpatriotic. In the field of education teachers' unions were blamed for declining standards of literacy. Pupils were suffering as a result of disruptive tactics in pursuit of unrealistic pay claims, shorter hours and even longer holidays. Worse still, they were teaching subversive subjects -- describing the British Empire in a negative light rather than acclaiming its glorious achievements.

When it was the turn of health, striking NHS ancillary workers blockading hospitals and clinics were portrayed as holding the lives of desperately sick people to ransom. Millions of pounds had been poured into the health service annually. There was simply no more money left.

In the debate on agriculture, the enemy was identified as the farm workers' union whose relentless demands were responsible for ever-rising food prices and the resultant effect on inflation. If they went unchecked their unscrupulous tactics would bring the nation to its knees.

By the time they got round to transport Irving could have written the script himself. This time the villains campaigning for wage rises to keep pace with inflation were the bus and train drivers. They cared nothing for the misery they were inflicting on long-suffering commuters in the form of escalating fares and cancelled services.

At the end of day three Irving was scheduled to cover an evening fringe meeting organised by the Clean-up TV movement, which at least promised relief from the ongoing anti-union propaganda. This time the theme was the subversion of acceptable broadcasting standards on television, the main culprit being the BBC.

In a well attended meeting in a local hall various speakers drew attention to explicit violence and sexual imagery in programmes passing for drama, transmitted at times when children were watching. Some speakers, including ministers of religion, also complained of an insidious anti-Christian agenda creeping into the BBC's wide-ranging output. We were still a Christian country and our public service broadcaster should defend our culture and traditions not attack them.

Irving rarely watched television due to his working hours but the examples of prurience and crude violence cited by the speakers were pretty convincing. They called for a watershed time in the evening before which children at least should be protected from watching content that was frankly vile.

A petition organised by the National Viewers and Listeners' Association had attracted thousands of signatures and once they reached a million the association would present their demands to the Prime Minister in Downing Street. Irving took copious notes and was writing them up ready for telephoning to the copy-takers in Manchester when he felt a tap on his shoulder.

'Hello, lover boy.'

He recognised the voice instantly although he had not seen her for at least 20 years. 'Rita Kennedy,' he said, turning to face her.

'The same. Always said I'd track you down.'

She took the seat next to him and they shook hands warmly. Although middle aged, like him, she looked the same as she did when he left the Brawton Chronicle for the last time -- same auburn hair, bright blue eyes and slender figure. 'You haven't changed a bit.'

'Neither have you, Irving, but you've put a bit of weight on.'

Must be all the rich living at the Telegraph.' They laughed together as one, just like old times. 'Who are you with -- and why haven't I seen you at the conference?'

'I'm a staffer at the Guardian now. Just arrived -- covering for a colleague who's been taken ill.'

'Where are you staying?'

'Grotty B and B. No room at any hotels. Are you filing much?'

'One thousand words. It's a story dear to the hearts of Telegraph readers.'

'You're late for the first edition, aren't you?'

'I'll catch the second -- the one the delegates read in Blackpool. How about you?'

'Night off... no interest in cleaning up TV at the Gaydian. They're happy to keep it as dirty as possible!'

Irving was aware of the paper's unwholesome doctrine. Nicknamed the Gaydian for obvious reasons, it could be as prurient as the BBC when it tried.

His copy safely despatched in time for the second edition, they adjourned to a nearby pub. It was packed with loud voiced Tories and some locals keeping their distance round a darts board. They sat at a table, drinking pints of best Lancashire ale and munching potato crisps and peanuts.

'Are you married?' Rita asked.

'You could say that. Emily, my wife, and I rarely see each other."

She smiled sympathetically. 'Difficult isn't it, the work we do, the hours we keep. Children?'

'One daughter, grown up...well almost.' Then he remembered. 'One more on the way.'

'I get the picture.'

'What about you?'

'Divorced. No children. Homosexual husband.'

'Sorry. Forget I asked.'

'It's OK. As we used to say on the Brawton Chronicle, you have to take the rough with the intolerable.'

They drank their beers in silence. Then Irving said: 'Speaking of the intolerable, it's

Thatcher tomorrow -- then all over for another year.'

Rita grimaced. 'Appalling woman. Anyone who robs children of their school milk is capable of anything. People say it's time for a woman prime minister but I find Tory women worse than the men!'

'They're all as bad,' Irving said 'More taxes for the poor, more handouts for billionaires.

They're fixated on money aren't they. It's more important to them than blood!'

Rita coughed, reached into her handbag for a handkerchief and coughed again. She dabbed her eyes with the handkerchief. 'It's a bit smoky in here.'

Irving had half expected her to take out a packet of cigarettes and light up. 'Didn't you used to smoke, Rita?'

She shook her head 'Never smoked in my life. Horrid habit.'

'You're kidding, aren't you?'

'No way. You must be thinking of someone else.'

Perhaps he was. He cast his mind back to the smoke-filled newsroom at the Brawton Chronicle and tried to visualise Rita battering away on her Remington. Was there a cigarette between her lips? The picture was unhelpful but he felt sure there was an overflowing ashtray on her desk next to the piles of paper, spiked copy and empty tea cups.

He walked her back to her guest house along the brilliantly illuminated seafront with its slow moving trams, fish and chip shops and burger bars. The tide was coming in and it was a fairly mild autumn evening. The promenade was still bustling with intoxicated night life, mostly conference delegates letting their hair down before the big finale next day.

'More of the same tomorrow,' he grinned when they reached her guest house. 'More flag waving. More gory Tory glory!'

She pecked him on the cheek. 'Sounds like fun.'

The soft light from a streetlamp high-lighted her swept back auburn hair and played havoc with his suppressed libido. 'Well, good night then.'

'Good night, lover boy.'

The look in her eyes suggested the feeling was mutual but he couldn't be sure. The 'lover boy' had always been banter. He wondered if it still was.

'I'd invite you up for a nightcap but the landlady wouldn't approve.'

Celibacy certainly was a hard thing to handle, he thought as he strolled back to the hotel. As a journalist you had to keep your emotions under control so as to remain objective. But that only applied to work situations. You were still human. You still got hungry for food and drink -- and for love. Right now, he was on the verge of starvation and he suspected Rita's life was as loveless as his.

He paused, leaning on the promenade rail

and looked out across the Irish Sea, vast and motionless in the moonlight. In a cloudless sky the stars shone with a brightness only visible in pure unpolluted air. There were billions of them, even trillions. The universe was teeming with them and from what he had read on the subject of quantum physics, it had to be teeming with life. Out there countless multiverses contained mirror images of ourselves. At this very moment in time (and space) other Irving Breens were leaning on a promenade rail looking out across the emptiness and wondering about Rita Kennedy, about their wives at home and intractable problems of life in general.

Spray from a large wave splashed him back to reality. It was getting late but there was no sign of any winding down on the Golden Mile. Revellers in varying degrees of intoxication were still milling around fish and chip shops and takeaways, enjoying their plastic-wrapped suppers and scattering litter into the gutters. The ice cream stalls and hot dog salesmen were still doing a brisk trade along with the strip clubs, tattooists and fortune tellers.

On an impulse he ducked inside a palmist's booth, not because he believed in commercial clairvoyance but out of journalistic curiosity and mainly for a bit of fun. A swarthy elderly lady beamed in the half light and gestured for him to take a seat and extend his hand.

'You are very worried about something,' she said with a strong east European accent. 'You have travelled a long way in search of something... a very long way,' she added, her brow furrowing deeply. 'You do not belong here. You are from another place but you can never return. You are at a crossroads in your life. Your family need you but so does someone else. Put your family first. I see very dark times ahead. Do not despair... you will find what you are looking for in the end.'

The palmist released Irving's hand and smiled. 'That will be one pound please, sir.'

He paid the money and thanked her. It had been an interesting glimpse into the paranormal although much of the reading could have been guesswork and conjecture. The *nil desperandum* advice at the end was probably standard practice. But he was no stranger to ESP himself and he had to admit he was impressed. The reference to 'coming from another place to which he could never return' was uncannily accurate. For someone with no knowledge about him at all, she had helped him clear his mind and go forward. There could be no going back. As for dark times ahead, they were par for the course for a national newspaperman.

When he reached the Metropole the Moon was perched above the brightly lit Blackpool Tower, both reflected in the calm sea. There was a gentle breeze but the air was still mild and faintly redolent of fish and chips and beer. Oddly, mixed with the salty sea air, it was a relaxing combination. He decided to stop worrying. Months of frustration and concern for his mental health would ebb away with the tide when it went out.

Paddy, the doorman from Dublin, touched his splendid peaked cap. 'It's a fine evening, sor.'

Irving stood for a moment, breathing deeply. 'It's the ozone, isn't it? Something special about the ozone.'

Paddy held the door open and winked. 'Bottle that and you'd make a fortune, sor.'

Hugo was nowhere to be seen in the bar when Irving arrived for their late-night confab but it didn't matter. The final day's timetable was already fixed. Irving was scheduled to delouse the advance copy of the leader's keynote speech to conference before she delivered it, then write a resume before Hugo covered the actual speech with his own erudite and inimitably witty commentary.

Irving didn't wait around for Hugo to show up. His senior partner was probably win-ing and dining some impressionable delegate in a pretentious nightspot. It was a fair bet that fish, chips and beer did not figure on the menu. He ordered his usual whisky and ginger nightcap and watched a few minutes of the day's boring conference coverage on a large screen TV before taking the lift to his distant bedroom.

It was too late to phone Emily. She needed all the rest she could get. He'd be back home with her the following night anyway. All the media had been invited to the traditional end-of- conference ball at the Winter Gardens but most of them, Irving included, couldn't wait to go home. He undressed and changed into his pyjamas. The night was still mild so he lay on top of the bed and gazed through the open window at the star-packed sky.

Somewhere out there -- even beyond that inscrutable universe -- replicas of him were doing the same. Would they all have the same dreams, he wondered. Now there was a thought but he was too tired to think it. He turned on his side and slept. He didn't dream of Emily. He dreamt of Rita Kennedy.

When it came to public relations you had to credit Conservative Central Office with a flair for showmanship. On the final morning of the Blackpool conference its talented team despatched Mrs Thatcher to the town's famous Pleasure Beach for the benefit of the TV cameras and a select group of media grandees including H B Berry. Along with her sheepish husband, Denis, the dazzling, freshly coiffured leader was filmed driving a dodgem car, riding a roundabout horse and firing a rifle at a shooting gallery although she drew the line at the Big Dipper. Denis declined a donkey ride but appeared to enjoy a large pink candyfloss.

Throughout the bravura performance the arch manipulator flattered the egos of her entourage by addressing them individually by name and asking after their families. Then after a further photo opportunity with Blackpool Tower in the background, she bought them all ice creams. Just to show her generous nature.

Meanwhile, Irving and Rita were poring over advance copies of the leader's closing speech, distributed to journalists in the Press room. The party's PR team had done their usual professional job, seamlessly weaving the work of different speech writers into a passionate diatribe guaranteed to unite the party in a rapturous standing ovation. But to neutral observers it was little more than emotive rhetoric and sophisticated spin heavily reliant on a ritual appeal to patriotism.

Lurking just below the surface was a barely disguised theme of class warfare based on references to 'the enemy within', the enemy being the trade union movement and working class 'benefit scroungers'. It was a reminder of her unhealthy preoccupation with the class divide and an ominous indication of what to expect if the Tories won the next general election.

The keynote speech was embargoed for later in the evening, to be released as Mrs T had actually delivered it. It was the job of Irving and Rita to sift through it for 'highlights' to be featured alongside the substantive reports in their respective newspapers. These would be written at great colourful length by Hugo and his opposite number on the Guardian.

'No easy task is it?' Rita observed drily. 'Like searching for diamonds in a coal mine.' 'Nice one.' Irving conceded. 'They're hooked on money and patriotism aren't they.'

' Last refuge of a scoundrel -- who was it who said that?'

'You did -- and Samuel Johnson. It sums them up perfectly.'

Working together they trawled through Thatcher's rabble-rousing dross, identifying turns of phrase likely to interest readers of their respective newspapers. References to 'going soft on crime' and 'life should mean life' for murderers would go down well with Telegraph readers over their breakfast kidneys and kedgeree. The same applied to vague assurances to crack down on sex, violence and swearing in BBC television programmes plus, of course, repeated promises to zap the trade unions.

There was rather less to appeal to Guardian readers over their yoghurt, lentils and meat-free sausages although legislation protecting homosexuals from discrimination in all walks of life and moves to liberalise 'women's reproductive rights' would be introduced in the event of winning the next election.

Their work finally done and their copy phoned through, the pair didn't hang around for the main event. They headed for the exit like children released from school, pushing their way through the protest groups outside and heading for the promenade. Mistaking them for delegates, the feminists screeched and jeered and the animal rights campaigners blew their hunting horns but the two waved their Press cards and laughed it off.

A watery sunshine was percolating through the grey clouds, the tide was going out and the beach was almost deserted apart from groups of donkeys. 'Donkeys inside and donkeys outside,' Irving laughed. They paid their money, mounted two of the docile animals and trotted off towards the sea, a handler keeping a respectful distance in the rear. Maybe it was the bracing salty air, the smell of the animals, the tinkling of their bells or the sight of rippling waves washing across the shining sand that triggered it but Irving suddenly felt a moment of déjà vu.

He was once again peering between two pointed ears at a desolate emptiness of sea and sky as a very small child. It awakened the trauma of his birth and the blank oblivion preceding it from his subconscious mind. He felt dizzy, swaying in the saddle and pulling tightly at the reins. The donkey stopped abruptly and he lurched forward.

Rita reached across from her mount in an attempt to steady him. 'Are you all right, Irving? Don't fall off.'

The moment passed. 'I'm OK. Just felt a bit sick.'

With the aid of the handler they managed to turn the confused animals round and head back to their pitch beside the pier. 'You've gone very pale,' she said as they dismounted. 'Sure you're alright?'

'I'm fine, thanks. It was just a glitch... a bad memory...'

Did all the other Irving Breens have the same bad memory, he wondered. Had some of them fallen off the donkey? At least he hadn't done that.

Rita thought it best not to ask about his

bad memory. She had enough of her own. But he still seemed a bit unsteady. She held his arm re-assuringly. 'What you need is a good lunch!'

It had to be fish and chips, of course, at one of the popular seafront restaurants. With mushy peas and plenty of salt and vinegar. Washed down with strong tea, the sort you can only find 'up north.' It was something to do with the hard water they drank down south, Irving explained. It was the same with the beer -- suitable only for wimps and women.

Rita gave him a hefty jab with her elbow. 'Chauvinist pig.' They set off on a stroll along the promenade. The clouds had lifted and it was warm in the afternoon sun. She was laughing and the offshore breeze caught her auburn hair and whipped it across her face. Irving thought how youthfully attractive she still was. He remembered the mixed feelings he'd had about her all those years ago at the Brawton Chronicle. They were still mixed now. Disturbingly mixed.

They reached the spot where Irving had consulted a palmist the previous evening and he stopped in his stride. The booth was no longer there. He was sure it was the right place because it was nextdoor to a florist's stand. The florist's was still there, colourful flowers and plants spilling onto the pavement. But the palmist had vanished. Maybe she'd decided to move on. It was the end of the season after all. But if the booth had been dismantled so recently it would have left some traces, some sign of disturbance to the pavement. There was nothing. The paving stones were as smooth and unmarked as the day they were laid.

Another mystery! He decided to ask the florist what had happened to her neighbour but there was only a young girl assistant looking after the stall who knew nothing about anything. Could it have been another hallucination just when he thought he'd heard the last of them? Hardly, the experience was still fresh in his mind. He could remember the palmist's words verbatim: 'You are at a crossroads in your life... put your family first.'

Dabble in the paranormal and this is what you get, he thought. It became a struggle to cling to the normal. What was normality after all if it was being played out with slight variations in other dimensions by clones of himself? As usual at such times, the tinnitus kicked in like the sound of a rushing wind and he slapped the side of his head repeatedly in an attempt to silence it.

Rita was perplexed and asked what it was all about. He shrugged and shivered at the same time. No point in burdening her with his weird hang-ups. 'It's nothing really,' he told her unconvincingly as they carried on walking and near-normality was restored. It was just another bizarre moment in his increasingly bizarre life.

They found a bench overlooking the beach and watched some children building a sand castle below. At least Rita did. Under her light topcoat she was wearing a blouse and tight fitting skirt and as she crossed her legs the hem rose above her knee. He couldn't help noticing. As they said in the newsroom, celibacy gave men a very hard time, in every sense of the expression. He shifted uncomfortably and tried looking elsewhere but his eyes kept returning to the elegant curve of her thigh. It just wasn't fair. You may be a journalist -- an objective observer of human frailty -- but you were still human and frail yourself. She crossed her legs the other way and the hem rose higher. So unfair.

They sat in silence broken by the sound of the children and the plaintive cries of circling seagulls. One of the birds perched on the promenade rail in front of them and stared at him aggressively. It took Irving's mind off Rita's knees but at exactly the same moment the tinnitus returned and he became aware of the words: 'Never mind sex. You should be going home. Your wife needs you.' He couldn't be sure he heard the words or whether they formed in his brain subliminally, the sort of interior locution he'd come to recognise at stressful moments.

The hairs on the back of his neck rose and he started to sweat. He glared at the seagull. It glared back unflinchingly, as if to say: 'That's right, Buster. You heard.' The plot thickened when Rita said: 'That bird's trying to tell us something.'

That was just too cute, he thought. Women's intuition never ceased to amaze him. He wiped the sweat from his face and neck with a handkerchief. The seagull remained motionless.

Rita said: 'What do you think it's trying to tell us?'

'No idea,' he said irritably. 'Something like there's a storm coming, I daresay.' Right on cue, the sun moved behind a bank of cloud and it grew chilly.

After an awkward silence Rita asked: 'Will you be going to the junket tonight?'

He certainly hadn't planned to attend the farewell ball. The prospect of socialising with all those Tories filled him with acute discomfort. He'd intended to return dutifully to his pregnant wife.

'I'll be catching the evening train to Manchester. Emily will be expecting me home late tonight.' That had been the plan. But if Rita was going...

'Are you going?'

'Why not? All those free drinks. It might

be fun.'

The seagull flew away.

'Why not indeed!'

TWENTY

The Winter Gardens ballroom had been suitably decorated for the conference delegates' farewell shindig. There was blue drapery everywhere, blue ribbons, blue balloons and miniature Union Jack bunting festooned across the balconies and ornate ceiling. On stage was a 16-piece dance orchestra, its musicians wearing blue uniforms, complete with a female vocalist in a sequined blue dress.

The same theme was reflected among the women guests in ball gowns of varying shades of blue with their escorts wearing tuxedos of the same colour, although others wore traditional evening dress. Irving and Rita struck a revolutionary note. He wore his Harold Wilson-style brown tweed jacket and she had changed into a coffee coloured creation in figure-hugging Jersey wool that left little to the imagination. The conspicuous couple attracted dubious glances as they sat at a balcony table until word went round that they were members of the Press. That explained it -- they didn't know any better.

No strangers to hostility as a professional hazard, Irving and Rita were too absorbed in each other's company to notice. They drank their ale from posh tall glasses and had more important matters to talk about. Like their lives since leaving the Brawton Chronicle and their marital relationships or lack of them.

'I worked there long after you left,' Rita said. 'Impossible for a woman to break into Fleet Street in those days. Still tough now. Then I met Andy at an air show in Cheshire and my life changed, as they say. He worked for the Guardian and wangled me in as a freelance to begin with. They must have liked my work because they offered me a staff job only six months later.'

'Fast tracking,' Irving said.

'I was on a roll, or so I thought. We got shacked up and then decided to get married as we had two wage packets coming in.' She paused and took a long drink of her ale. None of your delicate sipping for Rita. 'Seemed like a good idea. But then he told me he was bisexual...' She ran manicured fingers through her hair.' 'I mean, if he'd told me beforehand I'd never have married him.'

She took another swig. 'Downhill all the way after that. You wouldn't believe what he wanted to do... threesomes and worse. No way, Hosea! Anyway, he then ran off to join his boyfriend at the BBC. Divorce was inevitable. Messy but can't say I had the slightest regret.' She drained her glass. 'Same again, lover boy.'

As Irving signalled to a waiter they were joined at their table by Hugo, resplendent in his sky blue Dior lounge suit. 'I'll get these,' the star columnist said. 'Two pints of best bitter and a large single malt,' he told the waiter, pulling up a chair. 'You didn't tell me your good lady would be here, Irving.'

His deputy hastily corrected him. 'This is Rita Kennedy, she's a Guardian journalist, covering for a colleague who was taken ill.'

With a mock courtly gesture, Hugo took Rita's hand and air kissed it. 'Enchante. One does have to say you look ravishing, my dear.'

'One doesn't have to say anything of the kind, Hugo,' Rita snapped. 'I've heard a lot about you from colleagues.'

'Nice things, of course.'

'Far from it!'

It was all in fun. Just banter.

Their drinks arrived and they talked shop. For a third month in a row the Daily Telegraph's circulation had gone up and the Guardian's had gone down. 'No future for you on the Gaydian,' Hugo told Rita. 'Come and work for us at the Telegraph, a *proper* newspaper. I could get you a job in London.'

She realised he was flirting. It was still just banter. 'No way. Couldn't afford to live there.'

'We'd pay you more than you're getting now -- a lot more.'

'You're several drinks ahead of me, Hugo, so I'll overlook your attempt at poaching -- in front of a witness.'

'Don't drag me into this,' Irving protested.

Hugo grinned. 'Just having a larf, my dear. How about a dance instead?'

To turn the offer down would be embarrassing, Rita thought. So with a show of great reluctance, she complied.

The band was playing *In The Mood*, a Glenn Miller favourite popular with older guests. Irving watched from on high as the incongruous pair improvised their own version of quickstep mixed with jive on the crowded dance floor. Rita looked stunning in her erotic dress and Hugo clearly fancied her. Irving felt a twinge of jealousy. Despite their professional relationship as working journalists he'd started to fancy her himself. And the feeling was growing stronger by the minute.

She returned to their table alone, flushed and flopped into her chair. 'He made a pass at me, would you believe! Invited me back to his hotel. I told him I don't go out with Tories. He said: "I'm not asking you to go out with me, I'm asking you to stay in with me".'

The word-recall was precise and professional. Everything remembered verbatim without the aid of shorthand. Irving imagined she'd given Hugo a suitably robust rebuff. 'What did you tell him?'

'I told him to naff orff!'

'That's my girl.'

'He repeated the job offer -- in London. I've a good mind to report him to the NUJ for poaching.'

'He's not in the union, he's in the IOJ.'

'The Institute, those management arse-lickers... it gets worse!'

'And he's married, of course. But then so am I.'

'Yes, but you're not chatting me up.'

He looked at her steadily and smiled. 'I wouldn't bet on that, Rita.'

The intense blue eyes regarded him with a mixture of doubt and amusement. 'You're drunk!'

'Sadly not yet. But I soon will be. Then

you'd better watch out!'

Rita laughed. 'You're not serious are you? I can never tell,'

'You bet I'm serious.'

'Emily wouldn't like this conversation. She's expecting you home.'

'Change of plan. I called her. We're barely on speaking terms.'

She sighed deeply and pushed the fingers of both hands through her hair. She'd always fancied him, there was no denying it. Back in their Brawton Chronicle days she'd found his innocent boyishness a refreshing contrast to the dark cynicism of her male colleagues. His handsome looks and brown soulful eyes had charmed her into working on her appearance and changing her hairstyle but he'd shown no interest. Now all these years later he was showing plenty. He was married now, of course, but pregnancy had turned his wife frigid. He was sex starved and drunk. They both were. And the handsome devil was looking at her with those soulful brown eyes...

'Oh God, Irving, I need another drink.'

They ordered more beer this time with whisky chasers. Something had changed. They both knew it. They were no longer cynical working journalists with copy to file and deadlines to meet. They were two lonely people deprived of human love, drawn together by insatiable hormones, romantic music and alcohol.

Rita sighed and swirled the whisky round in its glass while staring intently into its depths. It had been almost six months for her too. 'I guess I'm as lonely as you, Irving. Feels worse on my nights off... nobody to talk to and you just can't watch the telly -- too juvenile for words.'

'I know, they've dumbed everything down to zero.'

'So a few months back I decided to try a dating agency... disastrous! I met this guy at a restaurant in Salford and guess what he ordered...'

'Caviar.'

'Rabbit pie! I should have known then it was a mistake. His idea of a night out was ten pin bowling and a latte. And guess what car he drove.'

'A Ferrari.'

'A Volvo.'

Both fell about. 'Show me a Volvo and I'll show you a bad driver,' Irving said. It was a standard newsroom joke.

'Anyway, I did a bit of research on him...'

'As you do...'

'... and it turned out he was not only married with children and a Tory but one of those...' she unbuttoned a sleeve on her dress and rolled it up with a shudder.

Irving was incredulous. 'You don't mean...'

'Yes... a mason. How naff can you get!'

'Toxic more like.' The secret society had once tried to suppress a report of his into a dodgy property deal. Two of his car tyres had been mysteriously slashed around the same time.

She drained her whisky in one gulp. 'So I dumped him -- and the agency. They're all a rip-off really.'

'You had a lucky escape.'

'You get over it and move on. There's always next day's paper to get out.'

You couldn't stay serious for long with Rita. She took both his hands in hers. 'Bet I can drink you under the table.'

'You're on.'

They touched glasses and laughed together. Just like old times, only different.

The lights dimmed and the band played a slow foxtrot, *Once in a While*, a Nat King Cole classic, sung by the glamorous star-spangled vocalist.

Once in a while,
Will you try
To give one little smile to me,
Though someone else may be
Nearer your heart?

Rita smiled at him affectionately. ' If I wasn't such a cynic I'd say they were playing our song, Irving.'

'Let's dance,' he said. 'While we still can.'

On the dance floor they clung together unsteadily, the fragrance of her lustrous hair arousing his senses, the closeness of her body annihilating restraint. The inner voice telling him to go home to his wife had fallen silent. Months of emotional deprivation were slipping away, along with what remained of his conscience.

The music stopped but they continued shuffling, along with other similarly entwined couples. The lights went up and then down again for even more inspired lyrics from the vocalist. *Temptation*, a famous Bing Crosby ballad.

In their intimate huddle, Irving and Rita yielded willingly to temptation, their pent-up inhibitions abandoned. Dancing was forgotten. Words were superfluous.

You came, I was alone
I should have known you were temptation
You smiled, luring me on
My heart was gone, you were temptation...

The taxi took only five minutes to her guest house. On the way they kissed, tenderly at first but then passionately, her dress riding up above her knees, all inhibitions forgotten. On arrival Rita fumbled in her handbag for the fare then as the cab drove away, for her pass key. Irving swaying under the streetlamp watched her, grinning.

'The landlady won't like this.'

She found her key. 'Fuck the landlady.'

The shock of her words took his breath away and sent an erotic charge through his body. That was it. The Rubicon had been crossed. There was no way back now. Too late to go home. Incapable of doing so anyway.

'She's gone to bingo. There's no problem.'

They climbed the stairs like furtive young lovers and she opened her bedroom door. 'Welcome to the boudoir.'

She switched on a bedside table lamp. It dimly revealed a plain seedy room but he neither noticed nor cared. He slumped into the single armchair and watched her pour two glasses of vodka from her secret supply in a wardrobe.

'Here's to us, lover boy.'

They tried to touch glasses but missed and Rita giggled. 'Have I won our bet?'

He groaned in resignation. 'Let's call it a draw!'

But his conscience would not give in that easily. For a moment a vision of Emily, pure and angelic but frigid, crossed his addled mind and he almost sobered up but not quite. This was lust not love, he told himself sternly and knocked back the rest of his vodka.

They kissed with an intensity driven by uninhibited desire, two wordsmiths finally lost for words and concentrating urgently on action. Slightly less drunk than he was, Rita guided him to the bed. He sat and struggled clumsily to undress. She helped him until only his shirt remained.

Then she stood and slowly, sensuously unzipped her dress. It slipped down over her elegant legs to the floor. Just as he'd thought, there was nothing else to remove except her tiny pants and high heeled shoes. She sat next to him and kissed him gently, the taste of vodka lingering on her soft lips. He lay back overwhelmed and let her make the running. Perhaps it was the combined effect of the vodka, the beer and whisky but he suddenly felt drowsy. Poised above him her perfect breasts brushing his chest, she slowly unbuttoned his shirt... then froze.

What she saw drew a loud sob from her throat and she recoiled in shock. Gleaming faintly in the half light was Irving's crucifix, the gold cross and chain his mother-in-law gave him on his wedding day. Rita collapsed in the armchair gasping for breath, her eyes welling up. She had no idea he wore a crucifix. They'd never discussed religion. She'd assumed he was an agnostic like she was... like most journalists were.

She'd attended Sunday school as a child but when both parents died within months of each other from tuberculosis she'd given up on God. Corruption and immorality were endemic in society from its highest ranks to its dregs. The concept of sin had lost its impact on her. Yet Sunday school had not been entirely wasted. Deep down but rising rapidly through the alcoholic haze, was the realisation that what they were doing was wrong. Very wrong. He was married with a daughter. His wife was in the advanced stages of pregnancy and waiting for him to come home.

A loud snore from the bed helped to concentrate her mind. He was not up to it anyway -- in every sense of the expression. Brewer's droop had taken its inevitable toll on him and her own desire had wilted as suddenly as his. She sighed deeply before buttoning his shirt and pulling up his trousers.

It took an age to waken him, then call a taxi from the telephone in the hall. He was too drunk to say anything, not that there was anything worth saying. With the help of the cab driver he was bundled on to the back seat. He waved feebly and blew a kiss as the taxi drove away.

Rita blew a kiss back and smiled bravely through her tears. As one-night stands went it had been more of a one-night slump. But then, you had to take the rough with the intolerable.

Somewhere a bell was ringing. It rang intermittently in perfect synchronisation with a deep throbbing pain in Irving's head. He turned over and tried to go back to sleep but neither the pain nor the ringing would stop. It took an agonising effort to raise himself on one elbow, open one eye and look at his bedside clock. The time was 7.35am and the ringing was coming from his bedside telephone. He tried reaching out to it but the pain in his head shot into his neck and shoulder. He sank back into the pillow, then tried again.

With a supreme effort he clutched the receiver and lifted it through the pain barrier to his ear. It was his daughter calling and she sounded distraught.

'Oh Dad, I thought you were never going to answer.'

His throat felt wrinkled like an overripe grape. He croaked: 'Sorry, Dawn. Rough night.'

'It's Mum, Dad. She's had a miscarriage. She's in hospital;' She broke off, sobbing. 'And I've crashed the car...'

He sat up abruptly and a blinding pain seized his forehead in an iron grip. But at least he was wide awake. 'Dawn, are you all right?'

'Yes, physically I'm OK.'

'Is your Mum OK?'

'Yes, they say she'll be fine. But she's lost a lot of blood so they're keeping her in. It was a late term miscarriage. The baby was stillborn. It was a boy.'

Just when he thought the pain could not get any worse the blow hit him like a lump hammer. A son. They'd had a son. And lost him.

'Are you still there, Dad?'

He tried to clear his throat. 'Yes, just can't believe it... that's just terrible... '

'I can't believe it either. It feels unreal, like a nightmare.'

'What time did it happen?'

'About one-o-clock this morning. She started losing blood and I phoned the ambulance. But she got worse and they didn't come. So I tried to drive her to the hospital myself...

'Her voice cracked again and she tailed off.

'What happened, darling?'

'I'm just no good at night driving... I hit a bollard at the junction with the main road. The car stalled and I couldn't get it going again. I just panicked. Then a police car arrived and they took us both to Wythenshawe Hospital. That's where I am now.'

'Is Mum awake? Can I speak to her?'

'No, they've put her under sedation. I could do with some sedation myself.'

'Ask them if you can rest there until I arrive. I'll catch the next train. Should be there early afternoon.'

There was no way he could stomach breakfast in the hotel's restaurant but several cups of black coffee and a double dose of codeine phosphate helped to partially tame the hangover. Recollection of the previous night's events amounted to little more than the image of Rita's dress slipping to the floor and a frighteningly fast taxi ride back to the hotel. He vaguely remembered being helped to his room by the night porter after collapsing in the lift.

He penned a note to Hugo explaining his hasty departure, packed his holdall and hurried downstairs to the reception desk. The desk clerk took the note and his room key, and prepared his bill. If he was aware of his guest's nocturnal indiscretions he showed no sign of it. But Irving felt some form of apology was called for.

'Sorry about last night. I was a bit worse for wear.' As euphemisms went it was a classic.

The clerk finished totting up Irving's hefty bar bill and asked him to sign it. 'No problem at all, sir. I understand you were feeling unwell. Our night staff were able to assist you and left a note in the diary. I trust you're feeling better now.'

Irving winced as a knot of pain twisted in his neck. 'Just about. I'm grateful for their help.'

'Always a pleasure to assist gentlemen of the Press, sir. Especially representatives of the Daily Telegraph.'

There was a bitter irony there, Irving thought as his taxi sped towards the railway station. Right now he did not feel like a representative of the Daily Telegraph. He felt more like a representative of a very low order of humanity. Who was he to condemn far-right, flag-waving racists as scoundrels when he was no better than one himself?

The crowded train rattled and lurched towards Manchester. Seated in first class, only marginally more comfortable than other carriages, Irving reflected on a dramatic human story that would never make the newspapers. He was its central villain. He'd messed up big time. He'd cheated on Emily and she'd suffered unimaginably as a result. Instead of returning to her as soon as the conference had finished, as he had planned, he'd allowed himself to be seduced by an irresistible redhead. He'd been sex starved for months and they'd failed to do the deed anyway but those were unacceptable excuses. They were a flimsy form of mitigation.

Dawn had told him that Emily's miscarriage had happened at 1am the previous night and after searching his fragmented memory he worked out that at that time he was locked in a passionate embrace with Rita. What made the tragic scenario even worse was the fact that if he had been at home at the time of Emily's first symptoms he could have driven her to the hospital himself.

There would have been no accident and no delay in reaching the maternity staff. Possibly the miscarriage might have been averted and the baby saved. The thought was unbearable. In his misery his eyes misted over and the pain of his hangover returned more violently than before.

On reaching Manchester Exchange Station he ran for a taxi and sat impatiently as it trundled through the dense traffic and heavy rain towards Wythenshawe Hospital on the city's outskirts. Still overcome with remorse he thought about the son he'd always wanted -- the son both he and Emily had given up on having. This had been their big chance and he'd blown it. For the second time in his life a vision of taking his son to Maine Road to watch City, both wearing blue and white scarves, appeared then crashed out of his mind forever.

At last they reached the sprawling hospital complex. It had stopped raining but the air was still damp and melancholy to match his mood. At the maternity unit he was told his wife had been wakened from sedation and was in a private room along with the body of their stillborn son. A nurse showed him in and five pairs of eyes turned to look at him. Emily, haggard and dishevelled, sat in bed propped up by pillows. Grouped round her bed and a cradle containing the lifeless baby were Dawn, Lilian, Daniel and a pregnant Megan. Their 'hellos' were muted and distress was plain on all their faces. They also shared another expression. Reproach. Where had he been when his wife needed him most?

But what really cracked him up was Emily's attempt to smile when he bent to kiss her. She almost made it but then her pale face collapsed in a flood of tears. He lost it himself then and they clung together in mutual grief, oblivious to their surroundings. Everyone else fled the room reaching for their own handkerchiefs. Daniel was the last to leave after patting Irving reassuringly on the shoulder.

It was a long time before they'd dried their tears and Irving could look at his son. The little face, deadly pale and tinged with blue, was the picture of serenity. He held a tiny hand but the fingers did not curl round his as Dawn's had done all those years ago.

'Do you want to hold him?' Emily said.

But he couldn't. Still struggling for self-control he shook his head. 'I just can't. Not now. It's too much.'

She took his hand. 'I know... I know what you mean.'

'What will happen to him?'

'They want to do a post mortem. I've refused. They've offered to "dispose of the body" but I've told them we're having a proper funeral.'

He bit his lip and shuddered. He had a good idea what "dispose of the body" meant. The thought sickened him. 'Of course, our son must have a proper Christian burial. What about a name... what do you want to call him?'

'What about "Irving?"'

He subsided into a chair and held his head in both hands in a feeling of utter wretchedness. It was just too much. After all she'd been through -- in his unexplained absence at a time when she desperately needed him -- she still wanted to name their son after him. It was too humbling for words.

He pulled himself together, sat on her bed and held her slender hand with its wedding and engagement rings. 'Darling, I let you down last night... I should have been with you. I don't deserve to have a son named after me -- alive or dead.'

Emily knew all about the unpredictable nature of her husband's job with its frequent absence from home. But intuition told her that this time there might be some other reason. In her trusting love for him she brushed the thought aside. 'It all happened so suddenly... you weren't to know.'

'All the same, I'd rather we named him after someone worthier. We could call him Fred -- after your father.'

She sank back on her pillows and closed her swollen red-rimmed eyes. 'I'm just so tired, Irving. If that's what you want. We'll call him Fred.'

In happier circumstances they would have all gone for a drink and chatted about their lives. It had been ages since Irving had seen Daniel and Megan, who were now an 'item' and living in an apartment of their own. As expectant parents themselves the day's events had been particularly upsetting for them. But the time was not right for a social gathering. After emotional hugs Lilian, Daniel and Megan said their weepy goodbyes and their taxi drove away into the gloom.

Emily, Irving and Dawn remained, waiting for a consultation with the doctor. There were formalities to be completed and arrangements to be made with an undertaker -- more mundane details that compounded their misery. At least the sympathetic young doctor offered a friendly face and some good news. Emily was given the all-clear but they were keeping her in another night for rest and observation.

Then he turned to the question he knew was on all their lips: had Emily's delay in reaching hospital contributed to the baby's stillbirth? Would their son have survived if Emily had reached the hospital earlier?

The uncertainty principle kicked in again. The answer was equivocal. The baby was several weeks premature and there were complications. It was possible but extremely unlikely.

Dawn's hand flew to her mouth.' He might have lived?'

'Only a very slim chance -- little more than one per cent. And then perhaps not for very long.'

Irving's worst fears were confirmed. If he'd been at home when it happened the outcome might have been different. Albeit not much different. There was only a one per cent chance the boy might have lived. That was negligible in terms of their present existence but in a quantum context it was vast. If there were one hundred multiverses the boy would have been alive in one of them. *But there were millions!*

After the doctor left the three of them talked it over in the gathering twilight. To

Emily and Dawn one per cent meant they were clutching at straws. It was neither the time nor the place for speculation about Irving's 'other worlds'. It was, after all, God's will. They would light a candle for Fred at St Peter's and Mass would be said for the repose of his innocent soul.

A nurse brought them cups of tea and biscuits. They tried to relax but Irving sensed one more question was bothering his wife and daughter: why hadn't he returned from the conference earlier, as he'd said he would? Telling a lie did not come easily to him. He never forgot one of his first lessons as a cub reporter: journalists were servants of the truth. They didn't tell lies. But there were exceptions to every rule. His present dilemma was clearly one of them.

He decided to blame Hugo and say his celebrated colleague had been tipped-off that Mrs T herself intended to make an appearance at the ball. All the media's cameras would happen to be there to capture the 'surprise' moment. Hugo expected to be pictured chatting to the party leader along with other sycophants. He'd insisted on introducing Irving to her as a reward for his assistance throughout the conference. It would help to 'enhance his professional image'. Irving had no interest in meeting her but reluctantly agreed on condition he could catch a late train to Manchester.

But the great leader's surprise appearance failed to materialise. Her Press officer put it around, off the record, that Denis was feeling too tired and emotional -- the standard euphemism for legless -- so the waiting media just carried on drinking on expenses. They included Irving who could still have caught the last train to Manchester but by then was feeling too tired and emotional himself.

He had to admit it sounded plausible and the last bit was certainly true. Emily and Dawn listened sympathetically and seemed convinced. They had no reason to doubt him because they knew he never told untruths. It wasn't in his nature.

Their willing acceptance of the story brought a lump to his throat. It was the first time in his life that he had told Emily a deliberate lie. The knowledge that he'd abused the trust of his soulmate and her unconditional love for him brought more tears to his eyes. He would do his level best to make it up to her. But deep in his heart he knew it would not be enough. Their lives together would never be the same again.

TWENTY-ONE

People say they're 'devastated' for all kinds of reasons. One of Irving's first stories as a reporter for the Brawton Chronicle was about an allotment holder whose outsize vegetable marrow had been vandalised. He blamed other jealous growers as he was sure it would have won first prize in the local agricultural show. Months of devoted cultivation had been in vain. He was devastated.

Another Chronicle story concerned a pigeon fancier whose favourite bird took off in a prestigious race and never returned. He suspected members of the shooting fraternity whom he described as 'heavily armed hooligans'. The loss of his beautiful pigeon had left him devastated.

More recently, in the Telegraph, Irving had covered the case of a severely depressed youth who had been referred for counselling after being eliminated from the finals of a televised talent contest. The lad was said to be devastated.

None of them knew the meaning of the word.

It was only at the funeral of their baby son that Irving himself discovered its true meaning. The ceremony was at St Oswald's Church, Wilmslow, after midday Mass on a wet and windy Friday. Many of the Mass-goers remained as two undertakers carried in the tiny white coffin and placed it on a trestle in front of the altar.

Irving and a heavily tranquilised Emily sat holding hands in the front pew. Emily was all in black and Irving wore his dark lounge suit and black tie. Immediately behind sat Dawn, Daniel, Megan, Fred senior, and Lilian, all grim faced and wearing dark clothing. Handkerchiefs were much in evidence.

The priest, Father Simon, solemnly lit a candle and placed it at the head of the coffin. Then he gently taped a rosebud to its polished surface along with two miniature ferns, one on each side.

He began the service with a special prayer for the loss of a child:

God of all mystery, whose ways are beyond understanding,
lead us who grieve at this untimely tragedy
to a new and deeper faith in your love,
which brought your only Son Jesus
through death into resurrection life.

We make our prayer in Jesus' name.
Amen.

Then everyone stood and sang the hymn, All Things Bright and Beautiful:

All things bright and beautiful
All creatures great and small
All things wise and wonderful
The Lord God made them all

In his homily Father Simon told the tearful congregation: 'Not every flower can open. Many are the unopened rosebuds that make up a beautiful bouquet. Fred has not died because he has never physically lived. But of course he has lived spiritually as a unique person in his mother's womb for over seven months. Now his soul lives on as one of God's angels -- completely pure and untouched by our corrupt and sinful world.

'To borrow a line from a famous poem: Age will not wither him, nor the years condemn. Fred has been spared all the trials and tribulations of life on this Earth, all the avarice, depravity and temptations, all the disease and pain of death. He has gone straight to heaven. Emily and Irving have one member of their family in heaven already!'

Tears flowed as freely as the Wilmslow rain. The priest's eloquence touched the hearts of everyone. All became mourners and queued to offer the stricken parents heartfelt condolences on leaving church. Overwhelmed by their support the couple braced themselves for the graveside.

Thankfully the rain had relented and weak sunshine filtered through a gap in the clouds. But a cold wind plucked at Father Simon's cassock as he read the closing prayer over the white coffin with its single rosebud and brass nameplate:

Fred Breen
Ageless Timeless Sinless

'Eternal rest grant unto him, Oh Lord,
and let perpetual light shine upon him.
Through the mercy of God, rest in peace.'

Irving and his wife stood arm in arm as the tiny coffin was lowered into the ground. Both were shivering with cold and numb with grief. The ordeal suddenly became too much for Emily. Her knees gave way, the cemetery seemed to gyrate and with a low moan, she fainted. Irving caught her and prevented her from falling. Fred and Daniel rushed to help. Between them they carried her to a nearby seat. Fred, who always thought of everything, produced smelling salts and she quickly recovered.

Her father breathed a prayer of his own: 'Heavenly Father, have mercy on us all in our frailty and distress.'

Irving whispered: 'Amen.'

He finally understood the true meaning of the word 'devastated'.

When Godfrey Myers heard of his reporter's loss the ageing but still sprightly editor called him into his office and poured him a stiff gin. It wasn't long since his own mother had died from cancer and for all his innate resilience he still felt the sadness of bereavement. He was also deeply worried about his son who was in hospital with mental health issues. He'd decided to allow Irving two weeks' paid leave in view of his long service and professionalism. 'It will help you get over the worst,' he said. 'Give you a fresh perspective. The world keeps turning, you know. News keeps happening. Life goes on.'

Not for me it doesn't, Irving thought, although he thanked Godfrey for his kindness. Life had become a meaningless existence. Emily had never cried so much in her life. She could not bear to look at other mothers pushing their prams in the street. It didn't help when well-meaning friends told her she was still in her prime and could always have another baby. At her age the chance of becoming pregnant again were fast receding. She had lost all interest in sex. And anyway 'this baby was the one that I wanted.' Why couldn't other women understand something as basic as that?

'Practical people' with a utilitarian approach to life at the expense of human empathy, would tell her that all she had lost was 'a well-developed bunch of cells' not a son. How insensitive and downright ignorant could you get? Her 'bunch of cells' was an almost perfectly formed boy *with his own DNA acquired at conception.* His identity was unique. There was nobody else like him in the whole world.

As an observer in the midst of humanity's ongoing dramas and crises, Irving was expected to suppress his own innermost feelings. When tragedy struck close to home it was a different matter. The trauma was still raw and his role in it too painful for a philosophical overview. His most important function was to become a figure of strength in adversity -- provide a shoulder to cry on although not far below the surface he was crying himself.

The need for a domestic memorial became paramount. Along with Dawn, whose own loss of an unexpected baby brother had left her reliant on anti-depressants, the couple searched garden centres for inspiration. They didn't know what they were looking for but it had to be something they could install in their garden, something beautiful and permanent. They bought trays of forget-me-nots and an ornamental stone planter for them. Something else was still needed. Then Dawn spotted it -- an elegantly shaped rose tree covered in buds. 'For our own rosebud' and they agreed it was the perfect choice.

All that remained was the question of a headstone for Fred's little grave in the children's section of the town cemetery. They selected a small white cross mounted on rough-hewn stonework and searched the Bible for a suitable epitaph. They decided on:

Fred Breen
Of such is the Kingdom of Heaven

There was no such thing as 'back to normal'. What was 'normal' after all? A world full of conflict, cruelty, poverty, exploitation, greed, fears... none of it seemed important any more. Irving had heard it said that after the death of a child something inside you also died. It may be a cliché but it was so true. Your personality took a negative twist. What was the point of going on if God treated you in this way?

Emily's answer was to sit for hours cuddling Samantha, the cat, and stroking Betsy, the Labrador, on the top of her head. Worst of all, she started smoking -- one or two cigarettes a day to start with but then 10 and rapidly up to 20. Meals became few and far between as her appetite vanished. A meagre breakfast was sometimes her only meal of the day. Irving came to rely heavily on the Telegraph's staff canteen and its chips with everything.

Their relationship, over the years secure and positive, became strained to a point where all intimacy drained away. Love and affection were replaced by politeness, as if they were strangers. They stopped going to church but avoided any meaningful discussion implying a loss of religious faith. They could no longer turn to each other. It was like touching a nerve. Emily was more sensitive than he was. If the subject arose, however briefly, she would relapse into tears. He suspected they were as much over her loss of faith as the loss of her baby.

Dawn had her own anxieties as she prepared for her university finals. She blamed herself for crashing the Rover on her mother's fateful journey to hospital. No amount of reassurance would convince her that she was blameless. She'd been fitted with spectacles for long sightedness but they failed to give her confidence. After saving hard to buy her own car she had now abandoned the idea.. The GP had put her on anti-depressants. Some days they worked and some they didn't.

When they worked she did her best to comfort her parents, taking over cooking and domestic work. She sensed the strain they were under, especially when they stopped going to church. When people did that it was serious. She stopped going herself for a time but resumed when friends at the youth club sent a deputation insisting that she return.

On the day Daniel and Megan, now heavily pregnant. visited in their second-hand Morris Minor, Emily took an extra tranquilliser and managed to keep her composure. Megan's 'bump' was well disguised by a loose-fitting floral dress and her cheerful outgoing personality helped Emily to forget her cares, at least for the moment.

Dawn made tea and served crumpets and cream cakes helped by Megan. Daniel, now a professional musician and in robust good health, sat with his arm round his sister. It never failed to comfort her when they were children and she'd fallen and hurt herself or her friends had upset her.

They all relaxed when Irving opened a bottle of amontillado. Emily was persuaded to entertain the guests on the piano. It was the first time she'd played the instrument since her world fell apart. She began with some mournful Schubert. But then Daniel remembered he had his clarinet in the car and went to fetch it. He and Megan leafed through Emily's huge selection of sheet music and came up with a copy of *Ave Maria*. Daniel had a good look at the notation and improvised some passages for his instrument. Then brother and sister performed a magical impromptu duet of Gounod's masterpiece.

The spiritually uplifting performance left its listeners spellbound and they responded with rapturous applause. Irving had always loved the clarinet with its amazing range, from mellow base notes to stratospheric trebles. But a note of discord lingered at the back of his mind. Before he suffered his brain tumour, didn't Daniel used to play the guitar?

It was a long time ago and he could be mistaken. Either that or his imagination was playing tricks with him again. The thought did not linger for long. It was not important. What was really important was how happy Emily looked at the end of the performance. For the first time in weeks she was smiling. Something had been found to cheer her up at last.

The couple's next visitor a few days later was Father Michael Keenan. Their dear friend and former priest at St Peter's in Brawton had heard about their sad loss from Fred and Lilian. Now starting to look his age, the grey hair thinning and streaked with white, he'd taken a train, a bus and a taxi to reach them in Wilmslow but was as cheerful and sprightly as ever.

'Finally tracked you all down,' he said with a twinkle as they all shook hands warmly.

Out came the best china tea service and buttered crumpets. They asked how he was and about the homeless shelter at St Peter's. He was 'hanging on' after heart valve replacement surgery. He now had a pig's heart valve in place and had developed an aversion to bacon! As for the shelter, demand for its services was as high as ever. It made no difference which government was in power, the words of Jesus remained forever relevant. 'The poor you shall always have with you.'

Father Michael knew from long experience of counselling the bereaved what sort of questions to expect. In cases of a deceased infant, the first question was always the same: how could a loving God allow the death of an innocent child? His answer was always the same. It was *because* he was a loving God. The child was allowed to die as an act of mercy.

'In his infinite wisdom God knew what lay ahead for Fred if he survived -- some unimaginable tragedy or some chronic disease leaving him handicapped or wheelchair bound. How would he have coped with that -- for the rest of his life? And how would you both have coped with it?'

Emily dabbed her eyes with a handkerchief. She wanted to say they would have managed somehow but was starting to accept that God knew better than she did.

Dawn, holding her mother's hand, asked if Father Michael could be sure that her baby brother was in heaven and that they would meet again when she died. It was an interesting theological question and he did his best to console her as tactfully as possible.

'I am as sure as anyone can be that little

Fred is now in heaven as his soul was entirely without sin. If you live a good life yourself you will spend only a limited time in purgatory on your way to heaven. Then you will meet your little brother again -- and enjoy eternal happiness with our heavenly Father.'

Emily squeezed her daughter's hand. 'So it's up to you, darling.'

Irving thought it best not to dwell on the subject of purgatory, which was central to Roman Catholic doctrine but not to other Christian denominations. Despite all his good intentions to convert, he was still technically a Methodist and for them purgatory played no part in their vision of the afterlife.

When it was time for the priest to leave, Irving insisted on driving him back to Brawton. Still overwhelmed by remorse and in need of spiritual advice himself he took the opportunity to unload all the details of his sordid role in the family's tragedy, including his dalliance with Rita. He hadn't actually committed adultery but he had tried to, which he understood was the same thing. He ended by saying: 'God only knows how desperately sorry I am, Father.'

Father Michael listened patiently to an account of human frailty he had heard so often before during his ministry and sensed Irving's genuine repentance. It would have been sufficient to grant the penitent absolution as part of the usual sacrament of confession. That was not possible as Irving was still not a member of the Catholic Church.

'I hear you Irving but I can't hear your confession in the normal way for obvious reasons. In the absence of formal absolution, I'll pray for God to grant you his forgiveness.' Irving knew that was as much as he could hope for. It was like a heavy weight being lifted from his shoulders. 'Thank you, Father,' he said. Once again he resolved to 'sign up for the real deal'. There could be no more appropriate time than this. Yet he knew from past attempts that when it came to the crunch he'd find an excuse to back out -- like a horse baulking at a formidable fence. Memories still took him back to Brawton Methodist Sunday school with its tiny chairs and pennies dropping into a glass jar. One day he would take the inevitable step -- but not yet.

They drove north through Manchester city centre in silence. Then another line of enquiry occurred to the journalist. 'On the question of purgatory, Father,' he began.

The priest turned to him and beamed. 'You don't believe in it... is that the stumbling block?'

'It's the whole issue of the afterlife that's causing me problems. I've been thinking a lot about quantum physics. The scientists tell us there are many different worlds out there, all with different versions of ourselves in them. It's like a whole new ball game.'

To Irving's surprise Father Michael did not dismiss the line of questioning out of hand. 'You're right, quantum physics is a whole new ball game. Nobody understands it, not even the scientists themselves. Maybe God is rewriting the rules, I don't know...'

'Could the scientists be wrong, do you think?'

The old man laughed heartily. 'It has been known!'

'They say quantum theory is making religion redundant.'

'They would say that, of course. I'm sure God has everything under control. It's more like another method of looking at religion.'

'As if God is revealing himself through science?'

The car had stopped in a traffic jam. Father Michael turned in his seat and faced Irving squarely, looking at him over his gold rimmed spectacles. 'This has to be off the record, Irving. Please don't quote me.'

'Of course not, Father.'

'Purely as speculation I believe God may be revealing himself through quantum physics. The Bible gives us a clue. It tells us: "God exists in all planes at the same time." There's a striking similarity there with parallel universes -- so many different worlds, with God existing in all of them. Many priests I've talked to speculate along similar lines. The Catholic Church, however, does not allow speculation. It demands strict adherence to orthodox teaching. So we all keep our personal opinions to ourselves and concentrate on preaching the Gospel -- our primary function after all.'

TWENTY-TWO

History is written by the winners, as the saying goes. Future historians studying the decade of the 1980s will consult 'newspapers of record' for reliable details of its major news stories. They will evaluate the facts, as the publications' journalists reported them, along with the comments and interpretations of various columnists. Their trust in the integrity and objectivity of these observers will ensure, as far as possible, that they discover the truth of events described. But will they discover the *full* truth?

The 1980s threw up many long-running and deeply controversial events including the Falklands War, the Heysel Stadium disaster with 39 fatalities followed by the tragedy of Hillsborough in which 96 mostly young people died. But no news story defined the decade more powerfully than the miners' strike of 1984/85.

With the benefit of hindsight many historians view the nation's longest-running industrial dispute as the culmination of Margaret Thatcher's class war. After winning the general election of 1979 she began flexing her muscles in a long-running battle against the trade union movement, which she described as 'the enemy within.'

The Russians labelled her 'the Iron Maiden' for her uncompromising leadership style but this unflattering description with its Gothic connotations did not linger long in the UK media. Instead, Conservative Central Office subtly converted it into 'the Iron Lady' thus turning a deep insult into a compliment.

With disingenuousness of this high order at her command, the Iron Lady proceeded to inflict unladylike havoc on a section of society she regarded as her sworn enemy. Her campaign took a sinister turn when trade union offices were found to have been illegally raided by nocturnal spies seeking evidence of subversive activity.

Adam Richardson reported that even the Manchester office of the NUJ had been targeted by spooks using duplicate keys, carelessly leaving documents disturbed. What could they have possibly been looking for? The answer was: nothing, it was just a warning that the journalists were under surveillance.

The Iron Lady raised the stakes when it came to the miners. She famously likened them to the enemy in the Falklands War. There was no doubt in her mind that, as such, they had to be defeated. The inevitable trial of strength arrived in March 1984 when the loss-making National Coal Board announced plans to cut coal output by 4 million tons. As a result 20 collieries would be closed with the loss of 20,000 jobs.

Faced with this draconian threat to their members' livelihoods and the prospect of further widespread decimation of their industry, the National Union of Mineworkers had little option but to call a nationwide strike. By April 136,000 miners were on strike, closing 132 collieries across Britain, although several pits remained open in the Midlands.

As the dispute became increasingly bitter some of the most violent clashes between strikers and police occurred at the British Steel Corporations' coking plant at Orgreave, in Rotherham, South Yorkshire. Thousands of extra police were drafted in from forces throughout the country and Arthur Scargill, general secretary of the NUM, led 7,000 pickets laying siege to the plant. With battle lines obviously being drawn up, national newspapers reinforced their presence with additional reporters. Among them were Irving Breen and his left-wing colleague, Dave Leonard.

Sniffing out the real human stories behind the dispute, as they had been taught, the pair heard harrowing accounts of wives and children suffering from the miners' loss of income. Although their families united in self-support groups they faced widespread delays in receiving state aid for acute hardship and it was no exaggeration to say that many victims were on the brink of starvation.

Irving and Dave were billeted at a guest house in Rotherham. After covering the day's dramas around the coking plant and using the house telephone to file joint reports including casualty figures provided by both sides, they watched the evening television coverage of the dispute. Some of the police brutality they had earlier witnessed on the picket lines was conspicuous by its absence. A TV cameraman also lodging with them said it was the policy of the programme makers to edit out scenes of explicit violence as they would be likely to upset viewers.

The following day, 18th June 1984, turned out to be the day of the Battle of Orgreave, one of the most brutal clashes in British industrial history. Viewers were not only upset but horrified by the violence even after heavy editing. The massed ranks of thousands of heavily armoured riot police charged the crowds of pickets in jeans and T-shirts, armed only with sticks, stones and bottles.

After vicious hand-to-hand fighting the outnumbered pickets were scattered in disarray. They were chased by mounted police, seemingly out of control and lashing out indiscriminately with their batons. Arthur Scargill was among the miners knocked unconscious. The conflict spilled on to the Orgreave village streets where even onlookers found themselves under attack by the 'cavalry'.

One of the unlisted casualties was Irving himself. A charging police horse threw up a small stone that caught him on the forehead. It caused a tiny cut with slight bleeding. He dabbed it with a handkerchief and grinned: 'Occupational hazard.'

Both journalists were overwhelmed by the savagery they had observed. They filed vivid reports of the battle with Irving describing it as 'open warfare with blood everywhere' without mentioning that some of it was his. Dave's verdict was more trenchant. The battle had been 'legalised state brutality against its own citizens'. There could be no doubt about the outcome, however. The strike would drag on for months but the miners had lost their fight to save their jobs and their communities. The Iron Maiden had won her class war.

The reporters' landlady insisted on bathing Irving's 'wound' and applying a small circular plaster. 'We'll never forgive our police for this day,' she said vehemently. 'The terrible thing is that they were not all real coppers.'

Irving pricked up his ears. 'How do you mean?'

'Our lad Chris is a miner. He was there today.'

'Not injured, I hope?'

'Not badly no, but he got the shock of his life. A so-called policeman hit him with his truncheon and Chris just fought back. As they rolled on the ground Chris caught a glimpse of the man's face -- it was his brother, Matthew!'

'How odd.'

'It was more than that. Our Matthew has never been a policeman. He's in the Army.'

The significance of what she was saying took a couple of seconds to register. Had the government dressed up soldiers as police officers to strengthen their fighting force? Had he stumbled on an exclusive?

'Is Chris here now?' he asked.

'Yes, he's upstairs. I'll call him.'

Irving signalled to Dave who was watching events on television and his colleague joined him. 'It seems some of the police officers may have been troops in disguise. The landlady's son Chris was there. He's coming to talk to us. I'll ask the questions. You take a note.'

The landlady performed the introductions. 'Chris, these gentlemen, Dave and Irving, are reporters from the Daily Telegraph. They were at Orgreave today and witnessed everything.'

Chris was about 20, bearded, short and stocky, the build of a miner. He shook hands and they sat round the dining room table. He seemed utterly dejected.

'Do you want to tell them what you told me?' his mother asked.

'I can't Mum. It'll get us all into trouble.'

'You can speak to us in complete confidence, Chris,' Irving said. 'No need for names. You'll just be referred to as a miner or one of the pickets.'

'It's not just me it's my brother as well. He's in the Yorkshire Regiment. He's signed the Official Secrets Act. He could be court-martialled for blowing his cover.'

'There's no danger of that. Both you and your brother will be fully protected. As professional journalists we never reveal our sources of information under any circumstances.'

'What if they *made* you -- under duress?'

'Many journalists have gone to prison to protect their sources. So would we.'

Dave looked up from his shorthand notebook. 'I endorse that, Chris. Your identity is safe with us.'

'Can you guarantee that -- for all of us?'

Irving showed Chris his NUJ Press card. 'We're trade unionists like you. As members of the National Union of Journalists we guarantee complete anonymity for you and all your family.'

Chris finally relaxed. 'Well, I can tell you it fair shook me up. This copper came at me with his truncheon -- hit me on the shoulder. So I punched him -- it were self-defence. His visor came loose and I saw his face. It were our Matt.'

'You are sure it was your brother?'

'Course I'm sure. I know my own brother. He said: "I'm sorry, Chris... they made us do it." Then he said: "Run like hell." So I did.'

'Sounds like there were more of them. Have you heard of any other bogus coppers?

'No, not likely to. People are too scared to say anything in case they bring the tanks out next.'

Dave stopped writing and said: 'Thank you Chris. You've made a very important contribution.'

'Won't save our jobs though, will it? We're finished... all washed up.' He strode out of the room, followed by his mother.

'This is big, Dave,' Irving said after a pause.

His colleague smiled thinly. 'What's the betting they spike it?'

Spike it they did, of course. In the following days Irving and Dave could find no corroboration for Chris's disturbing revelation. Most people they spoke to felt they knew what was going on but were too scared to talk on the record or even off it.

In a response to a reported leaked complaint to the Daily Telegraph, the Defence Department held a Press conference in Manchester when a spokesman demanded to know the source of the outlandish allegation. Naturally, Irving declined to comply with the demand despite threats of dire consequences levelled at all whistleblowers.

Since no witnesses were prepared to come forward the department could take no further action, the mouthpiece added. He categorically 'refuted' (another shyster abusing the word) the allegation and condemned the paper's 'irresponsible' reliance on conspiracy theories. These were based on nothing more than rumour and hearsay. Given time they would fade into folklore.

Future historians carrying out research into the Battle of Orgreave would have no time for folklore. They'd study newspapers of record and discover the official government's version of the truth, which was:

'It was an act of self-defence by police who had come under attack. The police were upholding the law in the face of intimidation from thousands of strikers.'

That's how it was, folks. Take it or leave it.

TWENTY-THREE

Irving had his own personal legacy of the historic miners' strike. The cut on his forehead caused by the stone chipping thrown up by the police horse soon healed. But it left a small scar above his left eye. It was almost imperceptible except when he shaved. When he turned the light on above his bathroom mirror there it was attracting attention as if trying to tell him something. He'd almost forgotten the misgivings he used to have about his facial appearance but now they resurfaced more powerfully.

You'd think after all this time he'd accept it was just so much fanciful nonsense, his imagination playing tricks, which was how Emily described it. He was still a handsome dude, she'd say and he had to admit she had a point. He stroked his smooth chin as he shaved. Not bad for a middle aged newshound, perhaps a bit fuller in the cheeks and round the eyes. Then he came to the tiny scar and that was when his moment of truth finally arrived.

Below the scar towards the side of his eye *there was something missing.*

It still made no kind of sense. But then, in

a long overdue flash of enlightenment, it came to him: didn't he once have a natural birthmark there... a tiny, heart shaped brown birthmark? Of course. It was his beauty spot, as Emily called it. Now there was no sign of it. But birthmarks couldn't just disappear. You were stuck with them for life.

He returned to his room and sat down heavily on the bed. One more mystery. One more sleepless night, his mind in turmoil. Then the penny finally dropped. Fantastic though it seemed, the birthmark must have been in another life. People often said light heartedly that in another life they were different in some way. He felt light headed, lay back on the bed and closed his eyes. What did it all mean? Could it be that in a parallel universe he'd had a tiny, brown heart shaped birthmark next to his left eye? Had some metaphysical force propelled him into a different multiverse, losing his birthmark in the process?

All right, it was way out, far-fetched speculation but it would explain everything. It started with Daniel's logic-defying recovery from brain cancer. All the family had prayed for a miracle and a miracle happened. Everyone agreed on that. Even the most sceptical doctors admitted they had never seen anything like it. So that must be how miracles happen. You pray for one and if your prayer is answered you're transported into a different multiverse *where the desired outcome exists but other things are different.*

Other things were certainly different. There was the bizarre spectacle of Jamie knocking in breaks of 50-plus at snooker when his previous breaks had been confined to single figures. No amount of secret practising could have transformed his game in so short a period. Also deeply strange was his friend's sudden change from a diehard Manchester United supporter to a 'true blue' Manchester City fan. In a city where football was virtually a religion that sort of conversion just did not happen.

Which led to the mind-boggling transformation of the Manchester City team itself. After decades of mediocrity, a laughing stock of soccer, they became unbeatable champions almost overnight. There was no way even the most fanatical City supporters could have dreamt that up in their wildest dreams. It was out of this world -- literally!

Almost as strange was the performance of the England cricket team, for so long a source of national embarrassment. Suddenly the team started winning. Not just one Test match but a whole series including the Ashes. Cricket lovers wondered if they were living in a different world. Which, of course, they were!

Even the baffling mystery of Popsie was resolved. Nana's pet was a cat in one multiverse and a dog in another. There was clearly a metaphysical wit at work. Also explained was a non-smoking Rita and Trevor Unwin speaking 'in tongues' -- southern accent one minute broad Lancashire the next.

Everything had fallen into place like one of those giant jigsaw puzzles that took years to solve. This was a puzzle that had baffled scientific and theological minds for centuries. The excitement of being on the brink of a mind-boggling discovery made him light-headed and he began to sweat profusely.

If quantum physics explained miracles surely it held the key to life after death.

Eureka was the only word for it.

It called at the very least for champagne. He'd break open a bottle and share the world-shattering discovery with Emily. Fred could be alive in another multiverse. Might it be possible to reach him and hold him in their arms? He sprang from the bed and rushed downstairs in excitement. But as eureka moments go, his didn't last long. Before he'd opened the bottle, the spoiler kicked in. According to the quantum scientists, movement between multiverses was not possible.

Yet it had happened to him. Strangeness ruled the quantum world in every sense. There was even an electromagnetic particle called a *strangeness.* How strange it would be if he were to prove the scientists wrong -- as Father Michael suspected. He replaced the unopened bottle in the wine rack. It was a case of back to the drawing board. He needed to take Grandpa's advice and learn some more big words -- return to the library and persevere with his research into this infuriating enigma.

In the lounge Emily was playing a particularly beautiful classic the name of which eluded him for the moment. He waited until she'd finished then asked her its title. It was Elgar's *Enigma Variations*. He shivered. How weird was that? The quantum gods, if such existed, were not only the most perverse of all time they also had a wicked sense of humour. With an effort he brushed the strangeness aside. 'Bravo, darling. You really should be playing with the Halle Orchestra, you know.'

Emily smiled appreciatively. Her music had worked wonders on her mental state since the dark days of Fred's stillbirth. She dressed in cheerful light coloured frocks and had her hair permed regularly. She refused to have it dyed, insisting the grey and fair hairs should blend naturally. The effect was that in middle age she was still as strikingly beautiful as in her youth.

She closed the keyboard lid and rose from the piano stool. 'It just so happens that I may do that one day. I've been offered an audition with the BBC in Manchester next month. They phoned this morning.'

He knew she'd been sending out performance tapes for some time without success. 'That's great news, Emily. I've always said you were a natural. Your playing matches that of any professional.'

They relaxed together on the settee. She had not looked so happy for a long time. She held his hand. 'You've been very quiet today. What have you been up to?'

'I'm struggling with an enigma of my own. I've been racking my brains about quantum physics and every time I think I've cracked it I find I've just lost the plot!'

It took another three months and several visits to Manchester Central Library's science section before Irving believed he had retrieved the plot, this being the primitive pre-Google information era. Each day before his research began in earnest he studied all the daily newspapers out of habit, their science pages in particular.

Startling advances in computer technology were making the headlines. The latest sensation in America was the development of artificial intelligence capable of challenging the human mind at the highest level. It included rapid single flux quantum (RSFQ) superconductors able to resolve deep logical and philosophical differences. Advanced examples of the runaway technology could be controlled by the human voice, but what Irving found most staggering was the prospect of high-powered quantum devices that responded to human thought.

It sounded like an electronic version of metaphysics in action. If you thought of something with sufficient energy you had a chance to make it happen. 'Fantastic' didn't come close. It was like something out of Alice in Quantumland, a book he'd read in his vain quest for enlightenment. The possibility of movement between universes clicked into credibility at a stroke.

It appeared that what needed to be moved was mind, not matter. There was a fascinating parallel in the world of finance. Take the case of an automatic transfer of money from one bank account to another. No cash actually moves. All that happens is a change in the balances of the respective accounts due to an electronic impulse. In a similar way a transfer of cerebral energy between characters in different multiverses could change minds and identities.

There was no stronger example of intense mental energy than prayer -- as miracles down the centuries demonstrated. What if all you had to do in the modern age was pray hard enough and a keystroke on the celestial supercomputer known as God could make it happen? The uplifting concept helped to restore Irving's flagging morale. His dogged endeavours were beginning to pay off. After centuries of scorn and mockery by cynical atheists the power of prayer had come into its own, bright and shining in its new cloak of scientific respectability.

In his new more sanguine mood he felt his research had taken him far enough to explain his theories to Emily, who'd become as curious as he was.

Armed with photo-copies of the relevant newspaper articles and two helpful reference books, he chose a sunny afternoon on his day off to join her beneath their garden parasol.

Eying the documentation, Emily put aside her Daily Telegraph crossword. 'Let me guess. This is something to do with the uncertainty principle?'

'Right first time. I've done more research and I think I might have cracked it. Quantum physics is all about uncertainty. It might explain things such as ESP, déjà vu and intuition. In scientific terms the bottom line is mind boggling -- a beam of light focused on one of two targets. The moment you look at it it changes direction from one target to the other!'

Emily was sceptical. 'Nobody touching any switches or anything?'

'Nothing like that. In laboratory conditions. No deception involved. A high powered beam of photons minding its own business until it's observed by humans when it reacts... spooky or what!'

'Almost as if it's trying to tell you something,' Emily said intuitively.

'That's exactly right. Scientists are busting a gut to find out what.'

'Have they come up with anything?'

'Yes -- parallel universes. Don't ask me how... higher mathematics and Max Planck. There are literally millions of universes out there as well as ours.

They're called multiverses and there are people in them -- mirror images of ourselves -- but other things are different.'

'Can they prove it?' `

'Not yet but I can!'

'Well hello, Einstein!'

'Seriously, I've come to the conclusion we've switched from one multiverse into another.'

'Is *that* all... what makes you so sure?'

'I feel different. I know you think I don't look different but I've worked out what was wrong with my face. I used to have a birthmark next to my eye but I don't now.'

'I don't remember you ever having a birth-mark.'

'That's because you've no memory of our other life. I *have!*'

'It all sounds whacky to me, Irving. You sure you've not been working too hard?'

'Think about it, Emily. Do you feel any differ-ent now to the way you used to? Has there been any change in your life that you can't explain?"

His wife's expression of tolerant disbelief slowly dissolved. A light breeze had sprung up and surrounding trees were stirring gently. They seemed to reflect her wavering feelings. Reason told her to dismiss what he was saying as beyond weird. But he'd touched a nerve. Something had, in fact, changed. Something she couldn't explain.

'Since you mention it, I *have* noticed something... my playing technique, the dynamics have improved dramatically. My rubato and my phrasing are more sensitive and una corda, that used to be a closed book, has opened my eyes. I know it sounds crazy but there are times when I feel the composer is guiding my hands... '

It was exactly what Irving needed. 'That clinches it for me, Emily. We've all made a quantum leap without knowing it. Completely painless. All I've lost is a birthmark.'

'I still can't believe it. It's incredible.'

'I know but it explains everything -- things that have been puzzling me for ages. It even explains miracles. Remember when Daniel had his brain tumour and the doctors said it was terminal -- that nothing could save him?'

'I remember it only too well.'

'What did we all do?'

'We prayed to God.'

'That's right. We prayed for a miracle. And we got one. The very next day your brother was sitting up in bed drinking a cup of tea.'

'I agree that was a miracle. But only God can

perform miracles.'

'I'm not disputing that. All I'm saying is that quantum physics shows how miracles happen. We're zapped into another dimension where what we wish for exists but other things are different.'

'The zapping... that would still be an act of God?'

'Of course. God's still driving the car. We just think we know how the engine works.'

Emily was almost convinced.   'It's just so weird but it feels like it could be true.'

'If you remember, Daniel began to recover the very next day. There was a tropical storm during the night. You slept through it but it was like a cosmic firework display. That was our miracle happening. It was us being zapped!'

`It's starting to sound like a real scoop, Irving!'

'Not really. It has no news value at the moment -- it's just a theory. It would only make the news if it won something like the Nobel Prize for science.'

'Maybe it will!'

He laughed. 'No way. There's a big problem. The scientists say all multiverses are self-contained. It's impossible to move from one into another.'

She sat up straight and pushed back her hair.

'But you've proved them wrong haven't you. You've done it. We've both done it.'

'Yes but they need empirical evidence, something that can be proved in an experiment. All we've got is anecdotal evidence. It's not enough. For scientists to accept anything you have to give them facts that can be tested and measured rather than just theory.'

Emily sighed deeply and stood up. 'I'll make some tea.'

The afternoon had cooled down in the breeze so they withdrew to the kitchen and drank their tea. He put on his reading glasses and picked up one of the books. 'This book is mostly about singularities and partial wave duality... it's heavy going but it comes to a startling conclusion. It says the world *does not so much exist as happen.* It's *happening* all the time. We don't notice but nothing's quite the same moment to moment.'

'Bizarre!'

'I know, it takes some thinking about. But then you ask the question: why do things keep happening?'

'Does it tell you?'

'No but I've got my own idea. Things can't happen on their own. Something *makes* them happen.'

'Go on then Einstein, tell me what it is.'

'The power of prayer.' He turned to the photo-copies. 'There will soon be such things as quantum computers that can respond to human thought. No touch control or even voice control. All you do is think something and it can happen. Mind over matter in electronic form. It's the perfect explanation for the power of prayer. If we can do things by thinking about it on our natural level, then God can do the same at a supernatural level -- move our conscious identities, our human souls, between multiverses.'

'In response to prayers.'

'Exactly. And as prayers are being offered up across the world all the time that's why the world's happening all the time.'

'So every time a prayer is answered it changes the lives of the recipients... but everyone else feels nothing?'

'That's the theory, yes.'

She leaned back and clasped her hands behind her head. 'I'd go along with that, Irving, but I can see why scientists wouldn't.'

He turned to the remaining book. 'This one's different. It's called Quantumanity. The author says all space is permeated by force 'fields' -- neutron, electro magnetic, gravitational and quantum. What religion describes as the human soul could be a quantum life form entwined with our genetics. When we die the life form leaves the body and returns to the quantum field from where it came...'

'You've lost me, Irving.'

'What he seems to be saying is that the quantum force field may be another name for purgatory.'

He topped up their cups and sat back in silence. Emily stirred her tea thoughtfully. As a devout Catholic, purgatory was a half-way house to heaven. It was a place of penance where souls went to be purified on their journey. Some had to spend more time there than others. For the worst offenders it would be a lot more time.

Irving sensed her unease. 'It's different names for the same place. The quantum interpretation is that when we die we get another chance to come back and go round again ... correct our mistakes and remove the guilt. That's not a million miles away from Catholic purgatory is it?'

It began to make a kind of theological sense to Emily. If the object of the exercise was to cleanse yourself of your sins then there was hardly any difference between the two interpretations. 'So we live our lives over and over until we get it right -- is that what he's saying?'

'That's about it.'

'What if we keep getting it wrong?

'We keep going round on the eternal carousel until we learn not to.'

'Some are going to take an awful lot longer than others.'

'Tell me about it... I meet them every day!'

'Then finally we're ready for heaven?'

'That's the theory. You could say God's like a celestial scientist conducting an experiment. So science and religion are not so far apart after all.'

It had all started to make sense, Emily thought. 'You've done your homework on this Irving but I think we should talk to Father Michael.'

'Fair enough.' He removed his glasses, leaned forward and kissed her gently on the lips. 'You know the reason I'm doing this, don't you... the real reason?'

'It's to do with Fred, isn't it?'

'Yes, in another multiverse he could be alive, you see.'

Tears filled her eyes. 'But he might not be, even if we could get there.'

He gripped her hand tightly. 'If we could have got you to the hospital in time... if only I'd been here...' He broke off as a lump formed in his throat.

She clasped both her hands round his. 'The doctor said there was only a one per cent chance, remember?'

'That's one chance in a hundred. If there were

a hundred multiverses, he'd be alive in one of them. But there are millions!'

'Darling, let's not torment ourselves. We've been through enough already.'

He struggled to fight back the tears. 'I'm sorry.'

'Let's ask Father Michael, darling. If your theory is right, maybe when we die and go round again it might all be different... next time.'

As Father Michael had taken over two hours on public transport when he'd visited them, Irving and Emily decided to drive to St Peter's presbytery in Brawton for the next meeting with the elderly priest. It was a Sunday and they attended the evening Mass. It was the first time they'd been to Mass together since the trauma of Fred's stillbirth and Emily found it a deeply cathartic experience. Drying her eyes, she resolved to resume playing the organ at St Oswald's and cut down her cigarette smoking. Irving was also moved by the healing power of the ritualistic Mass. He took part earnestly in all the prayers although he still could not receive Communion.

Afterwards Father Michael ushered them into his comfortable quarters adjoining the church and they took their seats in the living room. It was exactly the way they remembered it all those years ago although the beige carpet was showing signs of wear along with the ancient three-piece suite. His housekeeper always had Sunday night off so he made coffee himself and served it with chocolate biscuits on a glass-topped coffee table.

'So tell me what's on your mind.'

Irving explained his limited understanding of quantum physics -- that the world did not so much exist as happen and what made things happen was the power of prayer. Father Michael thought it was an offbeat way of putting things but did not disagree. After that it became more complicated. When miracles were explained as a quantum leap between multiverses it seemed like an intrusion into the divinity of the Creator and was asking for trouble.

On the thorny problem of purgatory, he was prepared to allow some leeway. Catholic teaching was adamant that it was another dimension in which departed souls were purified on their way to heaven. He'd thought long and hard about it and believed quantum theory might be an acceptable scientific interpretation. You needed to pray for the souls making their way through purgatory and you could still do that for quantum life forms making the same journey.

Irving concluded his argument by saying: 'I firmly believe God is making himself known through quantum physics and that, far from being mutually exclusive, science and religion are in fact complementary.'

There was a heavy silence while Father Michael polished his spectacles before responding. Then with impeccable timing he said: 'Follow that!' They all smiled and lightened up.

'Is God revealing himself through quantum physics? It's a good question and you've made a powerful case in favour, Irving. In the Bible Jesus himself tells us: "Ye must be born again" and "In my Father's house are many mansions"-- both of which could be interpreted as portents of parallel universes.

'I've discussed these interpretations in depth with my bishop and he regards them as heretical. I can't say I'm surprised. But some fellow progressive Catholics seem to be quite favourable. In theory -- and strictly off the record -- yes, parallel universes may be God's way of answering prayer. After we die, we may get another chance to live our lives again and avoid making the same mistakes. I believe that God as a merciful and loving father would go along with that.'

Seeing that Irving was about to interrupt, the priest held up his hand. 'But when it comes to moving from one universe to another while we're still alive then that sounds more like science fiction to me.'

'Excuse me, Father, but we've all made the

quantum leap without knowing -- all of us, you included,' Irving said. 'Can I ask you to cast your mind back over the last few months... do you feel any different now to the way you did? Has there been any major change in your life... anything you can't explain... anything totally unexpected?'

Father Michael smiled patiently. 'Life for a parish priest can be very much a routine business... baptisms, weddings, funerals. But now you mention it there was something quite extraordinary. One of our parishioners won a lot of money on a TV quiz show -- and donated half of it to our church roof fund. Twenty thousand pounds! We've got a whole new roof -- completely waterproof! It was the answer to prayer obviously.'

'Sounds like a miracle, Father,' Emily said.

'You could say that -- a minor miracle certainly. We'd all been praying for it for years -- every time it rained, in fact!'

It was all the evidence Irving needed. 'I rest my case, Father. Thank you for listening.'

There was another long silence. Father Michael removed his spectacles, rubbed his eyes and sighed. He knew there was an underlying reason for his guests' visit.

It emerged almost at once. Emily said: 'We have to ask you Father. If there are so many other worlds out there and they're all different in some way, is it possible Fred might be alive in one of them? And if we prayed hard enough might God allow us to see him?'

The priest had tired of a discussion that bordered uncomfortably on heresy. But he knew how important the question was to the bereaved couple. 'I do feel for you both and I pray for you often. All things are possible to God. But your son's soul is at rest now with the holy angels and my advice is to let things be while you're still alive. When you die I think there's a good chance of a happy reunion with him, one way or another. You should pray for that and I will offer up Mass for God to hear your prayers.'

Emily sensed the old man's weariness. 'Thank you, Father. And God bless.'

He placed his spectacles in their case and returned it to his jacket pocket. 'And God bless both of you, my dears. We're living in an uncertain world. Quantum physics is itself based on uncertainty so we can't be certain of anything. We need to keep an open mind and pray for guidance. God will help us to understand if we ask him.'

TWENTY-FOUR

The spanking new red tiled roof at St Peter's with its small white cross and waterproof coving for the Mass bell clinched Irving's theory of the parallel universe they were all living in. It was the latest addition to his growing list of phenomena that began with Daniel's miracle, taking in the startling transmogrification of a cat into a dog and an accomplished performance of *Ave Maria* on clarinet by a guitarist avidly into rock 'n roll.

The list just kept getting longer. He heard on the office grapevine that Godfrey Myers' son had been misdiagnosed with paranoid schizophrenia as a result of a mix-up with a patient of the same name. He had narrowly avoided being sectioned and had since been discharged. In another world he could have been locked away for months.

At this point Irving decided to convert his list into a properly written-up dossier for consideration by more scientific minds than his. All right, the evidence was anecdotal and circumstantial but there was too much of it to be dismissed for those reasons. There comes a time when the cumulative weight of anecdotal evidence makes it compelling. He needed the advice of Prof Jordon about submitting it to a higher echelon of theoretical physicists.

Meanwhile, Emily was blossoming as a concert pianist. The BBC offered her a recital at its Manchester studios with options of future performances on Radio Three, its highbrow culture channel. A late developer, she decided it was time to take driving lessons, pass the driving test and buy her own car. His wife, whose broken spirit languished not long ago in the depths of depression, was on a roll.

She was not the only one. Goldspur, the Telegraph's racing tipster whose success rate was a constant source of embarrassment to the paper's owners, suddenly hit a winning streak. In his own Manchester City-style revival he churned out a series of big race winners -- some at lucrative prices -- for several weeks throughout the Flat season. The paper's circulation shot up. All was forgiven.

Irving was not slow to take advantage. His turf account with the bookmakers William Hill, for so long in the doldrums, took on an altogether healthier appearance. Some of Goldspur's selections went down like the old days but his winners came in at such outrageous prices it was like living in a different world -- literally!

Emily and Irving touched on the subject briefly on one of his days off. They were sitting on their patio on a blissful summer afternoon under a Mediterranean blue sky, drinking tea and eating strawberries and cream. Fred's memorial rose tree was in glorious bloom and the wide expanse of lawn had been freshly mown by their visiting gardener. A gentle breeze stirred Dawn's prized display of forget-me-nots and dahlias. Background music came courtesy of their resident blackbird which had a range of improvisation on a par with Charlie Parker.

Emily was going through a stack of bank statements before turning her attention to the Telegraph crossword. 'I didn't know we were paying money to the World Health Organisation,' she said, pointing to an entry for £25 in favour of 'WHO.'

Irving, who was applying the finishing touches to his dossier before submitting it to Prof Jordon for his opinion, thought for a moment then smiled. It was a nice idea but he needed to correct her. 'It's not the World Health Organisation, darling, it's the William Hill Organisation!'

She saw the funny side. 'That's all right then. For a moment I thought we might be wasting our money!'

She knew he was well ahead with the bookmaker. At such times you didn't query your husband's gambling habit. You made the most of his luck while it lasted. She took up her crossword and studied it at length. 'Some of these clues really are very clever. How about this one: MEAT IN GRAVIES, anagram, one word, 13 letters.'

He scribbled the words on his notepad. Then scribbled their letters in a different order.

'You've lost me,' he said at length. 'All I can get out of that is MIGRAINE -- and it's starting to give me one!'

'I'll give you a clue. It begins with a V... '

He scribbled some more. Then it clicked. 'VEGETARIANISM! How cute is that! It's straight out of my quantum dossier!'

'Here's another good one: Wicked light, six letters, ending in E.'

He thought long and hard. He scribbled synonyms from his extensive vocabulary but it was no use. 'I could struggle all day and never get it,' he admitted.

'CANDLE!'

He thought about it. 'Now that really *is* wicked!'

'You just need some lateral thinking. It's a great help. And remember what the words 'GREAT HELP' spell another way?'

How could he forget? 'TELEGRAPH of course!'

He collected his copious dossier together but before packing it in the documents case he scribbled a few words on his notepad: Lateral thinking -- could come in useful in cracking the quantum enigma.

The polarisation of British society was neatly encapsulated at Manchester University's assembly hall on the day of Dawn Breen's graduation ceremony. The richest man in the country and possibly the poorest were both present. They were sitting a few feet apart separated only by the building's brick wall -- the beggar huddled on the pavement, the titled multi-billionaire on the hall's platform along with the lecturers in their regalia. All the beggar possessed on a raw November morning was his thin ragged clothes and a battered tin mug with nothing in it. The ageing, morbidly obese aristocrat on the platform owned large chunks of London, half of Salford and a quarter of Scotland.

Known variously as the Duke of Cayman, the Duke of Jersey or the Duke of Liechtenstein, depending on which of his tax havens was under discussion, the duke had a reputation for ruthlessness in business dealings. Competitors did not compete for long. Some were forced into bankruptcy and one had been the victim of a mysterious accident involving a car with faulty brakes. But the magnate had made a donation of half a million pounds to the university (approximately 0.05 per cent of his gross wealth) and, despite his unsavoury image, it followed that he should be invited to present the students with their awards.

Perched high in the gallery, Irving and Emily

watched and waited as several hundred students marched up the steps to the platform to collect their scrolls (the actual degrees would follow later) tied with blue ribbons. The dark suited billionaire began the distribution at a brisk rate while standing but whether it was the unaccustomed action of repeatedly giving something away or the heat from the floodlights, after a time he began to wilt. As the procession of students lengthened, he sat down and asked for a glass of water. Then, dabbing his forehead with a handkerchief, he continued the arduous task while seated.

Finally it was Dawn's turn. The slim dramatic arts student, fair hair tucked under her mortar board, black gown flapping, waved to her parents as she mounted the steps and promptly stumbled. She recovered her poise but the perspiring capitalist, slumped in his chair, had noticed. Presenting her with her scroll, he patted her arm reassuringly. Dawn smiled and stroked his shoulder in return. There was nothing patronising about either gesture. They were acts of mutual sympathy and the old codger briefly applauded. The audience lapped it up. There it was in full view, dramatic arts in microcosm.

Up in the gallery Irving and Emily stood and applauded loudly. They knew how much their daughter's degree meant to her and her plans for a career in the theatre. They also knew how hard she'd worked to acquire it and the pressure her brother's stillbirth had inflicted on her .During the run-up to her finals she had grappled with the horrors of clinical depression which would have seen off a less tenacious student.

After a mercifully brief speech by the vice-chancellor on the power of learning and the need for hard work, self-discipline and perseverance to achieve the sort of success in life embodied by their distinguished guest -- without mentioning the equal importance of milking taxpayers on a cosmic scale -- the ceremony concluded with all the newly appointed graduates hurling their mortar boards skywards in the traditional manner.

'Thank God there was no national anthem,' Irving said as everyone trooped off for refreshments. He always made a point of sitting throughout the anthem while those around, including Emily, stood up. It invariably led to friction between them and occasionally with others who deemed it disrespectful. He'd long since given up on pointing out what was really disrespectful -- the gross poverty imposed on the masses by a ruling class presided over by the monarch.

To illustrate the point the beggar was still there when Irving, Emily and Dawn crossed the quadrangle on the way to the refectory for the buffet reception. Dawn dropped some coins in his tin mug. He gave her a big smile, reached out and gently tapped her arm in thanks. She smiled back. It wasn't every day you were touched by the richest man in the country and by the poorest.

They queued with their trays in the cafeteria along with a milling crowd of graduates and lecturers still wearing their robes and gowns. A saxophone soloist was playing a selection of Gershwin classics with the sort of mellow modulation Stan Getz himself would have approved. All very civilised. They chose coffee, croissants and celebratory waffles with maple syrup for Dawn. Today at least she'd ditch her diet.

Moments after taking their seats at a corner table the swish of a fur-trimmed gown announced the presence of a senior academic. It was Prof Frank Jordon, lecturer in science and astrophysics, one of the platform academics and Irving's long-standing contact for stories on scientific matters.

Still dynamic and youthful looking despite some grey hairs in his light beard, the professor was carrying a tray bearing tea and pizza. 'Hello Irving, mind if I join you?'

Irving gestured to an empty chair. 'Please do, professor. You're the very man I needed to see.'

With introductions completed the academic tucked into his brunch. 'I spotted you in the gallery. As you weren't with the Press I realised you must be here on personal business, so congratulations to you Dawn on your dramatic arts degree.'

Dawn smiled modestly but Emily could not contain her pride. Without going into the more traumatic details she filled him in on the struggle her daughter had had to achieve her degree. The professor was impressed. 'Sometimes we lecturers fail to realise our students' emotional problems. At other times we underestimate their strength of character.' He turned to Dawn. 'You'll go far, my dear, you're a natural. Enjoyed your little moment with the duke... the old boy took it well, I thought.'

'He can afford to, can't he?' Emily said.

'Yes, of course. I know it's only a drop in the ocean to him but half a million's a lot of money to us. Beggars can't be choosers.'

Irving thought of the beggar outside. He felt like saying he'd have refused the money if he was the vice-chancellor but he wanted to talk to the astrophysicist about parallel universes not politics. He'd brought his carefully prepared dossier of metaphysical evidence intending to leave it with the professor's secretary but far better to strike while the iron was hot. He opened the documents case and extracted the dossier. 'I've been meaning to contact you for some advice, professor.'

'Frank, please. Are we on or off the record?'

'Off. This is for my own personal research. We've talked before about quantum physics and I've read a few books on the subject but I have to admit I'm not much wiser.'

The professor swallowed a mouthful of pizza and wiped his mouth on a paper napkin. 'Join the club, Irving! We've got accelerators hurling sub-atomic particles across high-powered magnets throughout the world and we're still going nowhere. All we know for sure is that parallel universes exist and that nothing can pass between them -- photons, neutrons, kitchen sinks... '

'What about consciousness... human mental energy?'

'Nothing. They're all hermetically sealed for want of a better expression.'

'There've been some startling advances in computer technology in America. They suggest the power of mind over matter might help solve the problem.'

'Yes maybe there's a new rulebook on the horizon. We certainly need one. Quantum theory has thrown our old Bible out of the window!'

The saxophonist started playing *It Ain't Necessarily So* and Prof Jordon leant back in his chair and laughed. 'Well I'm blowed. How about that for coincidence...? Used to know the lyrics but I've forgotten them...'

Dawn came to his assistance. Gershwin had been one of her major subjects in the musical theatre syllabus 'It's from the opera Porgy and Bess. 'It goes:

The things that you're liable,

to read in the Bible,

it ain't necessarily so...'

When the song ended, they gave the saxophonist a spontaneous round of applause. He looked pleased and surprised. People were actually listening to his performance.

'That says it all,' the lecturer said. 'Quantum physics is sending us all back to the drawing board. It's broadened the definition of physics, given it a whole new meaning. In fact, I'm beginning to wonder if it's physics at all.'

Once again Irving had been intrigued by the musical nudge the others regarded as coincidence. The wit was clearly driven by a superior intelligence. But Prof Jordon seemed to be making a concession and he needed to respond. 'I think it's more to do with metaphysics.'

'You could be right. Something's going on that defies rational thought about our existence in time and space -- about our selfhood. Identical versions of ourselves in other dimensions pose questions about genetic code. I mean might they all share the same DNA as us -- like identical twins?'

Irving had swotted up on his philosophy, particularly Karl Jung. 'Maybe it's all in the mind rather than the DNA. The more I research this mystery the more I'm convinced we need to look at it from a different angle.'

'You're in good company. Albert Einstein

said, and I quote: "No problem can be solved from the same level of consciousness that created it." So it seems we need to move away from a linear model to a higher level of consciousness...'

'Like metaphysics? Could the key to open these impenetrable multiverses be found in lateral thinking? If normal keys don't fit the lock why not try paranormal ones?' Irving reached for his dossier of paranormal evidence. 'I've compiled some notes that might interest you, Frank. They make a strong case to show we've *already* switched multiverses in our minds at least-- all of us, you included.'

The professor drained his cold tea and took the neatly bound dossier. 'That's fighting talk, Irving!' He flicked through its pages. 'You've been busy, I can see. I'll certainly read it all carefully and I'll run it past my colleagues for their opinion.'

Emily and Dawn excused themselves. They needed the powder room and Dawn wanted to say goodbye to a fellow graduate before she emigrated to Canada.

Irving had been waiting to ask the scientist the same question he'd asked Father Michael. 'I need to ask you, if I may, whether there's been any startling change in your own life recently. Anything you can't explain, anything completely unexpected...'

Prof Jordon stroked his light beard and smiled thoughtfully. 'Well, it's strange you should ask that. Not long ago my wife and I were driving to the south coast on holiday and we stopped for a break at a motorway service station. When we returned to the car we found another car had somehow mounted a low dividing wall in the parking lot and crashed into ours.

'There wasn't much damage to our car apart from a broken headlamp. It appeared the other driver was unfamiliar with automatic gearboxes. It was a very low wall, only a foot or so high, but we couldn't believe such a crazy thing had happened. We exchanged insurance details, cleared the broken glass and went on our way. The incident had delayed us by some 20 minutes or so.

'A few miles further along the motorway we met a tailback. There'd been a bad accident -- a pile-up. Police and ambulances everywhere. Several cars and a lorry were involved and we learned later that two people had died. It was then we realised that if we'd not been delayed by the bizarre incident in the car park we might have been caught in the pile-up ourselves.'

'Strange indeed" Irving said. 'In another multiverse you may have been. You might not be sitting here now.'

They held each other's eyes for a long moment. Then Frank smiled. 'Ifs, buts and maybes... ordinary life is full of them. We don't need quantum uncertainty! But it did make us grateful for a rather careless motorist I can tell you. When we worked out approximate timings they placed us uncomfortably in the zone.'

'The uncertainty zone.'

'Exactly. And there's another very strange incident you can add to your dossier. My brother lives on the island of Kapas in Malaysia. I've been there... beautiful place. There's dozens of other islands all linked by ferries, some less seaworthy than others. He phoned me the other day to say he had to travel to the mainland on business. He'd waited in a queue of vehicles to board a car ferry and just when it was his turn to drive on to the boat it closed its bow doors. It had reached its capacity and he'd have to wait for another ferry.

'As I said, Irving, some of the ferries are quite primitive and often overloaded. Halfway to the mainland it sank. Some passengers were rescued but a lot drowned. My brother says he was either very lucky or someone up there is looking after him...'

'Divine intervention.'

'You could say that, although he's an atheist really. We both are.'

'I'm a Christian, Frank, and I believe someone up there is looking after all of us. He's shunted us all into a different parallel existence -- you and your brother included.'

'I only wish I could agree but as a scientist I

can't believe in a transcendental creator.'

'Understood, and it's good of you to read the dossier. I think you might find the evidence persuasive. Not all scientists are atheists, of course. Were you aware that Einstein believed in God?

'Yes, I do find that disturbing. Where did he go wrong!' He chuckled. 'Only kidding!'

'And here's a quote from a distinguished scientist that might interest you.' Irving took out his pocket diary and read from one of its scribbled pages: "All matter originates and exists only by virtue of a force. We must assume behind this force the existence of a conscious and intelligent Mind. This Mind is the matrix of all matter." Who said that?'

'Sounds familiar but I don't remember,'

'And again: "Both religion and science require a belief in God." Same scientist.

A Nobel Prize winner in fact.'

'Sorry, you've lost me.'

'Max Planck, the father of quantum physics, no less.'

Frank leaned back and winced. 'Ouch! You know how to hurt, Irving. We'd better start calling them quantum *meta*physics.'

TWENTY-FIVE

They may be in a new multiverse but in the memorable words of Godfrey Myers the world kept turning. News kept happening. Life went on. Everyone looked exactly the same as they always did. The rich were still growing richer and the poor poorer. People remained remarkably quarrelsome, self-justifying and money-fixated while the stream of stories about human frailty flowed on unabated.

But one minor issue had started to bother Irving. People were talking more quietly. He noticed it everywhere -- at home, at work, on TV and the radio. There seemed to have been a collective loss of voice. The problem came to a head when reporting a meeting of the Anti-Natalists Society at Manchester's Free Trade Hall. The group, dedicated to stopping human procreation, had been augmented by population control activists and pro-abortion feminists with exchanges occasionally rowdy.

The hall's acoustics were poor and there were difficulties with a microphone. Some of the speakers relied heavily on expletives and Irving's shorthand notes were decorated with exclamation marks. One speaker, a young lady with a feisty aversion to the act of childbirth, appealed for contraceptives to be made available free of charge to poorer people. Humans needed to stop breathing in order to save the planet, she declared to loud applause.

At least that was what Irving wrote verbatim in his notebook and typed up later in his report. It seemed extreme to the sub-editor who checked the story but, since those at the meeting belonged to the pro-death movement and time was pressing, he did not query it. The story appeared at the foot of an inside page and next day Irving was called into the editor's office. There had been an indignant complaint from the speaker at the meeting. She claimed she had not said humans should stop breathing but stop *breeding*. Irving produced his notebook for inspection and it was clear from the shorthand outline that the word was *breathing*. It was a simple case of mis-hearing.

Godfrey saw the amusing side. His paper was no friend of sociopaths in their varying guises. 'What she said was *stop breeding* not *stop breathing*. But that as well! We'll print an apology. It'll get more laughs for these fruitcakes.'

It had been more of a friendly chat than a carpeting but the message was not lost on Irving. As he had started to suspect, he was going deaf. The ear problems he'd experienced in his younger days had caught up with him. Tinnitus he could handle but not hearing loss which he knew was progressive. To stay on the ball as a reporter you needed to hear what quietly spoken people were saying, often in noisy situations. Still in his fifties he didn't feel old enough for a hearing aid though that was exactly what he needed. That and maybe ask for a transfer to sub-editing before he was pushed.

A standing joke in Fleet Street used to be that if a reporter went blind he was made the paper's art critic, and if he became deaf you made him the radio correspondent. Seriously, Irving realised that the time had come to make his own personal adjustment. A step up the editorial ladder as a grade four news sub-editor was beckoning. The job needed minimal retraining in editing and headline writing, and perfect hearing was not a requirement.

It offered regular working hours from late afternoon to early morning and was better paid, although without an expense account. It would be a timely arrangement all round as the news subs were below strength, with two vacancies on the subs' table. After discussing the move with Emily, he asked Trevor Unwin for a transfer.

Next up was a hearing aid. After tests at Wythenshawe Hospital's ENT department revealed a 24 per cent hearing loss in his left ear he was offered a 'state of the art ' digital aid free of charge. The same model supplied privately by hearing aid cowboys would have set him back hundreds of pounds. Irving was impressed by its high-powered clarity. If anything it was almost too powerful. As he drove away from the hospital the amplified sound of the Rover's engine was hard to bear. He needed to read the instructions and do some fine tuning. Removing the instrument from his ear he returned it to his jacket pocket in its case.

Before returning home he remembered he had to renew his road fund licence at the local post office. There was a queue of customers as one of the two counters displayed a 'position closed' notice. After some 15 minutes he reached the front of the queue whereupon he felt a prod in his back. A voice said: 'Oi, I'm talking to you mate... are you deaf or something?'

He turned to see a large hirsute gentleman with his hands on his hips and glaring at him.

'Yes, I am partially deaf actually,' Irving said. His hearing aid was still in his pocket. 'What did you say?'

A beefy heavily tattooed arm gestured towards the second counter which had reopened. 'It's your turn.'

As he drove home through rush hour traffic Irving reflected that life could only get better now he was the proud owner of a state of the art digital hearing aid. All he had to do was put it in his ear and switch it on.

To cut a long story short... that's the task of a newspaper sub-editor. To edit a reporter's copy to a specified length without reducing its substance. Then write a headline summarising the story in a few words across a calibrated width. Against the clock. Speed is of the essence but never at the expense of accuracy. A sub-editor is a journalist, a printer and a libel lawyer rolled into one. It helps if you're an experienced reporter in the first place with some knowledge of typography and the laws of defamation.

Irving's introduction to the specialist role was not as challenging as he'd feared. Seated alongside Cyril Baker, a long-serving stalwart of the subs' table, he studied his list of tools -- type faces and sizes -- enjoyed the witty repartee of his new colleagues and marvelled at the poor spelling of some freelance correspondents.

Cyril agreed it was deplorable. The university journalism graduates were the worst. 'They're taught all about politics, copyright and the law but they're not taught the basics -- elementary grammar and spelling. I'm surprised some of them can spell their own names let alone other people's.' Irving remembered his own 'on-the-job' training -- thrown in at the deep end. There was no better way of learning.

The evening started quietly with some down-column (one or two-paragraph 'fillers') for the arts page and other early pages. They were soon followed by single column 'tops' (more interesting stories for top-of-page slots) and radio and TV reviews. Irving was given the TV review and was astonished by its amateurish nature. Replete with OTT flattery for actors and producers alike, it read like a straight rewrite of the broadcaster's Press release.

After messengers brought the deskbound subs tea and bacon sandwiches from the canteen, they started receiving more newsworthy stories at a quicker rate. Among them were reports of widespread flood damage in Cumbria and updates from Manchester Crown Court on ongoing manslaughter and rape trials.

Next to land in Irving's in-tray was the tale of a love triangle involving a vicar, his wife and a church organist. The reverend and the organist had gone missing from their Yorkshire village and no word had been received from either of them for over a week. There was a tearful appeal by the vicar's wife for him to contact her and an even more emotional plea by the organist's husband as a large sum of money also seemed to have disappeared.

The staffer's story, carrying a DTR byline, included further comments from scandalised villagers along the lines of 'nothing like this has ever happened here before'. The pictures desk was processing shots of the protagonists and the ancient church taken by a staff cameraman, along with captions.

'Full of legals,' Cyril pointed out after glancing through the story. 'Have a care.'
Irving could see the pitfalls and skirted round them like a seasoned sub. Then he worked on a double column heading in 24 point Bodoni Bold eventually reading:

FEARS FOR VANISHING VICAR

AND CHURCH ORGANIST

There was no time to sit back and admire his first double column page 'top.' Seconds after a messenger had removed the story from his out-tray on its way to the revise sub-editor for a final check, a foreign page story about riots in Madrid arrived. The backbench certainly didn't hang about.

The tempo gathered pace as more foreign stories followed... troops clash on border between India and China... United States serial killer wins plea bargain to avoid death penalty... Galapagos tortoise retires from stud duties on reaching age of 100... ('there's hope for you, Cyril,' wisecracks went round the table).

All too soon the first edition deadline loomed and the pressurised atmosphere reached a new level of urgency. Alan Trent, the chief sub, and his backbench team presided over the noisy chaos with the calm of officers on the bridge of a ship in a storm. Theirs was the task of charting the front page, dispensing the splash and other breaking news stories to the understaffed subs' table.

Cyril was allocated the splash -- about an anti-cancer 'breakthrough' drug. Stories on a trade deal with the US, immigration curbs and the death of a soap star went to colleagues. Irving received a three-paragraph filler on rising unemployment, cross referencing to an inside page story on the subject but before he could make a start there was a major problem.

A cable from Reuter's agency reported that the 'vanishing vicar' had been found in Ibiza with his organist friend. Irving was told to put the jobless filler on hold while he rejigged his earlier inside page story with the latest development. The task involved finding a galley proof for amendment -- a process not yet explained to him, Cyril was tied up with his super-drug splash and the rest of the subs were equally occupied. He wasn't panicking just yet but in the newsroom's growing heat his forehead had started to perspire. You couldn't beat being thrown in at the deep end.

Fortunately when the predicament was explained to him Harvey, the chief messenger, came to the rescue. After searching through a sheaf of proofed stories he located the vital galley proof and Irving did his best to update the story as a front page filler with the revised heading in 16 point Bodoni Bold:

VANISHING VICAR
AND ORGANIST
FOUND IN IBIZA

Working regular sub-editorial shifts between 5pm and 1am offered distinct advantages over news reporting. For a start you could ditch the alarm clock. The day began when you decided it did. No need to leap out of bed at the crack of dawn, gulp a hasty breakfast and join the early morning rush hour to the office. You could lie in every day if you wished, rise in a civilised manner at the crack of noon and saunter downstairs for a leisurely brunch.

During summer afternoons Irving relaxed on the patio with the Telegraph crossword and a beer or watched England's amazing Test cricket performances on TV. In the winter there was snooker and national hunt racing. Then after a pot of tea and toasted teacakes with Emily he drove calmly through light traffic into Manchester, arriving promptly on time, to the satisfaction of Jim Keating, the night editor.

Keating, a charmless martinet despite (or possibly because of) shortness of stature, was a strict disciplinarian and a stickler for time-keeping. Around 5pm he would hover outside his office to check on his underlings' arrival. If they were late, they would get to know about it in a loud voice so all in the newsroom would hear.

Another bonus of regular shift working from Irving's point of view was the opportunity to improve his snooker skill in his supper breaks. While most of his colleagues would disappear into surrounding pubs after the first edition had been put to bed, he would take a short walk to the Press Club and enjoy a couple of frames along with his usual pint of bitter.

On one memorable night, while playing a frame with Jamie Lee, he surprised everyone including himself by scoring 72 in a single visit to the table. It was the highest break of his life and due celebrations were called for. He returned to the office several minutes late, slightly the worse for wear.

A scowling Jim Keating was waiting for him. 'Rather a long break wasn't it, Irving?' he bellowed.

Reaching his desk, Irving shouted back: 'Seventy-two actually, Jim. It should've been more but I missed an easy red.'

For the subs working on copy for later editions and keeping their heads down, it was a moment to savour.

TWENTY-SIX

It had been a long and arduous shift, with subs working overtime on a special late edition covering the US presidential election. The sky was growing light and the dawn chorus was in full swing when Irving's Rover crunched onto the driveway of his home. The question of whether or not to garage the car was decided for him because, parked in front of the garage doors, was a bright yellow Mini Cooper he had never seen before. It was fairly old judging by its registration plate but the bodywork was in good condition and there were several months left on the road fund licence.

Emily had passed her driving test first time a few days earlier. They had talked about buying her a car but nothing had been decided. He had assumed he'd be on hand to advise her when she did but it seemed she had gone ahead anyway. The mystery was solved the next day over brunch. His wife had bought the car off a musician at the BBC studios and driven it home the previous evening.

'It was a bargain,' she explained brightly. 'I got it off a cello player. He had no further use for it.

He'd bought a van to carry his instrument in. So he let me have the Mini at a cut price.'

'How much?' Irving asked, fearing the worst.

'A thousand -- on the credit card.'

He had to admit that seemed reasonable providing it was mechanically sound. 'Did you take it for a test drive?'

'Of course. We drove all round Ardwick. It's very smooth, you'll love it.'

'What about insurance?'

'He arranged a cover note... fully comprehensive. Don't look so worried. The fee for my first recital will pay for it!'

Irving tried to stop looking worried. It was about time she had her own car after all. Times were changing. Two-car families were becoming the norm as more wives went out to work. They took the car for a spin into Wilmslow and she was right. He could find nothing wrong with it. For a light car it was remarkably smooth, almost as comfortable as the Rover.

On returning home they found the postman had been. There was a letter for Emily from the BBC, one for Dawn, now working in stage management in London, a credit card statement. a gas bill and some junk mail. 'Anything for me?' Irving asked as Emily sorted through the pile.

There was nothing for him except the gas bill. He was expecting a letter from Frank Jordon. It had been several months since he'd left his dossier with the astrophysics professor who had been sufficiently impressed to submit it to experts at the Royal Society for their erudite consideration. The society included some of the country's most eminent scientists whose judgment in such matters was regarded as definitive. They could not be hurried in their deliberations.

But Irving was becoming increasingly impatient. A formal acknowledgement was all that had been received. Some kind of progress report would have been welcome. They were looking at a document that had the potential to intellectualise religion -- surely a proposition of interest to scientists. He toyed with the idea of a follow-up phone call to Frank Jordon but thought better of it. It was possible that no news meant good news -- although, of course, the saying did not apply to working journalists.

Fred and Lilian Shannon decided to call it a day after serving the good people of Brawton for nearly half a century. The area had been scheduled for redevelopment and they'd received an offer they could not refuse for their off-licence. It had been a traumatic move at their time of life but they were now settled into a luxurious retirement apartment in Lytham St Annes.

Emily and Irving drove in the Mini to visit them with Emily at the wheel. Irving was impressed by her careful but confident driving. He was happy to relax as a passenger after all the driving he did on a daily basis. The apartment was on the ground floor of a Georgian building on the seafront, not that the sea made much of an appearance now; it had been receding for many years. But the air was still exhilarating and just what the infirm couple needed after breathing suburban city air for most of their lives.

They were delighted to see their daughter and son-in-law, and thrilled by Emily's late blossoming career as a concert pianist. Both were still mentally alert but physically frail. Lilian was growing deaf and Fred suffered badly from rheumatism. But the ritual of afternoon tea was still faithfully observed with best china crockery, sausage rolls and thickly buttered crumpets.

Emily and Irving were updated on the latest news from Brawton. Father Michael had retired after suffering a minor heart attack and had gone to live in Rome. After a lifetime of service to the Catholic Church and his devoted parishioners he would now be lovingly cared for in his spiritual home. Daniel and Megan had become parents of adorable twins -- a boy and girl -- and had opened a food bank in the homeless centre at St Peter's to meet ever-rising poverty among working families.

Later the four took a short and very slow stroll along the promenade in the evening sunshine, pausing to admire Emily's Mini. Fred had been surprised to hear that his daughter had driven it all the way from Wilmslow without a break.

Irving assured him she was a very competent driver and Fred said he didn't doubt it for a moment. 'What have I always said about women drivers?' he laughed heartily. 'Don't answer that!'

It turned out that no news was bad news. When Prof Jordon finally phoned Irving with the outcome of his submission to the Royal Society he was full of apologies and condolences. 'I personally believe that you could be on to something Irving but the powers that be don't. In their report they tell me they examined your dossier meticulously. They had several in-depth consultations among their leading lights in quantum physics but at the end of the day.... '

'It goes dark!'

'I'm afraid so. They say the dossier is well written and closely argued but relies on anecdotal evidence and speculation of a spiritual nature. Although intriguing there could be rational explanations for much of its content... '

'Rational explanations!' Irving snorted. 'How does a birthmark vanish of its own accord? How does a cat turn into a dog?'

'They don't say, Irving.'

'Because they *can't*!'

'They call such things imponderables. They reiterate that all current scientific evidence points to parallel universes being self-contained. Nothing and no-one can pass between them. The only caveat they're prepared to consider is these multiverses may sometimes briefly overlap. At such times particularly sensitive people may feel a familiarity with something that shouldn't be familiar at all. It's known as déjà vu and the sensation soon passes.'

'I do mention déjà vu in the dossier,' Irving reminded him. I've experienced it myself several times -- usually when something bizarre happens.'

'Most probably coincidence, they say. Where the society's report comes down most heavily against your dossier is in the area of metaphysics and theology. You say you were transported into another multiverse by praying for a miracle. That's the big stumbling block. Scientists generally regard prayer and miracles -- anything to do with religion -- as off limits. The concept of a supernatural God is anathema to them...'

'But not to Einstein or Planck!'

'The Royal Society believes it knows better!'

What a classic line that was Irving thought, although it had been said in a jocular manner.

Prof Jordon did his best to explain: 'Einstein and Planck were products of their time. Religion was a more powerful influence in society than science. It's different now. Scientists are the new high priests.'

'And just as dogmatic as the religious ones.'

'I don't deny that, Irving. Anyway they do recognise your good intentions. I'm instructed to pass on their sincere appreciation.'

'Thanks for that, Frank. And thanks for trying.'

'You're very welcome, dear boy. I'll send you the society's full report. And I'll post the dossier back to you by recorded delivery. It's a valuable document. But it's time has not yet come.'

Not yet, Irving thought. But soon?

When one door closes...Irving's encounter with the Royal Society diehards may have dimmed his hopes but they were by no means extinguished. These were the 1990s after all. Science had distanced itself from religion but religion, embodied in the United Kingdom by the Anglican Church, was moving closer towards science and secularity.

Traditional Christianity, eroded by the innovation of women priests and the prospect of women bishops, had given way to liberal values on social issues such as homosexuality, divorce and abortion. There was even dialogue between the Archbishop of Canterbury, an ineffectual hand-wringing figure, and adherents of cultural relativism. With concepts of right and wrong, good and bad being challenged, God was being nudged steadily towards the margins.

Asking a church reinventing itself along these lines if the Almighty might be revealing himself through science seemed a timely move to Irving. He was so convinced by the prospect that he set about writing to the archbishop without delay. His letter summarised the salient points in the dossier, which he offered to send to Lambeth Palace for the primate's scrutiny. He'd never doorstepped a palace before but there was a first time for everything.

If his experience with the Royal Society was any guide, the wait for feedback would be a long one. But there would be plenty to occupy his time and that of his Daily Telegraph colleagues. Rupert Murdoch's defeat of the all-powerful print unions in the 1986 Wapping dispute had ushered in a revolution in newspaper publishing. It was called computerised technology. The old labour intensive 'hot metal' method of production had been replaced by slick electronic wizardry with its own esoteric language and a chilling ultimatum: retrain as computer operators or take redundancy.

The Telegraph management were calling the shots now and they had long memories. Manchester's NUJ chapel, for so long their obdurate opponents on pay and working practices, were starting to feel the pain. The new technology involved transferring northern publishing from central Manchester to a streamlined computerised plant in nearby Trafford Park, decimating their editorial staff.

Almost all the paper's pages would be produced in London and transmitted electronically to the Trafford Park presses. One token page of northern news remained to be produced by a handful of journalists at the new plant. Most of the displaced editorial staff opted for voluntary redundancy but some were offered jobs in the paper's London office. Irving was one of them.

It seemed there was a long-standing vacancy

for a royal correspondent. For some reason management could not understand, nobody wanted the job. So desperate were they to fill the post that they were prepared to offer it to an oik on the Manchester staff. It carried elevation to a grade five salary scale including London weighting, generous expense account, car allowance, assistance with relocation and gold-plated pension.

That was the upside. The downside involved sycophantic attendance on the world's most dysfunctional high-profile family, with its four divorcees and ongoing scandals. There would be fawning, scripted interviews on television, camping outside palaces and mansions across the country, and insatiable globetrotting. After retraining in the use of a laptop computer he would be required to write a steady diet of unctuous, uncritical waffle about the family's more positive activities, such as they were, while drawing a veil over the dark deeds behind their vast fortunes. Irving politely declined. The post of royal correspondent was a job no self-respecting journalist would accept.

It was only a matter of time before the paper's northern editorial presence expired. He resolved to stay until the bitter end and accept early retirement on enhanced terms his long service had earned him.

The end, when it came, was neither bitter nor sweet; neither dramatic, poignant nor memorable in any way. It came as a total anti-climax. Godfrey Myers had retired and was long gone. Jim, Charles,

Trevor, Dave, Cyril and the last of the reporters and news subs had accepted retirement or redundancy. The one token page of northern news met its inevitable fate. No more first, second, third or final editions. The deadlines had finally died.

There was no funeral, no obituary, no closing ceremony, no eloquent valedictory speeches by His Lordship or other luminaries from London. Almost five decades of publishing in Manchester as part of the hub of Britain's massive national newspaper industry ended with a whimper.

There wasn't even a farewell party. It was too depressing for one and Trafford Park was miles away from the Manchester Press Club. After a few drinks in a local pub and promising to 'stay in touch' (the sort of undertaking nobody takes seriously) the last few journalists, enriched by several thousand pounds but now jobless, drifted away.

Irving had to return to the office to collect books he'd been reading on quantum theory. It was almost midnight and eerily silent. Second edition time without a sound. He collected his books and other possessions, leaving cleaners to clear the desks of newspapers, unused copy paper, spikes and wire baskets. On his way out he paused at the door and looked round sadly. Something didn't feel right.

He was the last man standing -- about to switch off the lights for the last time -- and he had a nagging feeling that decency demanded one final act. He returned to his desk and scribbled a few words on a sheet of copy paper. Then he pinned the message on the notice board. There was nobody left to read it, of course, apart from the cleaners. But someone needed to say something.

The final words he wrote for The Daily Telegraph read:

And now for something completely different.

'Completely different' was right. Far from a leisurely life watching sport on TV, solving the Daily Telegraph crossword and listening to Emily's accomplished piano playing, Irving's normally eventful existence at once became empty and unbearably dull. The crossword had lost its addictive appeal. It was either too challenging or too childish. Emily's technical piano practice involved frequent interruptions to repeat a single phrase or passage. Even televised cricket and snooker seemed boring. What he missed was the buzz, bonhomie and wit of the newsroom.

It was the same every evening. As first edition time approached the adrenalin would kick in and he'd become restless. Emily would advise him to calm down but without the challenge of a deadline and the professional teamwork needed to meet it, the sense of anti-climax was physical. Throughout his career as a newspaperman, he'd complained about pressure. Now it was gone he missed it like hell.

News coverage on television was a poor substitute, relying on a presenter reading from an autocue and a stream of politicians and other professional talkers known as analysts offering conflicting interpretations. The object of the exercise was obvious: keep talking even if you've got nothing credible to say.

His hi-tech laptop computer offered another source of news if only he could get his head round it. Retirement was no time of life to be wrestling with such a bewildering gadget. You couldn't teach an old dog new tricks. The course in information technology provided by the manufacturer seemed to be couched in a foreign language. It was a crash course in every sense. With each setback he'd resort to the premium rate 'helpline' only to find it an expensive rip-off.

After much dogged trial and error he gradually acquired a working knowledge of the obdurate device. He discovered an alternative medium that had changed the face of journalism without his noticing. It was called the internet. If you wanted full in-depth coverage of home and foreign news free from the bias of cowboy media proprietors, this was the place to find it.

There was no shortage of material. The era of the 1990s and the Millennium was one of unprecedented social change starting with a rapid thaw in the Cold War and the dissolution of the Soviet Union. There were extreme advances in technology with the introduction of the World Wide Web, gene therapy and designer babies.

After almost 30 years in prison Nelson Mandela became President of South Africa, Bill Clinton was impeached and Dolly the sheep was cloned. In Manchester an IRA bomb caused £700 million damage but nobody was killed. The Channel Tunnel opened and the Euro currency was born. The Hale-Bopp comet swung past Earth for the first time in 4,200 years and those of a superstitious disposition speculated on what tragic events it might presage.

That same year Mother Teresa, the saintly nun of Calcutta and winner of the Nobel Peace Prize, died aged 87. Her sad passing was overshadowed by the untimely death of a much younger international figurehead. The death of Princess Diana following a car crash dominated the decade like no other.

The accident/incident, whichever individual editors preferred to call it, occurred in the Pont de l'Alma Tunnel in Paris on August 31, 1997. The 36-year-old princess died along with her fiancé Dodi Fayed and their driver Henri Paul when their Mercedes collided with a Fiat Uno and crashed into a tunnel pillar. Diana's bodyguard, Trevor Rees-Jones, suffered severe injuries but survived. He was said to have no recollection of events.

The accident/incident had been mired in controversy ever since due to circumstances which, when taken together, suggested there was more to it than met the eye. It took 10 years for an inquest to be held in the UK. Evidence given at the initial police inquiry was reprised. All 14 security cameras around the tunnel had been switched off at the time of the accident/incident.

The Fiat was never traced despite a nation-wide police search. Several independent witnesses reported seeing a bright flash of light at the material time. Their evidence was inexplicably discounted. Potential witnesses died, 'disappeared' or refused to testify. Many other crucial questions remained unanswered, not least the involvement of the British secret service.

The passage of time duly exercised its obfuscating influence and the belated inquest delivered a verdict blaming Paul's 'negligent driving'. That -- the powers that be decided -- was to be the official version of the truth and if the public wanted more they could whistle
for it.

Judging by ensuing public opinion polls a significant majority of the British people were far from satisfied. The establishment-controlled media went through the motions of protesting but without conviction and the expected public outcry failed to materialise. There were other important distractions to capture the public's outrage such as the plight of polar bears on shrinking ice floes. Once again the power of the Press as servants of the truth had been effectively circumscribed.

Irving shared the disillusionment of his rank-and-file NUJ colleagues. All but a gullible minority at the BBC, the Telegraph Magazine and other coffee table publications regarded the official verdict as a classic cover-up and a body blow to democracy. 'Stinks to high heaven, doesn't it,' Adam Richardson declared when they met at the Press club sometime later. Irving, Adam, Charles Clarke, Dave, Leonard and other Telegraph retirees held annual reunions at the club but their numbers were rapidly dwindling.

'The public's just told what's deemed good for them,' Adam added. 'We spend our lives as journalists digging out the truth... makes you wonder why we bother, if it weren't for the money. What makes it deeply sinister is the presence of the secret service spooks. They've got a finger in every pie and a key to every door as we discovered ourselves.'

Dave, now confined to a wheelchair after a stroke but as fiercely far-left as ever, said: 'They even warned the poor woman that accidents can happen -- that should have made her step-up security. It's the threat they use against all their enemies. That's why there'll never be an effective wealth tax. No chancellor of the exchequer would be brave enough. He'd become an instant target for a fatal accident.'

'What does it say about a society when even its political leaders are living in fear?' Charles asked.

Dave had the answer and as usual he was spot-on. 'It says that all these years we've been pissing into the wind as journalists. We've changed nothing. Half the world's wealth is in the hands of one per cent of the population. They use fear to control the other 99 per cent.'

It follows that in an oppressive social climate such as this what actually happened hidden from view in the Pont de l'Alma Tunnel will inevitably remain a mystery. Along with soldiers posing as policemen at the Battle of Orgreave, the story will gradually fade into folklore. What *really* happened -- the whole truth and nothing but the truth -- will never be known.

At least not in this multiverse.

TWENTY-SEVEN

Months had elapsed since Irving wrote to the Archbishop of Canterbury asking him if God might be revealing himself through quantum physics. He believed his dossier offered ample evidence in support of the theory and would be of instant appeal to the leader of the nation's Christian community. But he was wrong. He had received no reply, not even an acknowledgement.

He wondered if his letter -- sent by recorded delivery and marked 'confidential' -- had reached the archbishop or been lost in layers of bureaucracy. When he tried telephoning the number appeared permanently engaged. He left a message but nobody called him back. They must all be too busy, he thought. He decided to wait another month. If there was still no response then there would be only one place left to go.

Emily was still revelling in the joys of motoring. She drove her Mini to the BBC's Manchester studios to rehearse her chamber music, to St Oswald's which was only a short walk away, and further afield to visit

Daniel and Megan and their twins, Francis and Ruth, at their high rise Brawton flat.

On the day she drove Irving to see them they stopped off in Manchester to buy T-shirts and rompers for the toddlers. Daniel was working as a sessions musician and led his own group on alto sax and clarinet but engagements were irregular. Megan had given up nursing to be a full-time mother. Money was tight but they still managed to contribute to the food bank they operated at St Peter's where many families were worse off than they were.

Irving and Emily had seen the twins soon after birth and again on their first birthday. But now they were walking and their innocence and affection for each other was captivating. As they played together with cuddly toys they paused to give each other a gentle kiss on the cheek without any adult prompting. Sublime and spiritually uplifting were among the words that sprang to mind. They were the way God made them, still untainted by avarice and corruption. If only they could stay that way. All too soon the need to survive in a contaminated, money-grubbing world would rob them of their purity.

The month was up and Irving had still not been favoured with a reply from His Grace the Archbishop. The Church of England had had its chance of a modern makeover. The opportunity would not come knocking again. It would knock this time on the illustrious portals of the Holy See.

He checked out contacts in the Vatican Press

office and was advised against a direct approach to the Pope. Instead he needed to petition the Cardinal Prefect of the Congregation for the Doctrine of the Faith. His letter should be sent to the Vatican Embassy in Wimbledon who would relay it to Rome by diplomatic bag. That way it would be sure to reach him.

After establishing the correct form of address for the cardinal he reprised the same document sent to His Grace and despatched it to His Eminence the Cardinal Prefect along the lines the Press office had helpfully suggested. They advised him not to expect an early reply. Things moved very slowly in Vatican City but His Eminence would definitely respond 'in the fullness of time.'

Irving knew the Catholic Church was not the most dynamic of organisations. He recalled a story he'd covered years earlier about an outstanding school in Haydock, near Manchester, named after St Edmund Arrowsmith, a 17th century English Martyr. It had been three centuries before Edmund received his sainthood.

He just hoped the cardinal would reply during his lifetime. He was starting to feel his age. In addition to deafness his eyesight was deteriorating and there were times when agonising osteoarthritis in his fingers stopped him typing on his laptop. Thank God he no longer needed to work. The state pension and bus pass he and his youthful colleagues used to joke about, a blink of an eye ago, took care of retirement. Plus, the redundancy settlement he'd received from the Telegraph had been surprisingly generous by the paper's normally grudging standards.

Time was also taking its toll on Emily's fingers. Though still an accomplished pianist she could no longer play professionally. Her brief career as a Radio Three performing artist had come to an end. It had been fun while it lasted and it paid well. It had rescued her from the nightmare of clinical depression and she gave thanks to God every day for that.

The future for both of them lay in the career of their daughter Dawn, who was now making a name for herself in the theatre. After training at RADA she had worked as a production assistant in repertory and later with the Royal Shakespeare Company. Recently she had branched out as a director in her own right and was living in some style with her actor boyfriend in an upmarket West End apartment.

In a move marking her arrival at the top of the London theatrical ladder she had been chosen to direct a modern adaptation of a comedy classic at the National Theatre. When she phoned with the news Emily took the call. Irving had taken Alice, Betsy's successor, for her daily walk. Her daughter was in a state of high excitement. It was a long-awaited chance to make a name for herself as a leading London director -- something she'd dreamed of since her university days. She offered to book seats for them both on the production's first night. Emily warmly congratulated her. She was equally thrilled. She had never been to a first night before and it was years since she'd been to London.

'We'll be there, darling,' she said. She made a note of the date in her diary. She knew Irving would be as delighted as she was. When he returned and fed Alice her dinner he declared it was the best news he'd heard for months. It was high time they took a break together. They'd make a weekend of it. Stay at a five-star hotel. Meet the boyfriend. 'What's the title of the play?' he asked casually.

'She did tell me but I've forgotten,' Emily replied. 'Oh yes -- Educating Rita.'

His enthusiasm disappeared faster than the dog's dinner but he tried not to look totally nonplussed. More strangeness. There was simply no end to it.

He withdrew a substantial amount of cash from their healthy deposit account, pre-booked train tickets and after checking out five star hotels on the internet reserved a room at the Dorchester. They took the Inter-City express from Manchester Piccadilly Station to Euston. First class of course. Not that they had any elitist pretensions but over the years a Telegraph expense account had convinced him it was the only way to travel. He declined to change the habits of a lifetime although he was now paying the exorbitant bill himself.

The taxi from Euston to Park Lane took half an hour for the three-mile trip, so congested was the traffic. Irving barely recognised the city any more. It had been years since the last of his occasional visits to the Telegraph's Fleet Street headquarters. Much of the old character had been swept away and replaced by grotesque office blocks clothed in smoked glass windows.

What capitalist skulduggery lurked behind them? Banks milking customers with inflated interest rates... insurance cheats reneging on valid claims... arbitrageur spivs manipulating share prices... pharmaceutical cowboys exploiting the sick... among the more blatant rip-offs. A tiny band of investigative journalists fought a losing battle every day to expose them. He thanked his lucky stars he was well out of it.

A room at the Dorchester meant more eye-watering expense but once ushered into its plush ambience his view of capitalism mellowed slightly. Everything spoke of elegant refinement from the gold fitted en suite bathroom to the silk draped king size bed. Or rather sheikh size bed. Rooted in the deep pile carpet close to the bay window was an ornate bronze arrow pointing across Hyde Park. They rang for room service and asked the attendant, a charming young middle eastern woman, what the arrow was for. They were told it pointed to Mecca.

'Which happens to be in roughly the same direction as Rome,' Emily said.

The attendant said nothing but remained smiling. She handed the couple menus for afternoon tea and departed.

'The place may be owned by Arabs but they

certainly know about our fondness for a brew,' Irving observed, studying the elaborate menu.

They performed the traditional ritual in the Promenade tea room, surrounded by luxury and white gloved waiters serving plentiful supplies of cake. At £35 each the pair were tempted to over indulge but bravely resisted. In a few hours they would be meeting Dawn and her partner, Sebastian Lyngard, for dinner in the Grill restaurant.

Emily was girlishly excited. Her daughter and her young man had been living together for over a year. She was persuaded it was 'the modern way' but Dawn was in her forties and leaving things rather late. Could a wedding be in the offing? From what he had gathered about the actor in limited online research Irving doubted it. He'd been married twice before

First impressions were not promising. The couple arrived 20 minutes late, full of apologies. Traffic problems again. Dawn performed the introductions and Sebastian's handshake was ominously limp. A self-regarding bit part actor in a TV soap he wore shades in an optimistic belief he might be recognised. Tall, late forties, smart casually dressed complete with a cravat. Only moderately hirsute but the smile seemed professionally fixed and when the shades came off the eyes were a bit too close together.

'Why we bother coming by taxi I honestly don't know,' he told his fellow guests. 'Tube's much quicker and more environmentally friendly.'

Irving nodded in agreement. Oh Lord, he thought, not another eco-warrior.

Steering clear of currently fashionable dialogue on global warming and renewable energy, they ordered from the a la carte menu. As it was a Friday, Emily went for scallops with chestnuts and Irving chose lobster thermidor. Sebastian let it be known that he was a 'devout atheist' and ordered a rib eye steak with fries. Dawn chose a salmon tartare creation with salad as part of her diet. After lengthy discussion with Sebastian, who prided himself on knowing about such things, they settled for a bottle of Veuve Clicquot to wash it all down.

Radiant in a low cut yellow evening gown, Dawn was full of her play's premiere performance the following evening. The dress rehearsal had gone well which was always a good sign. 'There's a lot of me in the new Rita,' she enthused and Irving did his best to look keenly interested. 'North country girl comes to London... tries to better herself... changes her accent -- but then changes it back again in disgust at the shallow nature of her new friends. She goes from ee-by-gum to lah-di-dah and then back to ee-by-gum!'

Sebastian whose own accent was decidedly lah-di-dah, said: 'To be honest I think you'd be better staging the play in Manchester.' He knew all about drama as well as wine, it seemed. But not a lot about tact.

'It'll be alright on the night, darling,' Dawn assured him. 'There's a full house tomorrow, remember?'

Sensing tension between them Emily guided the conversation towards the play's romantic element and from there onto marriage. She wondered more in hope than expectation if the couple had any plans in that area.

'We're happy as we are, aren't we darling?" Sebastian said, raising Dawn's hand to his lips for a thespian kiss.

'Couldn't be happier,' Dawn smiled without conviction.

The actor turned to her mother. 'I'll level with you, Emily. I've been married before and, to be honest, it was a mistake. I wasn't ready for it. It's a life-time commitment. I love and cherish your daughter but neither of us is ready for that commitment yet. One day, maybe... who knows?'

After another bottle of Veuve Clicquot they parted amicably enough. Hugs and theatrical kisses all round and good wishes for the success of Dawn's make-or-break premiere. At least *they* were genuine.

All right on the night summed it up. It was all right -- but not the ground-breaking sensation they had hoped for. From their seats in the stalls Emily, Irving and Sebastian laughed at Willy Russell's original witty dialogue most of which Dawn had retained, but departures from characterisation were puzzling. Frank, the alcoholic university lecturer, had now become a drug addict and Rita, originally a Liverpudlian hairdresser, had morphed into a waitress from Wigan.

'Ambitious' was how Sebastian described the changes and most of the audience seemed to share his view. There was no standing ovation at the final curtain and the applause was restrained. The tone of the reviews in the Sunday newspapers next day was underwhelming, an ominous sign as critics held the key to box office success.

Dawn was still fuming over a review in the Sunday Telegraph when she saw her parents off at Euston Station next morning. 'He called it "A tortured version of Pygmalion on drugs" -- I ask you! Not a positive word to say anywhere. The others weren't much better but at least they weren't insulting.'

'The critics aren't infallible, believe me,' Irving told her, 'They often get things wrong.'

'Look at it this way, darling,' Emily added. 'You're sold out all next week so it's no flop is it?'

Their daughter brightened up after that and waved them a long goodbye as their Inter-City express glided out of sight. Disappointed but happy in equal measure, Irving and Emily relaxed in their comfortable seats and studied the Sunday papers. Disappointed for Dawn as her break into the big time seemed to have slipped away but happy to see her in a steady relationship with Sebastian.

At least Emily was. Irving was very quiet, she thought. He seemed reluctant to talk about Dawn's play. When she recalled amusing moments in the performance he remained non-committal. There appeared to be something on his mind. As they sipped mediocre coffee from the trolley she launched the big question: 'What did you think of Sebastian?'

Irving looked up from his sports pages. City had won again and were streets ahead at the top of the league. He thought for a moment, recalling the actor's views on marriage, the fixed smile and the tactless remarks. Above all he remembered something he'd learned a long time ago as a cub reporter. Anyone who said 'to be honest' as often as Sebastian had to be dodgy. 'That man will never put a ring on Dawn's finger.'

It was almost a year before the cardinal responded. Winter melted into spring, spring leapt into summer and the faith Irving had placed in the Holy See began to evaporate. It was not as if he was expecting a sainthood -- just a reply to his letter. He was about to telephone the Vatican Embassy in Wimbledon to give them a well earned nudge when it finally arrived -- a high quality envelope embossed with the Vatican insignia of two crossed keys.

Aware that this was the quantum moment in his campaign, Irving carefully slit open the envelope, releasing the uncertainty principle. It was that nanosecond in the space-time continuum when the result goes either way depending on which multiverse you are in. Would the cardinal prefect express a cautious interest and request to see the full dossier, or would he politely decline? Before he could scan the single sheet of typewritten cartridge paper, he knew the answer.

The cardinal began by reminding him that the Congregation for the Doctrine of the Faith had been founded in 1542 to defend the Church from heresy and new unacceptable doctrines. That was still its purpose today. After much prayerful consultation the congregation had unanimously concluded that Irving's proposals fell into the 'unacceptable' category. They were incompatible with its centuries-old doctrine on purgatory and as such amounted to heresy, albeit unintentional. In those circumstances the Roman Catholic Church must reluctantly withdraw from further consideration of his dossier.

The cardinal appreciated that it had been offered in good faith and a spirit of rapprochement between science and religion -- an objective with which the congregation had profound sympathy. Many of the world's problems could be solved by such an alliance, for which the whole of the Church would continue to pray.

He ended his letter with deep gratitude for Irving's submission and prayers for his physical and spiritual wellbeing.

Irving folded the letter and replaced it in the envelope with a deep sigh. When one door closes... they all close! Realistically he'd been punching above his weight with a layman's limited understanding of an impenetrable subject. His ambitious mission to narrow the gap between science and religion remained a distant dream. Neither side wanted to know!

Maybe not in this multiverse. There were plenty of others. And plenty of time. You were looking at eternity after all. In another existence his grasp of quantum theory would be more enlightened and his evidence more persuasive. At the same time the powers that be would surely weaken in their ironclad inflexibility

Prof Jordon's verdict on the dossier when they had last spoken was still fresh in his memory...

It's time has not yet come.

Sooner or later it's time *would* come. He just needed to stay on board the eternal quantum carousel for as long as it took. He was after all a regular rider. At the end of time and space, the end of everything, God must surely reveal himself through science

A wet licking sensation on his hand dangling over the arm of his chair brought him back to earth. Alice was telling him the time had come for her walk.

To cut a long story short...

... time marched unsteadily on from one crisis to another, heedless of the damage it was leaving in its wake. The much-hyped Millennium came and went in a haze of forgettable fireworks. To mark the passage of two thousand years of Christianity, a monstrous Dome was erected in Greenwich at a cost of £750 million to focus the nation's mind on... nobody knew what. Anything other than Christianity it seemed. Empty of ideas, like the puny minds that conceived it, the monstrosity lay desolate and in-solvent within a year.

Three thousand people were murdered in cold blood when individuals described as Muslim fundamentalists flew two jet aircraft into New York's Twin Towers, the single deadliest terrorist atrocity of the century -- so far.

Sophisticated cluster bombs caused massive civilian casualties when dropped on Iraq market places by forces under the command of 'Teflon' Tony Blair. Attempts to arraign him at the Court of Human Rights in The Hague proved unsuccessful.

Pushing back the boundaries of progressive liberal reform, the Parole Board released several murderers who went on to kill more victims. Sugges-tions in the Press that the penal system had fallen into the hands of incredibly stupid people were dis-missed as 'alarmist'.

Barack Obama became the first black presi-dent of the United States but failed to usher in im-mediate Utopia. The Queen Mother celebrated her 100th birthday with an extra large gin.

And Sebastian Lyngard ditched Dawn Breen.

Not only that but he relieved her of her modest life savings in the process. The rental agree-ment on their shared apartment expired and she had saved several thousand pounds in a joint account towards a house purchase. On the strength of their combined incomes they'd viewed detached four-bedroom properties before choosing one in Ashford. Her career had stalled after Educating Rita's modest box office performance and she'd settled for the less dramatic but more secure role of housewife and hopefully mother.

Or so she thought. There was no mention of marriage. He was still 'not ready' for the commitment but they agreed to buy their new home in joint names. He arranged for a survey and withdrew the balance of their savings ostensibly for the deposit. At that point the actor promptly exited the scene, stage left.

'He just did a runner. Nobody knows where he is. He's not answering his phone. I just can't believe it,' Dawn tearfully told her parents on returning to the family home in Wilmslow. 'We both trusted each other implicitly. He's ruined my life. I'll never forgive him,'

Neither Emily nor Irving could bear the sight of anyone in such distress, particularly when it was a middle-aged woman starting to lose her looks and especially as it was their own daughter. They did their best to comfort her. She'd had a lucky escape really and was well rid of him. Irving would track him down and try to recover her share of the missing money. Meanwhile she knew she would always have a home with them.

Her father feared the money had gone beyond recall but didn't say so. He checked with the TV company's Press office and learned that the actor had been written out of the soap cast. Rumour had it that he'd been under pressure to pay off gambling debts. One friend who declined to be identified said he'd recently renewed his passport. That sounded ominous. He could be anywhere. He'd keep chasing, starting with International Federation of Journalists contacts in the Costa del Sol and other Mediterranean tourist hot spots.

He'd been right about Sebastian. A ring was still absent from his daughter's finger and her life savings were likely to remain missing from her bank account. She'd been mugged in two ways, both emotionally and financially. It was up to Emily and himself to help pick up the pieces. With the mortgage on the house now paid off he'd transfer some of his remaining redundancy settlement to her account to help soften the material blow. The emotional rebuilding process would take longer but he knew she was a resilient character from the way she'd overcome the loss of a brother all those years ago.

They'd modernise her old bedroom. It was large enough to install an en suite shower and toilet along with fitted wardrobes straight out of Vogue magazine. They'd redecorate using silk finish wallpaper and round off the makeover with a built-in TV set -- something they both still lacked in their own bedroom. The height of luxury in other words.

Dawn did not stay depressed for long. Once the initial shock had worn off she realised it was not the end of the world after all. She was no longer homeless and thanks to her father's ever-loving kindness she was no longer destitute. Sebastian had been an unfortunate episode in a pretentious life, part of a city full of phoney people.

She'd always been a northern lass at heart. Manchester was her city and it was rapidly expanding as the country's media capital as it had the previous century, becoming the centre of the national newspaper industry. Opportunities were opening up in television and offered hope for a woman of her dramatic experience and qualifications. London -- along with Sebastian -- was fast becoming history.

It could all be for the best really. Her parents were both feeling their age and starting to look frail. Her mother in particular showed worrying signs of early dementia, forgetting important dates like birthdays and constantly losing things, then asking St Anthony, the patron saint of lost objects, to help her find them.

Her father's deafness and weakening eyesight were also sources of concern. Osteoarthritis was starting to restrict his mobility. He needed stronger painkilling tablets but was reluctant to consult his doctor. Both parents were losing weight. They were not eating properly. As an expert cook she'd soon correct that. It seemed the cruel upheaval in her life might turn out to be a blessing in disguise.

One advantage of doing the Daily Telegraph cryptic crossword was the mental exercise helped to delay the onset of dementia. Several scientific studies showed this to be true. So Irving was rather worried when Emily stopped doing the puzzle she'd enjoyed for many years.

'Can't be bothered any more,' she answered when he asked her why. 'Too many Americanisms creeping in. It was tough enough to start with but when they use words like "swell" meaning good and "penitentiary" meaning prison you just lose interest.'

He checked out that day's puzzle and saw what she meant straight away. There was a reference to Brooklyn Bridge that your average Telegraph reader would find impenetrable. Even the most well travelled of them would not grasp the significance of Madison Avenue as the home of US advertising. The compiler wasn't playing the game. If he was, it certainly wasn't cricket. More like baseball.

Irving still had Charles Clarke's telephone number and he called his old colleague in his retirement home. The former Telegraph chief reporter was as ebullient as ever. 'They've hired an American compiler, would you believe. How to alienate core readership at a stroke! No wonder circulation has dropped through the floor.'

'What is it now?' Irving asked,

'Less than three-quarters of a million, half what it was in our day. They've killed the goose that laid the golden egg. You could redesign the paper, change everything, print incomprehensible cartoons... but you didn't tamper with the crossword. Only the dear old Daily Telegraph would commit such a cock-up!'

TWENTY-EIGHT

The older you get the faster time passes. Tell a four-year-old child to wait a year for something like a puppy and such a wait will seem like an age. A year is a quarter of the child's life. Tell a 70-year-old to wait a year for a new car and there's no problem as a year is only a 70th of his/her life.

For Irving, time started to accelerate the moment he retired. And the faster the years passed the more the ageing process seemed determined to outstrip them. The osteoarthritis in his fingers spread rapidly to his knees, elbows and even his neck. Nocturnal visits to the toilet increased from once to three or four times. Both ears succumbed to deafness and distorted tinnitus and he needed two hearing aids. They were unreliable and made his ears sore.

His long-term memory was still vivid. He could recall the words of hymns he sang at Sunday school... the way his heart leapt when Godfrey Myers asked him 'When can you start?'... the impassioned speeches of NUJ chapel meetings in the Telegraph canteen... the trauma of Fred's stillbirth in painful detail. But ask him what year it was or what day it was, even what he'd had for breakfast and he was stumped.

He needed stronger spectacles to read the headlines in the Telegraph and a magnifying glass to attempt the adulterated crossword. He was fighting a losing battle in every sense and, like Emily, finally abandoned the puzzle. He couldn't bring himself to stop buying the paper like many disillusioned readers. For all its faults the publication still had its moments as a public service newspaper. When it exclusively revealed that half the MPs in the House of Commons were fiddling their expenses other papers were left trailing in its wake. The campaign lasted over a month by which time the legislators' credibility was in shreds with several ending up behind bars.

Only when unsteadiness struck and he started falling over did Irving finally take Dawn's advice and consult his GP. He had also developed a persistent cough and the slightest exertion made him breathless but it was the dizzy spells and falls that concerned him. The first couple of falls were in the bedroom and each time he fell on the bed but the third happened in the bathroom. He hit his head on the radiator causing a large bruise.

Dawn drove him to the surgery in Emily's ageing Mini as both her parents had long stopped driving. She had avoided driving since the night of her tragic accident until the need to care for her parents on a regular basis helped to overcome her nervousness. She sat with her father during his consultation, acting as his ears when he had difficulty hearing, which was almost all the time.

On hearing about his cough, the sympathetic young woman doctor sounded his chest and referred him for an X-ray. She inspected his bruise which was now healing, took his pulse and blood pressure and listened patiently to details of his falls and memory loss. There was little she could do about these health issues. They were described as 'wear and tear' (the polite term for old age) for which there was no cure. She prescribed stronger painkillers and a walking stick.

Wear and tear had afflicted Emily in a similar manner although she had no problem with balance. Arthritis affected her hands to a point where she could no longer play her beloved grand piano and her dementia had grown worse than Irving's. She would make a pot of tea and forget doing so until she discovered it had grown cold and wondered how it had happened. Crumpets and teacakes remained untoasted in the toaster unbuttered and unloved. Spectacles, pens, TV handsets, keys were mislaid to an extent where St Anthony was required to work overtime. In cases where she tried to remember what she'd just said his services were not always available.

She could no longer remember anything about her son's stillbirth and her husband and daughter both felt this was because she did not *want* to remember. They admired her for that. Some things were best forgotten.

She had managed to give up smoking, becoming addicted to television viewing instead. With the advent of daytime TV she watched a continuous stream of quiz shows, chat shows, soaps, travelogues, wildlife programmes and endless repeats of old films. The only programmes she would switch off were the news bulletins, which were the only programmes Irving wanted to watch. They finally compromised by installing a TV set in their bedroom.

They both became so heavily reliant on Dawn that their daughter registered with social services as their full-time carer, receiving a paltry allowance which in no way reflected the full-time nature of her duties. Care homes were briefly discussed and ruled out of the question. Too many of them were profit-orientated. Standards fluctuated alarmingly with stories of patients being neglected and underfed appearing regularly in the newspapers.

Years ago the family had lost Nana, its beloved matriarch, in one such establishment when a straightforward case of flu was allowed to go undiagnosed and turn into pneumonia. A year later Susan Breen had succumbed to a heart attack in a north Yorkshire care home lacking a basic defibrillator. Her husband David had lodged an official complaint but was too infirm to proceed with it. Within months he died from a stroke. Health officials claimed that care home standards had since improved but Dawn, along with most of the public, no longer believed a word anyone in authority told them.

Emily's descent into a nether world of apathy and inertia was desperately hard for Irving to bear. She had become a virtual stranger. Their once-deathless love may not have died but lay forever dormant, all romance having long evaporated. When he bought her a single red rose for Valentine's Day she said without a smile that she would rather have had some chocolate.

Neither wanted to leave the house for any reason, even to walk Alice. Churchgoing, birthday parties, weddings and funerals were things of the past. When Fred died of old age it was a major logistical operation for Dawn to drive the pair to Brawton Methodist Church and back, such was their walking speed of 0.10 mph, car sickness and frequent toilet requirements.

A few days later both asked her whose funeral they had been to and Dawn showed them the printed order of service with its picture of dear Fred in his younger years and the hymns including *Fight the Good Fight* that had been Nana's favourite. Irving remembered then and asked Emily to play the hymn on the piano. This she did with difficulty in a halting style and Irving tried to sing the words in a hoarse breathless voice but repeated coughing got the better of him.

It was the cough not the falls or memory loss that proved the deadliest of Irving's health issues, as the GP called them. He was diagnosed with lung cancer after a chest X-ray and scan showed a shadow on his upper left lobe. Further tests indicated an aggressive tumour and a matter-of-fact oncologist told him the condition was terminal. His expected life span could be measured in weeks or, at best, months. The news was the way Irving preferred to hear it -- straight from the shoulder with no punches pulled. His final deadline was fast approaching. He always delivered on his deadlines. This one would be no different.

Irving had covered his share of stories about cancer patients told they had weeks to live who were running marathons and jumping out of planes strapped to parachute instructors years later. The diagnosis was not always hopeless. Cancer could go into remission at any time. Daniel, his own brother-in-law, was living proof of that.

Confronting his mortality had been long overdue at his advanced age and infirmity anyway. Emily and Dawn seemed more dismayed by the diagnosis than he was. They resolved to step up their prayers and ask Father Simon to say Mass regularly for his recovery. And the time had surely come to be received into the Catholic Church without further delay. He had finally run out of excuses.

Life became a painful regime of tablet-taking, hospital appointments, scans, blood tests and sleepless nights punctuated by unsteady visits to the bathroom. One of his few pleasures was accompanying Dawn on her weekly food shops at the local supermarket. He found a shopping trolley an ideal form of support and hooked his walking stick on its handle as they trundled along the aisles. Problems only arose when he left the trolley to select items from the shelves.

He'd lost three stones in weight in as many months and his trousers were much too big for him. Even when fastening his belt to it's tightest notch he needed to hold on to the waistband with one hand to prevent them falling down. It was a constant source of discomfort but he managed to complete most of the shopping without incident when the inevitable happened.

On reaching up to a high shelf for packets of filter coffee he sneezed, his eyes watered and he instinctively used his other hand to feel for his handkerchief. Down came the trousers with speed of an actor's in a Whitehall farce. They dropped in front of a young woman shopper with a child in a buggy. A feisty feminist, she called Irving 'a dirty old man'. His behaviour was 'highly offensive'. She had a good mind to call the manager. Only when Dawn explained her father's distressing condition did the hysterics subside.

Gradually the painkillers became less effective and had to be increased in strength. When back pain spread into his chest and he could no longer breathe deeply, the weekly shopping trips, his only contact with the outside world, had to be dropped. The GP prescribed a portable oxygen cylinder which helped his breathing but could not be taken into a supermarket.

As his decline gathered pace a nurse helped Dawn and Daniel convert the dining room into a bedroom with a divan bed and wheelchair so he could be wheeled through the french windows and sit out on the patio in the long hot summer. The nurse, Elaine, visited daily with bottles, bedpans and increasingly strong painkillers.

Hopes of the tumour's remission grew weaker and everyone's prayers grew stronger. At long last he agreed to convert to the Catholic Church and Father Simon was called from St Oswald's. Now white haired and stooped, the priest performed a 'fast track' reception ritual with chrism oil and a small gold crucifix, followed by the sacrament of the sick, otherwise known as the last rites.

A few formalities were necessary. Irving's reception into the church was recorded in Father Simon's leather-bound register, along with his signature and that of the priest. Emily, Dawn and Elaine added theirs as witnesses.

'You're one of us now, Irving,' Father Simon said. 'Better late than never! Holy Mass will be said for you tomorrow morning.'

Irving's voice was cracking up along with the rest of his body but he managed to thank the priest. 'I'll try to remain sinless until then, Father!'

The priest chuckled and said he would hear Irving's confession if he was ready to make one. Irving had been ready to make a confession ever since the day after his dalliance with Rita. With Elaine's help he sat up in bed, trying not to cough.

Father Simon took the purple silk stole used for the sacrament of forgiveness out of his case and placed it round his neck. Everyone else left the room since confession was a solemn and strictly private dialogue between penitent, priest and God.

Irving cleared his throat and in a halting whisper described the night of drunken debauchery with Rita in all its squalid detail. He repeated everything he had previously told Father Michael since that conversation had not been a formal confession. This was. He had then compounded his sin by telling Emily and Dawn a deliberate lie about that night and why he hadn't come home as planned.

Father Simon, bending to hear his penitent's words, knew the rest of the tragic story -- of Fred's stillbirth and the deep distress it had caused. But in a world of gross immorality, blasphemy and widespread corruption the confession he'd heard amounted to weakness rather than evil. In his day-to-day ministry he heard far worse. Irving had suffered enough and was now dying. He would impose only nominal penance.

'For penance say three Our Fathers... and I absolve you from your sins in the name of the Father and of the Son and of the Holy Spirit.'

The priest made the sign of the cross and helped the exhausted penitent to lie back on his pillows. Then he went to the door and called to the three women. 'It's customary to have a celebration on such joyful occasions,' he said. 'So I brought you this.' He reached into his case and produced a large bottle of the finest scotch.

Irving grinned through his pain. Catholics knew how to celebrate.

Like a horse race entering the home straight when the jockeys reach for their whips, the pace quickened. Within days Irving's pain outstripped the power of his medication to control it and the GP connected him to an intravenous diamorphine drip. Along with the oxygen supply to assist his shallow breathing, it eased the pain and reduced the coughing up of blood.

The GP increased her visits to monitor his condition but on one occasion a locum deputised. The young man, barely out of medical school, was an enthusiastic supporter of doctor-assisted suicide, the controversial end-of-life procedure commonly known as euthanasia. If patients signed a consent form they would be assured that 'terminal sedation' would be available by injection if and when they requested it.

Irving knew the idealistic doctor meant well but he'd never been a fan of euthanasia, considering it a double-edged sword. He politely declined the offer. When you were standing at death's door you didn't need to knock. It would be opened to you soon enough. The analogy, albeit a dark one, was well-turned and he was quite pleased with it.

His physical strength may have drained away but his mind was as active as ever. Where had he gone wrong in his long-running mission to convince 'the powers that be' that the impossible had actually happened -- that a quantum shift had occurred and they were all living in a different world? It was something he knew from personal experience to be true but his impassioned pleas had fallen on deaf ears. There were none so deaf as those who did not *want* to hear.

God may have forgiven him his past sins and failings but he was still beating himself up over them. Mental images kept forming as if in a kaleidoscope... he was in his mother's bedroom as a boy, stealing from her precious savings. Years later he'd learned the money had been intended for his school uniform. And he never paid her back.

Another spin and he watched in horror as a racehorse called Too Slow romped past the winning post at 25-1. Poor Lilian had wanted to back it and in his youthful arrogance he'd stopped her. Then his darling Emily had been compelled to pawn her engagement ring after his disastrous night in Salford Casino.

But at the back of his mind was the assurance, the certain knowledge that never left him since he'd discovered quantum physics: in another multiverse we all got a chance to straighten our lives out and lift the weight of failure from our shoulders. No way would he ever steal again from his mother. Lilian could back any horse she fancied and casinos would remain forever out of bounds.

Above all else he'd make sure he caught the

evening train from Blackpool to Manchester at the end of the Tory conference when his son needed him. That was his most bitter regret. Somewhere out there in another multiverse, perhaps far distant perhaps the one next to ours, Fred was alive and still needed him. He'd tried desperately to reach him. This time he'd failed. But next time...

All too soon the coherent thoughts dissolved into a seething delirium of dreams and memories... 'Stand up straight, boy,' Grandpa was saying... then other voices: 'Elitist scum'... 'they spat at God'...'when can you start?'... 'Hello, lover boy'... 'Popsie's been as good as gold'... He could hear music and singing....'*This is the day that the Lord has made*'... '*You were temptation*'... '*All things bright and beautiful*'.

In his tormented imagination a brightly lit ballroom appeared. A female vocalist was singing *Dancing in the Dark, till the tune ends we're dancing in the dark...* And an enchanting young girl was asking him an ineffable question: 'Where've you been, Breen?'

Emily was sitting with him holding his hand, smiling and weeping in turn in her own disordered state of mind. In a rare moment of lucidity he gripped her hand and looked intently into her tear-filled eyes. With an effort he managed to lift the oxygen mask. Speaking was exhausting but there was something he desperately needed to tell her.

'We will meet again... you do know that don't you, Emily?'

'Of course, Irving.' She had long accepted his 'other worlds' philosophy.

'We'll go dancing together again...'

'I know, darling.'

He gripped her hand more tightly. 'See you at the Odeon on Saturday...'

'I'll be there, my love. Don't be late!'

She kissed his perspiring forehead and smiled, tears running down her face.

The heatwave grew hotter. Scientists were blaming it on global warming. We should all stop eating meat to save the planet. It seemed a bit late now. They opened all the windows and brought a fan into Irving's room. Emily, Dawn and Elaine took turns to bathe his forehead with cold water, helped by Father Simon on his daily visits.

As he did when ministering to all terminally ill parishioners the priest relied on the Book of Ecclesiastes for words of comfort and hope:
God has set eternity in the human heart...
Whatever is, has already been
And what will be has been before...

Irving found the passage inspiring, like a divine endorsement of his quantum version of reincarnation. It sustained him in the knowledge that his mission would live to fight another day -- and so, miraculously, would he.

Daniel, Megan and the twins brought a large basket of fruit but he could not eat anything, just sip ice-cold water. His breathing became shallower and a tiny dot of light had started to appear when he closed his eyes, which was most of the time. It grew perceptibly larger each day and he knew exactly what it was.

The thought that he was about to leave the world no longer troubled him. He was already working out how to live in the next. It would all be different. The old order would be swept away. There'd be no monarchy, no billionaires, no exploitation, no poverty and no politicians. Society would be governed by journalists in a spirit of openness and truth, with Dave Leonard as prime minister... There was more but he was too weary to think about it.

'Phew, what a scorcher!' Elaine exclaimed on arriving for another day's dedicated care of her dying patient. 'It's 90 in the shade -- must be all the global warming.'

Dawn fitted both her father's hearing aids into position and asked him if he'd like to sit out on the patio under a parasol. He was focusing intently on the spot of light that was now widening rapidly but he heard her and nodded.

Far too weak to move himself, the three women lifted his frail skeletal figure into the wheelchair and pushed him slowly, attached to the drip and oxygen mask, out into the sunshine. A gentle breeze wafted the scent of roses towards him. With a supreme effort Irving turned his head and gazed unseeingly across the garden. Then a vision of Fred's rose tree appeared in all its full bloom glory. Tears sprang into his eyes and he whispered: 'Next time, my son... I'll be there for you.'

The white light enveloped his whole being in a paroxysm of pain and euphoria. Then all was calm. He felt a hand holding the back of his head and he opened his eyes. A nurse was smiling down at him. It wasn't Elaine.

'Oh, isn't he gorgeous!' the nurse said.

Somewhere a clock was chiming the hour. Four-o-clock.

Could there be, "out there," an ultimate multiverse, a dimension where everything is perfect... where love rules alone in the absence of hate... where truth is the *whole* truth... where corruption and greed no longer exist... with people the way God made them -- like innocent children -- and where evil has been completely eradicated? Yes, it's called heaven. We can all get there. Some will take longer than others.

What Did You Think of Next Time?

*First of all, thank you for reading Next Time.
I know you could have picked any number
of books to read, but you picked this one
and for that I am extremely grateful.*

*I hope you enjoyed this book and found some
benefit in reading it, and it would be wonderful if
you could share it with your friends and family, e.g.
by posting something on Facebook and Twitter.*

*Also if you enjoyed this book I sincerely
hope that you would be kind enough
to post a review on Amazon.*